The Spirit of Cassious House

To Find Truth, Valour, and Honour,
One Must Find the Courage to
Search Among the Lies

LINDA KEY

authorHOUSE®

AuthorHouse™ UK
1663 Liberty Drive
Bloomington, IN 47403 USA
www.authorhouse.co.uk
Phone: 0800.197.4150

Published by AuthorHouse 12/13/2017

ISBN: 978-1-5246-8217-0 (sc)
ISBN: 978-1-5246-8223-1 (e)

Acknowledgements

Why did I write this story?

The story came from a dream I had about Peter Capaldi sitting in an office in a University and I came in to talk to him after the loss of his assistant and I was to get a homework assignment from him. (As you will see in the story)

His response is also in the story... I won't tell you the rest but I wrote it down to the best of my knowledge and kept it with me and tried so hard to surround a story around it but I had such writer's block and I was at the point of chucking in the idea that a story could come from a dream.

One cold and windy day by the sea at St Andrews Castle, during a mini break, I was sitting on a bench and resting and I looked at my dream scenario and around the beauty of the castle grounds; and then ideas came from all over the place and I grabbed my notebook and pen and started to write out notes for the story and finally got a plot together.

I was on a roll and as soon I was home I started to pencil out the reference page, collected photos, making some props getting characters and decided to put in my life experience and current events around the characters. Then from that I started to pencil the story....it was the inspiration I needed.

I also had inspiration of looking at performances from Tom Bateman, David Tennant, Catherine Tate, Richard E Grant, Matt Smith and

Benedict Cumberbatch (The Prince's name came from his middle name "Timothy Carlton") and many others that had a profound effect on me.

I started making other pages and finally after writing it all in pencil, I started to type it out. I was also learning Gaelic from www. learngaelic.net/lg-beginners/ and I used it to help me create the story and the Welsh and Russian came from the Microsoft Translator.

So in conclusion, I hope you like the story and I worked as hard as I could to make it easy and fun to read as well as understandable. I hope you enjoy it.

Linda Key

Prologue

The night was clear with stars dotting the black veil while the half moon was sitting like a hook waiting to be baited in the night sky, and the towns below were all aglow with pubs and nightclubs as the sound of partygoers and drunks filled the street with celebration of the conclusion of the World Cup victories and chatter as the pubs were about ready to close while revellers of all ages, were staggering home in present day Kelton Heights. The police were out in force making sure there was no trouble as everyone headed home. The stars were bright as the cool breeze danced about in the city streets and its party goers around Kelton Heights… and it was on this clear night that our story begins.

It began with the predicament of three happy drunks who were staggering home after being kicked out of every pub for running out of money and maxxing out the credit card. They sang so loudly through the night that the cats hissed and ran from them and while people who were trying to sleep, woke to the caterwauling of these men. The residents around them were fed up with their noise, told them to shut up or just simply threw something at them as they ran from the objects and complained what their problems were…but the townspeople knew them as the troublemakers named Nathan Baines, Dylan McAnelly, and Ross Queronaille; "Three Stooges of Kelton Heights."

Why were they called that, you may ask? Well, because they were always playing harmless pranks on others in and around the city centre on each other and on others and sometimes it would backfire badly; but on this night, this prank would cost them big time. Tonight they were celebrating their team's win in the World Cup Final as they were in their team's colours and scarves with lager in their hands and a song in their hearts.

The "Three Stooges" walked along the street until they were out of the city centre and made their way past a Haunted and Historic dilapidated building called Cassious House on their way home until they heard songs in the night as they joined in like a bunch of high-spirited teenagers after the prom while the three of them stopped and listened; it would have been the last thing they would ever do as Ross said to his chums rather drunkenly, "Hey fellas...*hic*... how's about we go in to Cassious House and take...*hic*... a look around? M-Maybe spend the night?"

The other two, even though they were drunk had common sense as Dylan staggered over to Ross and says; "You know the House is off limits...*hic*...people have told stories of people disappearing ...*hic* in there." Then Nathan says, "He is right," as he points to his face then takes another drink of his lager, "I heard that a man by the name of Sid-...*hic*-ney Preston was m-murdered there;" he said pointing at the night sky instead of the House." Nathan corrected him by dropping his arm to point to the House as he continued after they had a good laugh. "I wouldn't go in there except that I'm cold...*hic* and the House looks cosy, besides the group in there may have more lager. Let's join in the fun fellas..." they thought it was a good idea and started towards the House's back steps.

Nathan, Dylan and Ross go up the steps and towards the House unaware that a glowing figure stood at the window and watched the men...he moved away from the window to encounter them so he could warn them off as they reached around the back of the House. Nathan finds a concealed door amid all the vines and bramble and he opens it to let his fellow stooges inside after being pricked and stabbed by the bramble and bushes surrounding the place. Nathan helped his two friends up after Dylan and Ross fell into the bushes and they all laughed as the "Three Stooges" staggered down the steps and into the House and followed Nathan inside. "Come on fellas...*hic*... I-I gots the door open; let's get in and get warm." He left the door open to light the way as the Dark Spirits saw they had intruders as they hid in the shadows and waited for the right time to pounce on their prey.

His friends stagger down the stairs to get inside the front door and made their way to the main hall as the door slammed with a resounding THUD and CLANG and they looked back as it echoed through the House. "Must have been the wind," replied Dylan as he took another drink of his lager, "…but onwards to warmth" as he staggered backwards while his friends pushed him forward as they laughed and get into the main hall of the House. What they didn't realise is that they were being hunted while the trio staggered down the passageway that was filled with vines, moss, and moisture not realising that they had passed the front hall of the House. "Hello…" said Dylan loudly as the others shouted out with him as their voices bounced off the walls. "Hey…*hic*…got anymore lager?" There was no reply as they walked on through the front hall while creatures of the night watched their prey hungrily.

The vines, cobwebs, moss, snakes, beetles and worms filled the hall as snakes, rats, mice and spiders quickly got out of the way of the trio and slithered or ran into holes on either side of the passageway as the trio made through to the main hall where there was no plants or creepy crawlies like in the main hall; but dust, leaves and sheets that were covering the furniture as the leaves and paper blew around on the floor. Dust swirled around them like dust devils, pictures of the past stared down at the men as their drunkenness finally gave way to them singing at the top of their lungs and the Dark Spirits listened as they knew it was dinner time and their hooks were baited by these three drunken fools as the pictures seemed to roll their eyes at their off-key singing while they sat and peered into the grand hall like guardians from the past.

The men sat on the floor and started to laugh uncontrollably at their predicament while they looked around at the huge hall which was cold and barren. The three of them tried to build a small fire but the cold winds kept blowing it out so the men bundled their jackets around them unbeknownst that they were being hunted as the temperature of the House dropped drastically. Ross said as he looked at the Dark Veil behind him waving in the wind as if it was a flag in a gale and he asked his other friends, "I wonder…*hic*… what that is?"

He stood up and started walking towards the veil to examine it closer until a man, bathed in golden light with a hooded cloak, stood before them with a sword unsheathed by his side and poised to strike when needed as he says with caution, "Don't touch it! You will anger the Dark Spirits!" The three men laughed as the figure continued, "I want you to leave; you are not welcome here and you are being hunted as we speak."

The figure's glow intensified as if that would frighten them off but it didn't as Ross looked again at the figure as he asked rather crossly, "W-Who…*hic*…are you? And do you have any more lager around here? What gives you the right…*hic*… to tell us what to do?" the other men laughed as the spirit stood its ground as he dropped his hood as he looked at the trio as he spoke. "It doesn't matter who I am…sirs- but I am here to warn you to leave; this place is off limits…you are trespassing here. So I will say it again, leave now for your own safety, for you are being hunted as we speak."

The men laughed even harder as Ross said, "Why don't you go and …*hic*… haunt another House, Mr glow-worm-thingy, we will do whatever we want party …*hic*… pooper!" The figure shook his head sadly as he sheathed his sword and said, "Don't say I didn't warn you…" and the figure bathed in golden light left them because there was nothing that he could do to save them as Ross went to the veil and started to poke at it with a stick just as the figure left shaking his head. It was a thick veil which was black as tar and deep as the deepest night; waving and dancing as if the wind had entered through the first floor window as its occupants grew restless and hungry at what they had caught in their nets as Ross started prodding at it with a small but long twig as the men laughed. Ross turned around to his fellow "Stooges", tossed the stick down and said, "Nothing to worry about fellas …*hic*… it's just a piece of cloth. Shall I tear it down and …*hic*… we can share a blanket?" The others nodded as he yanked at the veil with all his might until a sinister pair of skeletal hands started reaching out while Ross had his back turned to ask his fellow "Stooges" as he yanked on the veil; "Hey fellas,*hic*… come and give me a hand."

The other two stood and were just about to help him until a pair of skeletal hands shot out, surrounded him, and clasped around Ross's mid-section as he cried out to his friends to help him as the hands held him firmly in place as he screamed; "Get off me! Get off me! Help me please!" Ross cried to Dylan and Nathan ran to help a struggling, frightened Ross as they got his hands and started to pull but the Dark Spirits grip was tighter and stronger as Ross started to panic.

"Pull Harder!" Ross shouted at them but Dylan and Nathan fell and rolled around on the floor as they got up and tried again until another two Dark Spirits emerged and came up behind Dylan and Nathan as Ross looked up terrified as the dark spirits grabbed his friends as they cried out for help while the figure in glowing, golden light appeared again as he watched helplessly as the Dark Spirits lifted the three of them above their heads while the other Dark Spirits gathered around their prey; licking their lips as the men screamed.

The golden figure watched, with a couple of his other friends, from behind a wall and saw that he couldn't do anything to help them. At the height the men were at, the figure thought logically, their spines would be broken and they would be paralysed forever even if they survived the fall to the floor as the other spirits patted his shoulders for comfort as one whispered, "There is nothing you can do... you warned them but they brought this on themselves."

The young spirit nodded as they watched in horror of what unfolded before them when the curse was placed on them as tears rolled down his cheeks as he looked back and came before them as the young men saw the figure sheathing his sword and begged him to help them as Dylan cried out to the figure glowing in golden light, "Please, Please help us; we beg of you." Nathan joined in, "We won't come here again, we promise. Tell them to let us go!" The men screamed again while the Dark Spirits licked their lips of the dinner before them as the figure watched in horror as to what was enfolding before him.

He remembered what happened over three hundred and fifty years ago, and now before his spirited eyes, he sees it unfolding again. "I did try to warn you and all you did was laugh... I cannot help you for I would be drawn in to its evil; enjoy the veil, gentlemen." The men watched him turn away as they shouted for him to come back but when he didn't, they cursed him as the figure said sadly echoing around the room, "I am already cursed..." and faded into shadows with his fellow spirits as the Dark Spirits held them high; drooling and hungry and with one crack, the men in their final breaths; screamed one last time through the dark moonlit streets as the velvet skies glowed brightly in the velvet purple starlight sky as all was quiet once again as the dawn started to creep in over Kelton Heights.

Thirty miles away from Kelton Heights, sat its twinned neighbour Welleston Village; a small village by the sea that was just like Kelton Heights but smaller. Its village-like atmosphere was soothing and a popular tourist spot for those escaping the big city as its folks were just as welcoming and peaceful with cafes, shops, antiques, restaurants and the best five star Bed and Breakfasts that had a view nestled in the sandy crag by the chilly North Sea. Beautiful scenery, quaint gardens and parks were in the tiny village and quiet but small city centre and most of all, there were less or no cars in the village because the village folks walked everywhere within its small square so it was the perfect retreat for the city dweller who needed to escape from buses, cars, honking taxis, lorries and the congestion charge and look for tranquillity near the shore as everything was close by.

The only time it was busy was when the summer came and fairs would come to the tiny village and tourists would come and swim, sun bathe or just walk by the sea as the dance halls belted out music from the hall to outside. Other times, there was a wedding in the early evening as its tranquil backdrop was ideal for the couple who wanted to take their vows, while elderly residents held hands and walked along the esplanade dreaming of their youth and days gone by as the waves caressed the shoreline as a mother touching her newborn baby for the first time after birth.

In this peaceful village lived Alyssia Anne Franklin-Jenkins who woke up from a nightmare that she had since she was a child as panic ensnares her young face and her features are frozen in a panic that turns her white as a sheet and drenches her in a cold sweat as if someone dropped a bucket of cold water in her and she could feel the tears of fear and anxiety envelope her as she tries not to waken Catriona Timrod who was still sound asleep next door.

Her mouth hung open as her shout was caught in her throat while the hot, stinging tears rolled down freely from her brown eyes, her long brown hair was matted to her head like glue as she closed her mouth and fell back on to the pillow; trying to normalise her breathing as her breaths came steady and calming after she turned on the light on her dresser. Her sighs were a welcome relief to her as her nightgown was soaked with sweat as she looked at the clock on her nightstand. *"Six o'clock in the morning..."* her brain told her as she looked back at the ceiling. *"I guess I better get up; no point of me going back to sleep now;"* she said to herself as she sat up, threw the covers off, and got out of the bed.

As she stretched, she went over to the curtains and threw them open to look out at the early morning; it was grey, misty and the dew sat heavily around the trees and shrubs as well as on the flowers. She opened up the window and let the cool air in as she let the early morning cool air blow in her face while she closed her eyes and forced the tears back as if the weather reflected her mood and she sat down on the window seat and watched the birds playing in the grass as they looked for worms.

Five days ago, her grandmother Jessica Esther Jenkins passed away in her sleep from heart failure in this house and Alyssia felt like dying too as she thought of her as tears threatened to overwhelm her once more. She pulled out the envelope that her grandmother gave her that sad night and she couldn't bring herself to open it because the pain of losing someone so close to her was too much; but since the early morning was quiet and good for contemplation, she decides to open it and found two pictures and a note. She looked at them and smiled as she saw her mother, father a friend and her brother in happier times, but who they were was a mystery. Then she read the letter from her mother and it broke her heart. It read:

"My dear Alyssia,

Please don't be sad at my passing...I have always loved you and tried to do what's best for you... but the worst idea was taking you away from you father and brother. Here are two of my favourite pictures of them. Please I beg of you; go and find them and live the best life you can. I know it feels like I betrayed you and if I did, please, my darling, please forgive me. I love you more than words can say. Goodbye my sweet girl and be good. -Emily-"

Alyssia looked up and let the tears fall from her eyes as she looked again at the pictures of them and smiled. She wished that her father and brother were beside her and holding her close, but she couldn't remember what happiness was because of the memories that kept her depression intact and where they were was another story because she has not seen them since she was seven. If she did find them, what would she say? How would she react? And most of all, would they even accept her? All these questions were rolling around in her head as she thought of her family and the way her mother died as well were constantly plaguing her as the screams she let out would haunt her for the rest of her life whether it was in her dreams or in her memories.

Taking in a deep breath, she gets up from the window, makes her bed and gets ready for a shower as her clean clothes were set out on her bed as she heard Catriona putting on BBC Alba to catch up with the news in the North of Scotland in the Gaelic community. Catriona was from North Uist and the people spoke mainly Gaelic and Alyssia loved her as a sister figure; she was the calm in the storm while Alyssia was depressed and Catriona was there when Jessica died peacefully as she took her out of the room, sat beside her, and gave her comfort even though she was hurting herself, the nurse had to stay strong for her.

A week ago at Jessica's passing, Alyssia became so despondent; refusing to eat, refusing to come out of her room, and not seeing anyone; she just wanted to be left alone in her grief. While neighbours were bringing over food, sending their condolences, flowers, cards; Catriona knew it was too much for her to handle so staying away in her room, she thought, was better than to be around all the attention.

The Reverend Father came to them and spoke to the girls during that traumatic week as Catriona told him that she needed to be alone with her grief and to come to terms with the loss of her grandmother; the Reverend understood for he knew that Jessica was the only family Alyssia had known. Catriona didn't know this as the Reverend Father took her aside and told her the story of how Alyssia came to live in Welleston Village as Catriona stood horrified at what she went through. Catriona never knew; she told the Reverend Father that she had never been told about Alyssia's past by Jessica, only told to take care of her and make sure that she was comfortable and making sure that she took her medicine.

He had asked Catriona if he could see Alyssia and to offer his comfort and Catriona, still shocked about Alyssia's past nodded as they went to see Alyssia in her room, but she simply refused to even see or acknowledge him as Catriona and the Father knew her only family member was gone and it was hard to bear; so they left her alone as Catriona says apologetically to the Reverend in Gaelic as she wiped away some tears of her own, *I duilich Maigster, eadh bi a cruaidh seachdain do Alyssia is mi. Mi tuig sios domhain gu i eáirlig gu bruidhinn gu sibh but a h-cridh is na annan eadh* "I'm sorry father, it's been a tough week for Alyssia and I; I know down deep that she wants to talk to you, but her heart is not in it."

The Father was very understanding as he patted Catriona's hand saying, *Na gu gabh drag, mise ais suc suc a-rithist is bruidhnich le a h-; Don bi ro cruaidh air a h-.* "Not to worry, I will come by again and speak with her; don't be too hard on her." Catriona nodded and thanked him for his understanding as the Reverend Father left her and Alyssia and returned to the church. He told her gently to give him a call when she has come out of her slump and Catriona said that she would and bade the Reverend father farewell as she went back to doing the house work after all the guest had left.

After a depressing couple of days, Alyssia came out and saw Catriona who saw her in tears and ran to her to offer her support and comfort. She apologised for the way she acted but Catriona didn't care; she was glad to see her as she held her close and welcomed her back to reality as well as giving her all the comfort she needed. She caught her up on what was happening while she sat down in the kitchen and ate some food and had something to drink and a good clean up afterwards.

While she was upstairs taking a shower and changing into clean clothes, Catriona called the Reverend Father and told him that Alyssia was out of her slump. He was joyous and relieved as he made an appointment to come to see them as soon as he was free, *Mise feum tè tiodhlacadh agus tè banais seothach seachdain;* "I have a funeral and a wedding this week;" said the vicar looking at his diary. Then he found an empty slot, *Cia mu ath-Diluain feasgar an cois dá o'noig?* "How about next Monday afternoon at two o'clock?" He asked her in Gaelic as Catriona thought and nodded. *A Jessica's dlighear is fòs teachd an cois aon trithead- ionnas gu áis bi foidhne.* "Jessica's lawyer is also coming at one-thirty so that will be fine." The vicar and Catriona came to an amicable agreement and said their goodbyes as they hung up the phones as Alyssia came downstairs refreshed as Catriona filled her in.

A week in and she was back to her normal self and it felt good... *"Well,"* she thought as she stands up from the window to stretch her weary bones, *"I better go and get ready for the day; we have got a lot to do in the house and arrange the funeral."* Taking one last deep breath and stretch, she gets into the shower and cleans up. As the water hits her body, her skin sighed at the coolness of the water on her sweaty skin and her hair was relieved to get the excess sweat off too as she steps from the shower and gets a pair of trousers and an old top on as she prepares to clean out her gran's home.

She leaves the room and goes downstairs and heads down the foyer and up to the front door where the mail lays on the mat. She picks it up as she sees that they are all bills and she placed them on the sideboard in the hallway along with a whole stack of bills which littered the top of the sideboard. She placed all the bills into a manila envelope, put it on the sideboard and leaned the envelope against the stairwell as she reached the kitchen and starts the breakfast by boiling the kettle and getting all the breakfast bacon and sausages and toast.

A while later, Catriona comes downstairs and when she sees Alyssia, her smile is as bright as the sun as she was also dressed in a pair of trousers and an old top to cover her slender frame and flicked back her long hair which sat in a pony tail as she greets Alyssia. ***Madainn mhath, a Alyssia,*** "Good morning Alyssia," Alyssia turns to her and says, ***madainn mhath, a Chatriona.*** "Good morning Catriona."

The nurse smiled and helped Alyssia with breakfast as she gets the scrambled eggs ready, while Catriona sees to the bacon, sausages, toast, tomatoes and beans. ***An do sibh agad a math codlach?*** "Did you have a good sleep?" Catriona nodded as she turns the food and replied happily, ***Math dha-riribh, tapadh leat*** "Very well, thank you." Alyssia smiled as she watched Catriona get the tea and hot chocolate out of the cupboard, sets them on the table, and then gets the milk and juice as well, puts them on the table while Alyssia gets the two warm plates out of the oven as Alyssia dishes out the breakfast while Catriona deals with the kettle which started to whistle and pours the hot water into the teapot then puts the kettle back on its stand and takes the teapot of hot water to the table and sets it on a hot plate.

Alyssia on the other hand, takes a towel and delivers the hot plates of breakfast over to the table after Catriona turns off the oven. Now, with all the hard work done, the girls get settled into their chairs at the table and start to eat breakfast after saying a prayer. Catriona asked Alyssia, ***Cia*** advisor, the jester and the prince watched from the Tower at all the melee around the House and the three missing men.

In the small house next to the haunted House, Sharlene is comforting, encouraging, and making teas for the mothers of the missing sons and police officers; she didn't know what to say, only comfort them in their grief and anxiety as the twenty-four hours turned into thirty-six hours to forty-eight hours of agony and disbelief. Kevin's wife, Sharlene Parks was a delicate woman in her mid forties with short dirty blonde hair and a skinny frame. Her face was rounded and her eyes were amber as she told the other officer inside the kitchen as the mothers had their teas, and they all went outside to help with the search as she continued. "My husband and I sleep soundly and we didn't know about this incident until this morning and he is a staunch believer in the rules which has been handed down from one generation of the Parks to another. This has got him rattled because we live near this Haunted House for five generations and he makes sure that no one enters the House next to us," she sighs and replied as she gets her coat and told the officers "…there must have been another way that they have gotten in; come with me." They nodded as followed the caretaker's wife around the back of the House where there was nothing but brambles and thrones as well as snakes and other creepy crawlies.

She led them to the back door and noticed that the wood covering the stairs was exposed the front entrance of the main hall. Kevin saw her going down the steps as she signalled to him and the other officers to follow and they did as they get around the back where the bramble and weeds all grew as the arachnids, snakes, worms and other insects scurried for cover. The officers and Kevin help the search party check the walls of wood that were put up to keep any homeless person out of the porch and the front hall after complaints from neighbours and as time went on the plants and shrubbery took over as the wooden wall became warped and weakened by years of wear and tear as Kevin joins his wife with another police officer as they pull back the vines and bramble to reveal a door.

"This may have been the way they got in," said the young officer as he tried the door and came back, "…but it appears to be locked now. The door must have been warped and unlocked at one time-that's probably how they entered." Kevin and Sharlene as well as the officers check around after noting down what the young officer had told them as they continued to search the property for any clues that may lead them to the missing men. Sharlene and the officers came back up the steps and put the warped wood around its entrance and they headed back around the front.

Just then, another officer found a lager can and called to his boss as he takes a pen and picks up the can, "Sir!" they come running and see the can of Tennants lager as one of the mothers' shouted out in hysterics, "That's my son Dylan's can; that is his favourite lager. But why did he do this? Why would he pull such a foolish stunt like this?" She started to cry as Sharlene and other two mothers come over and comfort her. Sharlene and the others take her back to the House as the lieutenant told him to 'bag it' and get it sent to the lab for testing. He nodded as the search party continue their search behind the bramble and brush as well as the back stairs which lead up to the property as one officer asked a devastated Kevin, as the police asked them, "Where do you sleep?"

"Come with me officer," Kevin says still devastated by this development as he takes the police back around to his front door and into the House while the others search the area outside of the bedroom as Kevin take the men into their tiny bedroom and shows them as Sharlene stays with the mothers and gave them more tea and comfort. The police go inside the bedroom and look at all the windows as Kevin opens the window for them and the officers gaze out at the vicinity of the area…the caretaker was right as the policeman said, "There is no way that you could have known; there is triple glazing on the windows and there was no sign of forced entry on the door, sir. They would have been awoken to it if there were noises and there is nothing to suggest footprints, just the bushes were disturbed and there are no scratches on the doors or windows around here." The sarge nodded as he asked Kevin, to go ahead and close the window and he did and locked it up tightly as they continued with their investigation.

The group of officers looked out and saw that the window was facing the garden and the view of the shed; not the back of the House as previously thought. Mrs McAnelly said, "We apologise to you for the rude awakening so early in the morning, Mr and Mrs Parks, our sons didn't come home last night and we thought that…" Sharlene stopped Dylan's mother. "It is fine; you have every right to suspect us after the tales and stories of the House and the past disappearances. That is why my husband takes his job very seriously and keeps everyone away and I would be suspicious too if it happened to my son or daughter." The mothers smiled and they said to the officers, "They are never going to be to blame officer; they are just doing their jobs. Our sons were always pulling pranks all around Kelton Heights and this is one that backfired big time; and they are right…they were trespassing on private property."

The police smiled and so did the Parks as the group left the Parks to their peace, "I'm sorry for all the disruption," said Mrs Baines. "…we didn't mean to disturb you." Sharlene smiled as she saw to the ladies while her husband talked to the police. "We are sorry to disturb you this early in the morning, sir," said the officer to Mr Parks. "We got a call from these nice ladies and we have to make sure because of the history of the House. We have to look at every angle and try to get to the bottom of this mystery."

Mr Parks replied with a smile, "I appreciate it and to know that we are not suspected in their disappearances. I will be going to the council to see about an update on my query for an iron gate that I can close at night and maybe a recommendation for the police would speed things up?" The officer agreed and would talk to his superiors about it as he thanked them and asked, "Anyway, why don't you check out the backstairs, you may find more lager cans there?" The officer said, "The search party did but found nothing; it's like they disappeared into mid air; but thank you for your time and I do apologise for the rude wake up call."

Kevin's face broke into a grin as he led the officer to the door, "That is not a problem, officer; you are only doing your job for the protection of our community, and I thank you for your service; I hope you do find the boys." The officer replied as he put his notebook away, "Thank you, Mr Parks, I wish everyone was that appreciative and hopefully they will turn up as well. Goodbye to you and Mrs Parks have a wonderful day and I will talk to the head of the Department and get that recommendation for you for the Iron Gate."

One man looked up into the eyes of the spirits and nodded politely, not letting on as if he was hiding a secret and then looked back at the sarge who clapped him on the back as they headed back to the car. He looked up again and found them gone as he took in a deep breath as he looked into his wallet at a small pewter angel and smiled as he closed up the wallet and sighed. There was a change coming; he felt it in the breeze, the woods whispered and the spirits all over the house felt it.

"She is coming… *'the key'* is coming…" whispered the woods as only he could hear it and he felt the wind on his bald head as it entered his ears and lodged into his brain as he got in the car with another rookie and headed back to the station. The police and the search teams left the House as Mrs McAnelly, Mrs Baines and Mrs Queronaille thanked Mrs Parks for her hospitality and support as they give her a hug and leaves the couple alone to get breakfast and cleaned up.

But in the Tower, two figures talk as they watch everyone pull away from the drive of Cassious House as the early morning light shines through the Tower's dirty windows. "Looks like the Dark Spirits have had their meal last night," said the advisor to another figure as they watched the situation unfold as he could hear them cursing him in his mind.

"Yes, but at what cost to those mothers, Marylebarne? They lost their sons to the evil of this House for I was the last one to see them and told them to leave; they refused and laughed. I couldn't risk them falling to their deaths when I saw them one last time; being held by the Dark Spirit's grip;" The figure at the window said as he drew in a sigh as the other spirits started to do their chores after breakfast as their day began, "…not at the height they were at Marylebarne;" he said to the dark figure next to him, "as their spines would be shattered and broken; I had no choice but to let the Dark Spirits have them." Marylebarne came into the light as he put a hand on his shoulder and says as the young charge watched the police cars and Incident vans pull out of the driveway. "Sometimes it's the best thing, my boy." The other figure looked at his advisor who just smiled as he told him, "My young Prince, you have to know that the choices we make may be painful and we have to make sure we weigh all the options before we make a decision. That is something you must learn Timothy, for when you become human again, just remember…not everything is fair, and that these events and things happen for a reason." The young man nodded and smiled, "Thank you for your wisdom and input;" Marylebarne smiled as he replied, "I better get to my studies, sir… Excuse me." The advisor patted his back as the young man bowed and left the Tower as he passed a fruit bowl, he took some fruit, filled his pockets, his beaten up water cup and jug, and went to his room to work on his studies.

Marylebarne was a wise and decent man as well as the records keeper who was caught up in the curse as he saw the fall of the House. He had grey hair and crystal grey eyes that sparkled while his stature was one of pride and resilience, and his spirit towards the young man was fatherly and caring, supportive yet disciplined. He had a temper yes, but he loved his charge and would do everything in his power to protect those he loved; especially the staff of the House and their families. He is a teacher, a friend, a fighter, a leader and the king's advisor to his son and he made a promise to the king that he would watch over his son and that's exactly what he intends to do.

Prince Timothy Andrew Carlton was a man in his late twenties; he was just at the age of marriage when the curse happened and now he has grown into a fine man. Born to the King and Queen Carlton, he was being raised as a Prince to follow in his father's footsteps and to take over Cassious House when the curse happened after he was falsely accused of the rape and murder of his bride to be. Now he is a man with a round face with brown eyes and brown curly hair and has the power to make spells, heal, and walk through walls, as well as telepathy. He is tall and his facial features were handsome as all the girls in the Tower had a crush on him; including the girl who gave him his mild ale as he took a break from his studies. His manner was polite, his smile was bright, well respected, and his voice was downright sexy and steady. But his spirit was broken and crushed as this curse had an impact on him and searching for the one he loves was proving to be trying.

Just then a car pulls up and they see a family as everyone gets back to work while the Parks welcome their guests while the spirits began their chores while the Prince went back to his studies in the Tower. Marylebarne had to pay a visit to the man who looked up at the spirits and reassure him that everything was well and that he was not to blame for those boys disappearances and to move on and not dwell on what has happened. He did that as the guests came into the house next to the Parks not knowing that the wind picked up and whispered of the change to Marylebarne as he listened and went down to the dark main hall to talk to the Dark King who resided within the veil as the morning wore on.

After Alyssia collected herself and all the breakfast dishes were washed and cleaned up, the girls were busy getting all the statuettes and clothes ready for the charity shop as Alyssia left Catriona to do that as she went to pack her stuff for University. She would be off in three weeks to start at Kelton University as she got her books and other possessions all packed away and put aside as the room looked empty and sad. This is where a brown eyed, brown long-haired, pretty, quiet and loving young lady lived the rest of her days. Her nightmare started at seven years old; during the time of her father's disastrous court case and inquiry into his assistant's death.

At seven years old, she was a beautiful little girl with fair complexion, dark hair, brown eyes, medium build, small and delicate hands, pretty to look at, a loner and relies on her big brother Paul who loves her with all his heart, and her most treasured item is a teddy bear she has kept since she was a newborn baby. Emotional, loving, kind, willing to help and willing to give, has a big heart, loves pets, loves to sing, disciplined, and knows Gaelic and Welsh, literate in Shakespeare, loves the music of the Carpenters, John Denver and Enya, classical music, loves to play the piano and she was just a child. But it was not meant to last for four years later, she was later sent to Welleston Village to live with her grandmother. After her mum's death at the hands of George Thackeray after she exposed Sidney Preston's murder to the police, she had witnessed the house explosion and she still has nightmares to prove it.

At eleven, she is a talented, dedicated, well-rounded young lady with beautiful, long, brown hair, brown eyes, medium muscular build, honour student, not a bother to Catriona Timrod (who is like a second sister to her) or her grandmother. She was not a typical teenager who would fight and argue or cause her family trouble; she was the type of girl who did her chores, was caring, emotional, and understanding but was a victim of bullying in high school which has led her to depression, and social anxiety; she has a slow learning disability in Maths where the bullying stems because others thought that she was stupid. She keeps to herself, still practices her Welsh and Gaelic, piano playing, sings, writes, reads, loves to laugh, research, and avoids conflict. Now all grown up, she was off to

University on a scholarship and she was okay with that as she packed her things and got them to the other empty room while she waited for the will to be settled.

Before and after Jessica Jenkins's death; Alyssia was preparing for Kelton University which is thirty miles away in Kelton Heights while she was a college student who has won a university scholarship for her paper on Celtic languages and life in Kelton Heights and Welleston Village, she has started a search for her father and her brother. Her grandmother's lawyer has found her the place she will stay at; away from every party and bad influence that is associated with University campuses; the drinking, drugs, hazing, sorority rooms and secret societies that could cause a student to break under pressure and it was a flat used for holiday accommodation and now will serve her as an off campus living quarters for the next year… Cassious House; and she doesn't know it but she is about to make the biggest change in both of the towns fortunes.

Just as Alyssia finished packing what she could for University, she went downstairs to see Catriona who went to the kitchen to make the tea while Alyssia was putting all of Jessica's clothes in a cardboard box along with the statuettes when there was a knock on the door. Catriona left the kitchen and went down the main hall to answer it. The Reverend Father and Jessica's lawyer came in to the living room as Alyssia stood up and greeted them after she taped the box shut and moved it over to the pile of boxes marked "Charity shop" as the lawyer and the reverend greeted her as she stood up.

"Alyssia good to see you out of your room and active; how are you feeling?" She shook hands with both men as Catriona came through with the teas and every one took a seat, "I can't say I'm feeling any better right now- the pain is still raw, but I thought that nothing will get done if I stay in my room and cry and so I thought I better come out and get the place cleaned up and ready for selling. Catriona is going home to be with her family in the North of Uist and I will be away to University so I was wondering what to do with the house?"

The lawyer understood and he watched as she left the room and came back with all the bills in a big manila envelope and gave it to the lawyer while Catriona handed out the teas. "These came after my grandmother's death and the ones on top are new, sir;" Alyssia said as Catriona gave her the hot chocolate and sat down. "I've also got the funeral to prepare and so I will have lots to do before I go off to University." The lawyer says, "Well worry no more, that is why we are here," says the lawyer as the Reverend father spoke up as Catriona gave her the hot chocolate.

"I have had a talk with your grandmother before she passed away and the funeral arrangement have been made and approved. The service is very simple; she asked to be cremated and her ashes scattered to the wind. She wants to have a small Communion during the service but no flowers; she has chosen a charity and the mourners will be asked to donate to the charity. The service will be held at the church and then, the coffin will be taken to the Crematorium afterwards and tea and a light lunch will be served immediately afterwards at the Crematorium and she has asked me personally to do both services."

Alyssia was relieved as she let out a big sigh while the lawyer said, "I have the will here and all I need to do is have it signed by you, Catriona and me. The will leaves you both an equal share; Catriona will get the house and the money, while you Alyssia will get the car and the other half of the money and if the house is sold, you two will get equal part of the sale of it as well. I am speeding up the process for the will right now and I will call all the companies she owes money to and get them to close all of her accounts as well as pay off all the debts. In other words, I will do the hard part-all you have to do is pack up everything. I have hired a cleaning company to come in after you have left and clean up the house… it's the company my wife and I use and they are very reliable. So how do you feel now?"

Catriona and Alyssia smiled, *Gu is a foochadh, tapadh leat.* "That is a relief, thank you." Catriona replied, "A *Sinn feum gu lorg cathrannas bùth gu socair Jessica's rud is ma-t*á *fastaidh a sgioba-glanaidh gu t*á*r luis taigh e*á*rlaidh do luis ath- teagh lach gu teann ann an.* "We need to find a charity shop to take Jessica's things away so the cleaners can get the house ready for the next family to move in." The lawyer and the reverend father nodded as Alyssia asked, *Ma-t*á *theag sibh can cobair orm pacadh do oilthigh?* "Then maybe you can help me pack for University?" Catriona chuckled and said as the men listened, *Seadh gu fuiam coltach plana, a Alyssia.* "Yes, sounds like a plan, Alyssia." They stand and go over to the coffee table as the girls signed the will and then the lawyer added his name. Then when it was all done and checked over, he folded it back up and placed it in his coat pocket as the Reverend Father comforted Alyssia as she knew that once she signed this will, it was final; Jessica would never be with them except in thoughts and heart as she held back tears.

The lawyer then told them that he would hire the cleaners and as soon as all the charity stuff was away, "It will save you the hassle of cleaning the place yourself, Catriona... but what about the furniture?" asked the lawyer as Alyssia spoke up drying some stray tears. "I was looking up some furniture companies and they told me of a place which is a charity for the low income families and that I should try them. I have to call so they will come and look at the furniture, but I may have to make a donation. I would like you here to make sure everything is on the up and up and also I need movers to move all the stuff to the new place in Kelton Heights;" She sniffed and took out a folded paper from her pocket and handed it to the lawyer, "I have a list here of specific Items and it's not a very big list..."

The lawyer saw the list that she gave him and she told Catriona, in a brief whisper, that she would explain everything to her once the Lawyer and the Reverend Father left the house. Catriona nodded as the lawyer got Alyssia's attention. "This is a very short list indeed, but what about the boxes that is in your room?" Alyssia replied, "I want the movers to take them too as I will transport my clothes and smaller items like my computer, printer and other items by car and I want to have the furniture put in storage until I'm on the road and you or I can call them to let them know where to take the items before I arrive at the new place you have picked out for me... I will need you here as well to make sure that I understand everything."

"I would be happy to, Alyssia and not to worry, I will call them so you can concentrate on where you're going, okay?" said the lawyer, who took up the manila envelope and she nodded as the men stood and he replied, "Well I think the reverend and I have taken up your time so we better be going.... I will be in touch girls, and I will do as much as I can and get the will quickly sorted and look for a buyer or renter for the house, in other words, you leave all the hard stuff to me, girls." The girls smiled as the Reverend Father says, "I wanted you to know also that the whole village will be turning out for the funeral, is there anyone you don't want there?" The girls thought about Mrs June Caruthers and that she maybe should not come for she gave Jessica a hard time and made Catriona very uncomfortable as she asked Catriona quietly about June Caruthers. Then Alyssia says, "No, everyone can come, Reverend Father; I wouldn't want anyone to feel left out."

The reverend nodded and gave Alyssia and Catriona a hug as the lawyer smiled and opened the door as they went out to the car. "I will set the funeral for next week at one o'clock at the church and two o'clock at the Crematorium, is that date appropriate?" Alyssia repeated back to Catriona what the Reverend father had told them as they both agreed. "Wonderful. I will pencil it in and announce it in church and I will simply say that all are welcome." The girls thank them again as the men leave for their cars. As the men pulled away, the girls look at June Caruthers and simply headed back inside as Alyssia sat down with Catriona and told her in Gaelic what they have agreed upon as Catriona listened attentively while they get the rest of the stuff packed and start on dinner.

Prelude to Chapter One

THREE WEEKS BEFORE

<u>It was a beautiful sunny but cold day in Welleston Village and</u> Alyssia Franklin-Jenkins was with the whole village at the Welleston Village Crematorium outside of town at the funeral of her grandmother Jessica Jenkins with Catriona Timrod after a brief church service and Communion. Her friends, doctors, nurses, her lawyer and the whole town turned out for the service as everyone was waiting for the hearse and the undertaker to come. Alyssia drove herself and Catriona, her grandmother's nurse, to the Crematorium and they talked about things as they dried the tears of loss and grief away while driving down a country road towards the Crematorium.

Catriona was a beautiful lass with very long black hair, which was tied up in a ponytail, and the most beautiful amber eyes ever seen on a young lady. She was a slender young lady with a delicate pink and peach skin with a splash of tan on her rounded face and hands which were tiny and delicate while her black clothes fit on her slender frame as many of the women, especially cranky June Caruthers were a bit jealous of her to say the least.

At first when she was eleven, Alyssia didn't understand why her grandmother Jessica chose Catriona from Uist to be her grandmother's nurse but Jessica cleared up the confusion as she said to her when she was introduced to her the very first time. "Your mother wanted me to keep you knowledge of Gaelic up to date, and since Catriona only speaks Gaelic, I want you to talk to her in that language;" Alyssia finally understood and they became the best of friends at first but as Alyssia let Catriona help her with her studies on Gaelic, they became close as sisters and to Jessica

Jenkins; that was all right with her... but to June Caruthers, she was a really nosey, crotchety, cranky neighbour and saying to Jessica that she should get rid of Catriona and get someone from here to watch over her health.

Jessica didn't understand why June was acting that way and all the hate for Catriona fuelled the fire as Jessica would hear nothing of the sort and told June to mind her own business as an argument began between the two ladies. Jessica had told her time and time again why she chose Catriona, but June still made her life miserable as it came to a head at a bridge game as the other ladies warned June to stop her relentless attack on the nurse and Jessica. So finally she had enough; she stood up from the bridge table and folded her hand as Jessica said to her while she got her coat on, "Then stay away from me- don't bother coming to see me, in fact, our friendship is over. Goodbye ladies, I will not be returning to this bridge club anytime soon." Jessica left the table and went home; she never went back to her bridge partners ever again.

It was a couple of nights later that Jessica Jenkins was on her deathbed and her nurse was in attendance with the doctor, the priest, the ambulance crew, and the lawyer as she took her granddaughter to her and held her hand close to her chest. She gave her some advice and told her after the vitals were checked, "Alyssia I am very proud of you and I want you to do me proud at Kelton University, you understand me?" Alyssia nodded as she must hold all that pain inside her and it stirred within her like someone was baking a cake with anger, sadness, depression and tears as the main ingredients; then later baking it in a volcano until it burns into nothingness and she was trying her best not to shed any tears as Jessica told her, "No tears now, I want you to be brave and strong for me; just be the best you can be."

Jessica then gave her an envelope that she hid under a pillow beside her and it had her name on it as Alyssia listened, "Your mother gave it to me to hold for you; I was supposed to give you this on your eighteenth birthday but I thought I better wait; so before I go, I better give it to you now." Alyssia had a sad smile on her face as she was going to open it, but Jessica stopped her with a touch on her cheek. "No my sweet girl, wait till I'm gone and then open it; it's not long now my sweet granddaughter-I love you and so did your mother."

Alyssia was puzzled but did as her grandmother wished as Jessica smiled up at her once more knowing it was about time. "I love you grandmother," Alyssia said as Jessica smiled and patted her granddaughter's hand one last time knowing that she had done everything she could to fulfil her daughter's wishes as the priest administered the last rites, closed her eyes as she passed away peacefully in her sleep. Alyssia gave her grandmother a kiss on the forehead one last time, stood up, and placed the envelope in her pocket as Catriona took her aside and let the Doctor and the ambulance crew do their jobs. Jessica's lawyer and Catriona took her outside to the living room, sat her on the couch, and comforted her. "Your grandmother wanted it this way; she wanted no fuss, no mourning and no tears," said the lawyer. "She was always proud of you, never forget that." Alyssia smiled then they looked around and saw the body being carried off to the morgue as her doctor says, "I will get a death certificate ready for you, Alyssia, just when you are up to it, you can sign it and I will send it to the registrar's office for you. My condolences Alyssia and Catriona, I know how important she was to you."

He gave her one more touch on her arm and left everyone in peace as the priest says, "I know a friend who is a funeral director and we'll make the plans with your help as she said with a lump in her throat, "Thank you very much, father. I hoped that we could play her favourite hymn at her funeral, but come by tomorrow and we'll get the arrangements made." The lawyer who was with her says, "That's a good idea-for you go off to University in three weeks," Alyssia nodded as she tried very hard not to cry as the lawyer continued, "…so we better get it all done quickly and I will speed up the will and get that processed quickly so at least you will go away with some peace of mind, if it's okay with you ladies?"

Catriona nodded as he smiled and continued; "I would like to come here about early afternoon, father, we can at least get the funeral out of the way?" The priest nodded and said, "I will come by tomorrow afternoon with the funeral director and get the arrangements all organised." The lawyer looked at a despondent Alyssia and asked her, "Will that be okay with you, Alyssia?" She came out of it, even for a little bit and said, "Yes that will be fine, sir and Reverend father." He nodded as Alyssia went back into her shell as she sat on the couch while Catriona sat with her and the girls had an early night after everyone left the house. The next day, the Doctor came by and Alyssia signed the Death Certificate as Catriona witnessed it and put her name down as well. "My condolences to you both," the Doctor says after he signed it as well as Alyssia broke down while Catriona took her to the couch and held her close.

Now in the crematorium a week later, Jessica was being cremated and June was making a fuss all over again after Alyssia pulled into the parking area and they were greeted by the funeral director and the vicar. "Hello Alyssia and Catriona how are you today?" asked the vicar to Alyssia as the girls smiled, "We are well vicar, thank you." The Reverend Father smiled as the funeral director told Catriona in Gaelic, to follow him as she whispered to Alyssia where she was going; a prayer room within the crematorium. *Iongantach!* "Wonderful!" and followed him to the Reflection Room as she told the lawyer quietly, "At least it will keep her away from June Caruthers for a bit. I should have said that June Caruthers would not be invited, but then she would still make a fuss-I can't win either way."

The lawyer nodded and held her close to him like a loving father as she said sadly, "If I only knew where my brother and father were, they would be here beside me." She broke down as the lawyer hugged her as well as his wife knowing that this was ripping her apart having no family as Catriona joined in and felt for her. Jessica was her only family and she was as close as a sister, and for just a brief moment she would have loved to adopt Alyssia into her family, but never discussed it with her or Jessica as she had a family of her own back up in North Uist.

The Funeral Director and Jessica's friend and lawyer agreed as she calmed down long enough to say to her with a smile and low voice as she dried her tears, *Tadhail ann an am ceanachaidh sa rùm dè an luiathreachan agus guidh tostach agus fuirich thall bhò an June Caruthers. Mi àis bí sa cuibhrigte sèis a-mach.* "Go into the reflection room of the crematorium and pray and stay away from June Caruthers. I'll be in the covered benches outside over there;" she pointed to the covered seat near the Crematorium grounds. Catriona nodded and she went with the funeral director to the reflection room after giving each other another hug and as smile as the funeral director led Catriona away to a quiet room for prayer and meditation. The Crematorium got word that the Hearst was a bit late leaving the hospital in arriving at the Crematorium for the service so everyone had a talk and some laughs outside; but the vicar lost sight of Alyssia as he looked around the grounds and found her sitting in the covered benches near some trees watching the birds play in the leaves.

He saw a sad but a pretty young lady who was leaving for University in three weeks in Kelton Heights thirty miles away and even though the town was proud of her, the death of her grandmother had her shook up because of what happened when her daughter died in that terrible gas explosion in Kelton Heights several years ago and so the community did their best for her and her grandmother as it was the talk of the town. The sympathy that poured in was unimaginable…scores of flowers and cards flooded Jessica's home as Alyssia was only eleven and scared after she brought before the press and the townspeople as soon as they heard about Emily's death. The child was given stuffed toys and candy as the police and child services questioned Jessica and found that no charges would be filed against her. Rookie officer and friend of the family John Preston came to the little girl aged eleven, knelt before her and said in a soothing voice, "I will do everything in my power to make sure that you are safe and well cared for, I promise." John smiled as Alyssia hugged him asking, "But why? Are you going somewhere?" John told her, "I'm off to Afghanistan to fight for my country, but before any of that, I will make sure you and your grandmother is well taken care of and I will also make sure that Jessica has no worries with money or the mortgage. You are going to do great things, remember that…"

She looked at John and said, "I hope my angel will protect you," and she reached into her pocket and pulled out a small, pewter, circular imprint of an angel and gave it to John who smiled as he looked back at her. "I named her Angela…take her with you and she will keep you safe and watch over you." John took the small angel, clutched it in his hand, and gave her a hug as he held the angel in his fist and took it with him to Afghanistan.

Alyssia smiled at that memory as the vicar saw that she was a wreck with tears pouring from her brown eyes, drinking water like it was alcohol, sitting away from everyone, and watching the birds-not wanting anyone to see how she was hurting or feeling; the birds were keeping her mind off the funeral as she listened to them singing and watched them darting in and out of the trees above her. She thought of her family who were long gone; her heart broke in half, not knowing what she is going to do with all the pain inside.

The townspeople around her were laughing and recalling happy times and memories of her loving grandmother while she tried so hard to hold back tears drinking her water and thought: *"First my dad and brother are nowhere to be found, then my mother dies in a gas explosion at her home nine years ago…now my grandmother Jessica Jenkins passes away. Perhaps I should join them?"* Alyssia quickly shook the thought from her brain quickly. *"Really life, this is not the best way to start at Kelton University."*

Alyssia's heart hurt as if someone just stomped on it with spiky football shoes and she felt like a drunk drinking her water like it was alcohol as she took in a deep breath; she tried to stop her tears from flowing…saving them for the service, but they refused to stop as the vicar saw her holding on to an envelope that was in her hand as she puts it away as soon as she saw the priest came to her under the covered benches and sat beside her while she watched the two birds playing in the trees above her. They looked at her and she smiled at them and at their antics while she looked over to the vicar, smiled and then looked back at the birds.

Ciamar tha thu, a Alyssia? "How are you, Alyssia?" The priest asked as she looked back at him and smiles, ***Chan eil cho math, sagart…*** "Not so good, Reverend father…." He came over and sat with her as he placed a comforting hand on hers as they watched the birds fly away. ***Mi mamaidh, dadaidh agus mo beag bràithreil a bheil an seo gu sòlasaich meas an-duigh… Chan ann eile tho meas…mi faireach dainne glè aonranach.*** "My mummy, daddy and my big brother are not here to comfort me today; there's no one else except for me… I feel so alone." Then she sighs and tells him as they watch June Caruthers berate Catriona's good name to the others, ***Mo seanmhair cha coltach eadh gu a Chatriona is ti sàraichte air ti gobair June Caruthers.*** "My grandmother wouldn't like it that Catriona is being harassed by the busy body, June Caruthers." The priest nodded as she drinks more of her water and dries her ever flowing tears and then looks up at the sky, ***Tha an t-side brèagha ann agus mi gair eadh gu uisge.*** "The weather is beautiful and I want to rain."

The priest then looked up at the fluffy white clouds, blue sky and the warm sun as he pats her hand as he says, ***Gu dearbh!*** "Indeed!" They laugh as the priest gave her hand a squeeze and asked without upsetting her anymore than she was as he asked her, ***'S dòcha tha e mu tim sibh bonn-shuidhich ur n fhèin cuir san saoghal?*** "Maybe it's about time you found your own place in the world?" She gave him a small smile and asked as she looked at him, **Aois folbh gu oilthigh cuunt, sagart?** "Does going off to University count, reverend father?" He said right away as he chuckled, **'O shirrachd, tha.** "Yes, indeed!" She chuckled with him and says, **Ceart gu leor!** "Right enough." She sniffs and says gently, **Mi falbh oilthigh ann cola-deugh dèidh a h-uile rud tha seathigte air ti neach-lagha.** "I leave for University in two weeks after everything is settled by the lawyer..." **Gasta!** "Excellent!" he exclaimed and Alyssia smiled, even though her tears were still rolling down her face.

Then he asked her, **Tha fhios an tidsearans cò a bheil ag luis oilthigh bi ciall? Tha e mòr-eadarahm clach-mhile agus mi tha fhios agam seanmhair is glè motiel dè sibh agus luis beag sgoilearachds ais bi a mòr-eadarahm cuideachas gu sibh?** "Surely, the teachers, who are at University, will understand? It's a major milestone and I know that your grandmother is very proud of you...and the big scholarship will be a major help to you?" Just then they see the hearse and the undertaker coming towards the Crematorium in the distance as they all stand to take their places as she tells the vicar, **Tha fhios dòiche ionnas gu.** "I surely hope so." They smile and leave the covered benches to greet the car and the undertaker as the group of friends, family, and acquaintances head into the Crematorium for the service as Alyssia meets up with Catriona and go inside for the funeral.

A WEEK AFTER THE FUNERAL

Alyssia and Catriona were very busy going through Jessica Jenkins's stuff and Alyssia was packing for University in between times; but to say that the girls never stopped was an understatement-they only stopped to eat, sleep, and packed boxes for charity shops and to receive visitors like her grandmother's lawyer who came to see them and quickly to wrap up her grandmother's affairs as well as other townsfolk. The car and half of the estate belonged to Alyssia, while Catriona got the house and the other half of the estate as the girls thought that was fair and agreed with the lawyer and the lawyer himself got half and it was enough money to cover all the debts her grandmother left behind and the funeral expenses while the rest of the money was split between the two of them. *Mi àis bí folbh gu an Uibhist a Tuath gu bí le fear-pòsta agus mac; do mi feud gu bí a-sheo?* "I will be going off to the North of Uist to be with my husband and son; do I have to be here?" The lawyer told her, *Chan mur sibh coma leat togair gu, a Chatriona…mi àm na conbhail sibh muin. Ma lùigeas tu togair tadhail dachaigh, sibh tadhail air dachaigh…mi can do luis sorchan.* "Not if you don't want to, Catriona. I am not holding you back; if you want to go home, you go home; I can do the rest."

He saw that Catriona was upset as Alyssia told the lawyer about June Caruthers accusing her of murdering her grandmother, and to say that the lawyer was angry was an understatement! "That is completely out of line and not true, Alyssia," the lawyer said offended and cleared up the matter as he touched her hand gently. "Your grandmother died peacefully in her sleep and you knew yourself that she had heart trouble?" Alyssia nodded and said to him, "I did, sir. My grandmother and I have been through too much and you know of my background, do you sir?" The lawyer nodded as she continued as she took Catriona's hand, "…and I would never believe that Catriona would do anything to hurt Jessica; we are practically sisters and got along well as she saw that grandmother was well and took her medicine on time."

The lawyer agreed, "Thank you for clearing this up." The lawyer said to her, "I will handle Mrs Caruthers…not to worry." Catriona's tears rolled down her eyes as Alyssia patted her hand and said to her, *Chan gu dragh, nar luis neach lagha àis liath dearbh de June Caruthers.* "Not to worry, let the lawyer handle June Caruthers." Catriona smiled as Alyssia and the lawyer in Gaelic. *Raghaidh June Caruthers gu ma i buanaich gu tro chèile a Chatriona, mus mi folbh oir oilthig, mi àis pearsanta liath beatha cruaidh oir a h.* "Warn June Caruthers that if she continues to upset Catriona, before I leave for University, I will personally make life hard for her." The lawyer agreed and nodded… "Agreed Alyssia, no need for that nonsense; it has been a hard three weeks… for the both of you."

They change the subject as Alyssia said to her gently, *"Sibh feud mo ceadaich g ureic luis taigh ma sibh do reic; mas a do thoil e liath dearbh gu nar luis neach-lagha gu cobhair sibh.* "You have my permission to sell the house; if you do sell, please make sure to let the lawyer help you." Alyssia told Catriona smiled, *Tapadh leibh, a Alyssia.* "Thank you,

Alyssia." The lawyer told the girls that he would be as quick as possible with the legal affairs and that the money from the will as well as from the sale of the house would be split equally. The girls were happy and all the legal matters were settled and closed after he asked if there were any questions as the girls looked at each other and shook their heads. The lawyer had the girls sign the documents for legal purposes and the lawyer left them to their peace. ***Tioraidh, a Chatriona agus, oidhirp chan gu dragh, a Chatriona…*** "Goodbye and try not to worry, Catriona."

The nurse nodded and smiled a thank you as she got back to work while Alyssia showed him to the door and to the car as she told Catriona that she would be right back. Catriona nodded as the lawyer and Alyssia walked to the car, "Alyssia, I will make sure June Caruthers is told and warned about her attitude, leave it to me." Alyssia opened the car door as they shook hands as he said, "Goodbye, Alyssia and good luck at University." She smiled and watched him get in as she watched the lawyer's car pull away, and then went back into the house, and she closed and locked the door as Catriona and her wrapped all the statuettes in news paper and bubble wrap so they can send it off to all the different charity shops in Welleston Village, even the people who were picking up the furniture were coming to see her and getting the list of items together as they made a date to come back and pick everything up. A little while later, the first of the charity vans pulled up and helped take some of the boxes away, while another came and did the same. A little while later, another van pulled up and everything that belonged to Jessica was taken away to charity shops around Welleston Village and the only things that were in the house were Catriona's and Alyssia's things, food and the furniture as well as televisions and silverware, plates and cups, a microwave and other appliances as the girls got ready for dinner and bed.

AT CASSIOUS HOUSE IN KELTON HEIGHTS

That same afternoon, Prince Timothy was at his usual place at the window drinking his mild ale as he looked down at the angry couple and the undisciplined kids getting into the car. For three hundred years or more, he's been looking for the girl of his dreams and no one fit the description…

he hated being without a heart and soul and he vowed that the next person who took up residence near the haunted house, will hopefully be loving and kind as well as helpful. His loyal advisor Marylebarne, understood this as he watched the Prince sink into a deep depression sometimes; but somehow he broke out of it by giving his mind something to do; like learning to be a Prince; the laws and other royal duties of the Royal House, learning what each part of the household does and he's taken to his studies rather well Marylebarne thought as he gave him more studies and other lessons to keep his brain active.

Marylebarne was a wise but a fair advisor that made sure that things were done properly and that the House was running smoothly. His gray hair and wisdom along with his stern gaunt facial features and piercing blue eyes made him a dangerous man because he could see right through you if you were lying. His stature was proud and a man to be respected as he stuck to the old ways of doing things and the staff liked it and his no nonsense attitude made the good spirits love him even more. Since the stable boys and gardeners could not go outside, Marylebarne assigned them certain duties and they spent the daylight hours doing caretaker duties for the help (Butlers, DIY and janitorial positions, cooks and other household personnel) around the Tower; then at night, helped the remaining guards with watch duties; thanks to Marylebarne who made sure that they had something to do, many of them were entertainers or played instruments and they would put on small shows just to lift the spirits and hopes off all who were around them as they would sing and dance while Marylebarne would make sure that there was something for everyone.

Timothy was taking a break and drinking his ale as the men watched the family preparing to leave the property along with the other spirits who were watching and cheering on Kevin Parks, a fifth generation caretaker, as the couple charged out the door and went to the car as they argued with the caretakers after throwing their luggage in the car's boot as they argued some more as Kevin said quite firmly and steady. "I warned you and your children not to go into Cassious House and your kids didn't listen or you refused to tell them. I have been a caretaker here for five generations and so was my father and onwards and we have told people never to go into Cassious House; the most important clause in the lease, and your children disobeyed it!"

He remained calm throughout the whole spectacle while the woman was not so calm; she was so blinded by her own self-importance that she took what he was saying with offence; "How dare you, sir!" The mother said in such an arrogant way that Sharlene stepped up to argue with her but Kevin held her back while the kids got into their seats and started to fight as the father rebuked them harshly as she said to the Parks rather curtly, "Are you saying that I don't know how to discipline my own children?" Sharlene smiled as the spirits cheered Kevin on, "Yes...Yes I am! To be perfectly honest, you are the worst family to ever grace Cassious House and I hope that I never see you again for all that matter! Here is your deposit back in full and I bid you all...farewell!"

Kevin stood his ground as the woman got so hot headed that the spirits actually saw steam coming out of her ears as she snatched the money from him as she said, "Well I suggest another line of work, Mr Parks! The noise is unbearable and inconvenient, so I seriously urge you to find another line of work and have the city tear this place down!" Kevin was about to say something but held his tongue after the woman got into the car as her husband pulled out of the driveway with such speed that it kicked up dust and pebbles, while out the back window, the young children made faces at Kevin and Sharlene as the couple took cover while the spirits cheered.

"Good riddance!" Sharlene said as Kevin wrapped his arms around his wife after the Parks dusted themselves off as they went back inside and started to draw up another lease and flyer at the table. Up in the Tower, Marylebarne and Timothy looked out of the Tower window with and the other spirits and Marylebarne replied with a sigh of relief, "Good riddance to bad rubbish. That woman was appalling and horrible and her kids were terrible, undisciplined little brats. I am most relieved that they are gone and happy for someone else to live here that are more civilised." Timothy Andrew Carlton took another drink of his mild ale and he laughed in his cup as the Prince placed a hand on Marylebarne's shoulder as he said, "I quite agree, my friend," he said as he looked out the window again and continued with a bit of mischievous humour in his eyes joked, "I was about to put a sheet over my head, grab some chains, and use my spirit powers to give them such a scare-they wouldn't be sleeping for many years!" All the spirits laughed as he watched the car finally disappear down the tree-lined drive and into traffic.

But the Prince was troubled as Marylebarne asked his charge, "What's wrong my dear boy?" Timothy looked at Marylebarne and sighed. "For over three hundred years, I've searched for that one special girl and found no one, Marylebarne. I'm starting to think that she doesn't exist." The advisor placed a reassuring hand on Timothy's shoulder and said gently as Timothy looked at him. "Be patient, my dear prince, she will come, I promise." The Prince gave him a sad smile and said, "I really hope so. Well, I better get back to my studies, excuse me." Marylebarne patted his shoulder and he left the window as the girl took his canter, gave her a smile, took some fruit and asked the girl to bring some fresh cold water to his room. The young girl bowed to him and says, "Right away sire," and went to get the water as he left for his study to get back to work and restarted his studies as the afternoon wore into early evening. A moment later, the young girl brought in the fresh water for the Prince as he thanked her and she smiled, bowed, and closed the door as she went back to her duties.

In the Park's residence on the other side of the haunted house, early evening had rolled around once again as Kevin and Sharlene are having dinner. Kevin was writing the advert on a notepad and as he was writing, Sharlene says, trying to help her husband word it perfectly, "...and someone who will follow the rule of not going into the House next door unless by special permission." Kevin, who was writing the advert at the table, nodded in agreement and says, "It has to be a very special kind of tenant; someone who will make a difference to the towns and is very friendly...oooh, that's good;" and he wrote down what he just said on paper before it escaped him as Sharlene asked while she was about to take another bite of her dinner. "Is the tenant allowed any pets? We don't want to deny her a pet?" Kevin wrote in the advert to the University and said to her, "Wonderful idea, my dear. I don't want too many, maybe a two small pets limit?" Sharlene nodded as he wrote it down, "Perfect."

Kevin was happy with the wording and so was Sharlene, who looked it over as he said; "I will get a new lease sent over to the University with terms and clauses for taking the house next door. I will also give them the keys to the flat and they can give it to any student who wants it." The advert was written and Kevin looked at it once more, read it back to his wife, and she approved of it. It was typed up, printed and rechecked as both of them signed it as they ate dinner and relaxed before bedtime; and he also made sure everything was secure because of all the dark spirits haunting the land nearby. Sharlene then asked as he was reading the sports, "Kevin, when she said that 'you should find another line of work and have this House torn down' what does that mean?"

Kevin said as he took off his glasses and said, "What she means is that I should give up my duties as caretaker and find a meaningful job; but that is not going to happen. I am not going to give up on five generations of caretaking duties and abandon the spirits my father so dearly protected, just because some witch wants me to. This is also a listed House, Sharlene, it can't be torn down. The council said that 'tearing it down would be a desecration to our history and our past…'" Sharlene understood why he refused to live anywhere else; he had a duty and a promise to his family and no one was going to deter him from it.

"Well said, Kevin. Sometimes I do need reminding after that snobby, inflated ego, pompous windbag of a woman and her family of undisciplined brats and that snooty husband. She had enough hot air to fill a tire on a bike. Honestly Kevin, I wanted to punch her lights out for what she said to you." Kevin smiled and took his wife's hand as he said, "…that's my little prize fighter!" The couple kissed as he sat in his chair and got back to reading his paper while Sharlene brought him some tea and the couple relaxed as the night was filled with ghostly dance and music as night's dark veil surrounded the towns.

The same night, thirty miles away, Alyssia and Catriona were getting ready for bed and an early night as Alyssia's car was filled up with petrol, packed up safely and ready for the road, except for the clothes that she will be travelling in as Catriona gave her the guest room and she moved into it for just one night after the movers came and took Alyssia's stuff to storage until the call from the lawyer came to them. Just then, she heard Catriona call to her, **Dinneir air a'bhord!** "Dinner is on the table!" Just as she placed her clothes neatly on the chair, she heard her stomach rumble as she said, **Madha riribh! Mi àis nigh mo còigeachs agus bí cead le sibh. Mi àm lonail!** "Excellent! I will wash my hands and be right with you. I'm starving!" After the girls washed their hands, they came to the dinner table and started to eat after they said prayer. The meal was mince with carrots and green peas and mashed potatoes as they talked and laughed as Catriona asked her, **Cia fhada tha e gu luis oilthigh?** "How long is it to the University?" Alyssia cleaned her mouth with her napkin and drank some water as she replied, *Tha e...* "It is…" then stopped to think; then looked at Catriona and says gently, *Chan eil agam, air mionair, a Chatriona.* "I don't know honestly, Catriona."

She took her water again as Catriona smiled; *Uileag mi tha fhios agam tha e taobh a-muigh de baile...* "All I know that it is outside of town," Alyssia then said as the girls finished their dinner as she replied, *Tha mi air an rathad sa a'mhadainn…mi imir gu lorgadhcho guluath cho mi mi tair gu baile.* "I am on the road in the morning… I'll need to find the University as soon as I get to town." Alyssia looked at Catriona as the girls smiled and they gathered up the dishes and took them to the kitchen to wash them up. She told Catriona as she puts the plates down and starts filling up the wash basin with hot water and dish soap, *Abhàrr, mi togair gu tàir a-mach dè ur n falt ionnas gu sibh can soillerich luis taigh.* "Besides, I want to get out of your hair so you can clear up the house." Catriona smiled, *Dean na bi glaoicaeil; tha thu gu br*áth ann an a uidh. A bharrachd air sin, mi coltach sligeach thu an sheo. "Don't be silly; you are never in the way. Besides, I like having you here."

The girls smiled as Catriona gave each other a hug and she helped Alyssia with the dishes in the kitchen; Alyssia washed and Catriona dried as they laugh and talk, had a water fight, and put away the dishes, utensils, as well as the pots and pans in the cupboards and drawers. Finally, the kitchen is tidy once again and they went into the living room with their tea and hot chocolate as they relaxed before they hit the beds early.

Catriona said to her, *Mi àm moiteil dè sibh-folbh gu oilthigh air a'sgoilearachas...* "I am so proud of you-going off to University on a scholarship…" Alyssia smiled as she said; *...agus sibh a Chatriona feud a fear-pòsta agus mac... mi tha fhios àis bí buidhe gu sir sibh.* "…and you Catriona have a husband and son I know that will be glad to see you." She smiled at the thought of them as Alyssia says, *Dòmhnall agus Iain; iad* àis bí *a'feitheamh gu thig taigh…Chan nas June Caruthers; carson coma leat sibh thoir iad a f*òn? *Tha mi dearbh said e*àrling gu fairich fuaim bho sibh... "Donald and Iain; I know that they are waiting for you to come home; no more June Caruthers. Why don't you give them a call? I'm sure they want to hear from you."

Catriona smiled and said to her happily, *'S dòcha mi àis, tapadh leat, a Alyssia.* "Maybe I will thank you Alyssia." Alyssia smiled as Catriona says, *a aois fuiam saoidh ach tha mi moiteil de sibh...* "That does sound good, but I'm still proud of you." The news and weather were over as Catriona turned off the television and puts down the remote while girls stood and embraced once again as they got ready for bed as Catriona says gently as they head upstairs, *Mi àis comhlion eig in botal dè uisge oir sibh gu gabh ur n astaraich.* "I will fill up some bottles of water for you to take on your journey." Alyssia smiled and replied gently, *Sibh a bheil as caomh, a Chatriona, tapadh leat.* "You are most kind Catriona, thank you." The girls say their good nights and head off to bed after watching the news and the weather.

EARLY THE VERY NEXT MORNING

At seven in the morning, Alyssia awakens to Catriona clattering around in the kitchen downstairs and the radio on BBC Alba. She gets up, stripped the bed, showered, changed into her travelling clothes, puts her dirty clothes in a plastic bag as she placed it into a carry-all luggage; then brushed her hair, puts on her shoes and tossed the brush into the carry all and she placed her toiletries and other travel accessories along with her dirty clothes inside as well as she closed up the bag and left the guest room. She leaves her car keys out and she sits her bag and keys on the sideboard then went back into the guest room one last time, and brought out the bed sheets and wet towels and took them to the kitchen as she tossed them into the washer after she placed the mail on the sideboard.

Meanwhile, Catriona was busy fixing sandwiches and snacks for her as she got all the bottles of water and placed them into the old backpack. Alyssia the traveller came through and greeted her, *Madainn mhath, a Chatriona.* "Good morning, Catriona" Catriona looked around to see Alyssia's smile as she does the same, *Madainn mhath, a Alyssia...* "Good morning, Alyssia," she said as she was busy packing the old back pack with food and foil wrapped water with the last of the sandwiches and snacks as well as the crisps which either sat on top or on the sides of the backpack. After that is all done, she zips up the backpack while Alyssia sees to breakfast. Catriona helps her with the toast, eggs, sausages, beans, bacon and placed them on hot plates while Alyssia sees to the tea, hot chocolate and juice as she placed them on the table after turning off the oven.

The girls finally sit down and have breakfast as Catriona looked outside and told her, *An latha a bheil snog an-drástale fearthainn an-drásta's a-risthist a-shin bréagha as addéidh seo.* "The day is nice just now; with rain now and then; then fine later on." Catriona smiled but Alyssia was very quiet as she looked over and saw that she was deep in thought. Catriona touched Alyssia's hand gently, *Dè do trùma?* "How are you feeling?" Alyssia comes out of it and shakes her head as she smiled. *Tha gu math...mi farbhas mi àm nearbhach...tapadh leibh.* "I'm fine...I guess I'm nervous, thank you." Both girls smiled as Catriona pats her hand gently as the girls get the breakfast dishes washed, dried and put away and tells her to give the mail to the lawyer if he comes around, *Tuille post airson a Jessica...* "More mail for Jessica..." she told Catriona as the nurse nodded as she placed the mail on the side board.

Then Catriona put on her coat, grabbed the backpack and they both walk out of the kitchen while Alyssia grabbed her jacket, her carry-on bag, and car keys as they walked out of the house to her car which was heavy ladened with all her belongings. She opened the car door, set her carry-on bag and her purse on the passenger side floor, while the backpack sat on the passenger seat and Alyssia fastened the seatbelt around the backpack... while nosey June Caruthers watched the girls from across the street as she swept the sidewalk of leaves and dirt away from her home. The girls hugged and smiled as Alyssia stroked her cheek of a single tear while June Caruthers looked up again and scowled under her breath as she shakes her head as Alyssia tells Catriona, *Mi àis fònsibh dar mi tàir gu bail e gu nar sibh agam mi dèanta sàbhailte gu mo ceann uidhe.* "I will call you when I get to town to let you know I made it safe and sound to my destination."

Catriona nodded and as June scowled while the girls embraced again until her grandmother's lawyer pulled up as June quickly went back to sweeping the sidewalk at her house as the lawyer parks his car behind Alyssia's as the ladies look at him coming towards them. He greeted them with a smile and a warm handshake; *"Madainn mhath, a'chaileag...* "Good morning, girls..." Catriona says back at him, *Madainn mhath... Dè do trùma?* "Good morning...How are you feeling?" *Tha glé math. Dé* nì dhut ionnas gu madainn an-diugh? "Very good; what can I do for you so early this morning?" Catriona asked happily as Alyssia and her listened as the lawyer said gleefully, "I bring good news…the house has been sold and the money from the will and the house will be in your accounts at the end of the week."

Alyssia smiled and translated back to her, *Luis taigh greasaich is recite agus airgend bhò an tiomnadh áis sa an dá chuid banca aithris air ti am de seachdain.* "The house has been sold and the money from the will be in our bank accounts by the end of the week." The girls hug happily as the lawyer says to Alyssia as she hands the lawyer the small list and the mail, "Tell Catriona that my wife and I will be helping Catriona to pack and sort out the house before the weekend." Alyssia nodded and says to her in Gaelic while he looked over the mail and the list, *An neach-lagha agus a ciad-bhean áis bì cobhair air ti gu fòir sibh paca agus séor saich an taigh ro an ceann-seachdain.* "The lawyer and his wife will be helping you to pack and sort the house before the weekend."

Tapadh leibh, "Thank you," said an excited Catriona as she smiled and nodded as he put the list and the mail into his coat pocket, excused himself from the ladies and went over to speak June Caruthers. He went across to see her and her husband as Alyssia and Catriona embrace as she told her, *Coltach mi labhairte, mi áis fòn sibh dar mi táir gu baile gu nar sibh agam mi deánta sábhailte gu mo ceann uibhe. Tapadh leat, a Chatriona; uileag mo* mùim gu do fear-pòsta agus mac; *Buaidh gun robh leat agus gabh a cùram de cuair romhad.* "Like I said, I will call you when I get to town to let you know I made it safe and sound to my destination. Thank you, Catriona; all my love to your husband and son; good luck to you and take care of yourself." *Sibh gu… agus mi áis.* "You too and I will," said Catriona who nods and the girls embrace once again with tears of happiness and joy but of a parting friendship between the girls as they promised to keep in touch as best as they can.

Catriona gave Alyssia her address and Alyssia told her that she would get her new address to her as soon as she can. Just then, the lawyer came back to the girls, "Well, that's Mrs Caruthers warned; you are safe with us Catriona." Alyssia says, *Sibh a bheil sáihailte a nist, a Chatriona…* "You are safe with us, Catriona" she translated. *Tapdh leibh,* "Thank you;" she says to the lawyer as the trio smiled and tells her that she would be right back as Alyssia takes the lawyer aside. "Thank you for everything you have done for my grandmother, sir. You have been most kind and love to your wife. I did give you the mail from more debtors and the list, did I?" The lawyer smiled and said happily, "Yes you did, I have them in my coat pocket Alyssia and you are so welcome; it was a pleasure. Now off to University with you and my wife and I will watch over Catriona and not to worry about the bills, I'll handle the debtors."

Alyssia tells him, "Thank you and I have told her that I would call her to let her know that I made it safely to Kelton Heights..." The lawyer says as they walked to the car, "We'll be awaiting your call, oh and all your stuff is in storage and I will call them to take it to your new home as soon as you are on the road. The movers have your new address and they will bring your furniture to you as I call them, Okay?" He gives her the number and the envelope as to where she will be staying as she nodded. "This is the number for Kevin Parks, caretaker of the property; if you get lost, call him. They gave each other one last hug as they get back to Catriona and his car as the couple watch her get in and she put her seatbelt on as she says to them after turning the engine on and rolling down the window, *Tioraidh* "Goodbye." The lawyer and Catriona stood side by side and they watched the car disappear down the street as Alyssia pointed the car east towards Kelton Heights.

AT CASSIOUS HOUSE IN KELTON HEIGHTS

It was early that same morning; Kevin Parks was getting ready to go over to Kelton University with the lease papers, the advert and instructions for the next tenant. Sharlene was also up so she can let the workers into the flat and get it cleaned up for the next tenant. After the couple had breakfast, she handed her husband the advert, the lease papers in an envelope, as well as the keys to the house and he placed them in an old brief case as he told his wife about a dream he had.

"It was weird," he began as he closed the briefcase with a click. "I dreamed that a voice was calling to me and so I answered and it said; 'There is a girl by the name of Alyssia Franklin-Jenkins and she is on her way to Kelton Heights to attend University; give her the keys to the house,' but when I looked around to see who was talking, no one was there. It was like a distant whisper from long ago and then it says, 'she is **'the key'**...and that's when I woke up. If I knew what it meant, I would tell you, Sharlene. But alas, it's only a dream." He shook his head and smiled yet Sharlene was a bit worried about him.

"If it was only a dream, then the prophecy is coming true…" Kevin looked at her and asked gently, "What prophecy?" Sharlene thought for a moment and replied back to him, "It was about **'the key…'** it is a prophecy about the one who will break the curse on Cassious House." He looked at his wife strangely as she looked back at him, shook her head and smiled. "Oh never mind, it's just a silly prophecy, go on honey, and I'll have a nice hot bowl porridge waiting for you." He smiled and kissed his wife as he left Cassious House by using the back stairway and she closed the door and went inside to get dressed while waiting for the workers who would help her to clean up the flat.

In the Tower of Cassious House, the spirits began to awaken one by one as they all had breakfast and relaxed as the prince took his water, and a couple of apples and oranges as he started back to his study. "I have some work to do gang, so I will see you around." He got up from the breakfast table, tucked in some more apples and oranges into his pocket, and went back to his study when a child tugged on his pant leg. He looked down to look into the eyes of a little girl and smiled as he came down to her level as he took her hand and asked, "…and what can I do for you, my fair lady?" The child squeaked sadly, "I wish the curse was gone, your highness; it's been a while since I've seen and smelled the flowers outside."

Everyone looked at them, some cried, some sighed, while others just prayed when they felt tears in their eyes as she said sadly. "I miss running around outside in the springtime air, I miss listening to the real birds and the grass blowing in the wind around my feet. I also miss the wind blowing through my hair and the dance and song around the Maypole from long ago." The Prince sighed as he placed a hand on the child's cheek as he says as everyone listened while drying her tears with his hanky.

"You, my sweet child, are not the only one… I hate this curse, and I wish it was broken too. I do hope we find **'the key'** and that he/she will help us to break this curse that has held us here for over three hundred years; I miss all those things too…" He touched the child's cheek on her young face as she smiled. Then he replied; "but I feel like I have given up and I have no hope left. Maybe if I ask you if I can borrow some hope off you? Maybe…" The child smiled and lifted her princes' chin as Marylebarne smiled; "You know you can always borrow some hope from me, I would be honoured to give you some." The Prince smiled as the child came closer to him, and gave him hope through a kiss and a hug as he received them with thanks.

Everyone smiled as they were trying to keep their hopes alive too because they were always counting on Timothy to give them a miracle. It had not been easy for the House and its household these many years; and the Prince alone has been to hell and back as many times as they could count. The household wondered if this curse will ever be broken; others lost hope and fell into the Dark Veil, while others keep clinging on, hoping that the special day would come when the House was finally free and they could all be human again; but alas, they too were holding on by a thin thread that could snap at any minute.

Prince Timothy was the thread and the others were looking to him to keep it together as he smiled and put the little girl down and thanked her as she bowed before him, then the little girl ran back to her father; who welcomed her with open arms while he went back to his study with his fruit and water as the others went back to what they were doing and he went back to his room to keep his sanity and not cry in front of the household as he went back to his room. A little while later, Marylebarne found some more work for him to do to keep his mind active; a book on manners and family trees as he went to his study and gave the books to him. He knocked gently as he heard a 'come in' as his advisor came to him and closed the door.

He came to him and held up the books as the Prince looked at him with anxiety, "Thank you Marylebarne; this should keep me going for a while…" he replied with a tired look on his face and he put the books on to his cluttered desk as he went back to the window. He rubbed his face in frustration and anxiety as his advisor asked, "Are you okay, my dear boy? Come now, you can tell me." Marylebarne stayed to offer some counsel as the Prince says with frustration, "I feel like I'm on a tightrope over a huge cliff in dense fog; many of the spirits are struggling to follow and keep up with me and I don't know how long I can hold on or cross it without tipping into the canyon of fog below."

The advisor came to a frustrated prince, placed his hand on his shoulder and says, "I can understand what you are going through, your highness. You feel that there will be no way to break this curse that has hung over all of us for over three hundred years, and all our hopes are relying on you; but you are not alone," He looked at Marylebarne as the wise advisor said, "…just trust in me and all of us as we are walking this tightrope with you and we are bound to reach the other end. We all care about you and I promised your father that I would look after you and help you through this; no matter what comes our way. I will always be here; I'll never leave your side and neither will the other spirits, so my dear Prince Timothy, lay your burden on us and let us share the load. Will you allow us to do this for you?"

Timothy nodded as Marylebarne said to an exasperated prince as he looked up to his advisor, "Yes, if you want to share the load; but I brought this curse on the whole household and none of this was meant to happen…" Marylebarne says with sadness but feeling contented, "I know, my lord and believe me we all know you never meant to drop this curse on us, but we will see it to the end. Okay?" The men smiled and the advisor says as he picked up the books and hands them to him. "Now why don't you get busy on your studies; it will take your mind off things for a while."

The Prince nodded as Marylebarne patted his shoulder, and left him to his work as he got straight into it after the prince got a tankard full of water and his apple. But just as he left the busy prince in his room and closed the door, he felt a message being launched into his senses like a rocket hurtling towards Mars as he left the Tower and went into the main hall where the Dark King of the Dark Veil waited for Marylebarne to arrive and the advisor bowed before him as the King acknowledged his respect.

"I'm sorry to call you so early but I thought you should know *'the key'* is on her way, Marylebarne." The wise advisor knew never to question the Dark King of the Dark Veil as he says, "I see my dark lord, shall I tell the others or shall I wait?" The Dark King told him, "Until she gets closer, don't say anything to the others. I do not want to get their hopes up; I am giving the prince a job of guarding *'the key'*; he must protect her at all costs. I know he doesn't like us but he must try, and trust us if this curse is to be broken."

Marylebarne understood and nodded as he says to the Dark King, "I do understand, my Dark Lord. This curse has weighed heavily on all of us, especially my lord Prince Timothy. I guess without his heart and soul, the prince has lost all hope." The Dark King agreed as he says, "It's been a long three hundred years and I know it seems hopeless, but he must never lose hope Marylebarne, we must never give up." Marylebarne bowed to him and says, "Thank you my lord. Now if you excuse me, you must rest and I must get back to the Tower." He was just about to leave until he asked, "Will I know as well if *'the key'* has come?" The Dark King nodded as he replied gently, "As soon as she is close enough and I feel her presence, I will let you know too." Marylebarne bowed before him once more then left the Dark King to his rest as he disappeared into shadows and towards the Tower.

Meanwhile, Kevin Parks was at the University's Administration Building and gave all the papers to Kelly Preston; an elderly receptionist who loved everyone like her own family; whether it was a new student or a teacher, and even an administrator. A motherly receptionist, Kelly was given exact instructions about who should take the house across the street as Kelly agreed and says, "That's fine but I may have someone for the House already. Her name is Alyssia Franklin-Jenkins and she is on her way here now. Shall I send her over to you when she signs all the necessary paper work?" She placed the advert on the community board as Kevin says, "Sorry, haven't woken up yet…Alyssia Franklin-Jenkins?" the receptionist nodded and the caretaker of the House chuckled as he continued, "Well, I will leave it in your capable hands, Mrs Preston; can you send her over to Cassious House after she arrives?" Mrs Preston says gently and she got her hand kissed by Kevin as she shies away. "Oh you silly man, I will always be happy to help you; now run along back to your wife."

They both laughed as she thanked him as he started back to Cassious House to help his wife and the workers with the flat that was up for lease. Kevin was shocked to hear that comment as he wondered; *"Did you have the same dream as me, because I was told something similar?"* He smiled and left the offices as Kelly placed Alyssia's name on the envelope, avoiding the keys as she puts the envelope somewhere close on her desk. She was just about to sit down when Dean Pharrell Winchell came to Kelly Preston and gave her an official letter for the Higher Education Office to type up.

"Good morning Dean Winchell, how are you this fine morning?" Pharrell smiled and says, "I am well Mrs Preston, thank you." She smiled until he looked around and saw the back of Kevin Parks, caretaker of Cassious House walking away. "Mrs Preston, who was that gentleman that just left the building; it looked like Mr Kevin Parks?" Mrs. Preston put the letter on the desk and said as she looked over at the caretaker of Cassious House who was headed off campus as she says, "It was sir…" he looked back at her quickly as she replied, "Mr Parks was giving me some lease papers for a flat that has become available across the street."

Dean Pharrell Winchell smiled and asked quietly, "And who are the papers for? I will keep it quiet, promise…" he said with curiosity as Mrs Preston says with a smile. "Her name is Alyssia Franklin-Jenkins and she is new to Kelton University…" he looked at her shocked, "Why, do you know her sir?" He looked back at Kelly and replied sadly as the memories flooded his mind, "Yes I knew her mother and father, Mark and Emily Franklin…nasty business of his assistant's death a year ago." Kelly nodded, "I know and I followed the trial, Mark was such a good man to his wife and daughter and a good friend to Sidney Preston; no one had a bad word to say to him or his son. I was devastated when he was charged with his death, but when he got cleared and everyone started making life hard for him, I was angry and then they disappeared for a while until my other son found out what happened and told me. I'm just glad Mark is still with us…"

Pharrell nodded as he recalled, "So I gave Mark and Paul, his son and brother to Alyssia, a job here at the University a year before the work was completed. I also promised Mark and Emily at their graduation that if they ever had children, I would look after them. Their son, Paul is now a teacher and now the daughter will join them here at Kelton University." She nodded and told him, "I am so glad that Mark and Paul are here; they are such wonderful teachers and very professional." Pharrell just smiled, "I'm glad they are here too; so much bad luck but now I'm glad that they are settled in a job they so enjoy and I have a feeling this is going to be an interesting year." Kelly and Pharrell stood silent and looked at each other until he said as they got back to work, "Well, if you'll excuse me, I better see Kevin Parks before he runs back to Cassious House, Excuse me Mrs Preston."

Mrs Preston smiled and asked as she watched him leave to catch up with Mr Parks, "Sir, will you tell Mark and Paul?" The dean told her, "No, they don't know that she is alive and to drop this bombshell on the father and son would mean Mark would end up back in a mental hospital. No, it's best that they figure this out for themselves." Mrs Preston nodded as she got straight to work on the letter for the Higher Education Office while Dean Winchell caught up with Kevin and he talked with the caretaker of Cassious House. They were discussing how to protect Alyssia and her interests whilst she was at University, and with no family to be there for her; they needed a back-up plan.

Meanwhile, Mark and Paul were working away on their lesson plans for the first week of the new term as well as filling the paperwork and more forms for Edward Mangard and his admin team as they were busy as ever getting everything ready for the new term which starts next week not knowing what fate would have planned for them. Paul stood up and stretched as he went to make a fresh pot of tea for him and Mark; "Dad, want anything to eat? I'm just going to brew some more tea..." Paul asked as his father looked up at him. "Yes, yes, and Paul; if there are any chocolate digestives left, bring them will you?" Paul chuckled and says; "Coming right up, dad..." and he went to the kitchen and put the kettle on with fresh water.

He rinsed out the cups thoroughly and placed the two tea bags into them. Mark came into the kitchen as Paul puts on the kettle; "I know that this will be your first time as an actual lecturer, how are you feeling about that?" He asked as he leaned on the door frame as Paul smiled nervously, "I won't lie to you, dad. I am a bit nervous." Mark nodded as the young Franklin continued, "It will be the first time that I actually teach students, and I am a bit anxious to know what students I will have this term; but I know that you will keep me right dad...unless you're busy." Mark smiled and says, "I will never be too busy for you, remember that, son."

Mark placed a hand on his back as he replied, to him, "You have got me through a lot and I know that I have caused you some grief and put you through hell, but I will always be there for you; remember that!" Paul smiled with his dad and replied happily, "Thanks dad that means a lot." his father winked, patted his shoulder gently, and left him to prepare the teas and the digestive biscuits as he got the kettle on to boil. Later, the two men got back to work as Mark helped him with all the paperwork for admin which was a big thing for him as Mark checked all the forms and lesson plans and they were finally finished as Mark told him, "Leave the signatures until next week and I'll double check everything before we sign them. Let's just relax now; my brain is starting to hurt!" Paul laughs and went to get the teas as the teachers sit by the fire and enjoy the tea and biscuits as they talk and enjoy some quiet time with some soft music playing in the background.

Just then there was a knock on the door, "I'll get it dad," said Paul who stood up first and Mark nodded as he too stood up to greet his guests as Paul went to answer it as Mark came up behind him. "Who is it, Paul?" It was the elderly caretaker with a younger gentleman behind him as the lecturers let them in. "Hello Mr Hyman, what brings you here?" asked Mark stood by his son as Hyman got straight to the point as his young, muscular, and very bald assistant came up behind him. "This is John Preston; he will be my new caretaker assistant; I'm going around introducing him to everyone." The lecturers smiled and shook hands with John and got to know him as the elder caretaker says, "If you need anything at all and I'm not around," he gives him John's number to Mark and Paul as he jerks a thumb to John. "Just give John here a call and he will come a-runnin' as fast as he can."

The lecturers said, "Thank you and it's been a pleasure meeting you, John...we will keep your number close just in case." The burly man says, "It's an honour sir, talking to the author of many of books on subjects close to your heart," John says as he was standing just inside Franklin House's door as he said without hero worshipping Mark, "...old man Hyman has told me about them as well as you and your son and he has been helping me adjust to Caretaker duties here on campus so I hope we can be friends and colleagues as the term goes on."

Mark smiled and so did Paul as John turned his attention to a dilapidated, run down overgrown sad-looking House across the way, "But Hyman, I need to ask you;" he looked outside the lecturer's door. "Why can't we go over there to Thackeray House?" Hyman says, "He isn't exactly a lecturer friendly or Health and Safety conscious, my boy. We, on the campus, avoid him at all costs. One of these days, that dangerous house of his will fall in on someone; but we can't do anything until the principal can expel him from the campus. His name is George Angelo Sabacini Thackeray and he makes anyone feel unwelcome, including students and visitors as well as us Caretakers. Stay clear of him…he trusts no one, especially the lecturers here; they have been in a feud with him for a long time."

Then Mark looked at the House with tears and anger as he said with hurt and sadness; "It was over my assistant's death," said Mark who looked at the House with disdain as the elderly caretaker and his new caretaking assistant listen. Paul came to him and said, "Dad, come on, I'm sure John doesn't want to know about what happened…" but he refused to move as John listened and knew that he had found the men who disappeared off the radar and tapped on his recorder in his pocket as Mark replied.

"He was my wife's lover and he killed her when she found out something about him and my murdered assistant and during the trial after Emily had taken my daughter away when she was seven years old and it killed me deep inside. But then she disappeared again at eleven years old when Emily died in a gas explosion at her house. I feared my daughter had died and when they ruled my assistant's death *'accidental'* I was livid and driven insane with grief and anger; I was committed to a mental institution thanks to him." He put a hand on Paul's shoulder as he continued as Paul offered him moral support; "My son visited me every day at the institution, and then when they saw that I was better, my son took me in and nursed me, even during his exams and classes and on a student salary. He even saved me from a failed suicide attempt…I owe him my life, John. So, if I had sense, like I know you do, I wouldn't trust George Thackeray as far as I can throw him. Just don't go near him or even acknowledge his existence, he is nothing but a bully and a murderer!" Paul stood beside his father and puts his hand on his shoulder as the assistant caretaker looks at the father and son. John saw tears coming down his eyes and he patted his shoulder gently not letting on as John gently tapped off his recorder in his pocket.

"I'm sorry, I didn't know." He relayed his next statement to Mark who looked at him as Paul gave him his kerchief; "I never meant to upset you, Doctor Franklin, it was not my intention." Mark nodded a thank you as he said, "But I will do my best to take the advice you and Hyman have been giving me: 'If he speaks to me, I will be civil and keep my emotions in check' and I intend to do that." The lecturers looked at John and thank him. "Besides, he reminds me of someone I don't like either, like my wife's ex-boyfriend!" The men all laugh and shake hands with the caretakers once again as he replied once more. "It's just wonderful to meet you Doctor Franklin, I have read all your books and I look forward to reading some more of your book like your new one: "My Secret Pain." Mark was flattered and thanked him as the men shook hands the two of them leave the tutors alone as they got back to their quiet time while the caretakers got back to work.

Back at Cassious House, the spirits and the Prince as well as Marylebarne were looking out the Tower window at a moving van that has just pulled up. Sharlene greeted the gentlemen movers and she got the spare keys to the flat next to her home and opened the door for them as Kevin finally got back to the House and saw Sharlene helping the workers with cleaning up as Kevin looked about. "Well, I guess I wasn't needed after all…" she says with a glint of humour in her eye as he shoved his hand in his pocket and drew his wife beside him, "Well I'll need you to help me make the bed. A moving van pulled up and started unloading someone's things…a young lady by the name of Alyssia Franklin-Jenkins. She's coming from Welleston Village thirty miles away or so I heard from the movers."

Kevin nodded and said, "This dream is becoming a reality for some reason; I feel this year and the next, will be a year of change; not only with us, but for both towns. She's coming on a scholarship and Dean Pharrell Winchell knows her family." He stops for a moment as he says, "According to him, her family is no more; her mother died in a freak gas explosion with no body to recover…still remains a mystery to this day and her father and brother are still missing; so she has no one." The mover's boss heard him and said, "Well, she did have someone; a grandmother whom she lived with since she was eleven years old and now she's dead. Three weeks ago, died of heart failure in her sleep, I believe." They hand the couple the paper and read the circled obituary.

"Jenkins, Jessica Esther, seventy-two… died peacefully in her home surrounded by her faithful nurse and grand-daughter, Alyssia Franklin-Jenkins." The Parks were sad for her and they said, "This Alyssia Franklin-Jenkins is she coming here?" One of the movers says to Kevin as the mover finished moving the last of her stuff into the flat, "Oh yes, definitely. She had to stay with her grandmother's nurse, Catriona Timrod and her grandmother's lawyer to sort out the will and now the lawyer says she should be here by early or middle of the afternoon." The other mover came to him and whispered to him, "One of my men just got off the phone with her grandmother's lawyer, about a half hour ago and he told us to bring the stuff around as soon as she was on the road; I think this is where she'll be staying?"

Mr and Mrs Parks looked at each other and replied, "I hope so, and I have put in the lease papers over at the University so I hope she's the tenant we're getting and I hope she is really nice?" The boss of the moving company says, "According to her grandmother's lawyer, she is. High school honour student, good grades, never a bother to her grandmother or the nurse, polite, quiet reserved; the ideal neighbour; I know you'll like her." Sharlene asked the boss, "How do you know?" The boss says, "I've met her and she is a wonderful young girl, gave us precise instructions on what to take and what not to take that she did. Never met a customer like her in my entire twenty-one years I have worked as a removal man. Very sweet and kind and the lawyer has even met us. He told us about her and what she's been through so I told my men to be very kind and follow the instructions to the letter and the only young lady who read the Terms and Conditions with her gran's lawyer so she understood what was required and if she had any questions, she asked us. Intelligent girl she is and she even paid us in advance." The couple looked at each other as the mover says what they were thinking, "I actually feel bad of what has happened to her in the past; Bad luck, hurt, pain and sadness, so I just hope that she will have a better life than what she has gone through, and I wish her love and luck as do the rest of the town of Welleston Village; she deserves to be happy." Marylebarne was in the shadows of her flat unseen as he was listening and taking every detail in as the movers put the boxes down and the table and chairs by the front door and butts it against the couch and then placed the chairs around it and they were finished with the move and left the caretakers to their peace. Marylebarne smiled and was prepared to leave the flat to head towards the Tower and to the other spirits as they too were looking down at the movers who were cleaning up the van and folding coverings as they hear Kevin say; "We will make sure that she is treated with respect, kindness and dignity, thank you."

The couple shook his hand as one of the boys whispered that they were done as he got the clipboard and says with pride, "I need someone to sign these papers just to confirm that the furniture arrived safely; I have to give it to the lawyer so he can pay for our services." Sharlene did that for them as she asked, "Is that all the furniture she has?" The movers nodded as Kevin looked around the house, "Yep, she's bringing the rest of her possessions with her in a car her grandmother gave her." Sharlene hands the pen and the clipboard back to the movers and they tipped their hat to her as she gets the receipt from the movers. "Have a very good day, Mrs Parks, and to you too, Mr Parks. I better call the lawyer to tell him that her stuff has arrived safely and in good condition; good day to you…" he said and the movers tipped their hats to the couple.

After Kevin thanked them as they got into the moving van, left the house, and pull out of the drive slowly as the van disappeared down the tree-lined drive. "This is really odd, how can a dream just come true in under a few hours, Sharlene? I don't quite get it?" She took her confused husband back to their home and she gave her husband some hot porridge for lunch. The advisor had heard enough and he had to get back to the Prince but he wouldn't tell him anything until she was close and the suspense was killing him by not saying a word; but a promise was a promise and the Dark King would let him know as soon as she was close as he disappeared in shadows back to the Tower of Cassious House while in the Tower, the spirits greeted him happily.

"A new lodger it looks like?" said one spirit, while another said, "I hope she is not like that horrible woman from a week ago. I still have nightmares about those brats…" the other spirit told his friend as he smoked on his pipe. "Well, we'll just have to wait to see what she looks like and then, we can decide for ourselves." Marylebarne smiled as he replied as he came into the Tower, "Well whoever she is, she will be abiding by the rules that Kevin will give her 'not to go into Cassious House.'" The men nodded as the advisor left the men to talk and helped cook set the table for lunch as he said not a word while the other spirits continued to talk about a new arrival.

Just then, the Prince came through while all the spirits quickly changed the subject and talked about something else as Marylebarne saw him. "Ah, my dear Prince, come; we were just about to have some lunch." The Prince smiled as he came over to the table and the spirits had lunch and relaxed as they told stories while the Prince drank his mild ale. The cook gave them hot soup and sandwiches as well as bread and butter as everyone; including the children, listened and ate their lunch as they talked about other things until Marylebarne stood up and left the room unexpectedly as the Prince watched him leave. Timothy grew suspicious, so he finished his soup and sandwich, grabbed his sword and followed Marylebarne as he watched his advisor leave the Tower in shadows.

The Prince followed him not long after, to the main hall and kept well-hidden as he stayed close by with his sword drawn ready to defend his advisor if the need arises. He watched his advisor talking to the Dark King quietly as his advisor's voice echoed around the main hall; "…are you sure about this, my lord; I mean no disrespect, but we had these false alarms before?" The Dark King understood and says, "Even my own people can feel her getting close Marylebarne; *'the key'* is close and she is nearing her destination. But first she must face the ghosts from her past before she comes here…" Marylebarne nodded and said, "I will not tell anyone until she is in town; I don't want to bring false hope," The Dark King nodded and elevated himself to join his people and he says, "I will tell you in telepathy that she has arrived, go and attend to your people and the prince."

The advisor nodded, bowed and disappeared into shadows as Timothy waited until his advisor was safe until the Dark King sensed another presence as he stopped and said after Marylebarne had left him, "I know you're there, Prince Timothy Andrew Carlton. Come out and show yourself, but first put away your sword!" The bewildered prince did just that and came out of his hiding place as the Dark King looked at him as he walked closer to the first floor landing and bowed before him out of respect. "I need to know what you want with Marylebarne, and I want the truth." The Dark King came down to the Prince's level and smiled, "Speak to me now!" Timothy demanded as the Dark King's smile disappeared as he spoke while his robes danced around in the winds. "Marylebarne and I are telepathically linked; we have been for three weeks now." Timothy says to him as he bowed, "You are not to hurt him," he said to the Dark King angrily. "We have no intention of hurting him, my dear prince…it is not our intention!" His hissing voice was circulating around the room like a ceiling fan on full and he could feel it like a chilly wind in the Antarctic as he felt a slight chill while he stood in front of him by the huge pillar near the landing of the massive and elegant stairwell. "So tell me, why are you collaborating with him? He is supposed to be my royal advisor, not a traitor…"

The Dark King turned to him quickly, "A long time ago, the 'Sultan's' Advisor brought us here and ensnared us in this prison as you fled to the Tower. The advisor Marylebarne and I became friends and we discuss things that concern us and sometimes, he needs my advice, my dear Prince; he loves and cares for you. Sometimes we talk about you as he is worried about you losing all hope…don't give up, my dear Prince, for I was once a prince like you, until I was betrayed and later killed by my lover's jealousy." He was surprised to hear that confession, "Marylebarne never told me that," the Prince says as he sat on the floor in front of him leaning against the marble pillar.

The Dark King noticed tears in his eyes as he read his mind, "Marylebarne was right…you have lost hope!" The Prince looked at him as he sniffed, "I'm holding on to what little hope I have my lord, and it's fading fast. I don't know for how long I can walk this thin tightrope without falling into despair and the feeling of letting my people down, it weighs heavily on my spirits." He starts to weep as the Dark King comes to him and placed a comforting hand on his shoulder. "Now you know what I have to go through night in and night out and how hard it is to keep my own people's spirits up."

Timothy looked up at him surprised. "What do you mean?" The Dark King told him, "It's like a wound that has been ripped open so many times and even I have lost hope but it's thanks to my people that help me and share the burden I carry and it becomes an obsession to keep that little seed of hope alive until all hope turns to despair." The prince looked into his ghostly eyes as he sits beside him; "There are nights where I sit and cry too because I feel like I am failing as a king, but there is hope and I keep clinging to that hope and, as I was telling your advisor, that hope can come in the form of a young lady who is on her way to Kelton Heights and I need you to watch over her!" The prince looked at him and said, "Me? How do I know it's her? How do I know what to do?" The Prince asked anxiously as he was now on his knees as if he was praying for a miracle.

The Dark King replied gently as he lifted his chin to look at him, "You will know that she is the one, my dear Prince. Be there for her, love her, protect her and be strong; she will need you as Marylebarne needs us both; his allegiance is with you and no one else. Even I can't dissuade him from your side, he is loyal to you always as I am just now." The Prince looked at him and was about to say something, but let it pass as the Dark Spirit says, "Let me and my people be part of this adventure and we'll show you, we're not all that bad!" The Dark King and the Prince chuckle as the Prince nods as the Dark King lets go of his chin, pats his shoulder as he returns and heads towards the Dark Veil.

The Prince had no choice but to trust him and Marylebarne, who was standing behind a wall watching the events unfold. He waited until the Dark King elevated up to the dark veil and rejoined his people as he heard the Dark King say, "Marylebarne is a good man, my Prince…have faith in him and in yourself just like I have faith in you." The Prince was shocked at this revelation and watched the Dark King disappear into the veil. The Prince sat leaning on the pillar in the main hall and cried until Marylebarne stood before his Prince and he came over, knelt beside him, and placed his hand on his shoulder as the Prince looked at him. "Cry now my Prince it's what you need now before she comes," the advisor said and he sat with him while he cried as the morning started to fade into afternoon.

It wasn't long after the movers had left as the Parks had their bowls of porridge as they talk about the new resident Alyssia Franklin-Jenkins as Sharlene asked him, "Maybe we should be her family;" Kevin almost spit out his porridge as he looked at her strangely and said, "What…are you nuts?" Sharlene says putting him right, "I don't want to adopt her- I mean be there for her, be like a family to her." Kevin started to understand, "I see what you mean now; so just be like confidants to her, is that what you meant?" Sharlene nodded and said, "That's exactly what I meant! We could make her feel like she is one of the family and help her when she needs it, be there and listen when she needs an ear… that's all I am asking for us to do for her. She may be a student at Kelton University but sometimes, students need someone to listen to them." Kevin thought that it was a good idea and said, "Well then, let's be those ears and her hope." Sharlene smiled and thanked him as she took the porridge bowls to the kitchen and cleaned them up as well as the pan in which the porridge was in after she soaked them by the sink.

Back in the Tower, the advisor and the despondent Prince were back among their people as they had lunch with the rest of the spirits while talk and laughter filled the Tower. The men sat with the others but the Prince never said a word as Marylebarne kept him in his sights as the laughter and talk got a bit too much to bear as Timothy stood up and excused himself from the table after he picked up some fruit and took them back to his study to continue his lessons.

He got into his study, placed the fruit down and sat quietly on his bed as the strong wind blew through his open window as he placed the tankard by his water pitcher and lay on his bed as he tried to comprehend what the Dark King had told him about *'the key'* and what was going on between Marylebarne and the Dark King as he thought; *'How can I trust Marylebarne when I feel like he's betrayed me?'* He then sat up and rubbed his face of the new tears that threaten to overwhelm him as he got his tankard and filled it up with water. He looked out the window and took in a sigh in which he burst into tears again as there was a gentle knock on his door and he called out as he dried the tears on his sleeves, "Come in…" and Marylebarne came in quietly and closed the door as he got ready for a telling off from the Prince as he said flat out, "I don't expect an apology nor do I expect you to trust me ever again, but hear me out."

Timothy bowed his head as he began, "It started in the library when I was downstairs looking in the library and getting some books for you to work on while I was preparing you for royal duties. I was reading up on Family Trees until the Dark King appeared before me asking for advice on a book he wanted to borrow…" his advisor sat on his bed while Timothy just sat down in his chair at his desk and tried to be busy, but his concentration was gone and only tears blurred his vision as Marylebarne continued. "I told him about a book that sounded interesting and we started to talk about things and he asked me about you and I told him that I needed to keep you busy because of your deep depression and he told me that I was good to you and he recommended me those books that you have before you. W-We started becoming friends and he told me about his world and I told him about ours. But one day, he told me about a particular situation, about why he took people into the veil and why he stopped… Emily MacPherson and her friend Madeline Gratin."

Timothy turned to him as Marylebarne said, "It was like he knew there was something more inside young Emily that he would ever imagine so the Dark King gave her a specific task after she was married; to train *'the key'* when she had children; she agreed and he set the two girls free. It was on that promise that the Dark King stopped taking people in to the veil and after the murder of Sidney Preston…that was a year ago I believe;" Timothy was listening as he told him to continue.

"He told me that he was doing something so terrible and wrong and for that he is deeply sorry. He didn't go into detail but only to say that he has put all the innocents into a room on the first floor and his Dark Guards watch over them, feeds them and treats them with respect as he is prepared to release them once *'the key'* has shown herself to him." Timothy asked, "What did he do that was so terrible?" Marylebarne just shrugged and says, "I don't know maybe he will tell us, maybe not." Timothy was very confused but told his advisor to continue as Marylebarne stood up from his bed and goes to the window as Timothy turns his chair to face him as the advisor replied.

"But it was several months into our friendship that he told me that *'the key'* will show herself and we must be prepared and he placed his hand on my forehead and opened my mind to telepathy so he would tell me that she would be on her way. I told him that I was worried about betraying you, but he had no interest in me to come into the Dark Veil and he really cares for you…I didn't want to tell you because you may feel that I betrayed you and I would never hurt you, my prince." The advisor looked back at him and smiled and then looked back at the window while the Prince told him gently, "All you had to do was tell me Marylebarne," Timothy told him with no anger but understanding as his advisor looked at him while tears fell from his eyes. "I would have understood, my friend. I'm not upset that you made friends with the Dark King, but not trusting me enough to tell me, that's what really hurts. I felt that I was being left out and that you have betrayed me, but now I know why. You have always earned my respect and I just needed you to be honest with me, was that too much to ask?"

Marylebarne says as he looked at his charge with tears in his eyes, "No…and I do deeply regret what I did; you deserve to know what I was doing down there and not telling you was the worst idea ever. Since many of our people were taken, including Jesterson's family, I was afraid you would retaliate and if that happened, his highness would be taken to and I would never see you again after I vowed and promised your father and mother that I would look after you and that's what I'm going to do." Marylebarne went to the window as Timothy smiled and looked at him as he replied; "The last thing I wanted to do was to make you angry with me that you wouldn't trust me ever again."

Timothy comes to him and says, "I know you're my advisor and my protector, my teacher and confidant; how could I not trust you?" The advisor looked at him puzzled as Timothy continued. "I was just afraid that when you were acting funny, I thought that it was something that I did to upset you. Please Marylebarne, just tell next time." Marylebarne and Timothy embraced and the prince says, "I forgive you Marylebarne," they let go as he says, "…and keep that link open with the Dark King to let me know when she is near." Marylebarne nodded and says, "I will and no more secrets; I promise." The two men smile and shake hands as his advisor gives him some more work to do and he gets started on it as he tells him his assignments and left the Prince to his work.

Several hours passed and the day wore on into the afternoon as the sun started to sink slowly into the west as Dark King was sound asleep with the rest of his people. He was sleeping soundly until his mind woke him up as a car on a lone country road passed the sign: "The City Limits of Kelton Heights—twinned with Welleston Village…" and he saw the young lady drinking water and listening to the radio while she was stopping near the valley that overlooks the town in the distance. He awoke his people and says out loud in a hissing whisper which made Marylebarne freeze on the spot as he was giving orders to one of his workers until his brain exploded with the three words he longed to hear: SHE IS COMING!

Chapter 1

KELTON UNIVERSITY OF PARANORMAL STUDIES: NEW TERM—16 YEARS LATER

Early morning and the sun is rising in the East and in Kelton Heights, all the new and seasoned lecturers are preparing for their new term on Campus. Doctor Mark Franklin was a multiple award-winning, seasoned lecturer, an author and loved his job very much as the next person as the ice blue eyes and greyish black hair and stern facial features tell lots of stories joy, love and sadness. A kindly, older, very friendly, understanding, well-educated, bestselling author, Mark Franklin raises the bar when it comes to his students and the faculty around him. He is a man with grey fluffy, curly hair, crystal blue eyes, tall, slender, no nonsense, round faced gentleman, and he will go that extra mile for his students.

But he has a secret pain behind his eyes; about a year ago, when he was tried and found innocent of murder due to a lack of evidence as well as losing his wife and daughter, he goes out of his mind with grief and anger; so he is sent off to a mental hospital to pull himself together. After a failed suicide attempt and with the help of his son, he gets his life back together and is offered a job at Kelton University by Pharrell Winchell. Today, he still teaches, writes, listens to his students and his former students say that he still does it very well as he is the most popular lecturer on the campus and has won many "Teacher of the Year" awards from Kelton University many times over and he had just finished writing his autobiography "My Secret Pain."

His stature was tall and his medium frame stood straight as the weight of pain slumped his shoulder and wrinkled his brow and you wouldn't have know that he had been through hell by just looking at him and his son and new teacher Paul Franklin, are working away on some paperwork for the University administration forms and lesson plans while Mark brought over the teas as his son looks up at him with a smile. As he put his head back down, Paul hated the paperwork-he felt like he was back Teacher's College; but he had to get it done as Mark felt for him because he hated the paperwork too."Thanks Dad" he says with a smile as he takes a sip of his tea with milk which tasted like honey as it made its way down his throat.

Paul was a young fellow who had dark hair brown eyes and a slender frame which was covered with turtle neck sweaters, suits and a faux leather-patched elbow, tweed jacket and he was a welcome addition to the University; but down deep, he was also a carer for his father whom he almost lost over a year ago after a botched inquiry which ruined his career as Mark suffered a mental break down over the loss of his wife and daughter but strangely, he was never struck off the teachers' register as he heard his son saying to him, "Don't you forget to do your paperwork…" as he passed the toast and fresh fruit over.

Mark, who was a seasoned lecturer, replied happily, "It's all done; all I need is to sign all the paperwork and have breakfast." Mark and Paul laugh as he sees that his son is preoccupied so Mark gets his attention with a gentle nudge. "Hey…" Paul looked at his smiling dad still lost in thought as he continues, "First day as an official lecturer at Kelton University; how are you feeling?" Paul sighed as he shook his head, rubbed his clean shaven face from his tired features; "Nervous and happy, but I don't mind saying that it's going to feel weird not being a student teacher."

Mark nodded as they drank their teas and had their biscuits, "but I'm sure it won't be all that bad." He took a bite of fruit which was refreshing and sweet as it melted in his mouth while he listened to his father munching on a piece of toast as Mark says wiping away the crumbs off his jumper, "Can I give you some advice?" Paul nodded as he picked up some more fruit as Mark leans back and said with a sigh; "Paul, all you have to do is relax and never let the students see you nervous. Why? Because the last thing they need to see is a teacher quaking in his boots…that's a sign that that you have no confidence. Got that?" Paul nodded and let his advice sink in as another piece of fruit melted in his mouth as he listened to his dad (who always gave good advice) continued, "Just loosen up, take a deep breath and smile."

Paul says with reassurance, "Thanks dad. Would you like to check over my paper work? I know how strict the University is about this…" Mark nodded after he took the last of his tea and looked it over as Paul was told where to sign while Mark did the same to his paperwork as they stick it back into the envelope, stand up and stretch. "Well done. Now let's get this paperwork over to administration and then into the auditorium for the yearly "pep talk" as Mark rolled his eyes and moaned as they get their coats on as Paul laughs; "It's that good, eh?" Mark says annoyingly as they walk to the door, "Every year it's the same thing, Paul; it's like we're going to war! We are teachers, not the bloody Calvary!"

Paul laughs as they head out the door, lock up and head for the campus to work as Mark had an idea after he locked the door as the teachers make sure that they had their paperwork as they passed Thackeray House which made his father really nervous as he stops as his son puts a hand on his shoulder as he looked back at Paul and they share a smile as Mark gave him a nervous smile. "Sorry son…that place makes me nervous, that's all."

Paul patted his dad's back as he and his father continue to walk on as Mark says after passing Thackeray House, "How about lunch in town; I know a place that serves the best Macaroni and Cheese in Trouncil Terrace, hmmm?" Paul nodded and says, "It's a deal! We need to get some groceries for the house anyway." Mark nodded and they walk on over to the administration buildings and to the auditorium for their pep talk that was right next door.

JUST OUTSIDE KELTON HEIGHTS

The dew and mist cleared leaving blue skies, clear sunshine and a gentle breeze as the morning wore into early afternoon as a lone car driving on a quiet Kelton Heights country road from nearby Welleston Village thirty miles away as a grieving and alone Alyssia Franklin-Jenkins approached the edge of town. She pulled over and looked at the sign and the small town below in the valley thinking of all who have passed on as

3

a soft breeze danced in her hair. Before and after Jessica Jenkins's death, Alyssia prepared for Kelton University which is thirty miles away in Kelton Heights.

Once a college student who has won a University scholarship on her paper on Celtic languages and life in Kelton Heights and Welleston Village, she has started a search for her father and her brother after her grandmother died. Intelligent, classy, well-educated, lives on her own, has a car licence, loves the beach, and became an unexpected pet owner when she saw her jacket moving. She lifted it up and found a tiny black kitten which climbed into her car, cuddled into her jacket, and fell asleep. She stroked the kitten's head and names her Mystery, because she came from nowhere and Alyssia gave her some tuna and a capful of kitten milk from ASDA at a nearby town and then she drove on to her destination on a small country road and she stopped for a rest and looked down the valley at Kelton Heights.

"Alyssia," said a voice in her head as she tried not to close her eyes for if she does the bad memories wait to engulf her in more grief. Bad memories came flooding back like a dam that has already burst its wall as torrents of tears threatened to consume her heart again as she closed her eyes and saw her mum and grandmother racing into her bedroom, "Come on honey get up and get dressed." A sleepy eleven-year-old was woken up in the night and a coat put on her as she heard he mother say, "You are going to stay with Granny Jessica Jenkins." She could see her granny packing the last of her things as her squeaky voice asked her, "Why can't I stay with you?" Her mother never gave her a reply just a simple sentence which made her and her mummy cry as the words echoed through her head. "I wish I never taken you away from your father and brother; I've put you in danger."

She gave her the teddy she held so dear since she was a newborn and bundled her into Jessica's car as her mother hugged her one last time as she says in her ear, "Remember mummy loves you, go and find your father and brother." and she gave her one last kiss, loaded her into the car, got her seat belt on, and closed the door. Her mother gave her granny a letter and some pictures and told her not to give them to her until she is eighteen years old. Jessica nodded and hugged her daughter one last time and went back to the house as the car pulled away just as George pulled her back inside the house. Afterwards, Jessica saw him and his goons running from the house as Jessica turned on the engine of her car and prepared to pull away to take Alyssia away to Welleston Village… and suddenly, there was a loud explosion as Alyssia cried out "MUMMY!"

She opened her eyes and came out of it with tears streaming down her cheeks and she drank a whole bottle of water like it was alcohol as she cried and slid down the side of the car on to the grassy verge until she could pull herself together and drive on. *'Never drive when you're upset…'* she kept telling herself as her head was heavy with grief and pain which made her dizzy. Her grandmother and Catriona were gone and after them, there was no more family; she was alone with her nightmares and her sadness.

A moment later, another car came and pulls up behind her and this one was a police car as a kind young man came over to her and knelt beside her as she smiled. "You okay, miss?" He asked concerned as he took the bottle away and smelled it, "Yeah…water. I'm taking a break; trying to calm myself down after my Grandma Jenkins's death three weeks ago; so, I'm still a bit upset. Water is the best way to replenish after a good cry. Alcohol no, I never touch the stuff; Disgusting!"

The officer smiled and says gently, "Glad to hear it and I'm terribly sorry for your loss." He helped her stand and she took in a deep breath and says, "I saw your car here and thought I would check to make sure that you were okay." Alyssia smiled and got her judgement back as she replied, "Thank you for your kindness; bring out the Breathalyzer and I will do your test."

He did and the test began as he took note of everything and after wards, thanked her for doing the test and she had no alcohol on her breath. "I'll be fine Officer, really. I just need some fresh air and a bathroom break; then I'll be on my way. Thanks again for stopping and your concern." He smiled and looked at her car, "Off to University, I see?" he asked as they looked at the car, "Yes studying at Kelton University, don't know what yet but I am hoping it will keep me busy." The young officer smiled and gave her his card, "Well, call me if you need anything at all," she took his card gratefully.

"Thank you, oh and one more thing," he looked back at her as she replied. "I just wanted to know if Cassious House was still there." He looked at her odd until she said, "M-My brother and I used to ride our bikes near there when I was five years old and I was wondering if it's still up for demolition?" The young officer understood and says, "Nope it was spared and remodelled after a campaign to save it. It became a listed building over three hundred years ago and a caretaker of five generations of the Parks family lives on the property, or so I heard." She was relieved as she smiled as she thought of her brother. "Thank you Officer Thackeray," she says politely after she looked at the card. "You've been a big help;" He tipped his hat to her and says, "Glad you're feeling better; take care of yourself."

She smiled as he backed up and pulled away as she took her bathroom break as she went to the bushes near her car, pulled up her trousers and walked back to her car, then she got in, buckled up and drove on to Kelton Heights and the University/Research Centre; but first bad memories to face as she rolled down the window turned on the radio as the music and the cool breeze picked up her spirits as she looked around at all the scenery and the music danced away in her head while the car was pointed in the direction of Kelton Heights and a small house on Flagstow Street in the suburbs…it was time to face her past and her fears as she drove on to Kelton Heights.

THE BOROUGH OF KELTON HEIGHTS AND WELLESTON VILLAGE

Finally, she made it to the city limits as she got to the town centre and saw the citizens walking or driving past her as she stopped at a cross walk to let a mother and her child cross and then she was free to go as she remembered her mother and smiled as she pulled away safely. The big Elm and Oak trees lost their leaves of brown and gold so the dark branches waved to her as autumn was on it's way when she came to town and turned down Flagstow Street and into the tree-lined suburbs as she was looking and found her mum's old house and parked in front of it as she left the window open a crack for her small kitten Mystery as she continued to nap away after eating her tuna and drinking her milk. She was surprised at the fact that the house had totally been rebuilt as she got out of the car and stood outside on the driveway and looked at it.

It was painted with flowers all around it and a front porch swing sitting on its porch as she thought of the good times when her mother was by her side but then, she saw flames and her younger self crying out to her "MUMMY!" and a house on fire as she fell to the ground and starts to cry as the memories tortured her as she stood up and ran back to the car to compose herself and she leaned back in her seat and sobbed her heart out questioning why she was there in the first place. She looked at the house before her as she got some water and washed her face of all the tears and pain flowing down her eyes, then she blew her nose and leaned her head back on the head rest of the car seat and closed her eyes as her head was filled of memories and pain as well as the loss of her grandmother…it was all becoming too much. *'Why am I here?'* she asked herself as she closed her eyes.

An hour passed and an elderly woman, who was getting her mail, noticed a strange car outside her home and a young girl crying and so she went to the car to see if she could help. Alyssia saw her coming so she dried her eyes, took a deep breath, and came out of the car carefully as to not scare the old woman as she gave her a smile. The old woman spoke very gently to her and asked Alyssia, "Are you okay, dear? You seem very upset…" She didn't want to make her anymore upset than she was because down deep, she knew that there was something special about her, while a certain figure stood away off in the distance and watched the two ladies talk and he took out his phone and called someone as he said four words to the person on the other end: ***"THE KEY HAS ARRIVED"*** and then turned off his phone.

The old woman also knew that this was the girl who would change the fortunes and the future of Kelton Heights and Welleston Village; but now, she saw a very vulnerable young lady before her as Alyssia dried her tired, tear-filled eyes. "I'll be fine…I-I'm sorry to intrude, Mrs…" The old lady smiled and introduced herself, "Parker, Mary Anne Parker; and I bought the house a year ago." She shakes hands carefully with her and says, "It's a pleasure to meet you Mrs Parker; I'm sorry for the loss of your husband…I read it in the newspaper a while back." The old lady smiled and thanked her and then looked at her car heavy ladened with all her personal belongings as she looked at her Alyssia says, "I'm off to Kelton University, just on the outskirts of Kelton Heights."

The widow smiled and placed a comforting hand on hers and offers her some hospitality; "Why don't you come in for a cup of tea, some light-hearted conversation and a comforting hand? You can't go on to the University in the state you're in." Alyssia shook her head, "No, No I couldn't impose on you." The widow Parker said gently, "Think nothing of it," and she gently leads Alyssia to the house where her mother died; murdered by her lover as she hears the widow say, "You need some refreshment. Come now, you need to rest, have something to eat and get yourself cleaned up and calm; not another word." Alyssia wondered, *'How does she know about my grandmother's death? She must have read it in the paper…now is not the time of speculation.'*

Mary Anne Parker was a housebound widow with beautiful silver blue eyes and long grey hair that was put in a braid when she went to bed and up in a bun when she was sitting up. Her frail frame matched her delicate features as she was kind, caring, respected, a good listener, very well-educated, free-spirited and classy. She was an archaeologist with her late husband but before that, she was a spirited piano player in a band and orchestra, an actress and singer in her younger days; but she fell pregnant with Gwen when she was in her mid thirties and was forced to retire from show business. To keep making ends meet, she had odd jobs as a teacher of the piano and pursued her passion for archaeology with her husband and worked with the Kelton Heights Museum in which she and her husband served on the board and won many awards; her daughter grew up to be a nurse and is now taking care of her.

Alyssia smiled allowing Mrs Parker to lead her inside the house where a fire was blazing in a coal-marked hearth with a small living room that was cosy and full of charm. Alyssia was shocked as she saw no signs of the past with broken pictures or furniture strewed all over the yard as the police described it while a ginger cat sat in its owner's chair looking at the stranger. Beautiful decorative wallpaper and small fragrant flowers ensnared her senses and as she went to her window which looked out to the back garden and saw bird feeders of all sorts and bird houses with green grass and a small bench near a water feature.

But her mind flashes of violence, broken furniture, blood on the carpet and walls, fire remnants of her broken home and her mother's blood curdling screams as she was driven away to her grandmother's house in Welleston Village as she sobbed quietly until she hears the widow say, "COME AND GET IT!" as she took in a deep breath and dried her eyes as she thought: *'Just what I need a cup of tea biscuits with an old lady I barely know in the house where my mother was killed; damn horrible memories! Just go away and leave me alone! Quit torturing me!'*

She turned to see Mrs Parker's heavy laden tray with tea and cakes, "Here we are, tea time." Alyssia comes to her and takes the tray from her as she sets it down on the table with two chairs. "Aww thank you my dear…" she said to her as the student sat down on one high backed chair while Mrs Parker lifted her cat and sat down. But before the widow picked up her tea, the tabby jumped into her lap and Alyssia gave her the tea as the woman laughed gently, "Marigold loves my chair," she says as the cat fell asleep in her lap as she took up her tea and Alyssia gave the tabby a rub on the ears as she goes and sits down.

"Help yourself to some cake." Alyssia says to her, "Would you like some cake Mrs Parker?" The old woman nods and Alyssia cuts the cake and gives her a fork and her cake as the widow thanks her and then she takes a piece for herself as Mrs Parker sets her tea down beside a beaten up, small scratched up table says gently and lovingly, "Please Alyssia, call me Mary Anne." Alyssia nodded and she sat back in her chair as she placed her tea on another small table beside her and ate her cake which was very sweet, sticky and tasted of lemon and strawberries.

"Now my dear, tell me what you are studying at Kelton University?" Mary Anne began as Alyssia puts down her tea on the table. "Everything…" Mary Anne looked at her confused as she wiped her mouth with a napkin as Alyssia explained as she smiled gently, "I'm not sure yet what I want to do. I have been very emotional after my grandmother Jessica Jenkins passed away three weeks ago; so between packing the car for University and her funeral; I've never really thought about it."

Mary Anne watched as Alyssia dried a tear away as she sighed, "I'm sorry to burden you with my problems." Mary Anne smiled and says, "Not at all, Alyssia. I felt like you when I lost my dear husband; losing a loved one is never easy to bear that's why my daughter has taken care of me and no one else…she has gotten me through a lot of tears and doubt and gave me a reason to live. Her husband is over in Iraq so she is taking care of me." After a while of talking to her, Alyssia felt better.

Mary Anne smiled and asked her to come to the kitchen with the tray and help her clean up the kitchen dishes and Alyssia agreed. As they did the dishes as she explained her past to Mary Anne as she puts all the dishes away after Alyssia washes the dishes and Mary Anne sat on her walker and dries them. Mary Anne says as they put the last dish on the stack that sat on the counter, "Oh my dear I am so sorry that you have been through so much sadness. Use my facilities to wash up, go on." Alyssia smiled and said as she took the widow's hand into hers, "I'll not be long...I promise." The widow smiled as Alyssia lets go of the widow's hand and Alyssia finds the guest bathroom as she goes in and locks the door then leans against it.

She went to the toilet, washed her hands and face until she sees the face of her mother smiling back at her in the mirror and hears a scream as she turns around to see no one. Her brain screamed out: *Pull yourself together; it's this house and the bad memories. It's going to be okay when you leave...just hang in there.* Alyssia took in another deep breath, washed her face and hands again and after drying herself off, she dried the sink and hung the old towel back on the rail beside her, straightened her clothes, took in one more breath, and unlocked the door and leaves the facilities.

She goes out to the living room to see another woman there and Mary Anne introduced her to the young lady. "Oh sorry, Alyssia, this is my daughter Gwen Parker-Swanson; she is my nurse as well… Gwen, this is Alyssia Franklin-Jenkins." Alyssia smiled at the young lady and says as they shook hands, "It's very nice to meet you Gwen, your mother was telling me about you and yes, it's all good," The women chuckled, "…and I hope you don't think badly of me for being here with your mother."

She is a well-mannered lady and nurse who has the patience of a saint when it comes to dealing with her charge Mary Anne Parker; but Gwen Parker-Swanson is no ordinary nurse nor is what she seems to be alongside Mary Anne. Her long brunette and chestnut hair sat neatly in a ponytail, (for she hated scrunched up hair or buns unlike her fellow nurses.) Alyssia was reminded of Catriona as her beautiful hazel eyes, tall medium build, kind, patient, understanding, caring, faithful, anchor, polite, married, courteous and always hopeful with a touch of class has carried her with pride and her round face and porcelain skin was delicate to the touch as many men have looked at her features and have fallen in love with her.

Gwen says jokingly, "Well at least you're not a bad person or a cold caller...I hate those kinds of people who prey on my mother." The girls chuckled as the ladies shake hands as Mary Anne asked Gwen, "Will you feed Marigold Gwen, while I show Alyssia out to her car?" Gwen smiled and says, "Of course, mum," she says politely to her as her eyes turned to meet Alyssia as she says to her as she got out her car keys, "It was very nice to meet you; hope to see you around." Alyssia nodded, "I'd like that Gwen, thank you." Mary Anne and Alyssia got outside and helped Mary Anne down the steps of her home as Alyssia offered her arm to the widow Parker and they walk to Alyssia's car.

"Well, it's been wonderful to meet you Mary Anne and thank you for the tea and the cake was delicious." Mary Anne patted her hand, "It was so nice meeting you too, Alyssia. Good luck with your studies and trust me; you'll love it at Kelton University. I worked there when it first opened and it has everything; first rate lecturers, amazing facilities, good staff, restaurants and shops nearby. But I want you to do something for me Alyssia, come by and visit me...anytime." She was about to decline but Mary Anne wasn't going to take 'no' for an answer, "I insist!" Alyssia smiled and says, "I have taken up too much of your time already so thank you again for the tea but I better head on to the University and get into my dorm...thanks again for your company and hospitality." Alyssia hugged the old woman gently as she says as she lets go as Mary Anne pats her cheek gently, "Good luck at University my dear girl, all the best."

Alyssia got into her car, buckled up, checked on Mystery to make sure that she was comfortable, "Who is in your jacket?" Mary Anne asked curiously. Alyssia replied, "A small black kitten...she just got in my car and snuggled down in my jacket. I called her Mystery because she came from nowhere so now I'm what you call an 'accidental' pet owner." The little kitten stood up as they watched her stretch, bathed herself, took on more tuna and milk, then curls up back up to go to sleep. "Aww, Alyssia, she is beautiful and she could have chosen anyone but chose you instead. You certainly are blessed."

The women smiled as Alyssia stroked her small head gently as the kitten started to purr loudly as she started the car, puts on her seatbelt and she drove off leaving the suburbs behind and following the signs to Kelton University as the women go back inside. At first, Alyssia felt like she was being watched but shook it off as she talked with the ladies…something or someone was watching her from the trees as it followed her to Kelton University as it kept tabs on her until she reached her destination and then reported back to a strange House on the hill, knowing that she was safe.

When Alyssia saw Gwen coming towards the ladies as the spy who was watching the ladies called his employer. "She is headed to Kelton University…her car is heavy laden with her possessions. Shall I call the University sir?" His employer said, "No I will do that, you keep an eye on Alyssia and report back." The spy hung up the phone and puts it away as he disappears as he followed Alyssia all the way to Kelton University without her knowledge as the late morning gave way to early afternoon.

THE CAMPUS OF KELTON UNIVERSITY

An hour later, she and the spy arrived at Kelton University with a whole bunch of newbies, not only to study the paranormal but to do core skills, psychology, sociology, philosophy, literature, science, medicine and other subjects around the campus as the spy called his employer and told him that she has safely made it to Kelton University and the employer says, "Wonderful, come back to the manor and I will give you your next job and assignment."

He did as he left Alyssia safe at the University campus as she found a parking space and she went to the office at the Administration Building and sees a kindly lady receptionist at the front desk working away. She looked up at Alyssia and asked in a very gentle voice, "Hello dear, what can I do for you?" Alyssia was nervous but she said to her, "Y-Yes," she began. "I-I'm here to sign in and get the keys to my room?" The lady named Kelly Preston smiled up at her as she asked, "What is your name?" Alyssia nervously replied, "Alyssia Franklin-Jenkins, ma'am."

Now this is strange that a mother working at the University is the mother of an undercover cop John Preston as she is there for Alyssia for the first day and for the rest of term time. She also was the one person to give Alyssia her flat at Cassious House which is across the street from the University as the lawyer had called a head of time to help her enrol in University when she got the scholarship. She was a kind lady with beautiful grey eyes, medium height with dark amber hair and a round face; she is warm, loving, kind, motherly, has a friendly disposition, and loves everyone like her family (except for George Thackeray and his goons) and she doesn't like rudeness and is very good at making you feel welcome. Her son got the job on campus through her as Hyman was looking for a good gardener and maintenance man as he repaired some things for his mother, even though he has a wife who comes to see her on her days off, he still got the job and is glad to have him on the campus as well as a police officer.

The receptionist smiled as she looked at the board and says, "I'm afraid all the dorms have been filled but the caretaker Mr Kevin Parks can take you." The receptionist went over to the board and gave the flyer on the accommodation as Alyssia says, "That's fine, and I chose to live off campus anyway." The mother-like receptionist smiles and places a gentle hand on her back as the ladies go back to her desk; "Wonderful to hear, I'll get you the keys and you must sign some papers." Alyssia took in a sigh and said, "Thank you Mrs Preston; that's very kind of you."

Kelly gave her the papers and told her where she should sign and while she did that, she looked and found the keys to her small home on Cassious House property. Alyssia signed all the necessary paperwork and she was handed the keys as Kelly says, "Just across the street and ask for Mr Kevin Parks, he'll take care of you; then you can come back about one or two and we'll have your class schedule ready for you at Kelton Hall." Alyssia thanked her, "You have been a big help, thank you."

Kelly Preston smiled and winked at her as she left the office for Cassious House with the keys and paperwork in hand and finds her car as a figure watched her from the foyer and smiled as he goes back to reading the campus newspaper. She slowly drives her car through the crowd in the car park of the campus and gets across the street; then she finds the concealed entrance to Cassious House and drives up the driveway to a dark, foreboding House with a Tower as she pulls in and parks her car as she got out the address her grandmother's lawyer gave her.

The House sat on a hill that overlooked the University as its dark foreboding Tower stretched to the sky and pierced the thicket of trees as she looked about and she saw a hole in the thicket of trees as the woods echoed with voices of long ago. There were two small homes attached to the side of the House and they both looked out on the well-manicured garden and the overgrown back area that was covered with bramble and thorns, some snakes and insects and she dared not go towards it as she thought, *'You have got to be kidding me,'* she thought as she looked about. *'This place looks like something out of a Vincent Price horror movie!'*

Alyssia was nervous as she gets out of the car and looks around for anyone on the property unaware she was being watched by many eyes as the wind danced around her and the birds welcomed her with their song. **'She has come!'** said a whisper on the wind and it echoed in Marylebarne's brain and in the Dark Spirit's brain as well as they watched the young lady look around property of Cassious House. "Hello...Mr Parks; is anyone here?" she called out as she looked at the enormity of the House. She gets Mystery out of the car and placed the kitten into her jacket and kept her close to her and felt the kitten's purr on her chest as Mystery listened to her heartbeat and cuddled in as she stroked her small head as she looked around the huge house.

Prince Timothy came to the window and saw her from the Tower as he smiled and signalled for Jesterson and Marylebarne who joins him at the window as they look down, "She is lovely; looks like we have a new tenant," Timothy nodded and smiled as all the spirits look at her through the windows of the Haunted Cassious House, whispering as if to say, *'She is **'the key'**...she has to be!'* The other spirits were anticipating good things as news of her arrival was floating around the House causing excitement and happiness.

Outside, she looked about as Kevin looked out the window of his home and sees her looking around calling out for him; "Mr Parks? Is anyone here?" she called as she keeps Mystery warm while he gets his coat on and comes out of his home as he came to her after telling Sharlene that the new tenant has arrived and goes outside to greet her. After a minute or two, she turned to see a man coming towards her who sticks his hand out to greet her as they talked by her over packed car. Kevin came out to greet her as he says apologetically, "I do apologise for keeping you waiting so long. I should have told Mrs Preston to have you come to the door instead, Miss...?"

Her smile lit up her features as the Prince Timothy saw her smile and was immediately smitten with her as she said, "Alyssia Franklin-Jenkins." The Prince repeated her name and he watched as she gave him the paperwork and gave him the money, he read it as his wife came out after getting her jacket on; "Hello I'm Sharlene Parks, the wife…" she said gently and shook her hand as he looks over the documents. Kevin was a middle-aged man with brownish grey hair, amber brown eyes, tall, slender with a muscular build in his arms and waist area. He was a kind, but stern gentleman and Alyssia noticed that he doesn't take any nonsense from anyone and his smile was warm and bright as he greets her in the sunlight of Kelton Heights.

His wife Sharlene is a beautiful, resourceful woman with a twinkle in her eye and a smile to boot as well. Her short blonde hair, green eyes, tall, but delicate features and slender features, soft spoken gentleness and a heart of gold, makes her an ideal "older sister" figure to Alyssia who is all alone in this world. She knows that Alyssia is special and aims to put her to the test to prove that Alyssia is the one to change the luck and fortunes of Kelton Heights and Welleston Village.

He smiled and said, "It looks like everything is in order, Miss Jenkins. Welcome to Cassious House; come and I will show you your new home." He shoved the money into his pocket and took the keys from her as the trio head to the flats that were attached to the Haunted House. Alyssia follows Kevin into her new flat as Sharlene was right behind as he unlocks the door and opens the door to her new living quarters with her furniture already waiting for her with some boxes of some belongings. She looked around and told him, "It's beautiful, just I pictured it; thank you." The couple smiled as Kevin says in a whisper as he takes her aside, "There is one rule that I strictly live by and have been for five generations of Parks; I do not want you going into the House next door, it's off limits."

She looks at the curtain which was drawn back by Sharlene and behind it was a door as she looked at it curiously; the door was brown and it had a brass knocker on it while it had scratches and when she touched it, she felt all the dents and bumps within its wood. The door was crafted beautifully from mahogany and saw every intricate detail carved into it as the gold knocker was shining like a bright gem in the ocean when the light hit it just right and then she heard Kevin saying, "Many have gone in but they haven't come back," she looked back at him. "I don't want this happening to you as you seem such a lovely and polite young girl, okay?" She looked back at him and replied to him gently, "I understand Mr Parks; I have no intention of going next door to the House," he smiled as she concluded, "I'm here to study not to explore."

He smiled and pats her hand gently; "Thank you for your cooperation on this matter." She nodded as he says as he shakes hands with her, "Well Alyssia, welcome and if you need anything, just tell us and we will do our best to accommodate you. Now if you'll excuse us..." She did have one thing as she asked him, "I have accidently become a pet owner; are pets allowed? Sorry I didn't finish reading the flyer," He chuckled as he told her, "Yes there's a two small pet maximum...why?" She smiled as she pulled a kitten out of her jacket pocket. "Aww, she is lovely" Sharlene replied as she came to her and started to stroke the kitten's head gently as she slept snugly in her hand. "What's her name?" Alyssia said, "Mystery; she just climbed into my car and fell asleep in my jacket and I have no idea where she came from...thus the name."

They pet the sweet kitten as Kevin says, "She is adorable and yes she is welcome and so are you; Welcome to Kelton Heights, Miss Jenkins." Alyssia smiled and told Kevin and Sharlene, "Thank you and please call me Alyssia and I will make sure not to go next door as instructed." Kevin nodded happily as she places Mystery back in her jacket and gave her some food and milk as the couple leaves her to unpack as Sharlene says to Kevin; "I'll be there in a moment." He nodded as he waits for her outside as Sharlene waited till he was completely out of earshot as she turns to Alyssia who was about to call Catriona and the lawyer.

"Pay no attention to Kevin; he gets a bit paranoid;" she reached into her pocket and pulled out a silver key on a string and placed the key into Alyssia's hand and closed her fingers around it as she says to her gently, "This is the key to the door that leads into Cassious House..." She shook her head as Sharlene says, "I have a good feeling about you." Kevin called for her as she told him she was coming as she held her hand.

"Sharlene, I can't, I don't want to get into trouble with Kevin..." she said as she tried to give her back the key to the House as Sharlene says, "No keep it...you might need it; and if you want to go into the House, come and get our permission." Kevin called to her once again as she patted her hand and left her to unpack as Alyssia hung the key by the door on a hook and placed the kitten on the counter as she gave her some more tuna and some kitten milk after she hung up the key on a nearby hook, closed the curtain, and settled in to her new life and home in Kelton Heights as she calls Catriona and her grandmother's lawyer.

Shin? "Hello" said Catriona after picking up the phone. *Shin an sin, a' Chatriona.* "Hello there Catriona…" She smiled as she heard Alyssia's voice as the lawyer and his wife came over. *Tha mi feir fònadh gu abair mi déantatha gu Kelton Heights a gu an oilthigh…Mi ám sábhailte.* "I am phoning to say that I made it to Kelton Heights and to the University…I am safe." Catriona and the couple were happy to hear her voice. *Bha sin direach álainn!* "That's wonderful" Catriona said excitedly as Alyssia asked gently, *Ciamar a tha dol dhut le gu taigh?* "How are you getting on with the house?" *Sinn a bheil ach deas gu gluais a-mach. An obraiche a bheil an seo cnòdachadh an taigh do am ùr sealbhadair taighe is ais—thilleadh an tuath a-máireach."* We are almost ready to move out; the workers are here fixing up the house for the new home owners and I return to the North tomorrow."

Alyssia was excited for her as she says, *Uileag an rogh… Mo mùir gu do chuideachd.* "All the best…my love to your family." Catriona thanked her and they said their goodbyes and hung up the phones. While she was unpacking, she put all the pictures all over the place and finished each room and started on the car. Just as she was placing her computer table right where she wanted it, she looked at her watch, got her other coat and left the flat for the University to get her schedule for her classes tomorrow. She went down the back steps and over to the campus to collect her schedule as a man watched her pass while doing the gardening in a flower bed near Kelton Administration Centre while she was looking at a map of the campus for a certain building… Kelton Hall.

Just then, another lecturer who was going the other way knocked her down as the two other men keep her down and shouted profanities to her as the caretaker stood up and ran over to help her as the lecturer said rudely, "Why don't you watch where you're going, young lady?" Alyssia watched her map blow away and the men were laughing at her dilemma as she was almost in tears but then she saw a hand of a caretaker who came and helped her up as the rude man and his cronies walked on back to Thackeray House.

She felt a hand on her arm and saw a muscle-bound man looking down at her and he gave her a hand up with a smile as bright as the sun. "You okay miss; are you hurt?" Alyssia was startled but not hurt, "No I'm okay; no bones broken...and this is supposed to be a friendly University." She brushed the dirt off her pants and coat as she turned to him, "Thank you Mr...?" The man raised an eyebrow and smiled, "Preston, John Preston; Caretaker here at Kelton University." The man put his soiled gloves in the pocket of his overalls and shook hands with her.

Burly, guardian, friend, bald, with a round, chiselled features, a wrestler, and god-like physique, determined, kind, compassionate, always there to lend a hand, and the brother of murdered Sidney Preston, John Preston is a leader in the Kelton Heights Police and SWAT Department. He made a promise to Sidney's wife and parents that he would get Thackeray and put him away for life and starts working away on the case after getting the okay from his superior to investigate a secret conspiracies going on at colleges around Kelton Heights and is Alyssia's protector and friend.

She straightened out her clothes while the man looked at the lecturer walking quickly away from them as they watch the cronies pushing into others on the pathways of the campus. She was just going to ask him who he was but he saved her the time as he angrily pointed as if to stab him with a knife. "That's George Thackeray, one of the lecturers here and he has Karma waiting for him… One day when it strikes, I want to be there when it does!" She thought: *'my mother died and you lived, you coward! I hope John is right, I hope karma catches up with you.'* But she shook off the anger and smiled back at John as he had a strange feeling that she had met him before but he would not press her about it just now.

"Thank you so much Mr Preston" He looked at her and smiled, "Call me John." He took a deep breath and smiled at her as she looked up at him, "I'm glad you're okay, Miss...?" She smiled and says, "Jenkins, Mr Preston, Alyssia Franklin-Jenkins; new student here-just going to the Kelton Hall to get my new schedule for my classes; I lost the map as you can plainly see," the couple laughed gently and he checked her over, "…just scrapes and bruises, but nothing serious; but Kelton Hall is a different story." She smiled as the caretaker smiled and pointed the way.

"Down this path and follow the signs till you get to the entrance… you can't miss it; it's been all done up." Alyssia was brushing the last of the dust off says to him, "Thank you so much Mr Preston, you've been a big help." Marylebarne sent him a message to watch over her at all costs as he nodded at the advisor's message. He got back to his duties; and as he watched her leave and she walked on to Kelton Hall to retrieve her schedule. He took out his wallet and looked at the angel that was given to him; Alyssia had grown up and she looked so beautiful as John smiled, put his wallet away inside his overalls and zipped it up, got his gloves back on and went back to work.

Inside Kelton Hall was a different story; it was pandemonium as students and staff were everywhere as she saw tables and chairs with teachers and other faculty trying to get students names right and sorted into their proper classes; it was like an ocean of chaos as she pushed through the crowd, got in line as the noise was deafening, as she stood in line to get to the table and looked around at the enormity of the hall. It was like a small church, gym and recreational hall mixed together as signs and lights looked small compared to massiveness of the hall as she stood in line patiently and felt alone in a sea of people who were bumping her, pushing past her just chatting around her; but she finally made it to the front of the line.

When it was her turn, she came up to the table and told the lady her name and she was given her schedule of classes and a welcome bag as she asked where she could go to get help with her maths and she told her to go to Student Services in the Administration Building. She thanked her and walked through the lines and the deep sea of people to get to the exit as she felt that she was being watched as she got to the shallow end of the crowded hall. She got up the steps and looked about then exited and went back to the Administration building as she sighed and made sure that she was only bruised and battered except for the scars that Thackeray and his goons inflicted on her.

As she walked in, it was less crowded and she navigated her way to the front counter and she felt that she could breathe as she saw the same lady who gave her the keys to her home as she went to the front reception desk and Kelly looks up at Alyssia who looked like she had been hit with everything. "Hello there again; what can I do for you?" Alyssia smiled as she began to wonder if she had taken a liking to Alyssia as she shook it off and asked her, "I-I was told that student services were in here? I'm looking for help with my Maths, you see…" Kelly says, "Why yes, come with me." Alyssia followed her and lead her to another room as she asked Alyssia, "Did you find the House okay?"

Alyssia says, "Yes I did, thank you. I-I also met John Preston, the caretaker...he's really nice." Kelly nodded as she says happily, "Oh yes..." she knocked on the door as she continued. "I'm so proud of my son." She looked at her and smiled, stopped for a moment to check her welcome bag and placed her schedule inside as she caught up with Mrs Preston and stood by her side as Kelly knocked on the door gently.

After a few minutes, there was a voice from within the room, "Just a minute!" the voice shouted as a man opened the door as Kelly, who had placed her hand on Alyssia's back, told him that this young lady was looking for help with her Maths. The tutor saw her and smiled as he asked Alyssia to come in. "Thank you Mrs Preston, I really appreciate your help," she told the kindly receptionist as Mrs Preston walked away happy as Alyssia went inside and saw to support for her Maths and then went home after the meeting with the Student Support Advisor for Maths and Special Needs.

THE FIRST NIGHT IN CASSIOUS HOUSE AND FIRST MEETING

She finished getting her home in order by placing things perfectly where she wants them as the House was perfect and she had some dinner and fed Mystery. Then after doing the dishes and putting them away, she sat down at her homework table and read through the bag she got from Kelton Hall; from Fire Safety to assembly points and safety on campus...to her tutors and what to expect from the course she was about to undertake-she was taking it all in; reading her schedule and maps of the Houses and classrooms as well as reading about her tutors as she drank her hot chocolate and relaxing with Enya playing softly in the background while Mystery lays beside her and takes a nap.

The wind began to blow and the trees started to tap against the windows of her living room as a storm was coming from the west and would be heading east as it grew in intensity as Mystery woke up a couple of times but went back to sleep as she dismissed it as nothing as Timothy stood in the shadows and watched over her as the storm grew in intensity. As she was reading up on her tutors, she heard a noise from next door as

Timothy watched over her from the shadows as not to scare her while she ignored the noises at first; but as the noises got louder, the Prince watched in horror as she approached the key, drew back the curtain, and fit the key into the lock as Timothy's shadow flew across the room and went to stop the noises; but it was too late as he heard the click of the lock on the door as she went inside slowly and pulled her jacket close to her as the cold air drifted around her as he hid in the shadows and watched the veil intently as his sword was drawn and ready just in case.

She was inside the main hall of Cassious House as she looked around in awe at the biggest hall she had ever seen as the as a wind blew around the hall and stirred the leaves and dust as well as the furniture coverings around the hall as cobwebs held on for dear life. It was huge hall with black and white marbled tiled floor, a table that sat against the wall behind the door with an elegant curving staircase and nude busts on the railings' plinths and since it was dark, she had a hard time seeing what was in front of her. She had turned off her phone to charge the battery, so she turned it on and waited for it to come on fully as she placed the phone back in her pocket after charging it.

She looked above her and saw a massive skylight and looked up through the dome that stretched to the ceiling as the storm clouds raced by and she was amazed at the ferocity of the wind and the clouds speed while looking up at the storm from above in relative safety. "Wow the clouds are racing by very quickly tonight... they must be going at twenty or thirty miles per hour just now." She said out loud as she looked at the massive bay windows and the marble columns that held up the staircase as the rest of the hall was in deep darkness. The pictures from the past watched her pass by as she got deeper into the hall and they seemed to tell her to turn back but she pressed on hoping to find out who broke into the House on this stormy night as she felt someone or something watching her which made her feel a bit apprehensive.

Then lightning started to fork across the sky and lit up the room as the thunder rolled across the angry skies as the House temperature dropped even lower while she rubbed her arms through her jacket and looked around some more after she heard a noise. "Hello, is anyone in here? If you are, I must ask you to leave..." The lightning flashed into the house once again as if to take a picture of her as she went deeper into the main hall to look for the intruder. Beside her were massive bay windows which looked out on to the trees and bushes which blew in the ferocious winds and tapped against the pane but what she didn't notice was a very thick veil of darkness covering the first-floor landing of the stairwell as she called out, "Hello, is anyone here?"

She looked around again going deeper into the hall as the door of her home slammed loudly echoing through the House as she jumped and yelped wondering who shut the door behind her as Mystery even jumped but recovered to get back to sleep. Alyssia was very scared and she didn't want to go any further as she can help it as she continued to look around again and saw the trees tapping on the bay windows as if the trees were sending out a message in Morse code…'Get out while you still can…. get out while you still can…get out while you still can…' the message repeated as she shouted back as she tried to be brave but failing miserably as if someone was playing a cruel prank on her, "This isn't funny, you know, and if you don't leave; I will tell Kevin Parks that you're trespassing. So, leave now and do not return; this is private property…you have been warned!"

There was no one there, and just as she was turning back to head for home, a dark spirit came out of the veil and was closing in on her as it prepared to strike until she heard the clatter of a suit of armour and the shriek of a ghost being torn to pieces as she saw a young man standing with a sword in his hand just looking at her. "What the-?" she turned quickly towards the noise and what she saw she couldn't describe, a handsome young man dressed in medieval clothes with a sword! She looked at him and was about to confront him until they looked up and saw another dark spirit coming after her as the dark spirit knocked her off balance and on to the floor.

The Prince slashed at it as it turned back to attack her-and disappeared in a shriek of pain while another angry dark spirit came after him angrily. He shouted to her two words and they were as clear as day, **"RUN NOW!"** She didn't need to be told twice as she stood up and ran for the door which lead to her home and the young man kept slashing at them shouting, **"WHY DON'T YOU LEAVE HER ALONE? WHAT HAS SHE DONE TO YOU?"** he asked as he kept fighting them and stabbing all who opposed him while the dark spirits shrieked as they fell into dust; one by one each dark spirit tried to capture her and each time they met with his sword. He watched her dodge each spirit until finally she sees the door to her home within reach, "I'm almost there…" she said with breathlessness until a dark spirit blocked her way back to the House and she skidded to a halt.

She wanted to cry out but she was too afraid to as it got closer and the dark spirit started to reach out for her as another blocked her in. Timothy watched helplessly and he started to run to her aid as he called out; **"LEAVE HER ALONE!"** He slashed the first one blocking her way as the second one was close and she could smell its foul breath that was putrid and musty with years of decay and alcohol as its eyes glowed and it licked its lips at the prey he was about to feast on.

Its skeletal hand was almost upon her as she fell to the floor looking for anything to defend herself with but found nothing within reach and the spirit screeched and rushed towards her as she curled up into a ball to protect herself as it teased its prey. Timothy had to act quickly as he ran to her aid while a scared Alyssia was looking for anything to arm herself with as the dark spirit charged at her again. Scared and defenceless, she needed a miracle as she watched in horror as the dark spirit lunged for her once again looking for something that would be useful.

She patted her pockets quickly and thought that she was done for until her hand hit onto a cover and went into her front pockets of her jeans and found her mobile phone. It was fully on as she played with it, found the flashlight app on her phone, and quickly shined it in its eyes as the dark spirit stopped its attack.

The dark spirit shrieked with pain and tried to hide itself from the light; but it was blinded as he tried to smack the light from her as the Prince smiled and said to himself *'Good lass…'* as he got ready for his attack as the young prince made a running start and jumped as high as he could onto a chair and slashed it in two as he told her after landing in front of her with his sword at the ready as he kept an eye on the angry and vengeful dark spirits, **"GO NOW!"**

She nodded as he protected her from the anger of the deadly dark spirits who were starting their attack again. She stood and ran for the door, opened it, ran inside, closed and locked it, drew the curtain as she backed away scared to death at what just happened as she fell to the floor with relief and disbelief; *"Now I see why Kevin says the House was off limits!"* she said to herself as she got her breath back, her heart back in her chest and she went back to her reading still spooked as to what just happened as she stood up and dusted herself off and went to get some water.

It was midnight as she got ready for bed as she heard the wind howling mercilessly through trees as its branches were tapping against the window of her bedroom. The early morning brought heavy rain as the gusts slapped the rains against the windows of her bedroom while she got into bed and turned out the light as her stomach started to hurt. She tried to sleep until that nightmare returned and she sat up as the lightning flashed into her room as if someone was taking a picture of her again while she tried to settle down in her new bed.

She tried to close her eyes and sleep after turning out the light until a peel of thunder made her jump out of her skin and she shouted with fear and she cried like a little girl wanting her mummy as the lightning lit up her room again; forcing her out of bed to seek shelter and she was pale with fear and sweat while she prayed for the storm to ease. "Please no more…please no more!" she begged, "Please send a guardian angel mum; I'm scared... I'm so scared." She started to cry and pray as the storm grew fierce and just when she thought she saw everything, she looked up to see a figure of the same man standing before her while the lightning reflected his figure on the wall as he came to her. As he got closer, a loud peel of thunder bellowed through the House as if an earthquake had hit as she fell to the floor full of terror and cried out as he replied gently, "Hello, I just came to see if you were okay and if you would like some company on this stormy night?"

She looked up at him like a frightened lost child and nodded as he sat on the floor with her; holding her close while the storm blew with ferocity and she was clinging on tight to her guardian angel as he constantly reassured her. He was dressed in royal robes of Medieval Age and he held his sword beside him as she looked up at him like a child who has seen an angel as another loud peel of thunder shook the House again as she buried her face in his shoulder. She looked up again and saw that his eyes were brown and his curly, brown, long hair sat in place on his head as his full uniform suggested that he was a royal lineage… and the way he held himself told her that she was right.

He was tall as his muscular bulky frame carried him well and he comforts her by stroking her hair as his touch was soothing and his smile was warm and gentle. His dashing good looks were in his chiselled round face and rough stubbly beard showed that he was more like a pirate king than a royal and he held his hand out to her. "I'm glad to see that you are well and no cuts or bruises; except for these…" he saw the scrapes and cuts on her arms. "I-I f-fell on the sidewalk on campus w-when I-I was picking up my schedule."

"Ah, I see…" he said and kept her close to him as the storm blew harder and rattled the windows and the bushes. The lightning lit up the room, the peel of thunder, and the songs of the Dark Spirits was scaring her as her stomach was sore with all the worry and fear choking her as she buried her face into his shoulder. She was going to ask him something but she was too scared to ask him as he said, "Don't worry; those dark spirits will not come in here if I'm around guarding you."

She stuttered out with fear as she looked up at him, "W-Who are you?" She asked him as he stroked her hair; "I am Prince Timothy Andrew Carlton, it's a pleasure to meet you and you are?" Alyssia saw the lightning flashing, another huge peel of thunder made her hide and cry as the young man held her tightly beside him as she says as he placed a comforting, gloved hand on her cheek that was wet with tears of panic, sweat and fear as she looked at him and he smiled, "A-Alyssia F-Franklin-J-Jenkins, your highness and it's a pleasure to meet you too."

He placed his other gloved hand on hers; it was gentle as his gloved fingers wrapped around her tiny hand as he took it and he kissed her hand gently as he smiled. "It's a pleasure to meet you Alyssia Franklin-Jenkins." She smiled and jumps again as the thunder was peeling across the sky as he says to her, "It's okay; the storm is dissipating in the East and should end soon." She smiled and says trembling, "T-Thank you for your company, your majesty. I-I'm never this fearful of storms…"

He smiled and said gently, "Please Alyssia…" she looked up at him with eyes filled with friendship and kindness, "Call me Timothy." he said as she smiled at him. "I came to welcome you to Kelton Heights and Cassious House." She was still frightened as she smiled and looked into his eyes and said quietly "T-Thank Y-You T-Timothy;" she said kindly. "I-I appreciate your kindness and I-I hope we meet again soon and thank you f-for d-defending m-me." He smiled and said, "I would like that and you are welcome."

They smile at each other as he says taking her hand and he helped her stand, got her off the cold floor, and back into her warm bed as the lightning started to die away. He stroked her hair gently and told her as he planted a small kiss on her cheek. "I am always here with you; I am right next door if you need me. Close your eyes and think nothing more of the storm...sleep now." He pulled the covers up on her and passed his gloved hand over her eyes and she closed them as the storm passed and he took his leave of her after he turned out the light.

Mystery was too afraid to sleep alone as she struggled to get up on to the bed, so Timothy helped the frightened kitten up and on to the bed as the creature snuggled in close beside Alyssia as the spirited Prince disappeared as she awoke, looking once more to find him; but he was gone as she was still shaking from the events that took place while she lies back down with Mystery shivering beside her as she pulled up a cover on the kitten and they went back to sleep as the heavy rain fell through the early morning hour.

THE FIRST DAY OF TERM

The morning came and Alyssia's alarm went off as she got up and got ready for her first day at Kelton University. She got showered, made the bed, fed Mystery, dressed and had her breakfast, packed her back pack and checked to make sure that she had everything. She grabbed her keys and walked away to the campus as Timothy watched from the Tower window with Marylebarne his advisor and the other spirits, who watched the young lady, leave for the campus across the street.

Alyssia walked down the driveway to the campus across the street but she stopped for a moment and wondered if last night was a dream as she turned around to see the House and looked at it as the clouds were passing through the trees: *'More like a nightmare. My stomach still hurts from the events of last night. I can't tell anyone what I have seen or they will think of me as a loony bird and Kevin would think I breached his trust.'* She thought about it again and made up her mind, *'No, no one needs to know.'* She turns away from the House as Timothy watched her leave for the campus across the street.

Marylebarne says to the Prince, "So now we got a new tenant, no wonder you're smiling; she is very lovely…" then he turned to the other spirits around them and says firmly, "and I don't want any of you scaring her to death." All the spirits nodded as Marylebarne looked down at her with Timothy and says to the prince as she went behind the thicket of trees. "It looks like she has already been frightened enough and on the first day of term at the University too."

The prince nodded and watched him walk away over to a crate as Jesterson, the clown says as he sat on the floor, "Well, I hope she has a sense of fun and humour; someone to laugh at my jokes, my tricks…unlike someone I know!?" He was staring directly at Marylebarne who gave him a fake smile as Timothy hid a laugh as he told Marylebarne; "Anyway, I stayed with her during the storm, she was so scared; poor girl cried out in fright… not a great way to spend the first night in the house."

Marylebarne nodded and said with a smile, "No it wasn't. It was pretty blowy and stormy; the rain, the thunder and lightning…it was horrible; no wonder she was frightened, and that was very kind of you staying with her during its fury, I'm sure she really appreciated it-keeping her safe and secure…you did well." Timothy smiled as he thought of her and said to his advisor as he stared back out the window, "Thanks Marylebarne…very kind of you to say so." The advisor winked at him and toasted him with his drink as the young girl brought over the Prince's mild ale as he thanked her and took it gratefully as he looked back outside to see that the weather was calm once again.

MONDAY MORNING; FIRST DAY ON CAMPUS

At the campus with the rest of the newbies, she had found Franklin House and she gets into the sea of confused students who are looking for their first class until she bumps into a teacher. "I'm so sorry; are you okay?" She asked as the teacher smiled as she picked up a piece of paper and hands it back to him. "Yes," he replied as he takes the paper from her. "It's me that should be apologising to you; I wasn't looking where I was going; I was pre-occupied with this fax from Dean Pharrell Winchell." They both laugh as he says, "You look lost?" Alyssia says to him embarrassingly, "I am sir;" she shows him her schedule…"I'm looking for this room and tutor."

He smiled as he says, "Come with me; I'm headed that way." She thanked him as they head towards the classroom as they talk, "What's your name?" he asked as she says, "Alyssia Franklin-Jenkins, sir." He smiled at her as he says, "It's very nice to meet you Alyssia, I'm Paul Franklin and from your schedule; you are going to be my father's student and my student as well. So if there is anything you need or anything you want, just ask or seek us out; we'll always try to help if we can." They reach the classroom and he looks in the window and says, "It looks like my dad isn't back yet from his meeting with Principal Mangard, so I better open the door for you and the rest of students; I will also wait with you until he comes back."

She nodded as he gets the key, opens the door and lets her in to the classroom while looking for a light switch. He lets her in, flicks on the light and he told her to have a seat anywhere as he goes to the desk and gets things sorted as he goes over to the windows and lifts the blinds to let in the natural light as she finds a chair and looks around as the students began to arrive for class. He watched her looking at all the posters as Paul knows that she's been spooked as he watched her reading them closely as to find something that would make sense as to what she saw last night.

The paperwork was ready and he was just going to talk to her until his father came in cursing under his breath…should he ask? "So how did the meeting go, dad?" He gave him a snarl. "Oh that good, eh?" Paul asked with a smile as Mark says as he looked at his son, "I wish the principal would make up his mind to stop talking after he says "In conclusion…" five times leaving us ten minutes to get to class!" Paul chuckles and says to him, "All the paperwork is in order, I let the students in and all you have to do is start the class." Mark says, "What would I do without you?"

Paul was about to say it as his father shot him look and then laughs as Paul went to Alyssia and gently touched her shoulder as she jumped at Paul's touch as she looked at him, "I will see you here on Wednesday morning, okay?" Paul replied gently as she smiled and nodded, "Y-Yes, of course… till Wednesday morning and thanks again for your help." Paul could sense that she saw a ghost last night, but he shook his head and let

Mark get on with his class and leaves her to go and do his work in the office for Wednesday morning as she heard the door close behind him.

She looks to the older gentleman getting his work, student enrolment forms, and planner out of his brief case, closed it and looked up at her with a smile and a nod as he took his case into the office as the door closed behind him after she acknowledged him in the same manner; then he disappeared into his office. Alyssia took in a deep breath as she went to sit down away from everyone and reads her schedule until class started while her stomach was doing flips inside her body as the posters were not telling her pretty much anything about the spirit of Cassious House. It left her more puzzled than ever so she decided to try and relax whilst more of the students came in and nodded an acknowledgement to her and she did the same.

The class was filling up quickly and she watched all her class mates gather into their groups as she sat alone reading up on Paul and the older gentleman in her book until a soft voice interrupted her thoughts. "Ahem"... the voice said as she looked up and sees a young lady with a scared look in her eyes and a shy disposition about her. "E-Excuse me, can I sit here?" Alyssia liked her right away as she moved her bag, "Yes please, come sit down." She felt that she needed the company in a classroom full of strangers as the young girl sat down beside her as Alyssia says, "My name is Alyssia Franklin-Jenkins and yours?"

She squeaked out, "A-Amber R-Raulston, it's very nice to meet you; first time here?" Alyssia says as the girls shake hands, "It is; I'm just getting used to this schedule and our tutors." Amber smiled and says, "Yes so am I," as the girls laughed as she sits down as the girls talked. Even though she looks shy and reserved, nerdy with long black hair and deep brown eyes, smooth complexion and dimples on her oval brownish skin, don't be fooled.

Unlike Adrianne, she is athletic, spontaneous, funny, tall, and thin with long hands and fingers-she has a black belt in karate and knows self defence. She loves pets, singing, dancing, drama, reading, watching sports and working out. She is also very loyal, caring, understanding, hates being the centre of attention, has a loving sister and mum, a good listener, beautiful and an all-around good person- but just like Adrianne, she does have a temper and knows how to use it. She is also a worry wart; she knows that Alyssia lives near the Haunted House and she worries that Alyssia has fallen under its spell but her friends say that she must be imagining it, so she keeps her eye on her at all times.

Alyssia got her pen and pad out as the girls were just about to talk until another two voices got their attention. "Hello, hello…" said a male voice that had his arm around a lovely but a "not so" flattered young lady as he asked, "Can anyone join in or do we have to fill out an application?" Alyssia and Amber chuckled, "Nope have a seat. I'm Alyssia-Franklin-Jenkins and this lovely but shy girl is Amber Raulston. We were just about to get to know each other." Everyone shook hands and they all became fast friends; "I'm Milton Russell and this beautiful lady here who is beyond beautiful is Adrianne Falconi."

Milton Russell is a loveable jester who loves his girls, he cheers everyone up. The fringe-loving, brown-eyed, medium muscular build, and a boyish imp always has a joke, a gag, or an impression to make the girls laugh and loves them like girlfriends. He has a serious crush on Adrianne Falconi who just brushed it off as infatuation and his across the hall neighbour in his building. When he's not making the teachers and the rest of his classmates laugh, he has a caring side; a brotherly love for Alyssia when he met her on his first day of University and he will do everything in his power to protect her and his girls from danger and is very protective, brave, and loyal.

But Adrianne is the complete opposite of all three; Adrianne is a fiery redhead, with blue eyes, a petite body frame, small delicate hands, with an Italian/ New York attitude and independent spirit. This is one girl you don't want make angry and she is fiercely loyal to her friends and classmates and if you say anything bad about them or bully them, you'll hear from her! Every guy on the campus is in love with her but she simply takes it all in her stride and teases them. Milton Russell is her "across the hall" neighbour in her apartment complex as they became good friends and dismisses Milton's affections for her as infatuation but watch out; she has a temper and knows how to use it as well; especially against Thackeray and his goons and has fun and sarcastic side where Milton is concerned.

The two of them sat down as she says to Milton, "Don't flatter yourself or me with your compliments…we're all new here so let's take our time, shall we?" Milton bowed before her as the girls moved their stuff and the couple sat down beside the two ladies as Adrianne began while they waited for class to start. Alyssia was just about to ask how they met but the fiery redhead beat her to it as Amber and Alyssia listened while they took off their jackets as Milton took them to the hooks near the door. He comes back to the table just as she was ready to tell the two girls how they met.

"If you're wondering how I met this clown; I met him in Kelton Hall when we were getting our schedules and I was bored as we stood waiting to get our schedules. He was telling me jokes and making me laugh and the bombshell, he and I are in the same building, floor and our doors are across the corridor from each other." Milton smiled broadly as he said, "I thought that all my Christmases came at once and that I found the girl of my dreams." He said staring dreamily at her while Adrianne, who was not in the least impressed with his glances, just looked at him as Alyssia and Amber laughed as she continued. "Anyway, I was getting unpacked after I had my dinner, settled down for the night and was getting ready for the first day of University but while I was getting my clothes ready last night for this morning, this loony comes to my door.

I opened it, he was wiggling his backside at me like a bowl of jelly and singing at the top of his lungs, "Moves like Jagger" from Maroon Five[1] as the music from the radio, in his house, was blaring in my ears." The girls laughed as Milton felt proud of himself as she replied, "I actually thought that the landlord was going to put us out on our first day so I told him, "Go home Milton" and I slammed the door on his wiggling backside while trying not to laugh as he serenaded me through the door the same song as I was trying to relax." The girls laughed as Adrianne says taking a drink of her water, "Oh wait; you haven't heard the best bit yet," she said with a smile. "This will have you rolling on the floor."

The girls listened as she screwed the lid back on her water, "Then this morning, he packed seven people into a tiny car and drove here to the University as he asked me before if I wanted a ride and I told him, "No thanks, it looks like you got enough clowns in there," the girls chuckled as she went on. "Then he told me that he would meet me at the University and low and behold, guess who I met when I got off the bus? Mr Ronald McDonald here opens the car door and lets all the "clowns" out one by

---

[1] "Got the Moves like Jagger" by Maroon 5 with Christian Aguilera ©2011(June 21ˢᵗ) A&M Records/Octone Records

one as every student was standing watching this laughing their heads off; I just couldn't believe it!"

Alyssia faked a smile and a laugh when all she wanted to do was cry, but she kept it in as Milton smiled at her as Milton then says while she shook her head, "Come on Adrianne, I bet you were laughing under that face palm of yours?" She rolled her eyes as he looked at Alyssia and Amber and replied like an Italian gigolo at Singles night, "Besides ladies, I love keeping things lively around here when things get too serious." He says wiggling his eyebrows at her as she rolled her eyes as the girls laughed as Amber asked her in a whisper and a chuckle to Adrianne as she took a drink of her water, "Then where is his clown suit and floppy shoes?" Adrianne says in a low voice as she recapped the water, "I think they're in the cleaners!"

Amber, Alyssia and Adrianne shared a laugh as she told her, "It looks like you, Milton, Alyssia and I are going to be good friends; and as much as I hate admit it, but Milton did make my night in that hallway at my flat and this morning. I guess he sensed that I was a bit nervous for the first day here at Kelton University." Alyssia smiled and Adrianne gave her a back rub, "Nervous?" Alyssia looked at her and nodded as she smiled and said, "We're all in the same boat so just relax..." Milton drew a funny picture for Amber as she saw it and whispered to Alyssia, "On the other hand, I think his boat has sprung a leak." Alyssia whispered back, "I totally agree with you" as Amber chuckled with her.

In the office next door, Mark takes a deep breath after helping Paul with a couple of points on his fax and gets his act together. He looked through the student enrolment forms and looked at each student's photo until he came across one that attracted his attention: Alyssia Franklin-Jenkins's photo and he thought for a moment, "Nah, I'm only dreaming;" he said to himself as Paul looked up. "Are you okay dad?" Mark looked at him, "Fine son, just getting my act together before I greet the students; are you going to be okay now working away on your lesson plans, Paul?"

Paul says, "Yep, just getting some questions and a pack together on Haunted Houses; I'll have the pack ready for printing on Tuesday, and work out the rest of Dean Winchell's fax. Just some minor issues to clear up, that's about it." Mark said, "Well, I better get out there and if you hear scepticism and laughter, just ignore it!" Paul chuckled as Mark takes one last breath and heads out to the classroom and his new students.

Outside in the classroom the students wait for Mark as he comes out with his planner and other work as Milton put his drawing away as soon as he saw Mark Franklin coming out of the office and approach his desk. Mark then goes to the front door and closes it, signalling the start of class as the students settle down as he picked up a stack of papers and lifted them up as he said in a loud audible voice as it became quiet quickly. "Good morning class and before we go any further, I need you to fill in these forms so the University and I can keep in contact with you." Mark handed the students the form and as soon as the students got the papers, they filled them in…but to Alyssia, it hurt like a hammer to her heart as they were Emergency Contact Forms and she couldn't fill it in as she told the others to excuse her for a moment as she goes outside the classroom before she could cry as Adrianne went after her.

Mark was puzzled as he watched her leave as Adrianne followed, "I'll see to her Doctor Franklin, excuse me…" He nodded as Adrianne went after her while Amber and Milton were at a loss as to what just happened as they talked and got to know each other as they filled in the forms. Alyssia was outside the room, crouched down and huddled in a corner like a scared kitten on the street as Adrianne came, placed her hands on her shoulders and asked her what was wrong as she gave her a reassuring rub on her back as she looked back at her new friend and classmate. She told Adrianne, "I lost my grandmother three weeks ago and I have no other family…" she held her close and told her how overwhelmingly stressed she was feeling. "The form hit my heart like a hammer Adrianne; I just realised that I'm really alone now and having to move here and settling down quick…I guess I'm overstressed just now." She looked back at Adrianne and asked, "I bet the other two think that I'm a weird?"

Adrianne says gently as she holds her tight, "Aw damn, I'm so sorry Alyssia. I know that we've just met but you can count on me, okay? I'll explain to the others what was wrong and they won't think you're weird… Milton might, but not us girls." Alyssia laughed and nodded as Adrianne hugged her and gave her a tissue. "Look, leave it blank for now, and we'll let Doctor Franklin know. We'll have you de-stressed and relaxed in no time. Remember, it happens to everyone; trust me…new term, new place and the loss of a family member don't help either, but it will all make sense once things settle down. Okay?" Alyssia nodded and with Adrianne's help, she stood up as the girls shared one last hug as Alyssia takes a deep breath, dries her tears as they go back inside Mark Franklin's class room.

Alyssia goes back to her seat and Adrianne whispers to Mark that Alyssia has no family; "…her grandmother died three weeks ago, sir." He looked at her in shock; "What? Jessica Jenkins is dead?" She nodded but said, "I didn't know her name, sir; so can she leave it blank for now? I think she gave you her other details and maybe she can ask her landlord or one of us to be her emergency contact?" Mark looked at her shocked as he nodded, "Yes of course, thank you for telling me, Miss Falconi." Adrianne smiled and told him, "Just call me Adrianne, Dr Franklin and you got the other forms from Amber and Milton as well as myself?"

He smiled and nodded as she took some extra tissues that were on his desk and started back to her seat. She went back to the trio and gave her some tissues as Mark looked at her; something in his mind came back to him as he looked back at her photo. He still brushed it off as coincidence as Adrianne came back to the table as she took some water, "Feeling better?" She nodded as she gave Alyssia a back rub and tissues to calm her while Adrianne told the others.

Milton puts his arm around her as she blew her nose in to the tissue as the new friends rallied around her. "We're here for you and if you need a chuckle, my dear Alyssia; think of me as the brother you never had." Adrianne whispered to Alyssia, "I think that's a threat," she chuckled as Milton shot her a look while Amber says, "I'm so sorry Alyssia, I'm here for you too. If there is anything you need, just tell us…okay?" Alyssia took Amber's hand as she was going to say to give her family back to her, but she held her tongue and was glad of the support that was around her now as she dried her tears.

She watched Mark close the door once again and everyone quieted down as class started for real as he shook off the shock of hearing about Jessica Jenkins passing; he would deal with that later as he got the class started. He straightened his jacket, took in a deep breath and smiled at the class after all the forms were handed in to him. "I'm Doctor Mark Franklin, your tutor for the Understanding and Preservation of Spirits. My son Paul Franklin is also teaching you on Wednesday mornings and he will give you an all-out lesson on Haunted Houses." Alyssia's stomach tightened as she felt like fainting at the thought about earlier this morning as she rubbed her head of the dizziness. Adrianne gave her something to ease the pain while the class nodded and muttered nervously as Timothy came out of the shadows and listened while he kept his eyes firmly fixed on Alyssia who was still reeling from early this morning while many students were saying, "Ah good one Doctor Franklin..." while others laughed as he settled the class down.

Paul too was chuckling in the office as he made some tea and got back to his lesson plans after dealing with the fax to Dean Winchell as Mark says, "Oh I see we have a class full of sceptics and non-believers? That's okay...I completely understand." Adrianne and Amber gave Alyssia a reassuring rubs on the back and arms as he continued while Mark came from around his desk as the students settled down. "All of you will have George Thackeray on the Eradication of Ghosts and Spirits tomorrow..." he replied as they all quieted down as Mark continued.

"But I'm here to say to you that we all have to believe in something; heaven, hell, angels, Celtic, Pagan, atheists...we all worship at churches, temples, synagogues, Catholic, Mosques—whether you are Hindu, Sikh, Greek Orthodox it doesn't matter...we are all of different races, nationalities, countries, different views on death and the afterlife; we all are human with different views, opinions and understandings of the world we live in; I like and respect that." The students liked him as he comes away from leaning on his desk and stands in the front of them saying, "So let's get you in groups of four, I want you all to get to know each other by writing down something interesting about each other it's a great way to open up and learn with what or whom you share in common with."

But Mark had one more look at Alyssia and suddenly the memories of his long-lost daughter who was taken away at seven years old, screaming and begging for her mother not to take her from her father as Alyssia felt it too. He looked at her photo on the enrolment form and her name as the students watched him walking around the room and kept their eyes fixed on him. Timothy kept an eye on Alyssia who closed her eyes for a moment as the class relaxed while they were listening to Mark but kept his eye firmly fixed on Alyssia as Timothy was watching Mark intently as he started climbing the stairs towards Alyssia's table as he says with baited breath as if he was looking into the eyes of a ghost, "Maybe it's...maybe its family, friends or acquaintances that you haven't seen in such a long time and you just know that deep down you want to get to know them all over again."

The students looked at each other perplexed while Mark's mind raced with a flood of memories as Timothy stood upright and gripped the hilt of his sword; he was ready to defend her as he watched Mark climbing the stairs to her and looked directly at Alyssia in the eyes as the other three watched him as Milton got ready to stand between them as he thought: *'Can you be my long-lost daughter that was taken from me all those years ago? The one that I have searched for to find, to hold and never let go?'* The other students looked at each other confused as they watched as Milton stood between them as Mark looked at her intensely as he says aloud, "But it can't be...could it?"

Timothy tightened his grip on the hilt of his sword as Milton stood between them as her new girl friends held her close and she asked her lecturer, "Doctor Franklin, are you okay? Do I seem familiar to you?" Timothy watched and kept a tight grip on his sword's hilt as his hands were sweating and hurting from holding it too tight but wiggled his fingers to take away the pain as sweat beaded on his brow while Milton stood between them to keep her safe while the girls held her close protecting her as Mark came back to his senses and says while everyone looked at him. He looked around the room at all the confused students who were looking at each other as he says to her as the memory block took hold once again, "For-forgive me, I-I meant no harm."

Alyssia nodded as Mark backed off and patted Milton on the shoulder as he turned away while the whole class watched with nervous tension. Timothy let out a sigh as he lets go of his sword slowly and wiped the sweat from his hands on to his hanky and then wiped hilt of his sword with the same hanky that he carried with him. Milton sat back down and the girls loosened their grip on Alyssia's shoulders while Alyssia took in a deep breath. Mark was still in shock as he went back downstairs and said; never once taking his eyes off Alyssia, "I will give you the whole of the first half to break to write down something interesting about each other and then in the second half, we'll get the results; Deal?"

Everyone exhaled their relief and nodded as he left the class of students to do the ice breaker as the girls kept her protected while Milton took her hand after Mark left the room; not sure what was going on as they did their ice breaker as Alyssia watched the senior Franklin leave the classroom with a look of panic on his features. Prince Timothy who was also confused went back to the Tower and told Marylebarne what he just witnessed and to get some advice on what he needed to do.

In the meantime, the quartet talk about what was interesting about each other as Mark goes into the quiet room and takes in a deep breath whispering to himself: *'My God, di-did I just see a ghost or did I just see my daughter alive and well?'* He took in another deep breath and said to himself once again, *'I need to get a grip…Damn memory block!'* He felt those memories crashing against the memory block like waves that were eroding the sea wall as he rubbed his forehead of an imaginary headache and went into the office quite shocked as the group worked away on their ice breaker.

A moment passed, and Paul was working away on lesson plans in the office for Wednesday morning when Mark comes in and was still a bit spooked as his son looked up at him and took off his reading glasses. His father leaned against the door with his eyes shut as Paul puts his pen down, "Dad what is it? It looks like you've seen a ghost? Given what we're teaching that would be no surprise…" he chuckled as he picked up his pen and got back to work on his lesson plans after taking a sip of lemon tea. Mark opened his eyes and now was pacing around the room, looking out the office window as he told his son in a distressed tone. "I-I may have seen your long-lost sister who was taken away from us at seven years old."

Paul looked at his nervous father, put down his pen, and took off his glasses. "Dad, come on seriously, don't have a mental break down on me now…not on the first day of term!" Mark asked him to come to the window and he did as they look up at the young lady between the young man and the woman and Paul says, "Yes Alyssia Franklin-Jenkins; she is a new student here and I showed her the way to this classroom; she will be in my class on Wednesdays." Then Mark shows his son her photo for her student ID and the picture of her from when she was seven. "Paul, it's her…it's got to be!" Paul sighed and took the photo and form as he looked at them intently as Mark tells him about Jessica Jenkins's passing.

While in the class after they talk about interests, the four friends talk about what they like but what they witnessed between Mark and Alyssia. "Boy Alyssia, Mark's stare was very intense on you; I can't believe that he thought that you looked familiar to him." Adrianne replied as Alyssia was trying not to talk about it or she would start to cry; but she had no choice as the little girl inside her screamed for her daddy that one day in the summer as she replied, "I was taken away from my father and brother when I was seven when my father was accused of murder…" The friends looked at each other stunned as she continued.

"My mother feared all the media attention he was getting was too much so she thought that taking me away from him was the only way to take the heat off…she was wrong. Four years later at eleven years old, I was sent to live with my grandmother after my mother died in a gas explosion at her house. On my way here, I went to the house to face my fears and all I had was bad memories which crippled me and a kind old woman named Mary Anne Parker has her home now." The friends couldn't believe what they were hearing and neither could Timothy as she replied, "Now with my grandmother gone, I just realised that I have no other family… e-everything is just on top of me." She started to cry as her new friends gathered around her as Adrianne says, "We're going to be your family now so you can count on us."

Milton being serious says, "I'm here when you need a laugh and for me to pull a face," which he did as she laughed and dried her tears as he replied with concern, "…but whatever comes our way, we'll face it together, okay?" She nodded as he kissed her forehead as she tells them, "I guess with my grandmother's passing, packing for University and starting here at Kelton University; it's still a bit overwhelming." The friends all give her a group hug as they went back to work on their assignment as the trio looked towards the office as they could hear them talking about Alyssia. Did they know something that she didn't? According to Mark he must have-his stare was intense as to bring up those memories from her childhood as they worked on the ice breaker.

In the office next door, Paul is trying to make sense to what his father is telling him; "But she's a student dad" Paul said, "…how do you know that it's possibly her?" Mark says in a blind desperation; "I just do Paul, she has got to be." His son stopped him pacing as they took a deep breath and became calm, brought their voices down, took in deep breaths and they talked this out as Paul stood at the counter. "Okay dad, are you calm now?" He asked his father as Mark nodded and took in another deep breath as he says, "Good, now let's talk about this logically and rationally, what is it that you want to do?"

Mark said to him, "I don't know, Paul…" Mark says calmly as the older gent walked away from the counter in his office. "But one thing is clear;

I can't let on that I know or George Thackeray would hurt her if he ever found out. Remember that your mother and George were lovers…damn this mental block!" Paul agreed he has seen first-hand what his lies could do. "Agreed we should treat her like a student and a friend; we don't let on and we play it cool."

Mark took a deep breath as he said, "Look Paul I have to get the students on their break but will you be getting a copy of the picture as well?" Paul thought for a moment, "I could but that means I crossed the line from being a teacher to a stalker. I can't go up to her and say: *"Hey you might be my long-lost sister; can I get a photo of you?"* I would go from being a teacher, struck off the teaching register, to a prison uniform in a matter of moments and worst of all I might just scare her off…" Mark understood this and says, "No you were right, how stupid of me to suggest such a thing! It's not a wise idea," then he looked at his watch, "…and it's time for the student's first fifteen minute break."

Paul went back to his desk as Mark asked. "Will you do me a favour and make a fresh pot of coffee? I need to calm my nerves, two sugars and milk?" He agreed and he watched his father leave the office as he was still a bit shaken about what his father had told as he puts on a fresh pot of coffee and then goes back to his lesson plans. Mark took a deep breath and came out of the office as he told everyone, "Okay everyone, finish what you're doing on your ice breaker and go on your first of two fifteen-minute breaks…I think we all need a time out!"

The students chuckled as they get up and go on their first break of the term. Everyone left the classroom still talking away while Adrianne took in a sigh as she said, "Good idea, we all need it…" then she turns to Alyssia, "How about some fresh air, water and some sweets with us, it looks like you could use it?" Alyssia said with a sad smile, "That sounds wonderful Adrianne thank you." She stood up as the quartet left the classroom while Mark watched her leave as she smiled at him.

Mark went to his desk, scribbled a note on a blank piece of paper and would give it to Alyssia as she passed as he called to her and she went to him and gave her the note as they smiled and she left him to do other work as her friends huddled around her like bodyguards protecting a rock star as Alyssia read the note while waiting for Amber to get some water from the fountain:

"Dearest Alyssia;

Please forgive me for the way I acted this morning. I hope that we can be good friends as well as a good student/teacher relationship and that you will come to me if you need anything. Welcome to Kelton University -MF and PF.-"

The note said as she took it and went away on her break with her new friends to get some water, some sweets as well as fresh air while all the students were still talking away and getting to know each other. She came back into the classroom as Alyssia told her friends that she had forgotten her wallet and went back inside the classroom to get it. Mark looked up at her going back to the table and getting her wallet as she came back down, she left a note for him as she passed his desk. She left the classroom and saw a small note on his desk as he read:

"Dearest Doctor Franklin; It's very nice to meet you too and your son as well...and I hope we can be friends too but still have a student/teacher relationship in the University. And yes, I will come to you if I need anything. —AFJ-"

He smiled and choked back tears and he had to keep it together as he put the note in the back of his planner and his son brought out his coffee and he took a large mouthful. Paul was a bit concerned about his father but he knew down deep that his father would not lie about something so close to his heart as he brought out the steaming mug of coffee. "How are you now dad?" Paul asked as Mark says, "I'll be fine son, I promise. I'm sorry I lost it there for a while." Paul smiled, "its okay dad..." and gave his father a pat on the back as Mark took a gulp of his coffee thinking aloud, "Probably first day jitters; still getting back into a routine after the summer break..." Paul gave his dad a reassuring smile and says, "You're doing great; just relax as you always told me."

Mark looked up at his son, "Should have taken my own advice," he said as they laughed while Mark handed him the empty mug as Paul took it back to the kitchen in the office as the students started to make their way back to their seats as Alyssia and her friends came in with water and some sweets as she smiled at Doctor Mark Franklin who went back to his work as she gave him a paper in his hand and went back to her seat as the note simply says:

"Dearest Doctor Franklin, I have already forgiven you in my heart; it's really exciting to be here once I settle and get used to my surroundings. Thank you for making me feel so welcome at Kelton University. —AFJ-"

He felt happy and justified that she had forgiven him and she was talking with her friends as he took in a deep breath and slipped the papers into the back of his planner. The class began again as he closed the door and got the results of the ice breaker as the students laughed and listened to their other classmates' interests and it went on until lunch time.

While in the Tower of Cassious House, Timothy was telling everyone who would listen what had happened as Marylebarne and the other spirits found it difficult to believe. "Are you serious? Mark Franklin believes that this girl, who has just moved in on the other side of the House, is his long-lost daughter?" one of the listening spirits asked hardly believing what Timothy was saying; "Yes I am, in fact I couldn't believe it myself and I was ready to defend her if the time came. It was a shock to her apparently, and to the whole class." He said drinking his mild ale as the spirits muttered to each other as Jesterson says, "That's just too hard to believe and if I didn't know any better; I wouldn't be surprised if they were family and I am willing to bet my soul that they are father and daughter or even a part of us."

Marylebarne and Timothy looked at each other as Jesterson drank his drink and all the Spirits were shocked and talked about what they just heard as Marylebarne says to the jester with a bet. "Okay Jesterson if you're wrong, I will let you sacrifice yourself to the dark veil; but if you're right and God I hope you are, we have a new family member and also my dear Prince Jesterson can be a second guard to her." Jesterson smiled as Timothy says, "Good idea Marylebarne, that's if Jesterson is up to it?" Jesterson said, "I would be happy to do that for you, my prince." He took the bet as he toasted the advisor and the Prince.

"Then it begins, I will go through the records and look up the Franklin clan if anyone wants to help me and you two split your guard duties up." Jesterson and Timothy nodded as the Prince says, "I'll need to train you, Jesterson. Give me a few nights of guard duty and I will teach you as we go along; Sound fair?" The jester agreed as he got back to doing his chores in the Tower while Timothy went back to his studies in his room with some fruit as he asked the young girl to bring him fresh water and she bowed and the Prince went back to his studies as the servant girl brought him fresh water in his chambers as he finished his mild ale.

Back on campus, lunch time came and the four friends were talking about what had happened near the end of class. Milton, who was lying on his coat with sunglasses on, started off by saying, "Man I never saw Franklin go pale as he did-he looked like a ghost! This starting to become a very interesting first week here at Kelton University, something is definitely wrong at the University, don't you girls think?" Adrianne nodded and then says as she munched on some carrot and celery sticks, "Yep, He ran out of the room so quick and all we saw is the students slapping this guy on the head after he mentioned Cassious House. I heard someone say that he should have never mentioned it in Franklin's presence; what happened there anyway?"

The trio shrugged as Alyssia heard everything that her new friends were saying but she was not bothered about the House; she was bothered only by getting half of her homework assignment from Mark Franklin; but it was the fear and the sadness that clouded Mark's features is what stood out in her thoughts as she needed to talk to Paul and just as she looked, he was walking right by them. She stood and asked Amber, "What's our next class?" Amber says, "Maths in Franklin House at one fifteen p.m. Why?" Alyssia got her backpack and says, "I need to talk to Paul...I'll see you in class."

The friends saw her leave as she ran after him and she called to him, "Doctor Franklin?" He had his lunch in his hand as he turned and saw Alyssia coming to him quickly. "Oh hello again," he said with a smile as Alyssia smiled and asked, "Paul I need to talk to you, is there someplace private we can go without any interruptions?" Paul thought and says, "Follow me; I know just the place." The trio see her walk off with Paul away from eavesdroppers and gossips as she smiled back at them and they disappear around the corner. Milton was curious as he said as he dropped his sunglasses; "I wonder what that is all about?" Adrianne says, "Well it's none of our business and we should respect that." Amber nodded with her as Milton says with the roll of the eyes and a glint of humour, "My dearest Adrianne and Amber, have you noticed that this is a small University and secrets are hard to keep around here. I really thought you knew that..." He put his sunglasses back on and soaked up the sun until the girls smelled something rotten as they stood and turned up their noses. "What in God's name is that smell?" Amber asked as Milton said happily, "Oh that would be my Gherkin, Onion, Sardine and Brown Sauce with Garlic sandwich making it way out of my system…sorry about that, my dear ladies!"

They all recoiled in horror as he farted again as most of the students ran away while others covered their noses and walked away as the smell entered their noses again. "Ah that cleared the system!" Adrianne got her coat and bag and Amber's coat and bag as all the students left him while Adrianne said sarcastically, "Yeah and the half of the University. I see the flowers wilting, teachers dropping to the ground, students running away in fear!" Amber chuckled as the girls go off to the garden area after she handed Milton toothpaste and a toothbrush as she replied, "Go and brush your teeth afterwards you skunk!" The jester looks at Adrianne and says sarcastically as the girls went elsewhere to talk as Milton says before they left, "Yes Mom!" Adrianne heard it and smacked him on the belly as he let out a yelp and walked away with Amber who held in a chuckle as the slap let off more farts as he lies back down with a smile on his face at his relief while he thought of Adrianne and says dreamily, "What a gal!"

Meanwhile, Paul and Alyssia reached the private place and sat down on the covered bench and she gave Paul a chance to eat his lunch and she also finished her lunch with him. They were at a corner of the University where it was far away from students and other teachers. The woods behind the University were filled with noises of birds singing and the trees waving in the breeze and near one of the big elm trees was a covered bench that no one but Paul found and it faced the woods as Paul says, "I love coming here; it's quiet and sane when everything around me becomes insane; but I guess that that's not the reason you wanted to talk to me."

Alyssia smiled and she finished her lunch and had a drink of water as she said comically, "Ooh you got me!" Paul laughed as she joined him on the covered bench, "Yes it's quite serene here as well as a beautiful place to get your head straight, but no, this is not the reason I called on you. I need your help and please forgive me for prying." Paul nodded as she asked with a sigh, "Mark left the room really upset and in haste after a student posed a question to him about Cassious House; what happened there?" She then told him, "You don't have to tell me if you don't want to…that's perfectly okay as well." Paul nodded and finished eating as he dropped his trash into her plastic bag and drank his water as he tells her quite plainly, "There was a murder there a year ago and my father has never gotten over it. It was his friend and colleague Sidney Preston and it was claimed that he "accidently" fell off the roof; but my dad knew it was murder."

Alyssia was shocked as Paul told the story from start to finish; from the message he got to how he found his assistant impaled and he struggled to get him down, how he died in his arms, how he was accused of the 'accident', how the case and the townspeople ripped him to shreds in public, in the trial and how the case tarnished his image. The loss of his wife and daughter, after the trial and his attempted suicide and how he had to take care of his father during the time he was a student teacher and how he simply refused to go to the House this day as he tried to keep the tears out of his voice.

"Alyssia," he said looking at her, "I would give up my world to change what has happened this past year..." She listened as she put her hand on his as he smiled. "Everyone made his life a misery from start to finish; demonising him, taunts and beatings. The newspapers were no help as they slandered his good name through the mud while he spent months in a mental health clinic trying to deal with it; lost a great job, and when his wife and daughter left during the case, he had stopped living all together because he lived for them. Now that they were gone, I took him away until the trial was over. Then, while I was studying for my finals, he attempted suicide; so he was rushed to hospital and his stomach was pumped while he recovered as he woke up and saw me as I came to him and he told me how heartbroken he was and how he wanted to die. He was admitted to a mental institution for evaluation but all he really needed was help from a psychiatrist and he helped him get his life together."

Alyssia tried not to cry again as he continued as he took some water, "The day finally came when he was told that he was not guilty of murder and all the charges dropped; it still ruined him and I was living on a student salary at the time. That's when he promised me that he would clean up and get back on his feet but he didn't know how and he apologised to me for laying all this burden on him... but I took it all in my stride and the Teaching College gave me a helping hand filling out a Carer's Allowance form after I explained what had happened to my teachers and

Student Support Advisor who was very worried about me and my grades-it was approved so the payments started right away." Alyssia smiled and she asked him, "That must have been a load off your mind Paul due to what you have gone through?"

Paul smiled and said, "It was but the best news was yet to come for my father. I was away taking my finals at the Teacher's College when Dean Pharrell Winchell paid a visit to my father in hospital and told him that there was a post opening at Kelton University if he wanted the job because of his credentials and excellent record of teaching success at his other college as well as good references from his boss and all who worked with him but funnily was not struck off the Teaching Register as the teachers explained to the board that he was an excellent man with nothing but high praise. He said yes immediately and the University hired him after he went through rehabilitation and got better again. Dean Winchell said it would take a year to get the University up and running but he would let him know when it would open and he also gave us his old house until Franklin House was safe to move into and for my father to get better once more and back on his feet." She smiled as she touched Paul's arm while he smiled and continued as Alyssia listened.

"Pharrell even offered me a job at the University after I passed all my exams and finished Teacher's College and that he would talk to them right away about an internship with my father for the first year here at Kelton University. Both of us had an interview with Edward Mangard, principal of the University, and we both got the job here and as soon as the House was finished, we moved in around the year two thousand and one." He looked at her and smiled, "Pharrell has been good to us as dad paid off all the bills and got back on his feet as well as giving him back every penny of rent to Dean Winchell's old house to him as a thank you for his home while my father recuperated from his stay in the mental hospital…all I was needing to do was to make sure he took his medicine." He took another gulp of water which soothed his emotions and throat as he continued.

"After I passed all my exams, I would keep an eye on him…not as a carer; but watch for any and all warning signs of a relapse under the therapist's instruction. Then later, I was dismissed from Carer's Allowance after six months as soon as I got the job as the salary was enough for me to come off it quickly. It has been a very tough year for dad and me Alyssia, and now every time he sees Cassious House, it always reminded him of Sidney and what happened; he swore that he would never step on its land ever again."

Alyssia was impressed yet sad of all that had happened to Paul as Alyssia gently touched his hand and replied with compassion. "What happened in the past is in the past; nothing can change what happened-it was none of that student's business and Paul," he looked at her as she says with a smile. "…you are doing a fantastic job at keeping his spirits up and keeping him sane in the insanity you have been through and you are doing the best you can with what you got. I'm proud of you; I want you to know that, and to finish Teaching College while looking after your father…that is really impressive; I don't think I could survive what you have gone through."

Paul thanked her; "It's been a long time since I heard those words, thank you," she smiled as she gave him a tissue and he thanked her but then he saw another request in her eyes. "…but you have another request I believe." She smiled, "Ahh, you got me again," she says making him laugh as she gave him another tissue to blow his nose as she asked, "I need to see your father, I want to ask him about getting the rest of my homework assignment, but how do I go about it?" He chuckled at her innocence as Paul told her; "Just come to the class room and knock on the door of the office, then wait until he says "Come in" and then enter, he doesn't like it when people just barge in on him."

She smiled and said, "Thank you Paul, I will do that. But in the meantime, please let your father know that if there is anything I can do for the both of you; please tell me. I may be just a student, but I want to help in any way I possibly can." He thanked her again as they finished lunch and the couple took in some fresh air before heading back to Franklin House. Paul and Alyssia stood up and he placed his trash in her plastic bag and they walked back to the campus as he says, "I will let you know if there's anything you can do." She found a bin and placed the trash into it as they reach Franklin House.

Paul and Alyssia parted ways and asked him where the room for Maths were and he pointed the way for her as he said, "Maths, Philosophy, Psychology and Literature are in Franklin House, so you won't have to go too far to find those classes." She thanked him as she saw her friends waiting for her as they gave her a wave; "I will see you on Wednesday morning in the same room, Paul...and tell your father I will be by later tonight to get my homework assignment." Paul nodded and let her go as her and her new friends spent the rest of the afternoon in Maths.

The first day of University was over after she gave Steve Cosgrove her form for support for Maths and he says, "It will take time to get everything finalised but I will try to hurry up the paperwork so you have the support in place. Phil is away taking care of a sick family member at the moment and he will be back next week so I will pass the message and this form to him." She thanked him as the students left for the day as she went home, had dinner with Mystery the black panther, and then over to Franklin's Office to get the rest of her homework assignment.

It was the night after the first day of University and everyone was having dinner as all the teachers and students went home and talked about the first day. Many says that it went rather well for everyone; but for Mark it was going well until that question a certain student brought up as he tried hard to forget. Paul saw his father crying and upset as he tried to ask what was wrong but he had no answer to give and Paul left him alone to grieve as he went to his room and closed the door; he felt for his father as Alyssia's concerns rang in his ears. After an hour, Paul looked at his father who was still sitting at his desk-staring into space and he brought in a cup of coffee as Mark told him 'thank you' as Paul came with his coffee as he sat beside his father. "Alyssia told me what happened, no use in hiding it. She is worried about you and she told me to tell you that she needs her homework assignment so she'll be by later to pick it up."

Mark smiled at Paul and says, "That's really nice of her Paul, she is a nice girl...what else did she say?" Paul says to him as they drank their coffees, "She told me to tell you that 'if you need anything at all just to let her know; she may be a student, but she wants to help us...' just thought I would pass that message on to you from her." Mark took a sip of his coffee and smiled as Paul looked over his lesson plans for Wednesday as they had dinner and talked about the first day and what the principal had told them.

Then after dinner and the dishes were washed and left to dry, Paul says "I'm going to retreat to my room dad; if you need anything you call on me, I'm just going to sort out a confusing memo from Dean Winchell." Mark watched him stand and says before he goes, "Thanks Paul," and Paul gave his dad a smile and a pat on the back as he left the room for his small study in his room.

About an hour later, Mark was still in his office bemused and upset over the student's question which kept going around in his head: *'Why are you so afraid to go into Cassious House? Isn't there supposed to be a ghost or spirit that haunts the place?'* All that was flashing through his mind, in that moment and time, all he saw was his friend and assistant Sidney Preston scream as he was falling off the roof, the struggle of getting him off the stone sword as he held him close; and hearing his last words: *'It was Thackeray!'* His assistant dying in his arms and as he came back to the class, he had told his class their assignment and dismissed them.

Now he was sitting in his office with a glass of brandy and student notes scattered all over his desk as he couldn't focus as he looked at Alyssia in the photo; that day still haunted him and he added the loss of his wife and daughter and Jessica Jenkins to the list and he needed more than brandy to forget. He longed for a reunion with his long-lost daughter; but where she was, he didn't know and yet in class… he would have been staring right at her.

He poured himself a coffee and sat down at his desk as he tried to concentrate on his work thinking: *'No use of getting drunk anymore… better do something University oriented.'* He had just sat back down at his desk with his coffee and began looking over some of the work students did until there was a gentle knock on the office door as he was thinking away. "Come in" he replied as he rubbed his face of tears and frustration.

The door opened as he stood at his desk as a gentle smile greeted him from around the corner of the door from Alyssia Franklin-Jenkins who came into view and she came into his office and closed the door. "Doctor Franklin, I'm sorry to bother you at this hour of the night…" he asked her to come in, offered her a seat as he said, "No not at all, Paul told me that you would come by later; please come in and sit down." She came in, closed the door quietly and she sat down by his desk and pulled out a pen and pad from her handbag. He sat behind his desk and asked with a smile, "So what can I do for you, Miss Jenkins?"

She looked through her notebook and found the page that she was looking for and she began, "I-I was writing down my homework assignment from the board before you dismissed us but it got erased before I can finish it. May I get your notes to finish writing down my assignment, please?" He was embarrassed as he told her, "Of course you can. I didn't think that anyone was paying attention to what I was writing on the board."

She smiled gently while Doctor Franklin looked out his planner and found what he was looking for and happily showed her where to look as she wrote down the rest of her assignment as he looked at her. "There you are; I will let you get the assignment while I work on something else." She smiled and said gently, "I won't be long." He nodded and let her get on with it as he looked at her and thought: *'You have grown so much; you have to be my daughter and I will do whatever it takes to get you back…I missed you so much and so did Paul. When she took you away, she took my heart with you and if it's true that you are my daughter, I will walk you down the aisle on your wedding day and be there when you have your first child, make no mistake about that!'*

A few minutes later, he was buried in his work as she was finished and closed his class planner, while she put her notebook and pen away in her handbag. He never looked up until she cleared her throat to get his attention and he looked up and took his planner back from her as she smiled and thanked him. "Did you get everything?" She nodded and said, "Thank you so much Doctor Franklin; I will start this assignment right away."

She sat by his desk and asked quite simply, "Is there any other assignment I haven't written down that I must be aware of?" He looked at his planner again as he shook his head, "No not that I know of, but you can get me the Emergency contact when you can. I'm so sorry about Jessica Jenkins," he quickly corrected himself as she looked at him, "…your grandmother, I mean." Alyssia looked at him and smiled sadly, "She died of heart failure and went peacefully in her sleep as her lawyer sorted out everything quickly. I got the car and the money while the nurse got her home;" then she wiped her tears and said, "I have no idea why I'm telling you this," she said.

He smiled and said as he offered her a tissue after coming around from his desk and sat on the edge of the desk before her. "I guess I have an honest face," he said as they both laugh and he continued, "…and I'm a good listener." She grinned and said, "I guess you're right; my father was like that, Doctor Franklin; he was a wonderful listener when I was down." They smiled as he looked right into her eyes and thought for a moment:

'Can you really be her, my long-lost daughter?' He turned away and shook his head as he wanted to touch her cheek but he couldn't, *'No don't be nuts, she's a student!'* He came back to his senses and says as she stood up and placed her handbag on her shoulder, "Anyway, if you can think of anyone for an Emergency contact, you let me know, okay?"

She nodded and said gently, "Thank you Doctor Franklin, I will do that. I'll see if my landlords can be my Emergency Contact, but I better ask for permission first and that will be that out of the way...I know how important it is to you to keep your records intact, especially for the University's inspection." They walked to the door as he said apologetically as they look at each other, "Look, I'm sorry for the way I acted this morning, first staring you down and then that student's question. I-I was thinking of someone whom I lost many years ago and what happened a year ago. I-I just wanted to leave the room quickly..."

She glanced at the photo on his desk without letting on as she quieted him, "You don't have to explain yourself to me, Doctor Franklin. It was none of that student's business what happened. Yes, Doctor Franklin; there is a spirit in that House but whatever reasons you couldn't go in, or near it or under it," They chuckled as she concluded, "it's your own business, not mine; yours. I will never force you to tell me anything, okay?" He smiled and said gently, "Thank you for your kindness, Alyssia; it means a lot to me." He got out his hanky and dried his eyes and then felt her hand on his arm. "Thanks again for the assignment; I will now leave you in peace, because it wasn't your fault."

He looked at her stunned at those last words as she opened the door and said, "Good night Doctor Franklin." He smiled at her as she left the office. **"WHO ARE YOU?!"** He said aloud as she left Franklin House and headed back to her flat near Cassious House. She gets back to her home near the haunted house as Mystery, a stray who had jumped into her car at the petrol station, was getting used to her new home while Alyssia changed for bed as the weather had quieted down after a sudden shower.

She was glad to be home and that the storm was gone as she went to bed and pulled up the covers, switched off the light as her cat Mystery came in to her bedroom and cuddled up beside her on the bed and fell asleep. Timothy came from the shadows and he found a chair nearby as his sword was by his side and a book on Shakespeare sonnets was in his hand as he guarded her through the night and right up till dawn. He had to; as the dark spirits were restless and this time, he sat beside her to make sure they didn't get in as the noises got louder and then before the midnight hour, they were silent. He thought for a bit as he read his book and looked out the door: *'This is one person you are not taking away into your hell!'*

Chapter 2

THE NEXT DAY

Early Tuesday morning-and the first week of University continued. Alyssia is feeling better as she gets up, got showered and changed, makes the bed, and gets her back pack sorted with her folders already named and ready to go. She goes through to the kitchen and has her breakfast after feeding Mystery as she looked at her class schedule for this morning; she didn't like what she saw:

Time	Course	Where	Lecturer
9 am to 12 pm	Eradication of Ghosts and Spirits (optional)	Thackeray House	Doctor George Thackeray

This should be interesting,' she thought as she finished her breakfast. *'After knocking me down and his goons spitting on me on Sunday afternoon, let's hear him teach.* She washed her dishes and got her bag packed with the essentials; a wallet full of scrap paper, rubber banded pens and pencils, small and big index cards, post-it notes and her homework from Franklin's class and her homework notebook because, for some unknown reason and feeling, she would need them. She also grabbed a white plastic bag full of Halloween decorations that she was going to give to the Administration staff for their office party at the end of October but would use them in an unconventional, but educational sort of way.

Then she looked at the time, put on her backpack, picked up the white plastic bag, her house keys as well as her jacket and left her home for the campus unaware that Marylebarne was watching her in the shadows. She got outside in the cool breeze and looked back at the House and Tower thinking to herself: *Was I really dreaming that I saw a man in old medieval clothes sword playing? I must have been so no one should know; my landlord will know that I betrayed his trust if I told him that I was in the House looking for intruders.*

Just then she looked up at the Tower and saw him staring down and smiling at her as she reciprocated the gesture. Then she turned away and said out loud to herself, "It's true, there **IS** a spirit in that House! I have a Spirit next door to me...I've been working too hard!" As she made it to the bottom of the drive and disappeared into the thicket of trees, she waited at the crosswalk to cross the street. She looked back at the House as she waited for the crosswalk lights to go green and looked back at the Tower pierced the sky line and said to herself, "But it can't be...a Spirit? In Medieval clothes? Guarding me? But what for?" Those questions would have to be answered later as she shook her head, crossed the street, and became a logical student in Kelton University.

On the campus, she approached her classmates at Thackeray House and she saw her classmates huddled together as frightened fish being devoured by a pod of killer whales in the ocean. Amber, Adrianne and Milton all waited for her as the class stuck together and said their hellos to Alyssia as she hears Milton greeting her in his Mad Hatter voice."Well...well...well, if it isn't Miss Alyssia Jenkins," he made the nervous class laugh as he continued walking towards her as Amber and Adrianne join in. "Welcome to another day of learning courtesy of Kelton University."

She bowed to him as she asked as the girls came by her side, "I thought you would all be in class right now getting your seats?" she asked the group as they shook their heads like frightened little children on their first day of kindergarten, "Come on everyone, there's safety in numbers..." They all nodded nervously as they all followed her to the entrance of the House. Suddenly a huge, broken roof shingle fell and broke in pieces, pipes that were hanging down fell at their feet while others broke and sprayed water. Dirty broken windows, doors off hinges along with broken shutters just barely hanging on by one screw, fell or hung off as they creaked in the wind while the students froze on the spot. One student replied loudly, "I AM NOT GOING IN THERE!!!!" The others agreed as Alyssia looked up and saw George Thackeray who came to the window and saw that they were about to trespass on his property while Milton tried to liven up the situation as he whispered to her, "Boy Alyssia, talk about your fixer-upper!" and rested his head on her shoulder.

Alyssia smiled and stroked his cheek gently as she had to take the brave step to find out what it was like inside. "I hope the inside is not like the outside Milton, so I will go in and look around and it might calm everyone's fears." Nodding, Milton stepped back as she took off her backpack and set it, along with the white plastic bag, down by Amber's feet. "I'll make sure that it is safe to go in, everyone;" she said to her classmates then she turned to her friends. "Milton, Amber, Adrianne… you're in charge till I come back."

Her new friends nodded and asked everyone to step back as Alyssia made a careful approach towards the House. While up in the Administration building, Dean Pharrell Winchell saw the scene from his window as he took his coffee and he too was anxious at what will happen as he called Edward Mangard about the situation. The principal got in contact with his lawyers and building inspectors to be ready for his call.

Mark was also watching anxiously from the window of Franklin House as he saw his amazing, diverse students who were standing outside, but he was worried about Alyssia who was going in to risk her life to see if it was safe to go in as he watched the drama unfold before him. He was watching quite nervously until Paul called him over as he needed advice on a certain piece of work so a nervous Mark went to help him and told Paul what was happening at Thackeray House.

Pharrell watched Alyssia approach with caution until a worried Milton, putting his backpack down, got her attention. "No way," he said as she stopped with surprise, "…you are not going in there alone; it's too dangerous already…" Milton said as he dropped his backpack; "I'm going with you." Alyssia was just about to say something but changed her mind; "Okay Milton thank you," she said as Adrianne told them, "Call me if you need me and I will get help; in fact I'll call Dean Winchell and let him know…just be careful in there you two."

They nodded and the two friends go into the dangerous House while John, who was working in a flower bed nearby, watched the scene unfold as he kept his sights on the anxious class and their safety; staying close by if he was needed. Milton and Alyssia approached with caution until Milton saw a roof tile coming towards him and the couple got into the doorway just in time. They get into the front entrance as John and Hyman took off their gloves as they came to the class and stood with them while they waited for word on how safe it is-while George looked at them with disgust at this intrusion on his private property and now two students had the audacity to go poking around his place? This did not sit very well with him as he watched the class cowering in fear.

INSIDE THACKERAY HOUSE

The friends got through the front door and saw a nightmare before them; Broken furniture, sharp broken glass, wallpaper hanging off the walls, notice boards just hanging down by their screws, broken fire alarms and sprinklers that were dripping water-they had entered a Health and Safety nightmare! "How can someone let this place get in such disrepair?" she asked Milton as he just mocked, "I think I saw this in a horror movie once…" she chuckled nervously as Milton took her hand, patted it as they went deeper into Thackeray House. "Glad that you are with me Milton," he smiled, as he replied while they saw a path through the clutter. "Me too…come on my new friend; our fellow students are counting on us." The two students went deeper inside as wires sparked furiously at them scaring them as if it was a hissing snake that was about to strike while Milton calmed her down and encouraged her to go on as they looked about.

Ceiling tiles were barely hanging on, exposed electric wires that sparked endlessly as if they were cobras ready to strike; water damage and electrical light fixtures hung down on their last screw, electric sockets burnt out and broken, sparking away like sparklers on Guy Fawkes Night and hung dangerously close to water puddles, holes in walls with exposed levels asbestos and dust lingered in the air as they kept their mouths closed. Carpets with large humps and sharp floor tiles with sharp nails littered the floor…Milton saw the disbelief on Alyssia's face and tried to liven up the situation as he patted her hand.

"I think I saw this in Scooby-Doo[2] cartoon once," she said to Milton who chuckled, "until they found out it was a man in a sheet." Alyssia

---

[2] "Scooby-Doo" ©1969 (13th September) Hanna-Barbera Productions written by Joe Ruby and Ken Spears

smiled as they went on; carefully, steadily, and nervously they went deeper into the House of Horrors. "Glad this is an 'optional' unit," he said as she looked at him, "All it needs now is masked serial killers to jump out." She chuckled nervously as Milton looked around at all the cobwebs and felt something crawling up his arm-a small spider made his way up to another cobweb nearby as Milton flicked it off; "Bug off mate," he said making her smile. "Just easing the tension, Alyssia…" She smiled and patted his hand, "I appreciate it." He clutched her hand firmly as to reassure her and giving her the courage to go on through the nightmare House.

A few minutes later, she had seen enough as she stopped and looked at Milton with horror etched into her features; "I'm not going any further, Milton…it's too dangerous for anyone to be in here; let's get out of here." Milton couldn't agree more as he did an about face and he told her, "Stay close and don't let go of my hand until we're outside. Okay?" She nodded and they made their way back to the front door as he guided her through the messy obstacle course and hazards.

Suddenly and without any warning, the roof began to collapse as everything pummelled down on them. The roar was deafening while the students backed away horrified at the sound as John and told Hyman that he would be right back and he made his way in to the rubble to help them as the students' shrieked and cried out in horror. "ALYSSIA! MILTON! OH MY GOD!!" Adrianne and Amber kept them back with the help of Hyman, as John Preston ran inside the collapsed building while Mark and Paul looked at each other and ran to the window after they heard the roar and saw all the students shrink back in horror as the House fell down. "Oh my God Alyssia and Milton are in there, oh please God, please let them be okay." Paul and Mark prayed as the men ran out of the House, came to their students, and kept them calm as they waited with anxiousness.

While back in Cassious House in the Tower, Timothy sat up and he too heard the roof collapse in his mind. "ALYSSIA!!" he cried out as Marylebarne and Jesterson came running to him, "What is it, my prince?" The advisor asked anxiously after he heard his shouts as he told his advisor and friend what was happening in his thoughts as the men leave the Tower quickly and headed for the campus. A few seconds later, the three of them stood under the shadow of an old elm tree as they wait anxiously for any word.

Back on campus, Dean Winchell called Edward Mangard and told him about the cave in while inside Thackeray House, the roar died away and the couple were separated as Milton was the first to stand up. He coughed and sputtered out dust and asbestos as he heard John calling out "MILTON?! ALYSSIA?!" He came close and saw Milton coughing and brushing off the dust as the dust cleared and John came over to him carefully; "Over here!" He called out as he coughed and John came to him as he stood up and brushed off the dust off his clothes and hair. "I'm okay…" John quickly scanned the area of rubble, "Where's Alyssia?" Milton and John looked around and called for Alyssia, but there was no answer.

The men started to clear a path through the broken ceiling tiles, dust, and wires away until they found a pair of shoes and the lead them to an unconscious Alyssia who laid under a pile of ceiling tiles and wires as the men come to her as John checked her vitals. "She's breathing; let's get you two out of here." John said as Milton noticed Alyssia's feet was caught in some wires and quickly Milton took his pocket knife and cut through them and they heard more of the ceiling getting ready to cave in on them as Milton sped up and says as he quickly put his knife away as he replied, "I've got the wires cut, John…" just then the roof creaked and groaned, **"LET'S GO NOW!"**

John lifted the unconscious Alyssia into his arms and they both ran for the front door as fast as they could as the second cave in began and the frightened students cowered together and called for them to get out as the three of them emerged just in time from the falling House as the deafening roar died away leaving only creaking and groaning noises of tiles and walls falling in while pillars gave way under its weight as they too fell in as a mighty roar was heard once again as dust bellowed out of the front door.

John saw George looking out of the window and started laughing at them while John got her to a small bench and leaned her against it. Dean Winchell was in a panic as he left the Administration building quickly, telling his secretary to call an ambulance and the first aiders about a building collapse while Paul and Mark came over to keep the students calm and safe as they were worried about Alyssia.

The secretary was already on the phone right away to the building contractors and his lawyers while Edward got ready for a meeting with them as Pharrell ran out and before he reached the group, the ambulance, police and fire crews arrived as John tended to an unconscious Alyssia while Milton started to really brush himself off and ruffled his hair as the dust fell like snow out of his hair as the fire fighters and ambulance crew helped him get most of the dust off him. While John started CPR as the ambulance crew and first aiders worked on an unconscious Alyssia.

"She was hit by everything;" John told them as he put her in the recovery position, "…and she was unconscious when we found her," said John as the crew nodded as they gave her oxygen and checked her vitals. Mark, Paul and the rest of the students were worried; some cried and some prayed as the ambulance crew attended to her while fire crews went in to see if there was anyone else trapped in the rubble and thankfully there wasn't as they came out and made the area and building secure while police got statements from everyone.

After a few minutes of oxygen, she opened her eyes, coughed and started to sit up slowly while Milton and John brushed the dust from her hair and body while the ambulance crew saw to her as everyone let out a sigh of relief as they helped Milton get the dust off her. "Alyssia you okay?" John and Milton asked in unison as they looked at each other and she smiled and nodded.

She felt like she had been run over by a two-tonne lorry as she was sore all over as the ambulance crew checked her out for any broken bones or internal injuries and thankfully there wasn't any as Paul and Mark thanked Milton and John for acting very quickly. The men were about to say something until George said aloud from his window as he looked down at the group who looked up at him, "That will teach you to come on to my property!"

Coming from a long line of criminals, George Angelo Sabacini Thackeray has dark hair, murderous green eyes, slender with a muscular frame, tall, always in a bad mood, and is surely living up to the family's terrible reputation. Along with his two country bumpkin's goons, he is on the campus causing trouble again just like his ancestors before him. He is the most hated and unpopular teacher ever on the campus and around Kelton Heights and enjoys making people's lives hell, including the faculty who want him gone. His methods are questionable, he doesn't care about others, selfish, conceited, drinkers, drug dealers, evil, devious, sexiest, inconsiderate to others, womanisers, attention seekers, murderous (George killed Sidney Preston and Mark Franklin's wife), lazy, spoiled, rude to others who are trying to help, and has roots dating all the way back to 1754 when the family were under Mario Luigi Angelo Thackeray, the most dangerous man in Kelton Heights who were thrown out of the royal court after a failed assassination attempt on the King and the Prince.

George Angelo Sabacini Thackeray lost his son in a failed robbery at a bank that leads to a shoot out with police. But when he finds out that there might be treasure under the House, he murders anyone who tries to take the House away from him by implementing the 'Death Stare'; a tactic used by his ancestors to keep his people loyal to him. Adrianne, Amber, Milton, Mark, Paul, Pharrell, John, the Franklins, and the students as well as the police scowled at him as he disappeared from the window and went to teach his class. John wrote down what he said and would add it to the ever growing pile of reports on George Thackeray and then put his notepad and pen away discreetly. Milton continued brushing the dust from her clothes and hair while her friends, the ambulance crew, and first aiders worked together to help her sit up as Milton heard her sigh and looked up at the window.

"I'm really beginning to hate that man!" Alyssia said as she coughed and felt all the bumps and bruises as she looked at the mess she was in while Milton and John smiled with the other students who just chuckled. She turned to the group as she said, "I'll be fine everyone, but it's too dangerous to go in there, you're safer in Franklin's House than Thackeray House." Adrianne said sarcastically, "Oh you think?" Everyone laughed as she coughed some more as the ambulance crew gave her some water and brushed the dust from her. "You're going to be fine; you'll be sore all over but nothing broken;" said one of the crew. "…there is no need for you to go to the hospital."

She thanked the crew as Timothy, Marylebarne and Jesterson watched as they saw her trying to stand up slowly and watched from the trees as he saw Alyssia covered in dust but walking while the gentlemen spirits breathed a sigh of relief knowing that she was okay and they returned to the Tower to let the others know and to look up a healing spell to give to Alyssia while she smiled as she said sarcastically to the ambulance crew and Milton, "This is turning into the best first week I've ever had!" The group laugh despite her being sore all over as her friends came beside her and comforted her.

Then a fire fighter helped her stand as she limped over to the screens and got hosed down while Milton got checked over and he too, was hosed down as they got new clothes and were told to go and see their doctor. Just then, the building inspectors arrived at the campus and took her statement along with Milton and John Preston, who told them quietly that he was an undercover cop on a case. They put him down as a caretaker to keep his secret and he was appreciative of his bravery and that he should get a medal while Mark and Paul were also giving statements and Pharrell addressed them to come to see Edward Mangard for he will be waiting for them.

The building inspectors assessed the place with the police and fire crews as they were at a loss for words at what they saw and placed a **"DANGEROUS BUILDING"** sign on the door before another shingle came off the roof. They started to question why Thackeray was not keeping up repairs to Pharrell as the ambulance crew saw to Milton and he was fine as they cleaned him down with water and the same with her as she stood up and thank goodness Amber was her clothes size and gave her some new clothes to wear.

The ambulance crew took her old clothes and placed them in a bag while she changed into new the clothes Amber gave her while John had gone to the hut and found some old clothes for Milton to wear and gave them to Milton to wear as he dried off. "You okay there, Milton?" He nodded as John continued. "You did good going in there with her…Good job." Milton was still brushing off the dust out of his hair as he says, "Never better and thanks Big John!" The gardener shot him a look after Milton patted his back and looked at him scared as Adrianne and the class giggled… "I think you better keep quiet Milton before you're broken in half!" she replied while the rest of the students laughed until one of them say as he turned about. "Heads up everyone, it's Dean Pharrell Winchell and he looks angry or worried…brace yourselves!"

Pharrell came to the group as he walked briskly towards them as the other students thought as he made it to the group: *'Uh-oh, now we're in for it for cutting class and causing damage to Thackeray House and expelled on the first week of the new term…a new world record.'* Pharrell joined the students, the building inspectors, the police, fire fighters, Mark and Paul

Franklin, as well John Preston, who pulled out his notebook and pen again and recorded what the Dean is saying as he replied quite anxiously as he came to the worried, frightened students.

"I was watching what was happening from the window of the Administration building and came as soon as I saw John here running in. I called Edward Mangard about the incident and he is quite worried as well…" Mark chimed in angrily, "I told you Pharrell that someone is going to get killed or injured in Thackeray's House! I told you!" Paul calmed him down as the teachers waited to see Alyssia. Dean Winchell looked at the building inspectors and says to them, "He is expecting you and me as well as the police about the incident and his lawyers are in attendance for this meeting." The inspectors nodded and John took down the names of everyone involved as they waited for Milton and Alyssia to change.

Alyssia and Milton were changed into proper clothes as Adrianne and Amber came over and walked her to the bench and sat her down. "Is everyone okay?" he asked. The students nodded nervously as Paul and Mark came to see to her and she smiled gently and told them, "I'll be fine Mark and Paul, honestly…I just feel like I was run over by a two ton lorry, but I'm happy that there was nothing broken." The father and son gave her a hug and thanked God that she was okay and then they headed back to Franklin House as the police dismissed them, leaving her in the capable hands of her friends Adrianne and Amber as they with sat with her and comforted her.

Everyone listened as Milton described the conditions to them as the building inspectors, Pharrell and John recorded everything on paper. "How can you let a building get in such disrepair that it can cause death or injury to others?" Adrianne asked Dean Pharrell as the other students nodded while Amber stayed beside her and gave Alyssia a spare bottle of water as she drank it down. "Thank you Amber…" and she gave her hug and said in a low voice and coughed, "I will get you another one, promise." She smiled relieved as Amber replied, "I'm just glad you are safe and not seriously hurt…I was really worried about you and Milton and yet angry at Thackeray. The next time I see him, I will give him some karate chops in the nuts." The girls laugh, "Do you want me to give you back these clothes Amber?" Her friend shook her head and said as Alyssia drank the water, "They are old clothes Alyssia, you keep them. Besides, I have lost a lot of weight since then so I'm glad to be rid of them…" The girls heard all the fuss as they listened to Dean Winchell who was still shocked and horrified as to what has happened.

"I'm at a loss for words as to the condition and state of the House, in fact, we are at a loss as to what to do. We have told Doctor Thackeray time and time again to fix up the place and make proper repairs and alterations, but he simply refuses. We are at our wits end and if we attempt to make any alterations or repairs to his House, he would threaten to sue or kill us and he simply refuses to leave and he remains inside and unless he leaves the House; we can't do anything." John asked the Dean, "Do you have any of those copies of the meetings of when he threatened to sue you or kill you?"

The dean says sadly, "I do sir; we keep all meetings and emails for our records and for the police and building inspectors as well as when the University is being audited. I'll be glad to turn over all the documents you all wish to see and the attempts of companies and safety official's records on Thackeray House that you require." John smiled and said, "Thank you Mr Winchell." The building inspectors spoke to her and got her side of the story as she said to them to not be too hard on Dean Winchell and Edward Mangard. They thanked her and nodded and so did John as Dean Winchell came to Alyssia as she was signing the University first aid book and giving it back to the University's first aider as Amber and Adrianne sat and comforted her as she drank water and massaged her aching body as Dean Winchell got everyone's attention and everyone listened.

"Since this is an 'optional' unit, you can have a study group on Tuesdays and Thursdays mornings… but you have to do me a big favour all of you; you all must study very hard and do well." Amber says, "We will do our best Dean Winchell, promise…" He smiled and the students breathed a sigh of relief. "You can also make appointments for these mornings but make sure you tell the leader of your study group about these appointments so you can catch up." The students thought that was fair and they were even more relieved that the Dean was very understanding as he sat beside Alyssia with a caring smile while Amber and Adrianne left them to talk as he took her hand.

"I'm so sorry that this happened to you, Miss Jenkins; you have the University's deepest and humblest apologies." She smiled and said, "I forgive you and thank you for your concern. It isn't your fault that

Thackeray doesn't take care of the place," He smiled as she says, "…don't be too hard on yourself, Dean Winchell." He thanked her as he asked, "But I have a favour to ask you, would you like to teach the study group? I feel that you would be a great teacher…"

She was surprised as she asked, "Me? Why me sir?" The students gathered around her as one student confessed to her, "Because while we all cowered in fear, you went in before us to see if it was safe risking your own personal safety and for that; we are eternally grateful and we want you to help us study." She was speechless while all the students nodded as the fire crews and ambulance staff was impressed by her bravery.

All the other students, including the building inspectors and fire crews agreed as Milton came and knelt beside her, "All joking aside Alyssia, you are the perfect candidate for the job and we would like you to do this for us and since all of us and you are all newbies…teach us please?" She didn't know what to say as John came to her and knelt beside her and said, "Alyssia, I would like some help with writing and in return I'll help you with some Maths; what do you say?"

The students waited with baited breath and looked at Milton's puppy dog eyes and she giggled, "Dean Winchell, it would be an honour but I do have one request that I take a Friday at the end of the month off to go and see someone, is that okay?" Dean Winchell says, "I don't think that's a problem, Alyssia, I'll talk to the Doctors Franklin after I talk to these fine men." Everyone cheered and sighed with relief and thanked the dean as he said to all of them as he saw some students and faculty coming out wondering what was happening with the fire trucks, ambulances and police.

"It's break time and there is a coffee shop across the street; Maddy Everton is the manager of the coffee shop and business centre…I have called her to prepare a room for some students coming after Alyssia and Milton went into the building; she will be happy to lend you the room for free for your study group. From now on, you'll be called 'Franklin's Circle' because of the House you all are in." The students loved the name as the dean left them as he escorted the building inspectors, fire rescue, police and John Preston (with Hyman's permission of course) to the Administration building to see Edward Mangard in his office as John smiled and winked at her and left her in the care of her classmates and follows the building inspectors to the Administration building.

Along the way, they question Pharrell about the collapse as Milton and Adrianne helped her stand while Amber took her bag on to her shoulder and the white bag was given to Adrianne. Milton took her hand and shouted to the group, "Okay gang, who's for coffee?" The group laugh as he helps Alyssia to the coffee shop across the street with the rest of her classmates.

A short time later, they reach the coffee shop and Maddy greets the group, "Hello everyone, Welcome to Maddy's Coffee House and Business Centre. I'm Maddy Everton the owner of the coffee shop." They all shook hands with her as she continued. "Dean Winchell has called me ahead of time to greet you; come I will show you the room you will be using for the study group…" and they followed the owner to the middle room. Maddy was a woman in her fifties with greyish, brown, blackish short hair, grey eyes, thin arms, and wrinkled hands from years of working and dipping her hand in soapy water and a bulky frame.

She walked with a slight limp from a hip replacement two years ago and she wore a lot of jewellery and it jingled, jangled while she walked which didn't help her hip. Her clothes were stained with coffee grounds, fillings from muffins and other stains that never came out. Her apron was showing signs of wear and tear as there was a hole on the bottom of one of the pockets and her pad and pen sat in the other pocket which was already over flowing with used hankies, tip money, as well as coffee grounds, sifted cocoa powder, and sprinkles.

Her trousers were fitted and showed some signs of wear as well as the threads held on for dear life and her shoes were flat, black and also stained with her work. There were a couple of burns on the top of the leather but no hole while the laces were mere thread through many years of blood, sweat and tears as a warm welcome was guaranteed to greet you the minute you walked in.

As the group reached the top of the steps, they go into the middle room with chairs, tables and they looked about while Milton, Amber, and Adrianne all follow her inside and see how big it is as Maddy gets a very sore Alyssia a chair and they all help her sit down. The room was big enough to hold her class and they saw a projector attached to the ceiling as Milton used his muscles to get the tables into a semi circle while the girls get the chairs around them. Maddy got her comfortable and talks to her as Milton gave her a table and Amber gave her the backpack and the plastic white bag and sets it before her on another chair.

Maddy told her in a whisper, "I heard what had happened Alyssia from Dean Winchell and I'm glad that you and Milton weren't killed or seriously injured. Thackeray is an idiot and a lazy bum and I personally would love to see him booted off the campus and to Siberia…" The girls let out a chuckle as Maddy's feature became soft, "But enough of that nonsense, what can I get you Alyssia while my employees and your friends set up the room?"

She thought and asked. "Do you have hot chocolate with extra milk and whipped cream?" Maddy smiled and nodded as Alyssia says, "that will be wonderful and a muffin of your choice." Maddy had a glint in her eye, "Today's special is Chocolate Chip Muffin with a hot drink…" Alyssia's taste buds tingled, "Sounds delicious…may I have that?" she asked her and as Maddy nodded and wrote down her order, she told her the price. "Thank you so much Maddy…" she smiled as Alyssia sorely reached into her backpack, found her wallet and pulled out a ten pound note to give her. "I hope that covers it?" Maddy smiled and says, "It will and I'll bring it through, in a mug or cup?" Alyssia says, "Cup please Maddy…"

The owner leaves her after she pats her shoulder gently and left the room as the ladies from the cafe with her friends set up the room in a half-circle and Amber was called over, "In my backpack Amber, there is a wallet with scrap paper, pens and pencils in rubber bands. I want you to spread them out all over the tables for me once they are set up." Amber says, "Okay that's easy to do…thanks." Amber goes into her bag and sees the items and takes them out and spreads them around the table while Adrianne and Milton get the chairs out and all around the tables and after everything was set up, the trio went to get their coffees.

After they return she calls her friends over and asked them as they set down their coffees, "Will you three be my helpers? I would appreciate some extra support?" The friends agreed and she smiled as Milton told them as he takes off his jacket, "The room looks good, now all we need do is lead the students in here and we'll get started. We'll be right back…" Milton says as the girls told her to relax as she nodded and they went to get the other students to follow them to the middle room while Alyssia draws up a rough roll sheet. Maddy brings in her hot chocolate and muffin as well as her change as she thanks her and asked about the walls and if she could write on them. "Yes just on the wall behind you and marker pens, spray and a cloth is right behind you as well."

She thanks Maddy for everything as the owner brought the spray bottle and cloth over beside her as she and her girls get back to their work. The students start rolling in slowly and find a seat anywhere as Alyssia found a flip chart and drew her ghostly friend as she goes into her white plastic bag and checks for the props as she was going to shoot from the hip with this first class as she drinks her hot chocolate and has her muffin in between. After about fifteen minutes, Maddy says to them all, "Is that all of you?"

Everyone took their seats as one male student rushed in quickly and they all gave her the thumbs up as Maddy replied with a smile. "Good, I will talk to you all soon and just leave all your dirty dishes and plates stacked on this tray by the door." She said placing the tray down on the table, "Good luck all and to you too, Alyssia," she nods and smiles as she closes the door as class begins as Maddy turns over the sign on the door to **OCCUPIED** and went back to serving her customers.

Inside the middle room, the students settled down as Alyssia took a deep breath, steadied her nerves and thought '*Well, here goes nothing,*' as she smiled and stands up slowly as she introduces herself to the others. "Hello everyone;" the group grew very quiet as she continued. "Forgive me for being late this morning…I know we've all had a terrible morning; myself included," she said massaging sore bit. "But let's put it behind us and move on; now I'm going to pass around a piece of paper, and I know you all are sick of this, but will you all put your names down and pass it around plus I also want you to put away your folders for now and turn your phones on silent or off. If you must leave it on, please tell me; okay?"

They all sign the paper and turn off their phones until Milton's phone sounded; "Ring, Ring, Ring, Ring, Ring, Ring, Ring…Banana Phone!"[3] This cracks up the class, especially Alyssia, who really needed a good giggle after the morning they all had. Milton was embarrassed as he turned off his

---

[3] "The Banana Phone Song" sung by Raffi and Micheal Creber. ©1994 (27th of September) by Troubadour Music and "The Despicable Me Franchise and Minions" ©2010 by Illumination Entertainment by Pierre Coffin, Kyle Balda and Chris Renaud

phone as she said, "Oh Milton, you must have been a Minion in a previous life…" He stood up and went "BELLO" in his Minion voice which made the class and Alyssia laugh harder. "Thank you, Milton, for the laughs!" He bowed as he put his phone away and said to her, "Glad to be of service, my dear lady…" then sat back down.

Alyssia and the class calmed themselves as she reached in to her bag while the roll sheet was being passed around and got her homework for Doctor Franklin as well as her homework notebook and tried to make some sense of it while the class were passing around the roll sheet. A few minutes later, Milton brought over the roll call sheet as he wiggled his eyebrows at her, took a bit of her muffin, patted his cheek gently and went back to his seat as she signed it as well. She held on the table as she was still a bit wobbly and introduced herself as the students quieted down.

"Hello everyone I'm Alyssia Franklin-Jenkins and welcome to the first study group of the year called 'Franklin's Circle…' and like most of you, a newbie to Kelton University. As I listened to Franklin's lecture on Monday, I saw the confusion and bewilderment of what Mark's assignment does entail. Well on Tuesday and Thursday mornings as study group, let's see if we can make some sense of it; okay?" The group nodded as she smiled and says, "Wonderful, let's get started." She turned around and drew a ghost on the white board as the students gasped; she looked at them with a smile, "Marker pen board, I have the spray and cloth for it."

Everyone sighed with relief as she drew her ghost as everyone laughs… "Okay I'm no Rembrandt!" The students laugh as she puts her pen down and then she opened the flip chart and they saw another ghost. "Okay you all; one simple question: What is a 'ghost' or what is perceived as a 'ghost' to you?" The group looked at each other; they were still a bit confused as she told them; "In front of you are scrap of papers, pens and pencils, index cards, post-it notes and," she holds up the white plastic bag full of props and Halloween decorations, "…some visuals. I brought some friends with me who are in this bag," she held up the white plastic bag as she asked. "Would you like to meet them?" The class nodded as she says, "Wonderful, because they are 'dying' to meet you!"

Everyone laughed at her smile as she reached inside her white bag as Timothy and Marylebarne, who just arrived from the Tower, watched from the darkness of the room and listened as she pulled out a table top decoration with ghosts, a scaredy cat, pumpkins and a gravestone, set it up and placed it on the table. She then got out a lit-up ghost lamp, turned it on and set that on the table... then she brought out a ghost hanging decoration and pulled on it as it made a funny noise making the students laugh as she hung it from the chart easel.

She came out of the bag and put it to one side as she told the students comically, "I would like to introduce you to some friends of mine which I recently picked up at a party shop in town for the Kelton University Administration Halloween party happening in four weeks." She started to point to each one on of them and gave them silly names as all the students watched. "The table top is Creepy, the lit-up ghost is Lampy, and the noisy one here is Wispy..." and then she reached in to the bag and put a sheet over her head as the two spirits looked at each other with a smile as she placed a sheet over head with two eye holes and plastic chains as she said with a moan, "And this is 'You've got to be kidding me'!"

The spirits laugh with glee as well as the students who watch her take off the sheet as Milton jumps and shouts and then relief saying, "Oh my, oh it's only you, Alyssia...I thought it was a ghost!" The whole class laughed as well as Marylebarne and Timothy as she looked at him and throws a small ball of paper at him as he ducks and gives her a mischievous smile; "ANYWAY MOVING ALONG!!!"

The class settled down once again as she and the giggles continued, "All Doctor Franklin wants you to say- in your own words, what do you believe a 'ghost' is? I have our friend Speedy the ghost here and I want you to come up with ideas of what a ghost is and then we'll share our ideas and place them around him. So, get into your groups and brainstorm some ideas and write them down-and since this is an open report-don't worry if you get it wrong...off you go!"

She left the class to do their work as she sat down slowly and looked at her homework while she placed some of her ideas around the flip chart ghost as Marylebarne whispered, "Something happened this morning... oh the roof collapse." Timothy nodded as he conjured up a small spell that he found in the Cassious House library as a small ball of healing energy formed and glowed before him and he blew the small ball towards her as it quietly entered her body. Timothy then opened his hand as the ball broke up into small pieces and went all over her body as he looked at his advisor who smiled happily as he says, "That should help her heal faster."

The advisor saw him just staring at her and he was immediately heads over heels in love with her as the wise spirit smiled as he pats his back gently as Timothy replied without taking his eyes off of her, "I like her; she seems really nice, Marylebarne...but how do I get her to like me and maybe get her to help us?" Marylebarne says to him as he puts his hand on his shoulder, "Patience my dear Prince, one thing at a time; she is still a bit spooked from early Monday morning and she is still adjusting to living near a Haunted House plus the roof collapse doesn't help any, so we need to get her to trust us, then the rest will then fall into place. I would like to meet her, but right now you have studies to do, so let's head back to the Tower." Timothy looked at her once again as he agreed as they prepared to leave until he said as they watched Milton pull a face at the ghost on the board and the spirits giggled, "I think we should let Jesterson know that he may have competition!" The advisor said to the Prince, "You may be right..." The men laughed as they looked back at her laughing at Milton's funny face and they disappear into the shadows while the class worked away as they were having so much fun with this assignment.

A few minutes later, Alyssia puts up some movies, shows, series, books, haunted places, authors and dates up on the boards as the students, who were finished, wrote down what she had up on the board as she smiled. It was another five minutes later when students put all their plates and cups away on the tray at the door started to clean up the room and puts their trash in the proper bins.

Finally the students were ready to put up their answers around Speedy as Alyssia grabbed some pens and asked them to come up and write down their answers as she did the same and the rest of the class did too. Then the next group did the same as the students put their answers up and around their ghost Speedy, then the next group put up theirs and the last group did the same as everyone wrote down their answers and kept their list with them.

"Okay everyone, these are good answers; especially religion which is an excellent answer because of our beliefs, customs and understanding of our world, death and the afterlife...especially in Christianity. There has been so much debate around it and it can start arguments or open your mind to it;' another good answer gang." The group were happy to hear that they were doing well as she continued to read out the answers. "We also have 'it gives us a taste of our own morality,' that is true...well said; 'we like to be scared'; very true and in our world of terrorist attacks, suicide bombers, mass shootings and radical views, and Trump;" Everyone chuckled as she continued; "...it keeps us alert to everyone around us."

She looked at another slip and said happily, "We have 'television and movies and other entertainment media make money out of scaring people witless'...exactly! The movies and books, trick or treating on Halloween as well as haunted places I have up here, you should have these written down because this is part of the report; and special effects play an important part in the movie and entertainment industry as well as haunted trails, walks, London Tours of the dungeons of old...there is so much out there."

Then she shared her answers to see if the class agreed with her, "Okay, let's see if you smarty pants all agree with my answers;" the class chuckled as she revealed her answers. "I have my own answers on the board if you want to add these to your list; mediums and fakirs are also vital to the world of spiritualism and mysticism? Well, magicians have also played a part in the world of ghosts and spirituality and I have listed a few, so you can write them down along with the movies and the dates they came out."

They did and she continued, "Now you all were scratching your heads on mediums and fakirs and where does magic fit in with the subject on ghosts? Mediums are people who will conjure spirits from another world and do it for a fee, but watch out! There are a lot fake mediums who will charge an arm and a leg to take you for everything you got..." Milton added, "Yeah, just like Thackeray!" The group laughed as she continued as Alyssia laughed too as she added, "Yeah Milton good one; he's the biggest "fake"-ir of them all!" Milton, Adrianne and Amber giggled happily with the class laughed as the jester gave her a thumbs-up for that joke as she continued with her explanation of fakirs and mediums to the class.

"Fakirs are known in tribal communities who will conjure up the spirits to find answers for their village or tribes. India, Africa, The Amazon; these tribes use this to help the people of their village; Medicine men and women in American Indian tribes; Cherokees, Seminoles, Mohicans, Apaches; these tribes have ways of conjuring up the spirits. Pagans and Celts are also part of this group as well as Stonehenge in the English countryside so you can write those down." She slowly comes from around her makeshift desk and comes to front to sit on the edge of the table as she continues.

"Eskimos do the same by looking to the ancestors of old for answers and here is a film you should checkout, the Disney film "Brother Bear"[4] is an example of the spirits intervening on behalf of the tribe when the older brother and leader of the tribe is killed and his baby brother needlessly kills a bear out of anger; his brother then turns him into a bear to teach him a lesson, and sorry gang…you will have to watch the rest of movie to find out the outcome…" They all moaned unhappily as she says with a shake of her head. "Give Mark information; even if it's nonsense; just give it to him. The more information; the better. So gang, does this make sense now?"

Everyone was starting to get the idea of what Doctor Franklin was talking about as she gave her tongue a rest. The students nodded as they got to work on their rough drafts and mind maps as she says happily trying not to cry out, "Then I will sit and give my tongue a rest while I work on mine as well and we have twenty minutes till lunchtime so work on your answers for ten minutes and then we'll compare the answers." The students worked away as Alyssia sat down with relief as she put down her answers and then asked them, "Everyone have these? I'm about to erase them…" they all gave her the thumbs up as she started to erase them.

A few moments later outside in the Coffee shop, Paul Franklin had come in to see Maddy and she gladly served him. "Hello Paul, how are you?" Paul was getting his money out of his wallet as he smiled happily and says, "Oh not bad…the usual Maddy if you don't mind and dad says, surprise him with any muffins of your choice!" Maddy smiled and said, "Coming right up, handsome." Paul smiled shyly until they heard laughter and talking from the middle room as she looked up at the clock as Paul paid for his purchase until she heard her say, "That's nearing lunch time, and study period is almost over." Paul asked confused, "Wait… what do you mean 'study time is almost over'?"

Maddy told one of her girls Paul's order while Maddy lead Paul to the middle room and opened the door to see the class getting packed up and throwing away paper in the appropriate bins, cans, and broken pencils and dried out pens as well as pencil shavings were cleared up while empty

---

[4] "Brother Bear" ©2003 Walt Disney Productions

plastic bottles were disposed of in the proper bins and the students were packing up their belongings for lunchtime.

Then they heard Alyssia call out, "Okay everyone, you can turn on your phones; you all worked very hard today so you deserve your texts and apps. Thanks for putting up with me so sit and relax now; we have Paul Franklin as our lecturer on Wednesday morning so we might have more notes and keep in mind what I was saying about ghosts and write out a rough draft; we'll add more to it and put all together on Thursday morning…sounds cool?" All the students nodded as she felt her body wracked with pain as Milton and the girls saw she was struggling as they got her into the chair and cleaned the marker off the walls for her. "Thanks gang…I'm still a bit sore from this morning." Milton says, "Not to worry, we'll get everything cleaned up; you just relax."

She smiled until she sees Maddy and Paul standing at the door and they come in as she replied, "Hello you two; class is finished for the day and I hope we didn't make too much noise?" Maddy chuckled as she took her plate and mug and added them to the tray. "Nope not at all…my girls will do the rest…" She smiled as Paul comes over to her. "Thank you for the hot chocolate Maddy; it was delicious, can I have two bottles of water please? I owe Amber one." She nodded and gives her the money as Paul watched Maddy take the tray and the money out to the cafe as she told the students, "Leave the floors, and the trash bins; my staff will get them…" she told the students and they all agree as Maddy later came back with two bottles of water and Alyssia thanked her as Maddy gave her the change while Alyssia placed the change in her coat pocket.

"Thank you Maddy," The students nodded as she saw Paul; "Hello Paul, forgive me for not standing up or ignoring you…" Paul found his voice as he asked. "Hello again; why are you all in here?" Milton becomes angry as he says, "Oh you have never been in Thackeray's House of Horrors where serial killers could pop out at any time? Where Alyssia here was almost killed when the ceiling came down on her? The house that looks like a death trap? You mean that House where I'm still picking plaster and ceiling tile out of my hair?" Paul came to her and knelt before her as Milton joined her after he erased the board.

She nods as she touched Paul's cheek and said, "John Preston and this wise cracker here, got me out; I'm just sore all over. You saw us…" Paul says, "Yes I did, I am still in shock as to what happened, that's all." Milton goes back to his seat as he puts his feet up and says, "Dean Winchell excused us from the class; Alyssia, would you care to explain the rest or would you like me to play the theme tune from the movie "Psycho"?[5] "Amityville Horror?"[6] "JAWS?"[7] "IT?"[8] I take requests…" Paul shook his head while he and Alyssia were trying not to laugh; "So what theme tune would like to hear?"

Adrianne got his attention while everyone was chuckling as she spoke up, "I have a request, how about 'Sit down and shut up'?" Milton thought for a moment and said, "I don't know that one but if you hum a few bars, I might have it?" and he gave Adrianne a big smile as Alyssia and Paul and the rest of the class had to chuckle. Adrianne came over and said to Alyssia and Doctor Franklin, "Excuse me…" and Adrianne took him by the ear and led him to a chair as he cried out, "OW! OKAY I'LL LET ALYSSIA EXPLAIN! OW!!!" Maddy came in and gave Alyssia the two waters and her change as everyone laughs as Adrianne sat him down roughly in a chair while Paul took her by the hand and helped her stand as they go into another room. "Be right back you all; you got two minutes before lunch time so just sit and relax…I need to talk to Paul for a moment in private."

They all nod as they go next door as Paul leads her to a chair while Amber gather up the paper, pens, pencils and other material as Adrianne puts her props away in the white plastic bag, her homework and her notebook, the paper wallet and the other supplies were placed into her backpack neatly as Milton helped the guys clean up the chairs and tables after Maddy's girls cleaned them up and the students relaxed and looked up at the clock as lunchtime fast approached.

Next door, Paul and Alyssia sit and talk for a moment, "Milton is harmless Paul, and he's doing it to make light of a terrible situation from

---

[5] "PSYCHO" released 15th of September 1960 by Alfred Hitchcock made in the UK by ©Paramount Pictures

[6] "The Amityville Horror" based on a book by Jay Anson (1977) released on 27th of July 1979 ©Paramount Pictures.

[7] "JAWS" released 26th of December 1975 by Stephen Speilberg ©Amblin Entertainment

[8] "IT" based on the book written by Stephen King© released September 1986; Film for Television released 18th of November 1990 on ABC-TV and re-released in 2017 in theatres worldwide.

this morning. But he is right, Paul... Thackeray House is a Health and Safety nightmare." She told Paul everything from greeting the students to how she got hurt and how he and Mark kept the students back and calm when she was hurt. Then she told him how Dean Winchell gave her the job of taking over a study group after they left the group; "Dean Winchell and the students have appointed me to teach the study group called 'Franklin's Circle' on Tuesday and Thursday mornings so we can make sense of everything you are teaching us."

He smiled as he asked, "Do you mind if I tell my father about this? He would be thrilled..." Alyssia smiled as she said with a touch of humour. "Well, Dean Winchell was going to tell you about it anyway and see if it was okay for him to do this. He said that it wouldn't be a problem, but Friday at the end of the month I have to go and see someone in the suburbs." Paul was curious but never pressed the question. He helped her stand up as he pushed in the chairs for her as she thanked him as he asked, "Would you like some help on Thursdays? We can go over everything that we have done so far this week?" Alyssia says, "That would be an immense help because I have no idea what I am doing Paul, but don't you and your father have classes to prepare for?"

He grinned and said, "It would be an honour;" as he offers his arm to her as she took it and they go back next door and the students see them as she quickly gets their attention. "This is Paul Franklin and he's our tutor for tomorrow...Paul wants to give us a helping hand on Thursdays in the study group, will that be alright with all of you?" The students nodded as the chairs were put up while Maddy and her waitresses finished cleaning up the tables and the male students stacked up the chairs and tables.

After they were cleaned up and everyone got their backpacks on, Alyssia gave the list of student's names to Paul and he folded it up and placed it in his pocket as she kept a copy for herself. Paul then whispered, "I need to talk to you about yesterday." She looked at Paul as the class started to leave the empty room and go for their lunch. The students finished as she dismissed the class as she said to them, "See you all bright and early tomorrow at Franklin House and then on Thursday morning here in the coffee house."

They all said their goodbyes and left for lunch as they waited for all the students to leave and it was only her and Paul as her friends waited outside for her. Then she turned to Paul and says, "Now what were you saying?" Paul said in a low voice, "You seemed a bit spooked on Monday morning; you were looking at the posters eagerly in the class looking for an answer… tell me, what was it that spooked you?" She thought: *'Well you would be if you saw a spirit in medieval clothes running around slashing at dark spirits with a sword…'* her brain said as she shook it off. "I guess I was just nervous that first day Paul. I was so engrossed with the posters that you gave me a scare; I really thought you were in the other room."

Her brain thought: *'Good one, then why don't you tell him about the dark veil on the first floor landing as well, while you're at it'* as the logical side found a different approach as Paul accepted that comment as she said, "I-I didn't mean to jump, honestly…first day jitters, that was all." Paul smiled, "Well I'll go along with that; I remember being a student teacher in my father's class room for the first time, man was I nervous!" They laugh as he says, "Well, we have a great bunch of students here and I really hope that they do well."

She agreed as she got her back pack on and says to him as she picked up the white plastic bag after all the Halloween decorations were put away and they walked out together as Paul offered his arm to her. "All I want them to do is to study hard and come in here and ask for the help required and the dean and I want nothing more than that and really. I appreciate what you will be doing for me on Thursday morning…Paul, are you listening?"

Paul escorted her out as he said, "You remind me of someone…" she stopped and looked at him, "but who, I don't know." They looked at each other for a long time as he came out of it as her brain screamed: *'Oh no…not you too?!'* He shook his head and returned to his senses; "I do apologise…" Paul said, "Anyway, I better get back to Franklin House; dad is probably sending out the blood hounds for me." The couple laugh as the waitress brought over his order as he takes it from her as well as his change and thanks the kind girl as she leaves them.

"Would you like me to take the decorations over to the administration building for you?" Alyssia said, "That would be an immense help Paul, thank you. Give the bag to Kelly Preston…she will know what to do with them." He nodded and they get outside as they meet the others "So I shall see you over at Franklin House tomorrow morning and I'll make sure the ceiling is intact." They laugh as Alyssia says with a smile as her friends took her arm and they were ready to lead her to home as Milton took her backpack on to his back.

"Till tomorrow morning Paul and thank you and now I'm going home to grab some lunch and get ready for afternoon classes as well as change." Paul leaves the friends and they help her home to have lunch and change her clothes as Amber and her other friends help lead her home. They get to the edge of the drive as Milton gives her the backpack as they went for lunch and say their goodbyes to her and leave her and she waits until they were out of sight and starts up the back steps to Cassious House to her flat; unaware that Amber has turned to see her disappear up the stairs to the haunted house.

Meanwhile at the Tower of Cassious House, Marylebarne and Timothy see her once again struggling to walk up the driveway as Timothy noticed, "She is walking slower than normal again…" She finally makes it up to the top step and to the front door as she leans against the wall and looked for her keys and to get her breath. She found them as Sharlene sees her wracked with pain and tiredness as she was taking a break from planting the flowers and takes off her gardening gloves to talk to her.

"Oh hello there Alyssia, how are you?" She saw the smile of Sharlene Parks and says breathlessly as the pain got stronger. "Hello Sharlene, I'm a bit sore…no let me rephrase that; I'm sore all over thanks to Thackeray House falling down on top of me. Can you please help me in? I'm in agony!" She nodded got her keys and opened the door for her. Sharlene took her bag and slings it on to her shoulder, took her hand and guided her in as she sat her down on the couch with relief and a sigh as Sharlene puts her bag on the chair then she helps Alyssia get her feet up on the couch with a pillow under her legs as she asked the caretaker's wife who went to the kitchen and looked on the refrigerator to see what classes she has this afternoon.

After telling her, Sharlene goes to the bookshelf and sees all the folders clearly marked and placed the folders in another backpack along with her pens and pencils in the front of her bag. "I think that's it, would you like something to eat and drink?" Alyssia nodded and says, "I would like that very much… just whatever is ready; fruit, sandwiches (Cold) and maybe a drink of water." Sharlene does that as she says, "Coming right up and I'll feed Mystery while I'm at it." Alyssia says, "Thank you, Sharlene; Mystery's cans are in the refrigerator."

She nodded and Alyssia lays back and relaxed as Timothy came from the shadows and waited until Sharlene was out of sight as he conjured up another stronger healing spell and sends the ball of energy into her aching body and it got to work right away as he sees Sharlene coming towards her with her lunch as Timothy disappeared leaving the girls to talk as Alyssia tells her what happened as Sharlene says with a smile. "Wait let me guess…" Alyssia nodded as she thought it was odd, but indulged her anyway. "You saw Thackeray House, the exterior and interior changed your mind and the dean excused you." Alyssia and Sharlene laughed as she replied with a chuckle, "Close but no cigar, but you do get the booby prize!"

The girls laugh as Alyssia said, "This morning, the group was waiting for me to come and we would find this room in Thackeray House and go in together but when the exterior fell apart, Milton and I thought it would be better to inspect the interior as we dodged roof tiles. Then we made a conclusion that it was too dangerous while we headed for the exit and low and behold, the roof caved in on us sending John and Milton into hero mode. But how did you know?" Sharlene whispered to her as they ate lunch together as she sat down beside her, "You're not the only one to complain."

Alyssia had a confused look on her face as Sharlene got the cold water and tea ready for them as she came and sat beside her as Timothy listened, "You see," she began as she gave her the water; "When the judge ruled Sidney Preston's death 'accidental,' Doctor Franklin blamed Thackeray for wrecking his family and that's when this rivalry really began. Mark's wife ran off with his daughter before the trial and when she left, it killed Franklin and left him a broken man. He was never the same and to this day, he still longs for the daughter to return to him and furthermore, his son had to take care of him all the way through the time he was a student teacher." She replied gently, "Yes I remember Paul telling me yesterday, but he didn't tell me that Mark and George were rivals."

Alyssia was not sure how to make out all the new evidence before her as she sighed and told her, "I was taken from my father and brother at seven years old; forced to live with her and her lover. Then four years later, I was sent to my grandmother's home after my mother was killed in a gas explosion and there I remained until her death three in a half weeks ago." Timothy had come out of the shadows and listened to the ladies as Alyssia continued. "My mother and grandmother both told me to go and find my father and brother but never gave me any clues or names as to their whereabouts."

She stood up still in pain but it was bearable and went to the side board in the hallway and opened the middle drawer and got an envelope with her name on it and took it to Sharlene as Timothy hid in the darkness as he watched Alyssia sit back down on the couch and placed the envelope between them as Timothy came in and stayed out of sight as she says gently as she looked at Sharlene with sadness. "Before my grandmother died three weeks ago, she left me her car and money as well as this envelope; it wasn't to be opened until I was eighteen years old, but she gave it to me on her deathbed instead; it's a letter and two photos from my mother." Sharlene was surprised as she opened the envelope and showed her as the prince looked at the photos and read the letter.

"I don't know who the two men are in the photos, I just don't know where to start…if I only had one clue; the rest of the pieces would fall into place. I have to change, would you excuse me?" Sharlene nodded as Alyssia stands up, goes to her bedroom and changes her undergarments and clothes as Sharlene was shocked to find it was Mark Franklin and his son Paul as she thought: *'Either I need glasses or her father and brother are blind.'*

She asked Alyssia after she came back through to the living room as she pulled down her warm jumper, "If you don't mind Alyssia, I would like to show these to Kevin, if that's okay with you?" Alyssia says as she gets her bag on her sore shoulder as Timothy sees that she was still sore and conjured up a stronger healing spell and sent the ball of energy within her body and waited as the two energy balls collided within her as Alyssia says, "If you want to Sharlene, I'm not worried. I just need a clue or a point in the right direction so I can start my search. She thought: *'Have you looked right in front of you? He's right there; at the University…open your eyes.'*

Sharlene could only nod and she looked at the clock, "Is that the time already? I better get over to the University but I must clean up here…" Sharlene says, "You go and get to your class and I'll clean up here and you can come by our flat and get your keys later…go on." Alyssia smiled and Timothy flicked his hand and the two balls of healing burst with in her body as Alyssia says, "Thank you Sharlene; you're such a good friend." The Caretaker's wife smiled and she cleaned up the mess and washed up the cups and plates as Timothy heads back into the shadows and gets to the

Tower to watch her walk down the driveway to the campus and Kelton Hall. She arrived back on the campus and went to the middle of the campus as she looks at her map which she got with her welcome pack. She was confused as she looked at the schedule and then back at the buildings; "Kelton Hall… now which one of you is Kelton Hall again?"

John was mopping his brow from the work that he was doing as he saw Alyssia looking at her map and scratching her head. He decided to go over and give her hand and point her in the right direction but as he started to make his way to her, he saw George Thackeray who just came out of nowhere as he approached her but that didn't stop John as he came to her rescue as John had a soft spot for her. "Hello," said George as she looked at him with surprise, "Hello Doctor Thackeray…" and gave him a small nod as John was nearing the couple; "I was worried about you;" he began as Alyssia just stared at him, "Really, gee your concern is overwhelming after your House fell on top of me! Yes sir, I saw you looking through your window, scowling and shouting at us…but I didn't let on. Thanks to you, I'm sore all over…" She looked at him and that his mock concern was very unconvincing as he replied in anger as the sarcasm and rudeness built up within him, "Oh I'm so sorry…may I get you a bandage for you since you're walking fine!" She did feel better as she told him, "A bit of exercise never hurts anyone, Doctor Thackeray." George crossed his arms in front of her and said, "Are you being cheeky with me young lady?" Alyssia shook her head and said, "No sir, since you didn't want us on your property to take your class…"

George said to her, "Listen here you, my House is perfectly safe for the students and all you have to do is walk in and find the classroom, is that too hard?" Alyssia sees George getting into her personal space as she felt a presence behind her as she looked and saw John and she answered back gently, "But you said that we were trespassing on your property? So we decided not to come in…" George was about to say something as he saw John as the caretaker standing beside her and taking off his gardening gloves as he replied, "All these students wanted to do was to learn from you and maybe if you cleaned up the House and do the necessary repairs and work, you would have more students."

George was angry and harrumphed, "My House is fine, Mr Preston… it doesn't need fixing up!" Then he turned back to the couple as John kept her close as he came into John's face, "And for your information, I have two students so mind your own business and tend to your petunias!" He spits into John's eye and he walked away as John wiped his venomous spit out of his eye. He was going to go after him as Alyssia's gentle touch stopped him as if to say as she didn't look at him: *'John not on University property…He's not worth it!'* John said aloud as he watched him leave, "One day Thackeray, just you wait!" He said loudly as John calmed himself as he got her message and watched George storm off in a huff as she said, "Thanks John, my hero always."

He smiled, "Aw you're welcome…I see that you are feeling better?" she smiled and says, "Thank you, I went home to change and pick the plaster out of my hair and got some exercise." The couple laughed as she looked again at the map and then to the buildings as John asked, "You look confused; can I help?" She looked at the buildings as she nursed some sore muscles and says, "I must be getting senile, John. I forgot which one was Kelton Hall… a couple of other classes are in there and I'm running late as it is. Just a clue and a point in the right direction would be such a help and I'll know where it is for future reference."

John offered his arm to her and she took it with gladness, "Not a problem, come with me and I will point you in the right direction." She thanked him as she put her map and schedule away as he leads her over to a garden plot as he says and points to the building in front of them. "This is Kelton Hall and I see that someone is desperate for you to get to class." They saw Milton doing his 'hurry up and get to class now' dance as John and Alyssia chuckled, "I think I saw this in a movie once or in "Doctor Who[9]" I forget which!?"

He laughed and he points out the path to her as he sees the problem "No wonder you couldn't find the hall." She was puzzled until he picked up a sign and showed it to her; "Someone forgot to put the sign back up after the alterations to the hall were finished. It should have been put back up after you newbies were getting your schedules. I'll let Hyman and Dean Winchell know and we'll get that sign back up as quickly as possible but all you do is just go down this path and you'll see the front door."

Just then, they look up at Milton still dancing away and then they see Adrianne pulling on Milton's ear for the second time as they laugh as she

---

[9] Doctor Who ©1963 (November 23rd) BBC Worldwide

thanks him and gets on the path and heads into the building as they share a wave and he gets back to his work and she disappears into Kelton Hall for her class. "Thanks for all you are doing for me John," she says as she touched his muscular arm. "You saved me from a falling house, you were very kind to me when I needed a friend…those little things mean so much to me and I will treasure them always."

John smiled and says, "Just doing my job and I'm here if you need me…always. Remember that!" Alyssia smiled up at him and replied gently, "You know I will, John. My grandmother told me that I have a guardian angel and she told me that 'his name is John Preston and whenever you go back to Kelton Heights, he will be watching over you always.' He grinned as she replied, "Jessica has never forgotten the kindness you showed her after my mother died in the gas explosion and she picked you to watch over me and I will always thank her for sending you to me." He smiled as she gives him a hug after that and she lets him go as she walks towards Kelton Hall and he watched her disappear into the building as John gets back to work while he puts back on his soiled gloves as he gets back to the plot before him.

Inside, she gets into the lift and gets to the top floor and rounds the corner to see Milton still rubbing his ear replying, "Where have you been? We've been waiting for you…we were going to send Hercule Poirot, Sherlock Holmes, Watson and some bloodhounds out to look for you." Alyssia shook her head and follows Milton into the room as she puts her bag on to the table. "Well DAD, I got lost," and Amber and Adrianne smiled as the friends wait for class to start as they help her take her coat off and hangs it on a hook near the door as Adrianne comes back to the trio and they all sit down and she continued her story.

"But as I was looking for Kelton Hall, I was approached by our favourite grouch;" Milton jumped for joy as a kid who got a big lollipop from a candy store, "OSCAR!" The girls and the whole class looked at him as they chuckle as he looked at the class embarrassingly while Alyssia gets her notebook and pen out. Adrianne took the bait as she asked, "Milton, may I ask if you watch "Sesame Street" in the morning?" Milton looked at her in mocked disappointment as the girls chuckled gently. "Aw you caught me!"

Adrianne put her head on the table as the girls giggled. Milton smiled while Alyssia got out her homework notebook for Philosophy as Adrianne brought her head up and shook her head at him, "No, not Oscar, smart Alec…I think she means George 'the grouch' Thackeray!" Milton thought for a moment and said getting it, "Oh **THAT** grouch! What did he want?" Alyssia smiled and rubbed Adrianne's back as she wanted to choke him. "It's not worth it, Adrianne;" she whispered as Alyssia told them while they waited for their tutor to come in.

"I was reading the map to find Kelton Hall when George comes to me and asked where we all were showing his mock concern of how I got hurt saying that I'm walking better as John the caretaker told him off about not repairing his House before the start of the new term. He shouted back that his House was fine and that it didn't need fixing up, then he got right into John's face and spit in his eye as he told him to mind his own business and tend to his petunias.

As 'the grouch' stormed off, John was going to go after him, I stopped him and then he leads me here and points me down the path after we see Milton waving, dancing, giving me flag and smoke signals to where you were then we looked up again and saw Adrianne pulling on his ear to have him sit down." Everyone laughed as Milton rubbed his sore ear and said, "…and it bloody hurts as well!" Adrianne mocks her concern to him, "Aw did I hurt those big Dumbo ears of yours?" Adrianne pinched and slaps his cheeks as Amber and Alyssia were trying to hold in a chuckle as he looked at her with daggers and faked a smile.

He was just about to say something to her until the tutor for the Philosophy course came in and he starts handing out the text books as class began. "Saved by the tutor," Adrianne said dramatically as the girls and Milton took the books from the tutor while Milton pointed at her, "Just you wait, Miss Falconi, I will get my revenge" as she mocked being scared as class began.

At break time, Milton and the others were joined by their classmates out on the lawn as "Franklin's Circle" became close friends as they talk about George Thackeray and what he may be up to. One student says about Thackeray, "He's a grouch! That's all there is to it! He's a greedy, self-conceited, self-centred man!" Alyssia thought: *I bet he voted for Trump in the last election. He is a lot like him; greedy, self-centred, a grouch, a sexist pig, liar, a bigot…Hmm can't think of anything else.'*

The students continued as she came out of the fog while Timothy stands by the window in the darkened classroom to watch over Alyssia. He looks down on the group as the student continued saying, "He cares for none of his students or his House. Many of us chose to live off campus than at Thackeray House as he makes you feel so uncomfortable as if you aren't supposed to be here." Alyssia massaged a sore part on her neck as she says, "The feeling's mutual…trust me! I'm still feeling the aches and pains from that House collapse this morning!" The group laughs while break time continued as Amber rubbed her shoulders.

Milton speaks up, "I think he's up to something, if we knew what it was or get a clue as to what he's up to, we can do something." One student thought for a moment, "It might have something to do with Sidney's death or maybe Cassious House," all the students look at the dark foreboding House off in the distance. Alyssia looks at the House with them confusingly and asked, "What do you mean?" The student says, "We all know about the history of the House but I don't think you know why it's haunted, do you Alyssia?" Alyssia says, "I know it had to do with the prince being cursed, but that's the extent of it."

The student reached into her bag and gave her a guide book as she says after taking a gulp of water and starts her story as everyone listened as Alyssia looked at the House. "The House is being haunted by the spirit of a Prince Timothy Andrew Carlton, the only son of a King Stephen Antony Carlton and his beautiful wife Samantha." She shows everyone a picture of the Prince as she continued while Alyssia looked at him and stroked his face in the picture *'It's him'* her brain screamed, *'the man who slashed at those dark spirits that first night I was in Cassious House!'* Alyssia smiled as the young lady continued her story about Cassious House as she listened.

"Legend has it, that the king's son was wrongfully accused for the rape and murder of his own bride by a crime boss from India only named, 'The Sultan.' The advisor who worked for 'The Sultan' and was a friend to him, and he placed a powerful curse on the House and on the solid gold necklace that he was to give his bride, contains his heart and soul. According to legend, the Prince haunts the House looking for the necklace and his one true love and if anyone who frees him, the necklace would make the Prince human and it is worth a king's ransom. I think that is what Thackeray wants; he has been looking at the House and plotting something since he heard or read about the history of the House."

Then she remembered something Sharlene had told her *'I have a good feeling about you…'* and that got her brain chugging along and she was intrigued and quickly took down the title of the guide book as she asked where she got it. The student says happily, "I knew that would peak you interest, Alyssia; I got it at the Visitor's Centre near a fully functioning historic Harbour and Port on Welling Street in Kelton Heights by the sea, and right next door is a small art museum that houses old Kelton Heights run by a flamboyant man named Iain Margarida look out for him; and you seemed like the kind of person that likes history?"

Alyssia smiled and says as her brain was going a mile a minute as she looked back at her new friend, "I do; I am a member of Historic Scotland and love the history of the United Kingdom of the past," as she looked at the House and thought: *'Especially ones about a prince, magic spells and chivalry. Interesting…the game is on!'* as they all started to stand and brush off their jackets of the freshly mowed grass as the students got ready to go back inside for the second part of their class. Adrianne whispered to her, "Time to head back to class for Sociology… Ready?" Alyssia looked once again at the House and said to her, "Yes let's finish for the day," and the two friends followed the others back in as she hands the guide book back to her new friend and thanks her after she wrote down the title of the guide book as they make it back to the same classroom as the Sociology tutor came in and class began again with a new tutor and another text book to add to their ever increasing bookshelf of knowledge.

The end of the day comes as Alyssia says goodbye to her class mates and heads back to Cassious House and to her landlord/caretaker's home to get her keys. She made it to the door as her brain was filled with the history of Cassious House as she knocks on the door and Sharlene answers it. "Oh hello Alyssia, come on in," She wipes her feet and comes inside as she closed the door; "Wait here and I'll get your keys." Alyssia nodded as she goes to the next room and looks for her keys as Kevin comes into the living room to see her.

"Oh hello there," he said as Sharlene disappears into the kitchen while Kevin talks to her. "I heard what happened at Thackeray House this morning, are you okay?" Alyssia was still nursing some of the sore bits as she says, "Yes I'm feeling better, still sore some places, but I'll survive, Kevin. I've heard of bringing down the House; but Thackeray gave it a whole new meaning." They share a laugh as Sharlene found the keys and gave them to her as Kevin says gently not wanting to make her day any worse and bringing up the past. "I read your letter and saw the photos," he said giving back the envelope with her name on it, "…but Sharlene may be right about you being Mark Franklin's long lost daughter, but I want to make sure."

She looked at him with a smile, "You don't have to Kevin. You got enough on your plate as it is; like taking care of the upkeep of this House." He smiled and said "Please? At least it will be something for me to do. We're your family now, okay?" She nodded and sighed as she tells them, "I need to go to Kelton Heights Registrar's office and find evidence of births, deaths and marriages as well as divorce records…" Kevin says quickly, "Then us do that for you, please? We would like to help you as much as possible. I just need your full name and date of birth as well as a hand written note to tell them that you give me permission to do this for you."

Alyssia was given a pad and pen as she gave him the details and told him, "Keep it quiet okay? I'm not supposed to do this but if you are like family to me, I will do it for you; no one else is to know." Kevin puts a finger to his lips and whispered and winked, "Mum's the word!" She smiled and gives him the pad and pen as she gets back to the conversation at hand. "I do have another mystery on my mind-do you know where Welling Street is? A class mate told me it was a Port or Harbour near the sea?" Kevin nodded and says, "Yes I get you now; it's a Visitor's Centre and museum of the time Kelton Heights and Welleston Village used to be and still is a fishing hub of activity…the Harbour is still fully operational to this day."

Alyssia says to them as she pulls out a piece of paper and shows the couple a book a student recommended to her as she shows them a title of the book: ***"The Pirates, Vikings, and Celts of Kelton Heights and Welleston Village by Enscheda Taravel."*** She said to the curious couple as she continued, "I want to visit there; it sounds interesting," she replied happily as Kevin nodded. "Well Sharlene and I do most of our shopping for fish down there and we'll be happy to give you a lift there if you like?" Sharlene was intrigued and asked her, "Are you thinking that there's something more to Cassious House than meets the eye, Alyssia?"

Alyssia shook her head and says, "I don't know what I'm saying or thinking;" she tells the Parks. "All I know is that I love ancient castles and cathedrals as well as its history-but there's something not right at Kelton University and it's not the Spirit of Cassious House that's at work here." She felt a chill and rubbed her sore arm as Sharlene says, "Well whatever it is," Sharlene says as Kevin looks at her, "Thackeray has crossed the line by killing a man. Whatever is in Cassious House, he's willing to kill anyone to get to it!" Kevin and Alyssia agreed as she grabbed her book bag and slings it on her shoulder and almost let out a yelp as a shooting pain ran up her arm and into her brain.

"Well, I got a report or two to do and it's not going to get done with me standing here, so I better leave you to your peace, get into my house, feed Mystery and me and start on those reports." She turns and heads for the door, "Thank you for locking up and holding my keys, Sharlene and Kevin… you have been so welcoming since I moved in and I really appreciate your kindness." The couple smile as Sharlene says, "It's good to have you here and remember we are family." Alyssia smiled and says, "Thank you, it's good to be here too and I'll remember that you are my family. I'm still getting used to making it on my own." The couple smiled and say their good nights as she goes back to her home and locks up for the night.

She gets into the house and Mystery sees her, meows a hello to her, and rubbed her legs as she came through the door and placed the keys on a hook after turning on the main light. "Hello lover lump," she says to Mystery as she puts her bag down, bends down and picks her up as the kitten lays in her arms and purrs as she gets her ears rubbed. "Ready to get fed, my sweet girl?" The cat meows as she carries her through to the kitchen and gets her a can of food as Alyssia prepares dinner for herself while Mystery tucks into her favourite food…some tuna.

At Franklin House, the lecturers are talking about the day and Paul's shock at the new study group that was formed at Maddy's Coffee House after the roof collapse. Mark shakes his head wondering if George is of this planet let alone a human being while Paul cooked dinner for him as Mark was having some homemade Oxtail soup while waiting for the main course. "Is Alyssia okay, Paul? I mean, she isn't…" Paul says reassuringly, "No, she was just sore all over; she told me how Milton and the caretaker

John Preston got her out as more of Thackeray House fell in. No, she is well and teaching the study group and she handled it very well."

Mark was surprised but was still ranting about how George was so disrespectful to the students and not fixing up his House when he was told to." The men laugh as Paul says, "Well anyway, the dean has excused them to start 'Franklin's Circle' on Tuesday and Thursday mornings at Maddy's Coffee House." Mark was still at a loss for words at how George Thackeray could be so arrogant and he said with a shake of his head, "That man has no morals or conscious when all those students wanted to do was go to his class and he wonders why he has no students!" Paul smiled and brings over the dinner as Mark sits down after putting his bowl in the dish basin which was filled with hot soapy water as Paul dishes out the dinner and Mark pours the wine. He sits beside his dad and they all start to eat. "I'm sorry that I keep bringing up George, Paul. He just makes me so angry sometimes!" Paul calms his dad, "I love your rants dad; believe me!"

Mark smiled as Paul continued about the study group. "Anyway, I stopped a few of the students in our class and they told me that the group played a simple game and shared answers and ideas while trapping a 'ghost' to make it simple and fun. It's like the students could ask her things and she gave them a simple answer in plain English as well as gave them some of her own knowledge in simple chunks and they listened; they actually listened! I'll be going over there on Thursday morning to give her a hand; she doesn't exactly know what she is doing, she confessed so I thought I would go over as she was worried about me getting the lesson plans done for the next week and I told her that it would be an honour."

Mark was about to say something when there was a knock on their office door, "I'll get it dad," as Paul wiped his mouth with his napkin and puts it down on the table and goes to answer the door. "Who is it, son?" He brings Dean Pharrell Winchell to him as Paul dishes out another plate of food and a glass of wine, "Good evening Mark and Paul, sorry to catch you at your dinner but I have been in four hours of meetings with building inspectors, lawyers, the police, insurance adjusters as well as school officials with Edward Mangard. Finally, I am getting the chance to speak to you and Paul; but I see you are at your dinner…" Paul says, "Have a seat, Pharrell. I have enough food for all of us."

Paul dishes out the food and gives him a plate of food and a glass of wine as Dean Winchell thanks him. Paul sits down, spreads out his napkin on his lap once again as the dean got to the point. "I think Paul has told you about the study group that was formed today?" Mark says, "Yes he has and that is absolutely great news and the building collapse; I'm just glad that no one was killed and I'm sorry for having a go at you like that Pharrell, especially in front of the building inspectors…" says Mark as Pharrell smiled and says, "Its okay Mark, I apologise for not listening to you in the first place about Thackeray House and its eminent collapse."

Mark smiled as he said, "I was about to say to Paul here that I would like to go over to the café on Thursday morning to give her and the class a hand?" Paul was happy. "Dad you know that you are more than welcome and I would appreciate the extra help too." Pharrell was pleased that the men were accepting of the group as the men ate, drank, laughed and talked through the early evening as he told them about the meeting with the building inspectors and the study group until the coffee ran out.

Back at Cassious House, Alyssia was busy with her two reports as she got her plates cleaned up and showered as she changed into her night wear while Mystery was sound asleep on the couch dreaming of tuna and catching mice. Enya was playing softly on her radio as she worked on her mind maps and rough draft for her classes until she heard the noises again from the other side of the door. She was sure she was dreaming about a spirit in medieval clothes protecting her as she thought: *I was dreaming that early morning and the trick of the lightning made it all too real. But those noises are getting louder; I better go and see what's happening.'* She gets up and goes to the door until she is stopped by a male's voice, "Please don't go in there…" she turns around to see Prince Timothy in his medieval clothes with a sword strapped to his waist as he was staring at her as he continues "…the evil shadows are looking for victims tonight; using their mournful song as a lure."

She thought: *'I wasn't dreaming! Oh, my God…he's real!'* Her brain screamed as she moved away from the door and hung up the key as she looked at him. "H-How do you know those dark spirits?" she asked him as she approached him slowly. "They are the reason why I and my fellow spirits are trapped here; there's a curse on the House as you probably figured out. The dark spirits sing a mournful song to lure the victims into their nets and drag them inside the veil never to be seen again; it's been like this for over three hundred years and I want nothing to happen to you."

She was looking for a way to call it a night on her report for Franklin after she had finished her Sociology and Psychology rough drafts and puts them to bed for the weekend and Timothy gave her that break she so desperately craved and his arrival was just what she needed. She asked him, "That dark veil that is covering the first floor landing? Is that what you mean? And those three boys, they were taken?"

Timothy nods as she took in a deep breath, "I was there and I tried to warn them off but they just laughed…too drunk to care and when they were lifted high, their bones would have been broken or paralysed for life-so I had no choice but to let the Dark Spirits have them. I would have been drawn in as well if I tried to help; their song is powerful enough to lure us good spirits in. It's a living veil of dark spirits and death; once you are lured in and taken, you are never seen again." She was scared yet still amazed that there were spirits next door to her as she came closer to him. "I thought I was imagining it; you, the dark spirits…" she sat down in her chair as Timothy came to her and comforted her as he believes that she was too tired; besides, it's been a long day after the building collapse.

She looked at Timothy with love and sympathy as she asked if she could touch him and he nodded as she touched him gently on his face, his hands and arms, his clothes, his hair…he felt like a human once more as he smiled at her with tears rolling down his cheeks as he felt how gentle and soft her fingertips were on his skin. She touched his cheek and dried his tears as he looked at her with eyes of loneliness and hope as she said gently with a smile and love. "Thank you for protecting me, Timothy." He smiled big and bright as she kissed his cheek and a smile lit up his features as the night was quiet again; the song had ended. Timothy noticed it too as he says, "Looks like the dark spirits will not get a victim tonight-it's back to the shadows for them."

She asked him gently as she stood up, "…so where do you live, Timothy?" He sighed and walked about her home as he turned back to her as he looked at her with sadness. "All the good spirits and I live in the Tower of Cassious House because of 'the dark veil of evil'; it lures us in too and so we must stay up in the Tower for our own safety. I-I think you have seen us glancing through the window, have you?" Alyssia took in a sigh and says, "Yes I have. At first I thought I was hallucinating; I never told anyone because they would all think I was loopy," The couple laughed as she continued, "...but I can't even say anything to anyone, not even to Kevin Parks. He told me that the House was off limits when I moved in and I must respect his wishes and that no one should come here unless it was for University business only; I don't want to risk an invasion of your privacy or anyone getting hurt or disappearing."

The prince respected her decision and says as he touched her cheek, "I appreciate that, Alyssia Franklin-Jenkins; I will make sure the others know of your decision on this matter." Alyssia asked comically, "Others? Wait there's not seven of you?" The Prince laughed, "No, just one of me. The others are Marylebarne and Jesterson as well as my staff who were cursed on that fateful day. I think you know the story, do you?" Alyssia watched him turn away looking around her home as he looked at her as she felt very sad for him.

"Yes" she replied as she touched his hand, "One of the students told me that you were accused of the rape and murder of your bride to be; but I don't believe a single thing or word about it," He looked at her, "...because there's no truth or proof. You seem so nice Timothy;" she put her hand on his cheek as he touched her hand as she continued. "I can't picture you as a murderer..." He smiled and said as he came back to her as he took her tiny hand in his but then he walked away from her; "I never murdered anyone in my life Alyssia, and yet, I must pay for it with the loss of my heart and soul which in a gold necklace that I can't seem to find; waiting for my one true love to come and free me and the House. Many have tried but failed, but I feel down deep that maybe you Alyssia, may be the one to free me."

She came over to him as he looked deep into her eyes and placed a hand on her cheek as she fell for him hard as her love grew inside for him as she replied very gently, "The only thing you are guilty of is loving someone and that's a crime we all can be accused of. I can certainly try to help you Timothy; there's something not right at the University and I want to help you and your fellow spirits." She turns away and thought of the Franklins as she admitted to him as she walked away from him, "Both Franklins seem to know me but something is holding them back and what's more," she turns back to the Prince and says gently, "there's something sinister going on at the University and it's not you or this House but if you permit me to delve deep into the past, I may have the answers you need…it will take time and tears but it's the only way we can get to the truth. Will you trust me to do this, your highness?"

He nodded as he came close to her and stroked her hair gently. "I trust you," he said gently as he kissed her cheek again and hugged her tightly. She loved his hugs and she felt very secure when he held her close as he whispered, "I will introduce you to Marylebarne, Jesterson and the rest of the spirits in due course, I promise." She smiled as she looked back at him as she says, "I look forward to it." He smiled and they shared each other's company as the night made its way into the early morning as he asked her, "By the way, how are you feeling since this morning? I put a healing spell on you since you weren't feeling well and moving rather slowly." She said as they sat on the couch, "I am feeling much better, thank you. Whatever you did, the aches and pains went away." They sat down to talk about each other as she told him about her days as well as the roof collapse at Thackeray House and he held her hand and listened to her.

Marylebarne and Jesterson came out of the shadows and watched the Prince and her talking as they listened as Marylebarne said to Jesterson in a low voice, "Jesterson, she may be the one who will do the unthinkable…" Jesterson says, "And what's that Marylebarne?" The advisor looked at him, "to break the curse on us and the House, my boy!"

Jesterson is best buds with Timothy and the other spirits and he's the one who keeps everyone laughing in signs of trouble and sadness as he hides the pain of watching his family being taken from him by the Dark Spirits. This dark-haired, brown-eyed with Asian-like features, tall, funny, and whimsical friend of Prince Timothy's, is a clown and mischievous practical joker, but also a fighter and friend who swings a mean sword. When he meets Alyssia for the first time, he is totally taken with her and he knows that Timothy has chosen well. Loyal from beginning to end, he makes others laugh, becomes brave and comes to the aid of his family when the time is right.

Jesterson sadly nodded, bowed his head saying, "Sorry sir, it's been so long since hope has come to Cassious House. I have almost given up hoping until she came… forgive me, sir." Marylebarne patted his shoulder. "It's okay my boy I understand; it's been a rough three hundred + years, I have been praying that this curse would be lifted on the prince so he could be free and human again. He is learning to love someone other than Melandandari and for that, it's a step in the right direction; I'm proud of him."

Jesterson nodded and said, "Begging your pardon for speaking ill of the dead, Marylebarne;" he began as the advisor listened and looked at him, "I thought that there's been something wrong with Melandandari. She would always have an unkind word to say to him, no matter what he did for her and what's worst; he loved her and wouldn't hear sense of it or anything bad of her, sir. I mean you must have heard all the unkind things that she said about him, Marylebarne; and even you had to try and make him see sense…It was a nightmare!"

Marylebarne did remember and it hurt him to the core. "I did try, and believe me and if you hadn't warned the king and me about the assassination attempt on the king and his son, we would not be here today." Jesterson felt sorely scared about that day as he had nightmares and doubts if he ever had done the right thing; now he was sure that he did as Marylebarne smiled at him and said, "I am very proud of you and your bravery, Jesterson. I am sure that the Prince is too."

Marylebarne says as he looked back at the couple, "But I hope that with no heart and soul, he will learn what real love is and the more he spends time with Alyssia, the better. They have fallen hard for each other and let's hope it lasts until spring when the first full moon of the spring arrives and their love is real and true…this is the ultimate test, Jesterson. The test that will determine and prove that true love can happen to anyone, including the Prince who has waited for so long for the right one come along and break this curse that has plagued us for more than time itself. Come my dear Jesterson, let's leave them to talk; he will be doing his guard duty very soon."

Jesterson nodded and told Marylebarne, "I better brush up on being a guard, sir; it looks like I will be doing guard duty with the Prince very soon. I'm in training with Timothy and another guard right now, I pray I don't let any of them down or do something that I would regret." Marylebarne told the jester, "Listen and learn Jesterson, it's the only way you will get it right…we all have to do our part now to make sure that she is safe. I have a feeling that she is the one that we are looking for all this time and we must do our best not to scare her off or make her leave; she may be our only hope."

Jesterson smiled as he and the prince's advisor disappear into shadows leaving the Prince to talk with her. A few minutes later, he lets her go to finish her report and left for the Tower as he kissed her on the cheek and said his goodnights to her as she watched him disappear into shadows. She placed her homework away in her folder and Franklin's work in her book bag as she finished her report on ghosts and all the thoughts on what a 'ghost' was all around her spooky friend as she thought how it made the class laugh and helped her forget the dreadful morning at Thackeray House. But she also looked at the piece of paper with the book title written upon it; there was something nagging her at the back of her head and there had to be answers and pieces of the puzzle that she was presented with and now, she had made the promise and she was going to stick with it no matter how long it took and she would do it within the boundaries of her class work and reality.

Just then a yawn played across her features as she fed Mystery once more and headed to bed as she thought: *'Two more days of classes and I can concentrate on all my homework and get ready for the second week at University.'* She made out a to-do list and placed it on her homework pile and then, went to bed as she got into her bed and under the covers. She turned out the lights as Mystery jumped up on to the bed, curled up beside her and went to sleep as midnight came and the Prince sat with his book on Shakespeare's Sonnets and guarded her until dawn.

Chapter 3

The first Wednesday morning of the new term started out dark, rainy, and windy in late September as the red, brown, gold and orange leaves blew around Cassious House littering the grass and streets around Kelton Heights. Alyssia did her normal everyday routine: she got up, made her bed, showered, changed and went to the kitchen to have breakfast and fed Mystery.

It may have been wet and drab day for some people but for Alyssia, her world was sunny and bright as she got outside and put on her raincoat on over her backpack fixing her it to keep her backpack dry and getting her hood up as she headed for the campus to Franklin House for Paul's class with a smile on her face and a song in her heart.

Alyssia got outside, put her keys away in her jeans and started walking down the drive towards the crosswalk to get to the campus as she looked up at the Tower window and saw Timothy looking out with the others who were looking down as she smiled and waved to him while he reciprocated the gesture as she walked away and disappeared into the thicket of oak, willow, spruce, birch and elm trees which hung fully packed over the driveway of the Haunted House. In the thicket of trees halfway down the driveway towards the street, she saw a massive hole in the branches and wondered what it was there for, but she put the thought out of her mind and continued on her way to class at Kelton University.

As she got outside the grove of trees, which provided some temporary shelter from the elements, she fixed her raincoat and pulled it close as the weather turned very cold and breezy. The rain was becoming heavier and frequent after she fixed her jacket along the way and walked down to the end of the driveway of the Haunted House and made it out on to the wet, water-sodden, oil-slicked streets which endured the lashing rain. Vehicles of every size and speed sprayed the water about on the already wet-trodden pedestrians, unprotected bus shelters and other parked cars as she got across the street and on to the campus.

She pulled her hood close and tied it as she got to the cross walk and made the other pedestrians smile with her happiness as she crossed the street onto the University campus and on to Franklin House while heavy raindrops dripped onto her raincoat. Alyssia looked above her to see the rain clouds moving fast as the wind blew cold and merciless on everyone around her, but she didn't care and kept on smiling as she headed straight to class to see Milton, Amber and Adrianne waiting for her under the canopy entrance to Franklin House and waved to them happily.

They saw the biggest smile on her face as Adrianne whispered to Milton and Amber as she immediately assumed one thing, "Looks like someone's in love!" As the trio giggled, Alyssia had heard what she said but her remark didn't dampen her spirit. Milton, being the jester he was, perked up as he saw Alyssia in a strange mood and heard her singing away and smiling as he did a funny dance making everyone, who passed the quartet, laugh while he was listening to the song she was singing.

As he danced all the way to the classroom and got inside, they got their rain gear off as the rain came down heavily outside. The four friends and the other students around them hung their wet, rain beaten, soggy coats on the hooks by the front door of the classroom. More of their fellow students started to come in, greeted them, sat down at their tables, and waited for class to start as Milton says after she finished singing, "I'd give it a ten, but it's very hard to dance to!" He gave her a cheesy grin as she looked at him and said with a sigh, "Thank you Dick Clark!" she said in a sarcastic tone while the everyone laughed. Alyssia and her friends got their backpacks off, sat down, and opened their backpacks to get their notebooks and pens out while Alyssia reached into her jeans and got her house keys as she placed them in the front pouch of her back pack because the keys were digging into her stomach and leg.

Amber says to her gently as she sat down, "Alyssia, you're in a good mood…" Alyssia was about to say something until Adrianne nodded and says, "Yeah and we think we know why; it must be a guy who caught your eye; Ooh, I'm a poet and didn't know it!" Alyssia chuckled as she saw her friends leaning in to get all the juicy gossip as Adrianne nudged her on,

"Come on spill the beans, who is the lucky man?" She looked at all of them and said, "I'm not in love with anyone, I am just in a good mood," she says as she thought of Prince Timothy: *'Boy, you're in such a good mood and everyone thinks that guy has caught my eye! I'm still not telling them that I saw a spirit in medieval clothes defending me…might as well hand me the straight jacket and order the men in white coats while you're at it!'*

She tried to explain that there was no one who has caught her eye; but Milton followed Adrianne's hunch and he pulled out his deerstalker, his bubble pipe and his magnifying glass out of his bag. Timothy, who just came in to the classroom from the shadows, watched the friends and smiled as Milton says as if he was Sherlock Holmes, "We must investigate this further, Watsons!" Timothy started to laugh as Alyssia looked at her friends strangely and sighed while he peered at her through the magnifying glass as the girls look on her intently.

Milton said, "By Jove Adrianne, you may be right;" but Alyssia protested, "There is no one in my life, guys!" But they were not convinced as Milton looked her up and down with his magnifying glass; "Hmmmm, a smile from ear to ear, a song of happiness!" They look at him aghast, "Egad, Holmes how do you know?" The girls said together as she sighed, "Elementary, my dear Watsons…" as Milton "Sherlock Holmes" Russell observed, "it's pouring rain outside and yet, she is singing of sunshine, lollipops and bendy rainbows!"

Timothy held in a chuckle as Alyssia took in another sigh and looked at Milton with a strange look as she says, "Maybe I should order the men in white coats for you, Milton! They have a jacket in which you can hug yourself all day and you can bounce around in a padded room!" Timothy giggled as she got out her water while the girls laugh as she tried to explain. "I'm just in a good mood, guys. I'm not in love with anyone." Timothy continued to chuckle as the friends were not convinced.

Milton didn't listen or flinch as he continued to get more clues and she started to rub away an imaginary headache as Milton says startled, "Egad Watsons! More rainbows are popping up, and there's another one…wow look at them go! I thought I saw a unicorn jumping over one of them." Timothy and the girls laugh while she got her notebook and folder out of her bag as Milton excitedly says after seeing more bendy rainbows and unicorns, "Wow look at them go!" exclaimed Milton as she took the magnifying glass out of his hand and placed on the table as the trio and Timothy laughs as he heard her say, "Will you all cut it out?! I'm fine gang; I just woke up in a good mood-that's all!" Adrianne was suspicious as she says, "Nah, I still say that there's a guy in her life!"

The trio nodded as Alyssia put her head on her hands and thought out loud *"Oh I give up!"* while she emptied her backpack with more water and a white bag of sweets as she defended. "There is no guy in my life and that's the matter closed!" Timothy later said to himself; *"…Not while I'm around. I will make you mine one day… wait and see."* Amber and Adrianne smiled with a cheeky glint in their eyes as Milton picked up her small paper bag of sweets that she took out of her front pouch as she gave Amber the extra water to thank her for Tuesday morning while he stared at the bag with astonishment through his magnifying glass and says, "Aha! The mystery is solved, Watsons! Look at these pills!" He took one out and showed them as he replied still surprised, "…they are the size of horse tranquilisers!"

Timothy and the girls giggled as she took the bag from him and said, "They are **NOT** pills, Sherlock; they are Mentos mints!" She offered them to the group around her as they all took a mint or two each. While Milton took a mint, the girls take out their folders, pens and waters except for Milton who puts his feet up as he watched the clock, and placed the bag in his lap as the girls looked at him as he says, "I'm waiting up to the last minute for the teacher to come out." The girls all looked at each other until they saw Paul Franklin coming out of the office with his planner and work as Milton puts his feet down, pulls out his notebook and pen as he placed his bag on the floor in one motion. He looked at the girls as he asked, "What?" The girls laugh as Alyssia shook her head, Adrianne gave him a puzzled look and Amber was astonished at how quick he was.

"My God Milton," Amber began, "Were you raised by the Flash? That's the fastest I've seen you move!" He smiled, came close to her and touched her chin as he said, "I aim to please!!" Prince Timothy saw her bright smile and fell in love with her even more as he watched her with intensity while Alyssia gave Amber a gentle pat as Paul took roll and class begun. He called out each student's name and they answered…but not Milton, no…he stood up, cleared his throat, took a deep breath and operatically sang out in tune as everyone smiled: "H-E-E-R-R-E-E!"

Alyssia hid her face and giggled, Adrianne and Amber hid their laughs behind their hands as the rest of the class and the spirited Prince burst out laughing as he finished. Paul, on the other hand, was trying hard not to laugh as he watched him bow to his fellow students and says "Thank you, thank you, thank you. I'll be here all year and if you're driving today, don't forget your car-bye![10]" He sat back down as the class applauded and laughed even harder, Paul smiled and said, "Thank you Milton for making me laugh on this rainy day." Timothy bowed his head and dried the tears of laughter out of his eyes as Paul continued to mute his laugh and shake his head as he thought, *'Dad, we got a live one here this year!'*

The class calmed down as he introduced himself while the class got started for real. "Hello everyone, I'm Doctor Paul Franklin PhD and welcome to part two of the Preservation of Ghosts and Spirits. Now I want to start out first by handing out the text books. Dad told me that he forgot to do that on Monday afternoon and he expects you to take care of them… no writing in them, please! So, each person, from each table, please come and get the text books and put them away for Monday morning and then I got a pack for you all to work on so pick them up before you go back to your seats!"

Milton volunteered to get the books and packs for his table as he whispered to the girls as an interrogator, "Interrogate Alyssia and extract a full confession out of her and I will be right back!" The girls nodded as they whispered to Alyssia, "Okay, what's with the happy song and the biggest smile on your face? Is it that caretaker John Preston? He is yummy…oh god please tell me it's not Milton Russell?!" She calmed their fears as she thought: *'Oh my God, really? I can't be in a good mood for no reason? How do I explain a three hundred+ year old ghost in medieval clothing to my friends? They would be wondering if I'm on drugs!'* She had to re-iterate to them, "Amber! Adrianne! Calm yourselves…there is no guy in my life! I just woke up in a good mood that's all. John Preston is cute and is built like a God, but he is married and Milton makes me laugh and is a good friend like the both of you, but no one has caught my eye!"

Alyssia says to them calmly and happily as she sees Milton who came back acting like Igor saying; "Here are those parts you wanted, Master!"

---

[10] "Timon and Pumbaa" ©1995 Walt Disney Company/ CBS-TV. This line was taken from the story "Yukon Con" of Series 1 which aired on September 23rd 1995

He even had the laugh down as Adrianne looked at him and shook her head as he puts the books and packs down on the table while they chuckled as the trio took one book and one pack for themselves. Alyssia whispered, "Seriously Adrianne, I think he likes you…" Adrianne says to her sarcastically after looking at Milton and back at her, "Seriously Alyssia, I'd rather kiss King Kong."

Milton pounded his chest like a gorilla and made monkey sounds while she and Amber laughed gently as Adrianne gave the girls an eye roll while Milton sits down and Paul says; "Now does everyone have a textbook and a pack?" The class nodded as he said, "Wonderful, remember to keep your reports open on what a 'ghost' is because between us, you'll adding more to it. But now, here's the boring part of the lecture; Fire Safety." Just as he was about to speak again, there were moans and groans as Paul smiled while Timothy hid a chuckle under his hand. Paul then got on with it before the students moaned again. "I see I'm not the only one that hates Fire Safety talks, but the quicker I get it out of the way, the less painless it will be, okay?" The class nodded as he continued, "Now what do you do when you see a fire or hear the fire bell?"

Milton still in a silly mood shouted out, "Simple—yell and scream bloody murder as we run out the door to our designated assembly point!" Everyone erupted with laughter including Paul and Timothy as the class calmed down while Alyssia whispered to Milton. "Good one, I'd be the first one out the door!" Milton chuckled as he fists bumped her while Paul laughed and then took a deep breath and took off his glasses and rubbed his face as he thought: *Ten years without a class clown dad, and Milton Russell has broken that record in one day! Way to go, Milton…* "Close Milton, but no cigar!" Paul says with a sigh and a chuckle while the class calmed down and Paul puts his glasses back on. Milton says relieved, "PHEW! That's a relief;" he began, "I don't smoke!"

Paul shook his head while everyone giggled as he said before Milton said something else while Mark who was working away on his work, in his office at his desk, just shook his head while Paul began as the class settled. "You get up out of your chairs leaving everything behind in the classroom and in an orderly fashion, quickly and calmly, walk to your fire assembly point which is out the door to your left and out to the centre garden by the fountain; there are signs that will lead the way. **DO NOT** return to the building until the all clear is given as I will have the roll sheet and check to see if everyone is safe and not burnt to cinder."

Milton nodded as he whispered to Alyssia, "Mine was better!" She chuckled quietly as Paul replied, "Now shall we get started with Haunted Houses?" He asked directly to Milton who was looking over the pack and turns to page one while he gets a pen out as class began for real.

At break time, the quartet threw down their jackets onto the wet grass with the other students surrounding the quartet as they sat outside in the fresh air after the heavy rains. He answers questions about his comedy antics; "The comedy is to break the tension of being somewhere new during the first week like at University. My dad says, 'why don't you go to cooking school and become a chef?' I told him that I didn't have the 'Thyme'!" The students laughed as they pat his back but then; Milton then says, "I settle down a bit afterwards." The girls looked at him and they said in unison, "WE NEVER WOULD HAVE GUESSED!" Their classmates giggled as Alyssia said placing a hand on his shoulder, "But Milton, please don't stop making us laugh…" Everyone nods as she continued as Adrianne says, "Yeah, Alyssia is right; it's not the same without your comedy."

Everyone gave him the thumbs up for his sense of humour for he was the only one who could make a lecturer laugh and liven up a dull fire safety lesson, "We will need it at times when things get to serious or too intense," said another student as everyone nodded while another student quoted Paul, *"There will be sad stories connected to these Haunted Houses and historic events… so I will prepare you ahead of time for these sad stories; others will make you angry and lots of other will so spook you, that you won't be able to sleep for a week…"* so we will need that comedy after such sadness, anger and fright."

Everyone agreed as Timothy watched the group from the darkness of Franklin's classroom and looked down at Alyssia who looked up at him and they exchanged smiles until Amber finally spoke up. "I really hope and pray that he doesn't talk about TITANIC[11]; I'm so sick of hearing that story…" Adrianne, Alyssia and Milton and the rest of the class were aghast at Amber's comment as Milton says, "I will not hear such talk like that

---

[11] "TITANIC" and "My Heart Will Go On" sung by Celine Dion ©1997(December 19th) Nominated for 14 Academy Awards, won 11 and is the second highest grossing film earning over $28.7 million at the box office.

from a young lady!" The group chuckle as the whole class listens intently. "My sister loves that story…she'll sit there for three hours and memorise each line of that stupid movie, but the worse thing is when my sister sings that theme tune at the top of her lungs and she can't sing to save her life gang; I want to gag her sometimes!" Everyone gasped again as Timothy chuckled at their shocked expressions while the students get up and brush the grass off their jackets and rain gear as they start to head back to Paul Franklin's class to begin working on their packs on Haunted Houses.

As they get back to the classroom the class gathered around the quartet as they sat back down while Milton says with her hand in his, "My dear sweet Amber, I never dreamt that you; of all people, would think badly of your sister." Amber apologised as she said, "I know what you all are thinking, I do love my sister with all my heart; but when she starts singing…" she took in a sigh as she says embarrassed. "It sounds like a cat in a blender!" The group laughed as they sympathised with her as Milton patted her hand, "Wow Amber, she might sound better than some of these singers today and on the "X Factor[12]."

Amber smiled and nodded, "I think she would, too." The girls laughed as Alyssia had to ask, "What about your mother? What did she have to say about it?" Amber touched her hand and says, "…she actually agrees with me, Alyssia. There are times that she will threaten to throw everything "TITANIC" away if she didn't give it a rest! It's embarrassing to hear your sister caterwauling to a song that I so loathe." Timothy was looking directly at Alyssia as Adrianne says as she drinks her water, "Yeah and if you heard Milton's version of "Uptown Funk" by Bruno Mars[13]; trust me dear you're not missing much!"

Milton told her, "Hey, I may not be Pavarotti, but at least I can hold a tune!" Adrianne says sarcastically, "A tuning fork doesn't count, Milton! And trying to sing "Ode to Joy" like Beaker from "The Muppets Tonight Show" constitutes cruelty to Beethoven himself[14]!" The class laughs they

---

[12] "The X Factor" ©2004 (September 4th) ITV, ITV 2 and TV3 (Ireland) franchised by Simon Cowell

[13] "Uptown Funk" By Mark Ronson featuring Bruno Mars ©2014 (November 10th) RCA Records

[14] "Ode to Joy" by Johann Sebastian Bach/"Muppets Tonight" Episode 209 © 2009 Disney Television/Jim Henson Productions

joined in on the discussion saying how long the movie was the most expensive props and budget…many hated the film period! And how some sat for three hours watching a ship sink in a few minutes while their girlfriends cried their eyes out over the love story. Alyssia calmed all of her classmate's fears with a couple of facts.

"Well not to worry, my dear Amber and fellow classmates; did you know that Celine Dion hated the song? Practically loathed it! In fact she told her late husband René that she hated it and didn't want to do the song in a whisper." Amber and the class were shocked at that fact. "Oh yes, it's a true fact; the director, James Cameron asked her, 'just do it one time and let's hear how it sounded…' she did it in one take and now it's one of her signature songs!"

The classmates were amazed as she continued, "Here's another fact did you also know that James Cameron even went as far as to ask Enya to compose the score for the movie? She refused and did the songs "May It Be" and "Anrion (I Desire)" for the "Lord of the Rings"[15] movie trilogy instead and received many Oscar nods and the movie has been awarded over eight hundred times with half of them being awarded, I think forty-eight times and it's the only trilogy next to "The Hobbit" to not have nudity, sex scenes or a curse words in any of the films."

The class loved Alyssia; she was smart and caring as Alyssia as she told her, "So Amber my dear girl, you can relax and trust us not to sing it in class;" as the class said together: WE CAN'T SING EITHER!" That made Amber and Timothy laugh as did the others as Alyssia replied, "Come on gang let's get Chapter One or pack one done and if you need help before Paul comes back, I will do my best to help." The class agrees and they ended up back into their groups and got back to work on their packs and on their own while some had questions and came to Alyssia and helped them as much as possible while Paul was out of the room.

---

[15] ©"The Lord of the Rings"2001-2003 "The Fellowship of the Ring", "The Two Towers", and "The Return of the King" The books written by JRR Tolkien 1954/5 and "The Hobbit" by JRR Tolkien 1937; the movies "An Unexpected Journey", "The Desolation of Smaug" and "The Battle of the Five Armies" 2012-2014 directed by Peter Jackson for New Line Cinema Film Company and Universal Pictures. Enya appears courtesy of Warner Music Group (WMG) ©2012

In the office, Paul and Mark are talking as Timothy goes next door as he listens to Paul talking to his father about his first day with Milton and the class. He was talking to the class about the fire safety, how the students moaned because they heard it all before and what Milton's reply was. "He said, 'Simple we get up and run screaming 'bloody murder' down the hall to our designated Fire Assembly point!' It was perfect, dad; all the students roared with laughter."

Mark grimaced and moaned as he says, "Oh Paul, I really HATE class clowns; they are always making jokes!" Paul chuckled into his mug of tea as did Timothy until Paul says before he drinks his tea again, "Still dad, you have to admit, I think he's the first student to liven up a boring fire safety talk." Mark agreed with him there as he said, "Well, I have to admit that you do have a point, the boring fire safety speech really drives us lecturers to the brink of insanity; but we have to do it." Mark drank his tea while he worked on his files in the office as he nodded and admitted, "…but you are right; sometimes we need that bit of laughter to break the tension. So go on and tell me what happened next?"

Paul puts down his mug and reassured his father, "Well, after we did our fire drill comedy; which actually made all the students loosen up," Mark smiled gently at Paul. "It was afterwards that I saw the true, hard-working student who listened, took notes and helped the girls with their work." Paul looked up and saw that Mark was lost in thought as he went to the window and looked at Alyssia who was working away on her pack and talking to the others while Paul stands up and joins him and asked, "You okay, dad?"

He came to the window as the men look out at her working away and helping the other students with their work as Mark says to Paul while the lecturers have the rest of their tea as Timothy joins them. "I just know that Alyssia is my long-lost daughter and your sister and I would take every test known to man to prove it as well," they watch her laughing with her friends. "…she's got to be to be my daughter, Paul." The younger Franklin nodded and left him to go to the sink and he washed out his mug and his father's mug as he placed them on the drying rack and dries his hands as he gets his jacket on and prepares for the second half of the class.

Timothy was sad for Mark and Paul; to know that someone is your long-lost family and you can't prove it…"*it must be torture*," he thought.

Something was keeping Mark and Paul blind to the truth; and that can rip a person apart! So, he had a new mission; he was determined to make sure Alyssia was reunited with her family; but first he needed information and he would talk to Marylebarne about it and how to reunite her with her father. He remembered those two pictures and note that she showed to Sharlene yesterday and he needed to get his hands on them so he could show Marylebarne and the rest of the spirits.

He came back to Earth as he heard Paul say, "Well dad if she is family, she has the teaching gene…" Mark looked at his son puzzled, "What do you mean?" Paul told him, "After the cave in, the Dean and her classmates have elected her to be leader of the group; those three that are beside her, are her helpers of 'Franklin's Circle' at Maddy's Coffee Shop and what's remarkable, is that Milton 'the class clown' Russell and the Caretaker John Preston got her out of Thackeray House after his House fell down her." Mark was shocked, "You mean his House literally fell on her?" Paul nodded. "Pharrell said that the building inspectors deemed it dangerous and unsafe. Why do you think Dean Winchell created this study group and excused them from Thackeray class altogether? You heard him saying loudly to the class as the Fire and Rescue crews saw to Alyssia after she was brought out of Thackeray House; *'That will teach you to trespass on private property!'* was his exact words and I saw John writing them down for some reason." Mark says, "He's really gone too far this time," Paul agreed as did Timothy who kept listening as his anger seethed within him. "You're right, in fact, the dean and the principal are ganging up on him to fix up the House and he blatantly denies that there's anything wrong with it." Paul takes in a breath as Mark sighed and thought of Alyssia.

"Look dad, I better get out there for the second half of the class, will you be okay?" Paul asked as he fixed his jacket as Mark says as he placed a hand on his worried son's shoulder, "You do that and yes, I'll be fine. Knock them dead, son; I'm very proud of you." Paul smiled and took a deep breath, "Thanks dad," Paul says happily as Mark gave him a pat on the back, "…we'll talk more later." Mark nodded as Paul leaves the office for the classroom while Timothy left the office for the Tower and for Marylebarne; he needed advice and to tell the others about what he has learned about Alyssia and the Franklins as he disappeared through the shadows and went back to the Tower at Cassious House.

The break was ending as Alyssia and her friends talked as she caught Paul's eye and smiled at him; for this one student alone was on his mind and believing that she was his daughter without a doubt as he could feel his father's emotions being ripped apart at this revelation and not being able to prove it was worse. Paul thought: *'To believe in something and find out it isn't true is terrible, but to prove that you are the father of a child stolen away at seven years old and not being that father is catastrophic. This will demolish him if Alyssia is not his daughter and my long-lost sister.'* She had gone to the ladies room and has just stepped back in as she went back to her seat as class was ready to begin again.

While Paul looked at her and was lost in thought, Milton came up behind him and asked as Paul jumped at his voice. "Why not ask her out? She is beautiful, funny, and smart…" Paul looked at Milton over his shoulder as he said, "There's a rule that teachers are not allowed to date students," Paul asked Milton the same question, "…why don't you ask her out?" Milton looked at him, came from behind him, patted his back saying as he left him, "Sorry mate, not my type!" Paul shook his head and now he knew why his father hated class clowns as he said to himself while he watched Milton go back to his seat and chuckled out in a low whisper: *"Gee sorry I asked!"*

Milton had come back to his girlfriends as Paul saw to everyone was working away on their packs, talking quietly amongst themselves as Alyssia took in a deep breath and looked around as Adrianne looked up at her and asked, "Hey," Alyssia looked at Adrianne, "You okay, you seem a bit distracted?" Alyssia smiled and put her pen down as she stretched, "Just thinking of my lost family and how we used to be, Adrianne." She nodded as she took her hand as she felt a sob threatening to overwhelm her. "I just heard someone said that they were going to play catch with their baby brother; I looked up and choked back tears as I thought of my brother."

Alyssia took in another breath as Adrianne says, "Its okay…" she gives Alyssia a rub on her arm. "I know how emotional it must be for you right now, but we are here to help you see it through; especially what you have been through." Alyssia rubbed the hurt, the frustration and the memories out of her face as she continued, "Just hang on to us and we'll get you to the other side of this nightmare they call LIFE!" The girls chuckled quietly as Alyssia took a swig of water and they got back to work as Paul comes over to see how the quartet is doing and looks at their work…until the fire alarm went off as Milton dropped his pen and shouted, "Fire! Ah…I don't want to die!" He had practically ran down the steps, and out the door as the other classes were calmly exiting their classrooms while the class, including Paul, were leaving the room as the students left in an orderly fashion while they could hear Milton still shouting, "Put out the flames! Put them out!" Paul, still shaking his head as the others start out the door to the designated fire assembly area, gets his roll call sheet and they leave the room with his dad as he followed the rest of the class who were still chuckling.

They all came to the fountain feature while Milton sat on the edge of the fountain, "See…told you all my way was better!" Alyssia held in a chuckle, Amber face palmed and Adrianne wanted to push him into the fountain while Paul took roll and shook his head. "Adrianne finally said after a few minutes, "You are a mental case Milton Russell, do you know that?" Milton then gave her a goofy grin and says as he puts his arm on her shoulder, "Then go out with me! I can show you my mental health certificate to prove that I'm sane!" He wiggled his eyebrows at Adrianne as she looked at him and her friends chuckled while Milton gave her a kiss on the nose.

"EWWW MILTON LIPS!" she cried out while she wiped her nose and walked away as Milton felt her leave and he fell over on to his hands and watched her lovingly as Alyssia and Amber giggled at the scene before them. "What a woman! I am going to marry her one day!" Alyssia chuckled and said, "Not unless she drowns you first!" Milton looked back at Alyssia and said as he flicked some water in his girl friend's direction and they flinched and chuckled, "She can't drown me, I'm her mister right and one day she will be mine, what do you say to that?" Alyssia says, "Well Milton, if Adrianne makes you happy, I wish you luck in catching her because it looks like every guy on the campus wants to nab her so you better get in there and seize the opportunity when you can."

Just then, Paul is coming towards the trio as he reads the roll; "Alyssia?" he looked up and says, "Check. Amber?" he looked up at her as she smiled,

"Check. Mental case Milton?" He looked at the jester as the girls held in a giggle as Paul smiled and said, "Check!" Then he walked away as Milton shouted back, "Hey Paul admit it; my way was better!" Paul just lifted his hand and went on taking the roll leaving the girls hiding a smile under their hands. Adrianne got the girls together as the class came over, "We just heard from another class that Cassious House was supposed to be demolished about a year ago…but the council would not allow it!"

Another girl came forward and told them quietly, "Alyssia this is Becky, she's the councilman's daughter, just listen to what she had to say: "Alyssia, according to a general meeting held a year ago, some land developers asked the council that they could give them new houses on Cassious House grounds and make money off the rent, if they were given the go ahead from my father to demolish the house. But the "Save Cassious House" Project heard about it and planned a huge demonstration if father went ahead with it."

"So, they sent in the leader of the Project to speak to my father and made a strong case against it and my father was furious at the developers for suggesting such a thing and he told them at the general meeting that; '…with the land still cursed, it would scare off potential buyers and the land would be worthless.' The developers then argued that would not be a problem but dad said, '…the land is cursed and therefore no good to anyone until such time the curse is lifted. Many people have died needlessly or have disappeared including those three boys and until the curse was lifted, the House still stands. It's part of our history as well as being the first listed building in this area and if you tear it down, it would be a desecration to our history as well as our past and our heritage…the House stays!' and he adjourned the meeting as he gave more money to the caretakers to keep Cassious House safe from intruders and upkeep of the grounds.

The developers were furious and my father warned that if they continued to defy his decision, he would fire the whole lot of them! They backed off and father was praised by the Project for a "wise decision." I hope that was a bit of help Alyssia?" She nodded as she looked at the House and says, "It was Becky…I had asked an officer about it and he told me that it was still standing while I was on my way here three in a half weeks ago. Thank you, and if I want a transcript of the meeting, I will ask you for it, Becky and hope your father will give a copy of the general meeting. Again, thank you Becky I will keep that in my head and at the back of my mind!" Milton was running his fingers through her scalp and says, "Funny I don't see a filing cabinet drawer handle in your brain!"

Everyone chuckled as she told him, "You are too much Milton, and you know that?" He gave her a hug and said, "…but you love me?" Alyssia smiled, patted his cheek, as Paul came over and says, "That's the 'all clear' given to return to the building." They all nodded as Paul watched the group of classmates walked back to Franklin House to continue working away on their packs on Haunted Houses as they said goodbye to Becky while she returned to her classmates as Wednesday afternoon wore on.

After the fire drill, Paul watched everyone getting back to working away on the pack as he sat at his desk and tended to his own work until a few minutes later, he heard a gentle voice beside him and looked up at Alyssia who got a chair and sat beside him as she had a question for him in the pack. "I couldn't make heads or tails of it, Dr Franklin, and the students are a bit be-fuddled of the wording as well…can you help?" she told him. He re-wrote the question for her, "I can surely do that for you and the class, Miss Jenkins." He re-worded the question while he asked gently, "So how's it going for the first week?"

Alyssia smiled as she thought, "Well, let's see; a House fell on top of me yesterday, knocked down by a lecturer while getting my schedule on Sunday…meeting you and your father, and gaining three or more new friends on Monday…I say it's going rather well." He smiled he puts the re-worded question up on the board and lets the class know it and then he gives back the pack to Alyssia as she placed the chair back where it belonged, and goes back to her seat. "I hope that clears it up Alyssia, thanks for bringing it to my attention." Alyssia nodded and went back to her table as Paul got the group talking about what they had written down as others took notes and listened to what was being said.

The class talked about the answers they have written down, taking notes, listening, sharing views and opinions, asking questions, stopping debates and changing the subject back to Haunted Houses all the way up to lunch time. Mark had come out of the office and listened to all the debates and opinions and how Paul was handling the class as he looked at Alyssia afar off while Paul wrapped up the class. Paul jumped as he saw him sitting there, "Hello dad-" He smiled as he asked Paul quietly to have Alyssia stay after; "I have an idea of how she could help us…" Paul nodded as she turns back to the class. "I need you all to start on assignment two in your packs and for next Wednesday morning and for everyone to read up on chapter one for Mark's class and answer the questions at the end of the chapter for Monday morning. Remember, no writing in the textbooks!" Milton called out jokingly, "Yes dad!" The whole class chuckled as Paul wagged a finger at him. "Just do as you're told!" he scolded sarcastically at Milton.

Alyssia wrote down her homework assignments and closed the notebook as she and her friends got ready for lunch time as Paul calls out, "Alyssia," she looked at Paul who was coming up to her, "Could you stay for five minutes? My father wants to talk to you…" Alyssia asked, "Did I do something wrong, Paul?" He placed a reassuring hand on her arm; "Not at all, my dad would like to talk to you that's all." She nodded as Paul went downstairs as Milton says, "Watch he doesn't kiss you…" she laughs as Paul shouted to him without looking back; "I HEARD THAT MILTON!" She chuckled as she says while she pats his shoulder, "I will make sure of that, Milton!" The friends leave them as Amber says, "we'll wait for you outside."

She nodded as the men waited for the room to be completely cleared out as Mark came up and they all sat down as he got straight to the point. Mark takes her hand and says, "I need you to do me a favour," he said gently. "No doubt that you heard about Sidney Preston's murder at Cassious House from my son?" She nodded, "Yes, it resulted in the separation of my mum from my father and brother; Why?" she asked pulled out a spare pad and pen out of her purse while Mark held back tears as he continued. "I want you to dig up everything you can on Cassious House and any new evidence that you may have on my assistant's death no matter how small or insignificant it may be. I want to know everything; family background, history; anything you can find that will help. You know that I can't go near the House after his death…it still haunts me to this day, so I need you to do the research for me; will you do it? I need to prove that Sidney's death was murder and not of supernatural forces."

She wrote down all that is said as she showed them and the teachers approved it as she told them, "I'll be going away to Welling Street down by the sea on Thursday afternoon to pick up some material for a research project, if there are any books you could recommend to me before I go to Welling Street, may I have them? And what books are good to get out of the University library for this course? It's for the study group on Thursday morning and I will be getting the group to get their notes together for the open report."

Mark smiled and says, "I will get the list for you right now, hold on." She nodded as Mark left the table for his office while Paul spoke to her while they waited and replied, "You can get all the help you need for this report at the library at the Welling Street Museum…about the House I mean; and the University Library is good too and they have books about this class for the newbies such as yourself. Just give the list to the librarians and they will give you all the books they have for the report for first time University students."

She nodded as she asked Paul curiously, "Why do you want to prove that Sidney's death was 'murder'? I thought it was settled already?" Paul nodded, "I know but there is an inquiry being launched in May about some dodgy dealings at the coroner's office. If you can help us that would be a massive help to us and put my father's fears and Sidney's spirit at rest once and for all." Alyssia smiled and says, "I understand now Paul and I will do my best for you and I won't leave anything out, promise." Paul smiled as Mark came back with the list of books and gave the paper to her, "There you go…as promised, you can go now and get some lunch and we'll see you next week."

Alyssia took the list and placed it in her notebook, closed it, then placed in her purse as they dismissed her. "Alyssia," Mark calls out as she reached the door and turns around to Mark as he says gently with Paul by his side as both men stood up; "Thanks again for your help and good luck with your research; we're looking forward to what you have found out." She smiled gently and opened the door as she tells them, "Till next week gentlemen, have a great weekend. Paul I'll see you tomorrow at the coffee shop?" The men nodded a good-bye to her as Mark watched the door close behind her, "You too my sweet baby girl." Mark whispered and Paul placed a comforting hand on his shoulder as Mark looked at him with tears rolling down his cheeks as Paul had an idea.

"Let's go and get some lunch elsewhere. I know where there's a great place that serves a full English breakfast for a fiver and we also need to pick up some things at the shop while were out. I think we need to get away from here for a while;" Mark agreed as he rubbed the tiredness out of his features and sniffed away more tears. "That sounds like a plan, Paul... let's get cleaned up." They leave the room after Paul cleans up the desk and they get ready to go off campus as they turned out the lights in the classroom and head for their office.

Back at Cassious House in the modern part of the east wing, Timothy came out of the shadows and appeared into her home as he looked around to see what he could learn about her and get to know her better. Questions rolled around in his mind: What does she like? How does she spend her time? Is she funny, serious, a dreamer? What makes her laugh, cry, angry? Is she a child at heart? An intellectual? He had to know as he looked around her home only to find simplicity which meant she hated difficulty and complication as well as chaos. He looked at her books and DVDs and found out that she liked William Shakespeare, J.R.R Tolkien, Philip Pullman, Andrew Lane, Sir Arthur Conan Doyle, Agatha Christie, Jane Austen, Oscar Wilde, Robert Louis Stevenson, and Lewis Carroll. Her music ranged from Enya, The Carpenters, John Denver, Religious and Classical music as well as movie soundtracks. He nodded and thought: *'Literate and intelligent with a love for the arts... She's a dreamer with funny and serious side firmly balanced with a child-like innocence about her which keeps her grounded and happy.'*

She was a kid at heart from animation like "SHAUN THE SHEEP"[16], "THE MUPPETS"[17], "DISNEY"[18], "MINIONS"[19], "ANIMANIACS"[20] and other films like "TWISTER"[21], and "SAN ANDREAS[22]" which talked about the power and beauty of Mother Nature, and he chuckled at her GARFIELD[23] and SNOOPY[24] comic books, her stuffed animals, she loved her pictures and posters of her favourite actors that were dotted around her home as well as her display of dragons and craft work made him think as he looked at owls and cats displays as he thought: *'Needs to feel secure and have interests… also very imaginative and creative and loves animals.'*

He saw her cat Mystery coming into the living room and jumping up on her couch as she curled up and went to sleep after her lunch and bath as he stroked her fur and gave her a rub on her ears; "Aww" he said aloud as he smiled, "You're lovely and sweet…bet you love to keep her company, eh?" The cat loved a good rub on her ears as Mystery purred away loudly as he looked closer at all the books on her shelf and found that she was a lover of learning and knowledge and that was good to know and she also loved doing research and kept her mind open to new things.

He saw her family pictures dotted around her home as he went into the kitchen and saw how clean and uncomplicated everything was simple and neat. He kept his eyes on the clock as he went to the bedroom and glanced at more family photos on her dressing table as he saw a computer on her desk as he saw plays and scripts all around it as well as photos of famous people and her friends. *'She likes to read and write a story…strengthens her creative and imaginative abilities and loves to stay busy when boredom rears its ugly head.'*

---

[16] "Shaun the Sheep" ©2016 by Aardman Animation by Nick Parks 5th of September 2016

[17] "The Muppets" by Jim Henson ©1955 The Jim Henson Company

[18] "The Disney Company" © Walt Disney 16th 0f October 1923

[19] "The Despicable Me Franchise and Minions" ©2010 by Illumination Entertainment by Pierre Coffin, Kyle Balda and Chris Renaud

[20] "Animaniacs" ©Warner Brothers The 13th of September 1993

[21] "Twister" ©Amblin Entertainment/ Universal Pictures by Michael Crichton 17th of May 1996

[22] "San Andreas" ©Warner Brothers Pictures 21st of May 2015

[23] "Garfield"© by Jim Davis 19th of June 1978

[24] "Snoopy" "Charlie Brown" and PEANUTS ©Charles Schultz 2nd of October 1950

And just when he thought he knew everything about her; he saw photos of a place that was dear to her heart: Orlando, Florida USA and the Disney Theme Park EPCOT[25]and the HOLLYWOOD STUDIOS[26] in earlier times in pictures: *'She must have been there and these places are close to her heart'*, he thought as he saw one of the comic books on her night table as he placed the book into his pocket as he absorbed her surroundings quickly. He looked at the clock as he thought in fear: *'I better head back to Marylebarne; he might wonder where I've got to; and if he knew I was here, I would be in trouble-I'm supposed to be sleeping.'*

He faded away into the shadows and went back to the Tower with one of her books in tow and chuckling away at Snoopy and Peanuts until he looked up and saw Marylebarne standing in front of him as he jumped. "Marylebarne!" he said as he calmed down and held on to her book as the advisor says with an eye roll. "Oh come on I'm not that bad, I was wondering where you were?" The Prince smiled embarrassingly, "I-um…" he said it quickly, "I was looking around her home." He was about to say something as the Prince said quickly, "Yes I know-I'm not supposed to be there; but I wanted to get to know her better."

He stood like a bad child who broke the vase with a baseball and lowered his head in shame; but Marylebarne just smiled and chuckled happily saying, "That's wonderful to hear…" The prince was very confused and shocked as Marylebarne continued to cheer. "It is?" Here he thought that Marylebarne was going to scold him…but now he was cheering? He thought: *'What's wrong with this picture? First you tell me not to go to the East Wing and now you're cheering? Great I expect to be yelled at, but you're cheering me instead?'* "Marylebarne, stop cheering!" He shouted as the advisor looked at him as he calmed down. "I disobeyed you…I thought that you would be angry with me?" The advisor says still chuckling, "I lifted that rule a long time ago, my boy, you were a youngster back then and the small flats were getting built at the time; you must have not been told that the rule was lifted!?"

Timothy was exasperated as he took in a deep sigh and says annoyed, "No I guess I wasn't told about the rule being lifted," as he shoved the book

---

[25] "EPCOT Centre" ©Walt Disney Company opened October 1st 1982

[26] "Disney MGM Studios/Hollywood Studios" ©Walt Disney Company the 1st of May 1989

into his pocket. Marylebarne came to him and says gently with his hand on his shoulder as they walk back to the Tower, "I'm very much delighted that you are starting to care, share and keep her company. You have made me the happiest advisor ever, your highness." He went back to cheering for him as the prince smiled and says as he took out her comic books on "Snoopy and Charlie Brown."

The prince smiled at him as he replied, "Thanks, my friend; I appreciate your kindness and support." Jesterson then woke up asking as he opened the door to his quarters, "Hey, what's all the hub-bub?" The cheerleader Marylebarne told him the news as he asked the Prince, "Tell me; does she like to laugh? I can handle it!" Timothy says with a chuckle, "Yes she loves to laugh; in fact, she is practically a kid at heart." He was about to tell them what he had learned, until they hear a door closed downstairs.

"That's Alyssia coming back for her lunch before she goes to her afternoon classes; I better go and get some rest, goodnight." Jesterson called back, "Remember you owe us what you have learned…" Timothy says, "I have not forgotten, Goodnight Marylebarne and Jesterson." They all say their goodnights to him and he went back to his room with one of her "Snoopy and Charlie Brown" books after they all bowed as he closed the door and sits down on the bed as he looked at her book and chuckled at Snoopy's antics.

While back in the East Wing, Mystery jumped down from the couch and mewed at her 'hellos' to her as she dropped her bag on the couch and picked her up and said as she rubbed her kitten's ears, "Hello my sweet girl, ready for some lunch?" Mystery mewed happily as she carried her to the kitchen and gets Mystery's and her lunch while getting ready for her classes for the afternoon.

While she waited for her lunch and Mystery was fed, she placed all the work from Paul on the table along with Mark's and the paperwork on what the students should focus on was written down and placed neatly on the pile. Right now, she was focusing on her other core skills classes and looked at the schedule as she marked down her room numbers at Franklin House while she watched the time to get back to the campus as she thought that Monday and Wednesday morning work were coming together nicely: *Just like the pieces of a jigsaw puzzle were fitting together easily and nicely…* and her lunch beeped and she took it out of the microwave.

While she was having her lunch, she made out a 'to-do' list of what was needing done; then after that, she puts the pens and folders into her bag and got ready to go back to the campus until Timothy paid her a quick visit. "Hello Alyssia," he said as she looked up and smiled as she saw that he had her comic book. She smiled at him as he said looking down at the paperback, "I-I was just returning your book." Alyssia smiled and replied shyly, "Snoopy is very funny and so are his human friends." She observed, "You must be a very fast reader…" she said as she put her folders away neatly then her text books that sat above her folders on the bookshelf and closed the bag as she came to him to take the book from him.

Their hands touched and they looked back at each other and chuckled as they smiled rather shyly as he tried not to react while she replied gently, "I-I love Snoopy; he makes me laugh when I need it; like yesterday," and she placed the book back on the book shelf after he lets it go. She placed it with her other comic book as she turns back to him and quickly replied, "I-I'm glad that you're getting to know me better, Timothy," she said as she gets ready to go back to the campus, "I'm as harmless as a kitten."

The couple chuckled as she told him, "But seriously, Timothy; please help yourself to any of my books that are of interest to you." Timothy smiled and was rather surprised at her openness, "That is very kind of you, thank you." She smiled at him and then looked up at the clock and said, "Well I never had to live next door to Spirits before." He chuckled as she looked at the cat clock ticking away above the kitchen door frame as she replied not looking at him, "I'm not ignoring you, my dear prince; I'm just watching the time to go back to the campus." He looked behind him and saw a cat clock over her kitchen door frame and then he turned back to her as she was close to him; "…so I better go or I'll be late." She openly kissed him as she stroked his cheek as he smiled when he looked deep into her eyes. "Okay take care;" she wiggled her eyebrows at him, "I'll see you later tonight, handsome."

He smiled as he watched her leave for the campus as the door closed and he melted into a pile of goo just as Marylebarne came to him after she closed and locked the door and saw a pile of goo on the floor as he watched Timothy come back to his human form. "I think I'm in love, Marylebarne. I think that she might be the one to break this curse; but I better take my time and get to know her properly, not rush in where angels feared to tread.

I did that once before and look at what happened; cursed." The advisor gave his charge a pat on the back as the Prince looked at him, "I think that's a good idea and it's about time you introduced Jesterson and me to her and it's time to show her Cassious House as well."

Timothy was worried about the dark spirits on the landing-the thick black veil which covered the stairwell to the first floor like a swarm of killer bees or hornets ready to sting anyone that would dare get too close. "But what about the evil dark veil on the landing? No," he thought pacing back and forth. "No I can't risk it, Marylebarne; even the caretaker has told her that the House is off limits, she told me so herself." He stopped him and said wisely, "My dear Prince, it will be daylight so the evil cannot harm her. But if will make you feel any better, I will talk to Kevin Parks and see if we can get permission for Miss Jenkins to enter the House."

Timothy nodded but still had his doubts as Marylebarne says as he placed a hand on his shoulder for reassurance, "Just bring her to the House and we'll protect her." Timothy still wasn't sure as Marylebarne said, "The dark spirits can't harm her in the daylight, my dear Prince-trust me; she will be in no danger." Timothy reluctantly agreed and he nodded as they disappeared into shadows and back into the Tower as the afternoon meandered on. Timothy went to his room and paid attention to his studies until she came home while Marylebarne left him to his studies and understood Timothy's hesitation and his worry of the dark veil, but he would talk to Kevin Parks anyway and that should make Timothy happy.

Back on campus, she got to her classes in Franklin House as John caught her eye and she waved to him as he waved back as he discreetly took off his gloves and tapped on his earpiece and called on his superior and Stuart's father Kohl Thackeray at the Kelton Heights Constabulary. "Boss," he began as he said in a whisper while he was planting some flowers, "I need all the information you have on an Alyssia Franklin-Jenkins as well as everything on Doctors Mark and Paul Franklin and George Thackeray family; I'll be by to pick up the folders later." Kohl agreed and John tapped off the earpiece, put back on his gloves and got back to work.

Inside Franklin House, she joined Milton and the girls and they lead her to another room as they found the English Literature class she is to attend as they would be next door with Communications after he pulled a face to her to make her laugh. She gets into the classroom as the trio would meet up with her again in Philosophy class just down the hall as they agreed and said their goodbyes as they went their separate ways to their classes.

During her break time from English Literature, she went to the library and gave the librarians the list of books she would need for the study group from Mark Franklin and the elder librarians told her, after looking at the list, that the books would be ready first thing in the morning. She smiles and thanks the kind librarians as she went back to Franklin House for her last class of the day with her friends in Philosophy class down the hall.

After class, the quartet and her classmates all said their goodbyes and Alyssia told them that she would see them at Maddy's Coffee House tomorrow morning as they all parted ways. After dinner, Alyssia worked on her 'to-do' list and did all that was required of her; lesson plans, rough drafts, mind maps and notes were all over the table and somewhere in that mess were her text book on "Ghosts" and a pack on "Haunted Houses." While she got everything together and in a neat pile, she placed everything in the appropriate folders and placed them in the poly pockets inside and in order as the early evening went into ten thirty at night.

Timothy and Marylebarne were watching her as she worked; "My goodness," Marylebarne said shocked. "All this work to pass courses; how does these humans do it?" Timothy replied as he shrugged, "I don't know Marylebarne; maybe it's to prove how clever they are or maybe to make the world a better place." The men watched as she placed her folders back on the shelf and got Franklin's work put away in the back pack with all the mind maps, lesson plans, notes and other work in folders and into her backpack ready for tomorrow.

Just then, she saw Timothy coming out of the shadows with Marylebarne as she smiled while Jesterson ran out of the shadows and apologised for being late as Timothy smiled and the two gents finally met Alyssia. "This is Marylebarne my advisor and Jesterson; two of my friends from the Tower... they wanted to meet you Alyssia;" the Prince said as she shook hands with them. "It's good to meet you both; Timothy told me all about you... all good, trust me."

The men chuckled as Marylebarne kissed her hand and Jesterson gave her a leg up as she chuckled and Jesterson liked her right away and so did Marylebarne who gave her an invitation to come to House next door; "I would be honoured Marylebarne, but what about Kevin Parks; he is very protective of all of you?" Marylebarne says as Timothy took her hand into his as she briefly looked at him and then back at the advisor, "You leave it to me; I'll make sure you are free to come and go as you please." She nodded a 'thank you' to the advisor while Jesterson pulled a trick on her as she and his friends laughed. Timothy was happy that they had met her; but then a yawn played across her face as that was the signal that she was tired as Timothy says, "I think it's someone's bedtime."

She laughed and says as a small, whiny child, "But I'm not tired..." Timothy laughs gently as she said, "Just kidding, I have a half day tomorrow- it's a study group day so I better 'hit the hay' early tonight; got a lot of books to get from the library for the study group first thing in the morning." Marylebarne says, "Hit the hay?" She turns back to the advisor who looked a bit puzzled at the choice of words. Timothy smiled as she explained, "Its slang for, "I'm going to bed early tonight and to make sure that I take the pitchfork out first." Jesterson laughed at that joke with her as Marylebarne stroked her cheek as she laughed. "You humans are so fascinating, I don't think that I'll ever get used to your language or your world," Alyssia says to him in a whisper, "...it's better that way."

Marylebarne patted her cheek as she replied, "I guess to you, we are an odd bunch Marylebarne, and sometimes I don't understand humans too." He smiled and said to Jesterson, "...but at least we can laugh and have a good time;" Jesterson whispered, "He's the hardest man with a dry sense of humour; he never laughs at anything!" Marylebarne shot Jesterson a look as the jester hid behind Timothy as Alyssia laughed. "Well, I know one thing for sure that this is going to be interesting year for us all; I hope you don't plan to move, Alyssia? I have grown quite fond of you."

Alyssia touched the Prince's cheek, "Where would I go? I have no intentions of leaving; you all have made me very happy already and warmly welcomed; I thank you all for what you have done for me." The men smiled as she added, "But there is one thing; I cannot tell anyone about my encounter with you or I'll be sent away to a padded room!" The trio looked at each other as she continued, "I must respect your privacy and, in return, you can respect my decision on this matter as I don't want this House to be invaded by anyone. Kevin Parks has had five generations of

Parks guarding this House; I would not want to be the one to violate his trust for what he is trying to do for you."

They nod as Timothy says, "She is right, Stanley has been our guardian and protector since 1862 and telling anyone about her encounter with us would start an invasion; the dark spirits would be feasting for eternity and the curse would never be broken; I will respect her decision," Marylebarne and Jesterson also understood and said, "…then we respect your decision as well." They all shook hands as the advisor says his goodnights as well as the jester while they fade into shadows while Timothy escorts her to her bed chambers and he holds her close.

"I'm so glad that you like them, Alyssia; they will watch over and protect you like I do." He kissed her cheek and says his goodnights to her; "I will be back at midnight to see you through to the next day, safe and sound, if that's what you want?" She kissed his cheek and smiled, "I want that so much, Timothy; thank you for guarding me." He hugged her once more and then he disappeared into shadows…"Till midnight, my sweet maiden, sleep well."

He leaves her to get changed into her night clothes, sets her alarm, gets into bed and she reads her book, "Shakespeare in Love" before she drifts off to sleep. Mystery, who didn't want to be on her own, comes running into her room, snuggled beside her as she puts her book away and turns out the light as the kitten and her owner fell into a deep sleep and sweet dreams as Timothy comes to her and guards her till the dawn breaks in the East.

Chapter 4

Early Thursday morning came as her alarm went off at seven-thirty in the morning. She got up, showered, changed, made the bed as Mystery followed her to the kitchen to get fed as she checked her schedule and found that there were no other classes in the afternoon so the rest of the afternoon was hers; to do her homework and fill in gaps in her report for Franklin's class…even Adrianne recommended a book that she saw in the library and added that book to the list and she only hoped that the campus library had it.

But before she could do that, she had her breakfast; and with a bowl of cereal and a glass of Apple juice, which just hit the spot, she was ready to face the day. But what she couldn't help thinking about was the Spirit of Cassious House and its past; she looked at the key and curtain and just for a moment, it made her think that maybe, just maybe; there was something more to the House than meets the eye. Sharlene was right to ask the question about the history before the House was built; *That does it!* she thought, *I will make a stop at the Kelton Heights Visitor Centre and Museum to do my own research…then it's off shopping and bill paying;* she sighed and said aloud, "My work is never done."

She went to the sink and washed her bowl, glass and spoon, sets it on the drying rack, looked out for her folded book caddy, picked up her backpack and coat as well as her keys, and headed off to the campus; but what she didn't notice is that Marylebarne had appeared in the shadows as he thought with a smile: *Such a hard worker and curious to boot…it's time to introduce her to Cassious House, better go and talk to Kevin Parks about Alyssia entering the House.* He disappears into shadow as he heads back to the Tower to make plans as he sees Timothy and Alyssia waving at each other as she disappeared down the driveway.

At Thackeray House, Stuart Thackeray woke up to his alarm, got up, showered, changed and got ready for another boring, depressing day at the dangerous House. He sighs after leaving his room and heads down the corridor and into the messy kitchen to have breakfast as the rookie looked out the dirty windows at the birds and sunshine as he poured himself some coffee.

Detective Stuart Thackeray is a rookie cop doing a very dangerous undercover job for the Kelton Heights Constabulary: going undercover as George Thackeray's son. He is tall, reserved, sandy brown hair, green eyes, quite muscular, lean and very handsome, a gardener, and the fourth generation police officer of James Thackeray-Franklin, the first police officer of Kelton Heights and is the son to Kohl Thackeray, John's superior at the Kelton Heights Constabulary. A deadly sharp shooter, expert rock climber, served his country in Iraq and Afghanistan, he is kind, caring, understanding, considerate, and is well-trained SWAT officer. Even though he is a rookie, he appears a bit naïve and will give up easily; but with the right support and friends, he endures, does his job and sees the mission to the end no matter if it's a failure or a success.

He was bored and depressed; there was nothing to do, except sitting around and do nothing but play with his phone and being a teacher? Forget it! George wouldn't let him into the classroom as he thought angrily: *This undercover job stinks! All I do is play with my phone...'* he puts his phone down in frustration as he finished his coffee. *'I need work; I need to be free; I need to be busy. What is he hiding that is so secretive? I will find out and when I do, I will have to wait to get a search warrant to do it properly.'*

He pours himself another coffee and then sits at the table as he put his phone down next to him and hears more of the building falling apart as his frustration grew with the shake of his head; *'...or before the House kills me first.'* He listened to a ceiling falling in down another room as he began to wonder if all this undercover work will be worth putting Thackeray away for life as he looked out onto the campus and wondered what John was doing at that moment while the birds chirped away as another part of the House fell in on itself.

Just as he was rubbing the boredom off his face, George comes in to the messy kitchen whistling a tune as he sees Stuart and smiled brightly as he says in a cheery and jovial voice, "Good morning Stuart my boy. How are you this morning?" Stuart gave him a half-smile. "What's wrong?" George asked still in a good mood as he goes to the window and looks outside. "The sun is shining; the birds are singing..." Stuart looked at him as he said while another wall fell to the floor, "The House is falling apart, the roof caved in down the hall last night and another room has caved in just now," just then they hear the racket of fighting and broken furniture and arguing:"...and now the yokels are up as well."

George sighs and rolled his eyes as he goes over and pours himself some coffee, "Those two will be the death of me; they actually think that a 'spirit' is moonshine that you drink behind the barn." That made Stuart laughs a bit as he puts his mug on the table as George then changes the subject. "In any case, I'll be able to get a new House with expensive cars and all the luxuries I can imagine." Stuart thought as he sighed, *Oh here we go again, the 'when I get Cassious House' spiel all over again! He never shuts up about that House!* Stuart pours himself another mug of coffee and goes to sit down at the table.

Coming from a long line of criminals, George Angelo Sabacini Thackeray is surely living up to the family's terrible reputation. Along with his two country bumpkin's goons, he is on the campus causing trouble again just like his ancestors before him. He is the most hated and unpopular teacher ever on the campus and around Kelton Heights and enjoys making people's lives hell, including the faculty who want them gone.

George says as he joined Stuart at the table with his coffee, "Think of it, my dear boy...You will be able to train bodyguards, snipers, assassins, and bouncers on how to be ruthless and cunning!" Meanwhile, Ted and Ed Ezra were making their presence known as they heard tables and chairs being smashed, arguing, punching as shouted the House down with their ruckus as Stuart looked at George as he asked, "What about them, are they going to be part of your world?"

George heard more crashes and fighting as he said, "I'll give them something to do, yes. But son," he said excitedly as he continued over the racket, "I'll be able to take back Cassious House and re-claim what is rightfully ours. My forefathers were kicked out, shamed, and told that Cassious House will never be theirs so long as the King and the son lived... but now I can change all that, and become the man I've always wanted to be." Stuart's brain thought sarcastically: *Yeah, an annoying ass with nothing but that stupid House on your mind!*

Stuart nodded as he drank his coffee as George got in his face asking, "You doubt me? You don't think I can do this?" Stuart looked at him and as George stared back at him. "Dad," he says with a half-smile, "I'm not saying that…it's a wonderful idea but you do know that the House is haunted by the king's son, do you?" George sat back down as Stuart says, "And then there's the massive black veil of evil on the first-floor landing covering the stairwell with no way around it?" George stopped him and says, "Yes I know that the House is haunted and I know about the dark veil of evil…I've had men sneak in but have never returned, but that will be easily rectified with a secret weapon that I'm developing and then the House will be mine. Those dark creatures moan throughout the night; singing their eerie songs which have lead men to their deaths; but I won't let that happen to me and I will get what's mine."

Stuart smiled as he puts his mug down and says gently, "I'm not saying it's not easy or hard; I'm just making a point. I don't believe that we should antagonise the dark spirits…" George was about to say something until Stuart continued with his logical argument to appease this man. "But if you have something-a way of getting rid of them-then I'm with you, okay?" George smiled happily, "Okay…good. I like it when you speak your mind. It shows intelligence and cunning…" Stuart thought: *'Yeah unlike you who preys on the misery of others! Glad that he can't read minds and thoughts, or I would really be in trouble.'* his mind screams as he drinks his coffee. Then George stands and stretched as he said quite arrogantly, "Now, if you don't mind, Stuart," he said putting his hands on his shoulders and whispered, "I have a class to teach." He puts his mug down as Stuart calls to him, "Hey dad, do you mind if I go out for some fresh air?" George smiled back at him as he stood at the door, "Not at all, knock yourself out, my boy; I'm not holding you back!"

He nodded as he and George exchanged smiles while George turns and leaves the kitchen for his classroom to teach the two Ezra brothers then Stuart reached across the table, got his cup and George's cup, washed them while George leaves the kitchen for his classroom then he gets his phone and coat and leaves the House through the back way for fresh air and freedom as the back door creaked and moaned in the breeze. He gets outside and looked about as the cool air blew through his hair while back door creaked and moaned again as he cursed under his breath until his phone beeped; it was John who was off today and he texted him.

'Good morning'☺ *–JP-* John texted with a smiley face as Stuart smiled. *'I thought that you might need a smile this morning.'* Stuart chuckled as he took in some fresh air as the rookie texted back, *'Good morning, John. Are you off of caretaking duties today?'* -ST- John texted back as he looked out at Stuart who was right by Thackeray House cursing under his breath as another wall or room caved in while the back door creaked more and more as the burly cop giggled at all the curse words he was airing out.

'Yep... You bored? Need something to do? -JP- Stuart was intrigued as he began to think that John was a mind reader or was he looking out his window from the caretaker's hut and observing him? There was only one way to find out as he texted back: *'Yes I do. I'm so bored even the cockroaches and spiders know my name.'-ST-* John laughed his recent message as he texted: *'Ha-ha-ha...well, be bored no longer come by the caretaker's hut near the dean's office window and press in one-four-seven-one into the keypad; I'll let you in, and I will be very happy to give you something to do.' -JP-*'Cool...see you then; oh John almost forgot, have some coffee and a couple of croissants on hand; I'm starving! There's no food in the House that is edible.' -ST-*

John smiled and texted: *'Okay deal. While you are waiting to be let in, delete this entire conversation as soon as you're under the canopy of the hut; the boss man hates it when his number is given out!'-JP-* *'Will do; don't want you to get into trouble with Hyman, he seems to trust you. So I'll see you in a moment,'* Then he looks over to his right towards the Administration Building as he asked, *'...it's the black hut with the greenhouse on the right side, is that it, John?'-ST-* John nodded and was very appreciative of Stuart's help; Hyman would have a go at John if he ever found out about him texting the Caretaker's Hut security code as he texted back to the young rookie: *'Yes, the very one... You'll have to come around by the Dean's window as it's a concealed entrance...-JP-* Stuart smiled as he looked across the campus grounds to make sure he was going in the right direction. *'Understood John, see you soon.' –JP-*

His depressed brain and mood lifted as he put his phone away and leapt for joy and said to himself; "Finally, something to do…" as the rookie headed for the hut near the Dean's office window as his weary legs walked in freedom on the soft, well-manicured lawn while more of the House fell in, including the back door as he rolled his eyes, threw his hands up in the air and then shoved his hands into his pockets of his coat and walked towards the caretaker's hut near the Administration office.

John watched and laughed at all the curse words coming out of his mouth and he went and got the croissants and doughnuts ready to go into the over and the coffee maker percolating for them both so they could start reading over files. Crossing the lawn to the Caretaker's hut, he saw the greenhouse and it told him that he was just about there when he bumped into a familiar face from his traffic stop; "Miss Jenkins, hello…" he said in a cheery voice. She had an arm full of books, a pull crate full of more books and papers hung out from all over the edges of hard covers as a back pack full of her assignments for Mark and Paul Franklin's classes were on her shoulders. The fold-up trolley was heavy-laden with more books as he bent down to pick up a soft cover book that had fallen off the stack as she said, "Oh hello Stuart, it's good to see you again," He placed the soft cover on top of her pile in her arms as she continued, "…and thank you; such a gentleman. You don't see many of them around nowadays."

He smiled and noticed that there was a pretty smile that lit up her features as he asked rather stupidly, "I see that you made it to Kelton Heights safely?" as she tilted the pull trolley to an upright stance as she placed the book, that Stuart gave her back on the stack with her free hand while she replied, "Yes I did, and it's all thanks to a kind old lady, Mrs Mary Anne Parker, who has got my mother's house; I hope to see her tomorrow…so, how are you since that depressing traffic stop? I thought for sure that you would try and avoid me?"

They chuckled as her smile was contagious as he smiled back and said, "I am well. I am just on my way to see John; we got some work to do, and my, oh my, it looks like you have work to do as well?" She looked at all the books in her hands and sighed. "Yes, I do. I'm now in charge of a study group after the House literally 'fell down on me.' Dean Winchell has excused us from Thackeray's House of Horrors and class; I am now appointed to head up the study group as you can see." Stuart was concerned, "I heard about it from John, are you okay?" Alyssia says, "Yeah I'm okay…I've survived worse."

The couple laughed as she nodded her head to the right and said as if she was reading his mind, "…over there ahead of you. The entrance is hidden so go around and it's under a roof hatch which conceals the keypad and would you please say hello to John for me…from Alyssia?" He nodded happily, "I will pass the message on to John thanks. Are you sure you can manage all the books to Maddy's café?" Stuart asked looked and thanked him as she was about to depart, "I'll be okay and you have an appointment with John, I don't want you to be late so I better get going too; class to see to; I hope I see you again, Stuart and please stay safe." He smiled as he replied, "I will Alyssia and you better stay safe yourself crossing that street…"

"I will; thank you…goodbye for now Stuart." She smiled as they part ways as he quickly looked back at Thackeray House to see if anyone was watching after he watched her leave as she heads across the street and he headed for the hut before him. He gets to the black hut and gets into his persona of being an undercover cop as he pressed in One-four-seven-one into the keypad and waited for the door to be opened as he deleted all the messages from John on his phone and switched it off until he hears a click and pushed the door open and goes inside after the door closed quietly behind him after he checked to see if he had his keys and his notebook on George Thackeray in which he did as he left no trace of who he really was back at Thackeray House.

Before him was the greenhouse as he looked around and smiled as he goes inside and sprayed some plants with a water bottle nearby as he looked at all the different kinds of plants and flowers while he waited for John to see him. He explores the greenhouse with awe and amazement while John comes from the right and sees him looking at the plants. "If you get really, really, bored; I'll give you some gardening tips?" John says, as Stuart leaps out of his skin while John laughs. "Don't ever scare me like that again, Detective Preston!" Stuart says in a very low, aggravated voice as John chuckled. "I love seeing you jump; it tells me that you're on your toes…come on in."

Stuart followed John into another part of the hut and saw some living quarters which looked a bit messy but clean and tidy. A laptop with paperwork sat on a table while all around the living area and a small, clean, but tidy kitchen as John made some fresh coffee and brought out some frozen croissants and doughnuts as he placed them in the oven on low heat. John says, "Have a seat, Stuart; I'll be right with you." The rookie nodded as he asked John as he sat on his "low to the ground" couch as he looked around, "Nice place you got here John." The burly caretaker smiled as Stuart asked, "By the way, were you just reading my mind or did you observe, as you always do, that I was BORED out of my mind?" John was puzzled as he looked at the rookie and he said, "When you texted me a few minutes ago, you asked if I was bored?"

John says happily as he got some plates as the coffee machine was percolating away, "I saw you outside in the fresh air near Thackeray House so I wanted to give you a change of scenery with clean windows, plants, doors not falling off their hinges, pipes that are not falling off the roof, as well as rooms, walls and roofs not caving in all around as well as something to eat and something different to do." John came out of the kitchen as Stuart looked up at him. "…and yes I was also reading your mind! I read all the swear words you have said about Thackeray and his House; I agree with you entirely! Such colourful metaphors put very eloquently."

The men laughed, "Another two rooms caved in while I was coming to see you by the way and the back door fell over in a breeze, John…there won't be a House left John if Thackeray doesn't give in to his pride and let someone in to fix the place up, but I believe that's wishful thinking, is it?" John took a sigh and nodded his head at what Stuart has to go through; "Thanks I think," so the rookie changed the subject to a happier topic. "…oh and I ran into Alyssia; she says hello.

She was on her way to Maddy's Coffee House to teach a class and she told me about the House caving in on her and Milton?" Stuart said while John got the doughnuts and croissants out of the oven as he put another fresh coffee pot on the percolator while he brought over pot and placed it on the hot stand as the mugs and plates were brought over. Then he got the croissants and doughnuts out of the oven and placed them on the plates and brought them over to the table as he got the butter and jam as well as the milk and sugar out of the cabinet and placed it on the table as he said, "Yes and I'm glad that they survived the cave in, it would be another two murders added to the ever growing list of charges against George Thackeray."

Stuart nodded as John sighed and replied as he finally sat down after taking off his oven gloves while the young rookie got his notebook and phone out and placed it on the table."I was in a meeting with the Administration team and building inspectors for four hours, Stuart; and they have all said the same thing-Thackeray has threatened them all with death if they attempt repair; come on over to the table and I'll tell you more while we have brunch." Stuart stood up from the couch and came to the table as they cleared some work off and John put his laptop aside on an abandoned chair. Stuart came over and sat down as John puts his oven gloves down and they sat had breakfast and as they ate John tells him about the four hour meeting and what was discussed while he rubbed his face of exasperation and frustration.

He told the rookie that he went to the police station to make a report to the sergeant and the commissioner of police about the meetings and that he had to pick up some folders as he says, "I'm glad that you made it over, I need another pair of eyes to look over some files on Alyssia Franklin-Jenkins, the Doctors Franklin and the criminialistic family of George Thackeray that I got from the Constabulary. So, before we begin, are there any developments?"

"Really John, do you have to ask?" Stuart asked as he drank his coffee and as a rookie, he had a job to do and he told his boss everything as he went into his pocket pulled out and opened his notebook as he got his pen for he kept a written account of what was said and told to him as well as what was said between George and him as well as recordings; from complaining about the Ezra brothers to taking back the House. John started to laugh in an angry sort of way as he listened to all of the recordings from Stuart's phone. "Just as I thought…" John says as he shakes his head, as he chomps on a croissant, "…he and forefathers never learn."

Stuart looked at him confused and asked not to insult his intelligence… "I'm sorry John but what are you talking about? Who and his forefathers never learn what?" John could see the look of confusion on Stuart face as he got right to the point. "George Sabacini Angelo Thackeray belongs to a crime-lord family that dates all the way back to Renaissance Italy and they are recorded in the history books and in the Carlton Royal Family History here in Kelton Heights; I was reading up on the history of the town on my spare time to get some information." Stuart chuckled, "John the historian; has a nice ring to it."

He chuckled and continued as he plopped down one folder in front of Stuart as the rookie looked at the file while John gave Stuart a brief History lesson. "The head of the family at that time was a man call Mario Luigi Angelo Thackeray and they were notorious for using fear and intimidation to strike fear and obedience in to the townspeople, and how you may ask? Well, if you didn't as you were told or opposed him publicly; he'd give you the "Death Stare." Stuart looked at him and then back at the folder as John took back the first pot and brought over another fresh pot of coffee as he put the first one back on to percolate after he put in a filter and the coffee beans and then brought over three more full folders of the Thackeray family.

It was like reading the phonebook of crime as Stuart looked at John who brought the files and looked at all the graphic photos of the murders that the Thackerays have done over the centuries after he placed the pot on the coffee maker and flipped the switch as he came back to his rookie. Stuart was almost sick to his stomach at them; and in his head and in his thoughts, he could hear screams of death and torture as well as the people screaming in horror at their loved ones being killed in front of them and crying out for justice.

Stuart put the pictures back in the folders and shut the files quick as he shut his eyes for a moment while sweat poured down his face like Niagara Falls as John was a bit concerned and he placed a hand on his arm. "Stuart, you okay buddy?" He opened his eyes and saw his concerned boss looking back at him as he stuttered out, "T-The "D-Death Stare?" John gave him a half smile and sits down with him as he placed the Franklin Family files in front of him which was nothing compared to the Thackeray file as he asked once more, "The Death Stare?"

John nodded and says as Stuart came out of a nightmare while he quells his queasy stomach as John nodded as the burly caretaker explained, "It's a technique used **only** by the males of the family… it entices death throughout history; and it's been used on men, women and children but not immediately, the first is a beating or a good stern talking to, then it's the deadly "Death Stare" meaning that you are a threat to him and that you must be eliminated. Many people fled the village, others took it, while many others died and others he didn't bother with." Stuart was scared and shocked as John casts his mind back to the family history of the Thackeray clan as he stood and took the plates to the sink and he placed them in the basin of hot water which was already prepared and then, he came back to the table and told his story.

"One story was told, which made me sick, was that one day in Italy… and I still have nightmares! Mario and his thugs herded the entire village of people into a huge barn and burned down a village with animals and livestock, men, women and children; all because the villagers ran him and his people out of town after he failed to take over the town and its people who stood up for what was right. The survivors and relatives who heard about the tragedy said that the police turned a blind eye; eventually finding out that the police and soldiers were blackmailed and bribed to keep the incident quiet."

Stuart was horrified as John continued despite his colleague's shock. "The villagers and survivors of the doomed town were so furious; they formed a huge search party and when they were found the furious mob grabbed all the travelling party while they slept-including Mario, blindfolding them, throwing bags over their heads, tortured them, wrapped hanging ropes around their necks, tied their feet and legs, and hung them from two strong oak trees outside of the town and burned them alive," Stuart was more than horrified, he was disgusted. "Yikes talk about a 'lynch mob'!" Stuart said with disgust as the burly cop nodded.

John smiled to see that Stuart was feeling better as the burly cop asked, "Well if your family and friends were all murdered in that village, you would go after the people who did it?" Stuart nodded as he concluded his history lesson. "Anyway, after justice was served; they gathered all the ashes, took their remains, put them all in canisters and sealed them in an iron box and the men cast the iron box into the ocean in the dead of night; that was the end of the family…they simply died out."

Stuart was still nursing a squeamish stomach as John gave him something to ease the pain as Stuart still wasn't sure what he was talking about or what was going on; but he relied on John and what he was looking for as he looked at the massive files. "Boy talk about dishing out your own brand of justice!" Stuart says gently as John chuckled. "Did they ever get into trouble for it?" John shook his head and said, "Nope, in fact the mayor praised them because he was the one that issued the order from the king. After they heard about the incident of blackmail, all the guards and police who perpetrated the treasonous act of keeping quiet, were either hung, got their heads chopped off or were simply stripped of their titles and everything was seized and they were banished from the land with their families."

Stuart nodded then looked at the files before him as John sat beside him after he got a fresh pot of coffee and mugs. "S-So, what's with the files?" the rookie asked curiously as John says as he gave him a refill pad and pen as he got one for himself. "I want you to learn everything about Alyssia and her missing family as you possibly can. I'll deal with the Thackeray Family file as well as her mother and Sidney. Look over every little detail carefully and if you see something that we may have overlooked, write it down or tell me; no matter how insignificant. She also may hold the key to the past and open the door to the future that will put Thackeray and his goons away for good. So, shall we get reading, or do you need to throw up first?" Stuart mocked his laugh, "Ha-ha," Stuart says as he opens a file, "I'll be fine…" John smiled and patted his back gently and they were off on a reading spree until lunch time as John poured more coffee and the officers got busy.

Meanwhile in the middle room at the back Maddy's Coffee Shop and Business Centre, the tables were set up and ready for her as she dumps her books on the tables then she got the fold up trolley full of books and brought into the room. She shook out her arms and had everything from library books, lesson plans, mind maps, notes, rough drafts, outlines, Paul's important notes and other material needed for the study group, copies that were made and ready to be handed out as soon as the students were in and settled.

She got to work as she hung up mind maps on opposite walls and spreads the scrap paper, post-it notes, index cards and pens/ pencils out all over the tables. She was relieved that first week was almost finished and the aches and pains from Tuesday were almost gone; but her body still felt the bumps and bruises of the roof collapse. Whatever Prince Timothy put in that healing ball, it made a big difference… but today was Thursday and she put Tuesday morning far behind her as she made sure that everything was ready as she got a bigger table and used it to spread out and opened the library books while she placed the handouts in a neat pile on the table and last but not least; she got out her roll sheet and sets the roll call in front of her.

She placed a sign on the door for the students to find her after they got their coffees and it worked as many of her fellow students started to roll in; still sleepy and not awake yet as they said their hellos to her and she welcomed them. "This is the day to get your rough drafts finished," she said quickly as more students rolled in and started to take their seats as many of them told her that they had no idea what to put in their reports; how to word it or make any sense to Doctor Franklin and themselves. "Not to worry, she told them, "Paul and I will be going around the group to each person to see what they have written down, Okay?" they sighed with relief, nodded and they went to their seats.

More students were arriving as she went back to her ready-made desk as Amber and Adrianne came in. "Good morning you two" then she looked again, "Where's Milton? I thought he would be with you?" Alyssia asked as Adrianne got out her phone and began reading a text from him as she says, "Milton texted me saying he's on his way... he texted to say the following;" as she cleared her throat, *'The idiot next to him had his video games on quite loudly all night and that he woke up late because his alarm didn't go off. Would you let Alyssia know that I will be there as soon as I can? Thank you Miss Falconi. —MR-'* she turned off her phone and placed it in her handbag as she looked back at Alyssia and Amber.

"At first I thought he was talking about himself, but unfortunately, it was about his neighbour next to him." Alyssia and Amber chuckled as she looked up at the clock as she replied, "I'll tell him you said that, Adrianne..." Adrianne didn't care as she had a big smile on her face while Amber chuckled and went to find their seats and saved one for Milton. The girls chuckled as Alyssia says, "We still have time-half-day today..." Everyone cheered, "But we still have to finish our report for Doctor Franklin." Then big sigh of disappointment filled the room as the friends laugh.

Alyssia turned to them and told everyone, "Aww come on guys and gals, don't be sad or disappointed... if the reports are done before Monday, you'll have plenty of time to relax, deal with families, do chores or just simply relax. Use the IT facilities at the library or the study rooms that have computers; then you can finish and print them off either at home or at the University; you'll enjoy your weekends better!" Everyone settled for that as Amber asked, "What about you Alyssia? What will you be doing over the weekend?" Alyssia says gently, "I have someone to see tomorrow so I am doing mine tonight and putting it away for Monday."

Amber was just going to ask who until Milton came in with a tray of teas, coffee and a hot chocolate with pieces of cake on plates with forks, milk, cream and sugar. His hair all messed up and his clothes were just thrown on as his back pack was plopped on to the floor, "Oh, look at what the cat dragged in," said Adrianne with a cheesy grin as he shot her a look and said sarcastically, "…hello to you too, Adrianne Falconi!" The girls and the rest of students chuckled as they took their seats until Milton, with a tray of hot drinks, set the tray on Alyssia's table and gave Alyssia her hot chocolate on the table, Adrianne's coffee and Amber's Latte as he sets the tray on the table by the door.

He gave Alyssia a gentle but tight hug as he put his backpack on the table as he whispered, "Sorry I'm late… did Adrianne the sarcastic give you my text?" Alyssia chuckled and said, "Of course and I'm sorry that you had a rough night. What time was it when "Mister Gamer" went to bed?" Milton was seething as he said through his gritted teeth, "Three am…and the landlord was even fuming; this morning I heard them arguing, so I woke up, and got into my clothes, and got here as quick as I could… glad I had my shower last night." Alyssia smiled, "Its fine Milton," she began as she touched his shoulder, "I wouldn't start the study group without you." He smiled as Alyssia passed her hand over the coffees and hot chocolate and asked, "but what's all this?"

Milton says quietly, "I lost a bet;" Alyssia looked at him inquisitively as he explains in a low voice, "Amber and Adrianne made a bet with me that if I made John Preston laugh, they would buy me coffee, but if I didn't; then I have to buy them the coffees." Alyssia says slowly, "Wait, you told John Preston a joke and he didn't laugh?" He turned to Adrianne who just smiled and toasted him as he scowled at her smug smile and then turned back to Alyssia replying, "Hence the jester failed, the girls' coffees and your hot chocolate plus the sad puppy dog face."

Alyssia took his hand and patted his back gently as she took him aside while Adrianne and Amber relaxed with their coffees and cakes.

"Aww Milton, don't be downhearted..." she said gently. Did you know that most of the well-known comedians have had jokes or their stand-up routines bomb? They would go over all the material and look at where they went wrong. They would rehearse and rehearse until they fine-tuned and polished their routine, took all the bad jokes out, and tried them out again and again until success or they just threw them out and thought up new jokes!" He listened to her encouragement more and she continued. "Many have had bad days and they got right back in there until their act was perfect or they started over."

"Case in point; Michael McIntyre once said that he thought he was doing so well when he was performing for Prince Charles for the first time and in front of the whole nation on television. When he played it back, he noticed his jacket boobs and realised that the crowd was laughing at him and not with him. He has since cleaned up his act and polished his routine and still talks about that incident and today, he is funnier as ever." The jester looked at her as she continued making Milton feel better.

"Today, many of them are well-known on television, on the stand-up circuit and in movies...so do me a favour, the next time your jokes or material bombs; don't get down, get new material. Throw out all the old jokes and replace them or simply polish it until you have it down and it's shining like a diamond! Here are more examples for you to think on, Henny Youngman[27] was known for his quick remarks like "I read a book on how to stop drinking-so I threw away the book!" "Can I help you out? Okay, which way did you come in?" "Take my wife, please..."

Milton chuckled as she smiled and says, "Or from Rodney Dangerfield[28]; "I asked my wife if we can have a dog, she asked, 'Have you looked in the mirror lately'?" Or my personal favourite; "Odie is so stupid that he needs to stand on a chair to raise his IQ!" (Garfield by Jon Davis) or my all time personal favourite: - "I just got back from a pleasure trip: I took my mother –in –law to the airport!" (Milton Berle; a famous vaudevillian[29]) Milton laughed harder as she asked him, "You see? It's simple...feel better now?"

---

[27] Henny Youngman:16th March 1906 – 24th February 1998

[28] Rodney Dangerfield:22nd November 1921 - 5th October 2004

[29] Milton Berle: 12th July 1908 – 27th March 2002

The jester hugged her again and said, "Yes, I do…Thank you." The friends smiled as Alyssia waited for the rest of the group as they came in as she looked up at the clock briefly as she rubbed Milton's arm. "We have 5 minutes before we start so why don't you go and clean up and make yourself presentable…" Alyssia asked Milton and he said, "Good Idea, I look like I've been dragged through a hedge backwards." She chuckled as he leaves the room for the toilets while the students relaxed before Study Group.

A few minutes later, Milton came in looking more like himself with all his clothes neat and his hair brushed and clean shaven; "Feel better?" Alyssia asked him. "Much better, thanks." and he gives her a small kiss on the cheek as he finds a seat by Adrianne and Amber. Maddy then came to the door, "Okay is that everyone?" Just then a male student came in quickly with his coffee. "Sorry for the delay, traffic snarl up in the town centre…" she laughed and said as she pats him on the back, "That's not a problem; glad you made it, I wouldn't start the class unless everyone was in."

He smiled and he took his seat with his coffee as she signalled to Maddy, "Thank you Maddy…" she smiled as she closed the door as Alyssia got on with it as she took roll while in the café, Maddy turned the sign over to OCCUPIED and then went back to work to serving customers as Alyssia started to take roll as all phones were switched off.

But for one student; she has got to leave her phone on because she is waiting for a call from the hospital about some blood tests. Alyssia says, "Not a problem; your health is very important than anything else; if you just signal me that you're leaving the class that will be wonderful and we'll get you caught up on what you missed." The female student was thankful and she nodded and went back to her seat as Alyssia took roll. "Okay everyone, shall we get started?" Everyone nodded as she took roll.

Meanwhile on the campus across the street, Mark and Paul were walking over to the Coffee Shop to see the class until a woman named Cecilia Lambert joined them. Cecilia was a middle-aged woman, short, brown hair, glasses, and always in a skirt and blouse. Her brown eyes and sweet round face was always covered in makeup, in fact way too much makeup. Milton told Alyssia once, "The Avon factory exploded on her face" as she and the girls laughed but he meant it a harmless way because he liked her. She also had strict teacher demeanour which scared Milton, but the other girls didn't mind her as long as it kept Milton in line and she spoke in perfect sentences. She could hear every whisper as though she was an elephant, cat or bat hunting for his food at night the class joked, but she didn't care; she adored Franklin's class and took the banter happily.

She called out to Mark and Paul as they walked on; "Good morning gentlemen," she said as the Franklins looked over to see her coming towards the men. "Hello Cecilia," says Paul with a smile. "We're just heading over to the coffee shop to help Alyssia with the class, care to join us?" Cecilia smiled and says, "I love too, besides I have to check the student's communication levels except for Alyssia, she has already completed her Communications study." The men say, "Sounds good-the more help the better. Come on…" and they offered their arms to her, she took them gratefully and headed over to the coffee shop to help everyone.

As they arrive, Maddy greets them and gives them their order as she sees them to the middle room as Maddy knocked on the door while Alyssia was going to get the students to play 'Catch Speedy.' Maddy opened the door slowly as she heard her say, "I need your help -Speedy here is very hard to catch- oh hello Maddy; are we being a little too loud?" Maddy pokes her head in the door; "Sorry Alyssia to interrupt and no not at all-just to say you have visitors…" the owner stepped back and in walked the Doctors Franklin and Cecilia Lambert from the University. "Thank you Maddy… I was expecting them today." Maddy nodded and smiled gently as the teachers came to her while the owner closed the door and she greeted the teachers before her as they came into the room; "Hello there, please come in…" Alyssia said as the teachers came in and over to her make shift desk as Milton stands and bows before them.

"Hey look who's here gang! Our three all-time favourite people; welcome to Alyssia's World of Learning!!" Amber hid her face as Paul laughed, Mark shook his head and Cecilia just grinned as Adrianne face palmed thinking as all the students laughed: *Oh God, he's got his mojo back!* Milton made the class giggle as Alyssia hid a smile with her hand, *'God help us…he's back at it again!'* Mark looked at Paul and asked him quietly, "Let me guess; Milton Russell?" Paul nodded with a proclamation, "Behold dad, the fire drill comedian!" Paul chuckled as Mark grinned while Milton sat back down after bowing to the teachers. "He is harmless and a hard worker, he's just doing this to loosen the tension and stress of the students for their first week on the campus and term."

Mark and the two teachers agreed as well as giggled as they came to speak with Alyssia. "Okay everyone," she began as everyone looked to her, "I need you to relax and talk quietly amongst yourselves while I have a word with the teachers. Why don't you all go on a mini-break and then we'll begin again, okay?" She told the students as they all got up and stretched; some went to the toilets, including Milton, while others cleaned up their mess and placed their dishes on the tray beside the door as the teachers gathered around Alyssia.

"I'm so glad you all are here…we were just going to play a game of 'Catch Speedy the Ghost' by using ideas to trap and bind him; it is a game to help and to give the students ideas as to how to word their reports so it makes sense to you and to them." Then she held up the papers and replied, "I was just going to hand out these before you came in…" Paul said, "Let me do that for you" and she thanked him as she gave him the papers and he started handing them out while Mark looked on and Cecilia says to a nervous Alyssia, "I'm Cecilia Lambert; their Communications teacher. I hope you don't mind if I sit in and watch? I am trying to see what Communication level each student is at writing and spoken levels." Alyssia shook hands with her and says, "Yes I am glad to help you out with Communication and verbal assessment, Miss Lambert. Please relax and enjoy the class."

Cecilia smiled while Paul came back as Mark says, "We've got your back, we're only here to observe and look at the students work so far…" Then the teachers looked at all the students talking with each other as Paul observed, "…and it looks like everyone seems to be enjoying themselves." Alyssia smiled and said, "You don't know how much this means to me; thank you for helping me out." The teachers smiled and said, "We'll be at the back watching and observing, okay?" She nodded as everyone came back in from getting teas and coffees to the toilet breaks as the teachers got to the back of the room as she started again as the class settled down. "Okay everyone, let's start again…"

Just then, Marylebarne and Timothy come into the room from the shadows as they see Alyssia and the students relaxing and getting ready to start class but are surprised to see that they have guests, "The class has visitors, I see?" Marylebarne asked as Timothy looked at them and he looked at Alyssia's lecturers' pictures from the beginning of term as he had her brochure she was reading from the first day of university. "That is Doctor Mark Franklin, PhD on the right," he points to the older gentleman then moves his finger to the left, "and the younger gentleman is Doctor Paul Franklin, PhD; his son. But I do not know the lady beside Paul…" Marylebarne nodded as they stood listening to what Alyssia was explaining about a game to help the students get their reports ready for Monday as Timothy puts the brochure away into his coat pocket.

They listen in the shadows to Alyssia as she says, "As I was saying to you all, I am trying to stop Speedy here from getting out of his trap…" The trap wiggled and bounced in her hands as she continued as the students were afraid. "So we had a talk and he has told me that the only way he would get back in, is if you all come up with any more ideas about what a 'ghost' is from Monday and Wednesday mornings and place them on the mind maps on each wall beside you."

The students take down the notes from the board and placed them on papers, "Has everyone got these notes on the white marker board?" Alyssia asked them as they nodded as she erased the board so that the ghost is free to float around the room. "If you haven't got them, get them from the ones that do so you have them for your own notes. Now before I free the ghost and play this game, I want you all to know that Speedy was hard to trap and it only took a dozen chocolate chip cookies and a glass of milk to lure him in the trap. So if you have any cookies or muffins, better not let Speedy see them, he might gobble them up when you least expect it." The group laugh as Timothy and Marylebarne smiled.

"Are you ready everyone? Pen and papers at the ready…here he comes!" They all watch Alyssia free Speedy from his trap and the ghost floated around the room as she replied, "Then start catching him!" Timothy and Marylebarne laugh as they watch the ghost float around the room as students laugh, "Okay Speedy start scaring!" He makes faces and starts moaning as students' laugh or duck for cover and they start tossing out ideas, writing them on post-it notes and papers as they get to stop Speedy the Ghost in his tracks while they laughed and post ideas in each wall while Alyssia got some mini chocolate chip cookies and a small glass of milk and placed it in the trap. Milton, on the other hand, started to make faces back at Speedy as he slapped him with his ideas on the mind maps around them. The teachers and the spirits laugh as she did the same but Speedy went into panic mode trying to escape from the papers holding him at bay.

After an hour, the mind maps were full of the ideas as the ghost stayed where he was and he frowned. "Aww Speedy, don't be sad," she told the playful spirit. "Why don't you go and see your friends in here and I'll let you go later, okay my friend? I've placed some chocolate chip cookies and some milk in the trap for you... make sure you share those cookies with the others." She told him as the ghost nodded and dived right back into his trap as Alyssia closed the lid while all students believed that they did well in capturing Speedy. Alyssia got their attention and said as she placed the box down carefully on the table.

"You all did it, well done!" The students were chuffed and she says, "Speedy didn't think you would come up with so many ideas in this first week. But you gave him a run for his spirit life and I am very proud of it; especially Speedy who said to me that you all have been paying attention and taking good notes...keep it up!" All the students settled down and put all their notes from each mind map in their notes. She took down each mind map which were full of post it notes and placed them apart on the table as one student asked, "Miss Jenkins, I hear that there are spirits in the White House and in upstate New York as well throughout the history of the United States; is this true?" Alyssia says, "Yes this is true, well brought up! And I guess you all know from my accent that I'm American?" The students and teachers smiled as well as Marylebarne and Timothy as they listened carefully.

"There were stories of builders who died working on the White House, Presidents of the past, between the Revolutionary War and the Civil War, who died while in Office; and a Hessian mercenary who had his head cut off, haunt villages like Sleepy Hollow in upstate New York and was written in a poetic short story by Washington Irving[30]. You see, during the time of 1899 before autopsies were legal, it was against the law to cut up the body of the deceased whether it was a crime or sickness. They believed that souls of the deceased were waiting to be taken up in the final days of Earth to

---

[30] Washington Irving (Poet, short story writer) who wrote "The Adventures of Ichabod and Mr Toad", "Rip Van Winkle", "The Legend of Sleepy Hollow" Born 3rd April 1783- 28th November 1859.

be judged; but when the body has ceased to live, the soul has already left the body… or so I'm told and today that notion is now obsolete, but back in those days, people actually believed it and it was told that if you cut up a body; it was desecration of the soul but if you stole the head of the Headless Horseman, he will rise up and haunt the village to re-claim it."

The students all shivered at the story as she continued, "It was a Halloween story to scare the kids and now, there's a statue of the Horseman and Ichabod Crane who died battling the Horseman and his fate was never solved. You should read the poem sometime when you have a chance… it's very spooky and a lovely piece of work. Or for those who love Johnny Depp, get the movie "Sleepy Hollow" with Christina Ricci, Sir Michael Gambon, Miranda Richardson, Jeffery Jones, Casper Van Dien as well as Christopher Walken; the late Sir John Hurt and the late Christopher Lee[31].

There is also a series on it, I think it's out on DVD or on Netflix (2013-2017)…check it out when you have time." The students nodded and she gives them a quick History lesson, "Okay everyone, get out some paper and a pen, it's time to give you five influential people and a villain; sounds like a movie!" She heard the students chuckle as she wrote on the board:
-   Archbishop David Beaton 1538-1546 ©"St Andrews under Siege" from "St Andrews Castle, Cathedral and Historic Burgh by Chris Tabraham and Kirsty Owen (www.historic-scotland.gov.uk)
-   Alan Turing: the Breaking of the ENIGMA Code: 1912-1954 the Turing Trust ©**2009** (www.google.com/alanturing)
-   Dr Martin Luther King, Jr. 1929-1968 (www.biograhy.com)
-   President Abraham Lincoln 1809-1865 (www.biography.com)
-   President John F Kennedy 1917-1963 (www.historylearningsite.co.uk)

The students were really interested in the history as she says, "These act of defiance rings true today and if you want on your spare time or even add them to your report, look up these sites and these villain and heroes or

---

[31] "SLEEPY HOLLOW" ©Pathé/Mandalay/ 20th Century Fox Films directed by Tim Burton 28th November 1999. Las Vegas and Los Angeles Film Critics Society Awards, 2000, Academy Award for Best Production Design, 2 BAFTAS, 5 Satellite Awards, 1 Art Directors Guild for Excellence and 1 Costume Design Guild Award for Excellence

look up your own. The assassinations of President John Fitzgerald Kennedy in Dallas in 1963 and Martin Luther King in 1968 are examples of this all because they dreamed of freedom for everyone in the United States… and it was on that day we lost our innocence of Camelot and the dream of living in peace and freedom from harm and danger of others who had opposed us are jealous of what we have."

"John Lennon might be haunting the apartments which he lived in with Yoko Ono after he was killed by a deranged fan on the eighth December of 1980 on the steps of his home because he spoke of peace and unity. All these moments in history, all these spirits that haunt and shape our history is to help us learn what we have achieved in the United States as well as the progress that was made. But even in Britain you have spirits who shape your country's history…like the murder of Archbishop David Beaton; who was killed by dissidents and his mutilated naked body hung out the window of St Andrews Castle…how they dug a tunnel to break into the castle by an underground narrow tunnel that still exists to this day and in which I have to say, will not go into without a canary, pick axe, a hard hat, rope, flashlight and the seven dwarfs!"

The students and lecturers laugh and listened, took notes as she remembers one piece of history; "The one I remember the most is the assassination attempt on Ronald Reagan's life and the assassination of Pope John Paul II which lead to armoured cars and Plexiglas windows. Some have even told me of Custard's last stand, in which the Native Americans rose up and killed all his men, even Custard himself…" Milton says jokingly easing the tension and making the students laugh, "Maybe he didn't like spotted dick or Sticky Toffee pudding?" The group laughed as Alyssia says trying not to giggle, "You might be right Milton," as the other students, the spirits and the lecturers laughed as she continued.

"The point is we are all haunted by the past and how the past can shape our present or our future…quoting Benedict Cumberbatch's incarnation of Sherlock Holmes, "There are no ghosts in this world…save those we make for ourselves." (-The Abominable Bride 2015 -) Today, we have made history in 2005 and 2012; we had Barack Obama-our first black president in the White House. So, what influenced our past; has now influenced our future because as we speak, America and Britain is making so much progress that we can't turn back now or go back to the way we are… men went out to make the money while women stayed at home and took care of the children; no- times are changing and those events are changing the way we think, feel, understand and live.

Women are taking on roles that make our country stand out; Case in point- Angela Merkel, the first woman to hold science degree and now is Prime Minister of Germany now in her fourth term, Michelle Obama-first lady of the United States and a role model and motivational speaker as well to all the ladies and girls to every woman out there today. Hillary Rodham Clinton, who became the first female Secretary of State under Barack Obama, helped bring down Kernel Kaddafi and Osama Bin Laden...all these women play a pivotal role in the role of Women Rights who told girls and young women, 'You can be anything you want if you put your mind to it.'"

"Think about this and you can ask your grandparents...during the Second World War while men went off to fight for our freedom overseas, women took over the factories making ammunition, guns, bombs, planes, tanks...all sorts of warfare. They did this through bombing raids and even risking their lives to help others achieve greatness. Women are now entering the military and the police force, even NASA as well as the Secret Service and other careers where men played a dominant role and these women lay their life on the line every day: Christine McAuliffe, first female astronaut and teacher to reach for the stars, Rosa Parks, the first black woman who sat at the front of the bus and made a stand for the blacks in the South during segregation, Sandra Day O'Connor; First Supreme Court Judge, Susan B Anthony, who went to jail to fight for voting rights for women." Cecilia and the Franklins, as well as the Prince and Marylebarne, were impressed at her vast knowledge of history as Alyssia engaged the students who listened very intently as she continued.

"Here in Britain, Alan Turing was the first gay man and Mathematician, to help the Government break the German code at Bletchley Park and win the war before they were caught and executed. But instead, he was arrested for being gay, not congratulated for his efforts and given forced hormonal treatment as well as being the first man to invent the Personal Computer that we use today. He later poisoned himself in 1954 and his work is right now being acknowledged, many years after his death and a pardon from the Queen along with 46,000 other gays that were persecuted, as the man who won the war in the movie "The Imitation Game[32]" with Benedict Cumberbatch. I suggest you all to give it a watch; it's really sad but makes you proud to be British and whose name is now up there with Winston Churchill and Franklin Delanor Roosevelt as heroes of the Second World War; and we are trying so hard to right the wrongs of the past and move forward."

The students, who were all mixed races smiled; and the class at that moment; in that small room in the coffee shop…they were closer and stronger than ever before as Alyssia came from around the make-shift desk and concluded, "Now how about we get to those rough drafts of your reports to make some sense for the lecturers so I can give my tongue a rest, hmmm? Oh and one more thing, the paper that Paul has handed out is very important. Put it at the front of your folders and whatever you do, don't lose them!"

The students nodded as they got out their reports while the teachers made the rounds and looked over the other students work while Alyssia got started on her report. After a while as she looked around the room and at the clock, the students were busy polishing up their reports and correcting mistakes and spelling errors with the help of the visiting lecturers. Alyssia was just clearing up all the books and notes, quotes and references that she was writing down for her own information as Cecilia came to her after all the books she had were put away in the folding trolley and she was given pamphlets from Alyssia as Cecilia read them quickly. "These are great ideas….where did you get them?" she asked as she looked through them with interest as Alyssia says, "Dundee and Angus College had them out or put them in Fresher's bag to help them when doing a report and to protect them from plagiarism that may get them expelled. As for me, I use them, Cecilia, to remind myself what is required at times. The paper that Paul handed out is important information as what is required in their reports…"

Cecilia nodded and smiled. "I will look out these pamphlets and give them to the students, thank you for this. I think Kelton University have them somewhere; I'll ask Dean Winchell for them…thanks for the reminder and I will make sure that Paul gives me a copy of the paper for

---

[32] "The Imitation Game"©2014 (November 28th 2014) Directed by Morton Tyldum by Black Bear Pictures and Bristol Automotive…starring Benedict Cumberbatch and Keira Knightly.

my records." The ladies smiled and she gets back to working with the group while Mark and Paul helped the students get their notes sorted and in a proper place as the lady who left her phone on says, "I had a talk with the Doctor while you were talking with the teachers: everything is okay...my doctor gave me the all clear on my blood tests."

Alyssia was so happy and gave her a hug. "I'm very happy for you. How is your report coming along? Have you seen the lecturers yet?" The young woman says, "I have and I'm getting help with report writing from Student Services as well as spelling and sentence structure. Thank you for your understanding; I thought you would like to know..." Alyssia was happy and the ladies part as she gets back to her seat.

As the day wore into afternoon, the group were getting the last of their rough drafts finalised by Cecilia and the Doctors Franklin. The rest of the class, who were finished, gets the room cleaned up and places their dishes and cups on the tray near the door as Maddy watched the time to go in and pick them up while the class simply sat down and gave their final draft a good going over and put them away in their folders. Mark, who was looking over Alyssia's report, took the list of notes that the students had given during the game and puts them into her notebook says, "This is a good solid report, the only thing missing is your conclusion; but otherwise, a really good report." She smiled and said, "I will be working on the conclusion over the weekend along with other homework...I was just getting some help and quotes into a notebook along with the name of the book and date of publication."

He smiled as he added, "You did great out there; I'm proud of you." She smiled and says, "Thank you Doctor Franklin; I appreciate your kind words." Timothy, Marylebarne and Milton watched from a distance as they watched Mark put his hand on her cheek and said, "I'm so sorry to stare, but you do remind me of someone...but who could it be?" The group watched, including Paul, who looked up from a report as everyone watched. Alyssia stared at him intently as Paul watched too as he wondered who could she be as his dad stroked her cheek as tears rolled down his cheek as she brushed them away.

Mark then shook his head and says to her, "Forgive me," Alyssia looked at him and he withdrew his hand slowly as he patted her hand, "I-I-I'm sorry..." Mark left the room as Alyssia shed some tears as she thought: *'So close…I thought he was going to tell me.'* Milton came to her and offered her a hug as Paul went after his father. *'He knows me but something is holding him back.'* Milton came and held her close as she cried, "He knows me Milton, why doesn't he just tell me? End this torture?"

She cried harder as Milton gave her his shoulder to cry on as Adrianne and Amber came over and gave her some water as Paul left to see to his dad and Cecilia took over the Franklins post to see what was needed to be done as Marylebarne and Timothy did the same as they follow the men into the next room as Milton says to Cecilia, "Excuse me a moment Cecilia, I have to help a friend in need." Cecilia nodded as he left the room and went to see the Franklins while Timothy and Marylebarne watched as an angry Milton came in. "You know something, don't you?" Milton asked them both straight out as the father and the son looked at him as Milton came into the empty room next door. "Milton, go back next door, please…" Paul begged him but Milton refused to go anywhere as he walked towards them slowly as he says angrily trying not to shout and disturb the customers.

"I have a tortured girl friend next door begging to see her father and brother so she can be reconciled with them and all you do is play mind games with her? Now I like you two very much and I want to help you, but you must help me out here, you build her hopes up and then tear them down and there isn't enough glue in this world to fix her broken heart; now tell me what the hell is going on?!" Paul tells his father softly after Milton stood his ground. "I have to tell him, and he's right… we can't hide this any longer."

Mark looked at his son and nods as he helped his father into a chair to sit down as he cried. Then Paul came to Milton, "We believe that Alyssia may be our long-lost family member, but we can't say anything as long Thackeray is around. My mother and Thackeray were once lovers and she took Alyssia away from us at seven years old…the problem is that something like a blindness or a memory loss is preventing us from seeing or telling her the truth."

Marylebarne remembered Timothy telling him this as the men looked at each other as the advisor explained in a whisper, "When the curse was placed on the House, it must have spread to the townspeople as well…" Timothy nodded says, "So that's why they can't reveal or see their daughter who is sitting right in front of them?" Marylebarne nodded. "I may need to read up on it but if the curse is lifted, the memory loss or blindness will lift and if I am right, it must have started a year ago after the death of a local University lecturer. I'll have to look in the archives and get my answers; there has got to be something we can do for them." Timothy nodded as they turn back to the scene before them.

Milton was shocked but still angry; "So you just upset her because you simply can't tell her?" Paul says as he nodded while Milton walked away from him, "Screw Thackeray; just tell her for God's sake! Put her out of her misery, Paul...she deserves to know!" Paul and his dad look at each other as Mark says calmly and angrily, "You think we haven't tried, Milton? You think that we are so thick that we keep something like this from her? It's ripping us apart too and I have lived the regret of not fighting for her or my wife..." Milton was still in shock as he watched how vulnerable he was and he started to feel sorry for them; and friendship and demeanour grew softer and Paul placed a hand on his shoulder as Mark's voice grew softer, "We mean no harm to her, Milton; we had no idea how torn up inside she is until now."

Milton loved his lecturers and he told them as he sat with Mark as Paul stood beside him, "Then I will keep the secret with you and we'll work up to that day when you do tell her; just stop playing mind games with her and this report for court and Cassious House; we'll help her in every way we can; you can count on it." Mark and Paul were shocked as Mark asked, "What about George Thackeray? What if he finds out?" But Milton said to both of them as he stood up and placed his hands on both of their shoulders, "To hell with him!" His voice was softer as he sighed, "Yes, Thackeray must go and I think everyone in the University has had it up to here with 'the grouch of Kelton University.' Just let me tell her home girls so we can all work together with you, then you must tell John Preston everything; he wants to help to and get you reunited with her. Come on, let's work together, what do you say?"

Mark and Paul nod as Milton shook their hands, "You have a way with words Milton," says Paul as the jester of Kelton University shook both of the Franklin's hands and the deal was made. "I see why you care so much for her." Milton calmed himself, "It's about friendship and communication, Paul;" he said. "She has had it rough for this first week and all she wants is support and I will not let her fall nor will Adrianne or

Amber or the class; we are all in this together…she just needs to know the truth. Help me help her and we'll get through this together, deal? We will call you if anything happens to her, okay? At least you know that we'll be keeping her safe when you're not around."

The father and son agree with him and they smile as Milton walked away until Mark called to him, "Milton…" he turned to them as he says coming towards the 'jester of Kelton University', "Thanks for the scolding, you're a good friend to her." Mark placed a hand on his shoulder and smiled, "Take good care of her for us, please?" Milton nodded, "You know I will, you two." Milton left the room and the father and son calmed each other down before going back next door.

The spirits had heard enough and Timothy and Marylebarne signalled the Prince to follow as they head back to the Tower to plan their next move. "This changes everything, my boy. The Franklins have no idea that they are looking at their daughter, so there's more here that meets the eye plus I'm stalled on my search to find out more about her. I will need more information and a look through the 'Sultan's' advisor diaries and journals; but where to go to next, that's a different story."

The Prince thought, "I saw her talking to Sharlene Parks about her family and she had a letter and two photos that she showed her. Maybe that may give us clues or hit another roadblock…whatever the case; I will need extra eyes to help me search. She is off to see someone on Friday in the suburbs so we can start looking through her house for clues…" Marylebarne thought aloud, "I think you may have something there Timothy, we'll do it your way and see what we can dig up." The spirits head back to the Tower as he goes back to his study and continues his lessons with more fresh fruit and water as they wait until Friday to execute their plan.

Meanwhile, Milton comes back next door and sees to Alyssia as she was cleaning up the paper and pens all around tables and putting away chairs with the other students as he taps her shoulder. "Hey," he says as she turned and he wrapped his arms around her while she looked at him with a sad smile. "You okay now?" Alyssia sniffs as she says, "I'll be fine now, and I just wish I knew what was going on, Milton…that's all." He gave her one more hug and says, "Listen, I need to talk to the home girls and then the girls and I are going to show you a great time." She was about to say something as Milton stopped her with a kiss on her cheek. "The report can wait, Alyssia…you need a few laughs with yours truly." She chuckled and says, "Okay I just have books to take back to the University library and then, some fun with you, Amber and Adrianne!"

Milton kissed her forehead, "Good, I'll dismiss everyone and you," he said with his hands on her cheeks, "…no more tears, understood? That's an order!!" She saluted him as he took Adrianne and Amber aside and told them what was going on between Mark, Paul and Alyssia as they promised to keep quiet and help them be a family again. "I promised that we would take her out for some fun…" Milton said in a low voice and the girls nodded. "Great Idea, now all we have to do is let the gang go," Amber says as the friends watch her get back to cleaning up the room as Milton then straightens his collar and says, "Leave this to me." Adrianne face palms as Amber just chuckled while the girls stand beside him as Adrianne put an arm on his shoulder as he turns to the students around him as he got their attention and he bellows to everyone while Alyssia looked up as she puts away everything in her backpack.

"Okay everyone, get out of here, get that report finished and keep it open for we'll need them for Monday and Wednesday mornings! Have a wonderful weekend you all!" The class looked at Milton then back to Alyssia as she says to them with a chuckle, "Go and have a great weekend and remember everyone, use the IT facilities at the library or the computer room to finish everything… and you'll get an early start to the weekend if you do this." Milton was befuddled, "What she said!" While everyone laughed, Adrianne says to him in a whisper, "Admit it, she is better at it." Milton looked at her and says, "Oh shut up!" She smiled as Amber hid a chuckle under her breath.

Everyone said their goodbyes as the students leave Maddy's Coffee Shop and head home or over to the library to finish the reports while Cecilia and the Doctors Franklin, after giving her a hug and compliments, left the coffee shop with their order after saying their goodbyes to Alyssia and the students as they headed for the campus as the cool air surrounded them.

Cecilia says to them before they crossed the street, "You have a wonderful bunch of students in there including Alyssia Franklin-Jenkins." Paul and Mark smiled, "Thank you Cecilia…very kind of you to say." Cecilia smiled and said to them as they get across safely and on to campus property as they walked towards Franklin House. "She certainly has the teaching gene. If I didn't know any better, I say she was your daughter… Good day gentlemen." She sees Margaret, another Communications lecturer, and goes over to talk to her as the men looked at each other as Paul and Mark get back to Franklin House for lunch and lesson plans for next week.

In the caretaker's hut on campus, John Preston and Stuart Thackeray were taking a break from pouring over files and writing down notes as the morning turned to early afternoon as John stood up and looked out to see the Franklins headed back to their House as they were having lunch and Stuart joined him as he says to him, "It's just so good to be active again; taking notes and thinking." John looked back at him as Stuart continued; "Thackeray is so boring, John; I'm not even allowed in the classroom to teach Tweedle Dee and Tweedle Dum." John let out a hearty laugh as the men returned to the table to get back to work as Stuart says out of curiosity, "He's hiding something, John. I wish I knew what to do and how to get past him;" John tells him with a hand on his shoulder, "Don't you worry, I will let you know. We want to see what comes to light and then, we'll move in for the kill. But first, we need to know his plans;" he says as he walks away from the window as Stuart followed John into the small living room as Stuart nodded and changed the subject.

"So tell me John, what do I do if I get the "Death Stare"?" John looked at him as he remembers what Kohl told him: *Take good care of him, John, and let no harm come to Stuart. I trust you and your judgement.* Stuart sees him lost in thought; "You okay John?" John then comes out of the fog; "Stuart," John began, "I have told your father that I would take care of you and he knows that you are a grown man, but he's worried for you. This George Thackeray is dangerous so he gave me a briefing and told me to tell you this if ever I was asked that question, so listen carefully. I will call your father and the supervisor of undercover to have you immediately taken off the case and placed under my guard. I promised your family that I would keep you safe and I will risk everything to keep you alive, do you understand?"

Stuart smiled and nodded, "I do understand, John. This is a dangerous undercover operation and I must act like Thackeray's son and not let on that I am an undercover cop. I'm so glad that you're here John or I would screw it up and end up in a ditch or worse at the bottom of the sea. My dad told me about the case and what happened to the coroner so I will do my best not to screw this assignment up." John pats him on the shoulder and says to him, "Good man; now shall we get back to work?" He nodded and they began reading and taking notes on the files before them. Stuart was having trouble reading one of the reports as John helped him with the file as lunchtime rapidly approached.

Meanwhile, a tired Alyssia got home to Cassious House and places her notes, books from the library, and worksheets on the table and chairs as she gets in to the flat, washes up and has lunch since the University library was closed until one o'clock for lunch. She starts her report and follows the worksheet as to what Paul wanted in the report and doesn't stop until she was finished or her brain couldn't handle any more information.

One in a half hours later, she was finished and she typed it up on her computer, saves it, and puts all work away in the appropriate folders and notebooks; "Finally…" she cried out. With everything done and the dishes cleaned up, the notebooks put away neatly on the book shelf; it was time for her to do her housework chores as well as paying a visit to Kelton Heights Visitors Centre Harbour and Museum on Welling Street while she checks to see that she has everything and heads to the car with her shopping bags and purse as well as her backpack and piled them into the car.

She took in a deep breath and looked at the property around her and saw a large hole in the thicket of trees. So with a pair of binoculars, she looked at the hole through the branches and she could see George Thackeray looking back at her as he leaves the window as she lowers the binoculars slowly replying out loud, "So that's how Thackeray can see the House from his window…Damn him!" she said to herself angrily but she couldn't help it and left for town. "I will have to deal with this problem later…right now, chores to do!"

Back at the hut, the police officers finished reading all of their files as it was time to compare notes as John got his notes about Alyssia and her family. "Alyssia Anne Franklin-Jenkins born 1998, she was taken from her father and brother at age seven during the trial fiasco. Four years later was declared missing after an explosion at her mother's home until her grandmother, Jessica Esther Jenkins, called the police and confessed and said that her daughter was alive and given to her hours before the mother died and was told to take her back to Welleston Village. Alyssia Franklin was brought forward for the police, child welfare and the press. They reported that she was found safe and charges of kidnapping were dropped immediately as Child Welfare left her in the care of her grandmother until her death at age seventy-two; three-in-a-half weeks ago…"

Stuart says, "I was the one… and forgive me for interrupting," John nodded as he continued. "…she met when I was on my way here. She was nearing the city limits of Kelton Heights when I came across the car parked on the side of the road and I found her sitting on the grassy verge drinking water. She told me that she stopped for a bit of a rest and that her grandmother had died three weeks ago as she kept saying, "Never drive when you're upset" and she drank water." He looked at John, "I wondered if she was right?" John says, "She did the right thing; alcohol or being upset impairs your judgement when you're driving. So, when you stop anytime from any long journey, whether it's to take a break and rest as you calm yourself when you are upset; it clears your judgement."

Stuart nodded, "Clever girl!" John smiled as he gave him a wink and got back to the job at hand as John considered her criminal past. "This is interesting and quite a surprising;" Stuart came to him as he read, "No criminal record, no weapons or drugs possession, one very minor speeding violation but paid the fine-but other than that, she is a law-abiding citizen. The only thing she is guilty of is lots of bad luck as a child, got good grades, was an honour student at High School, very polite, received a scholarship from Welleston Village College for her paper on Pagan and Celtic languages and life in and around Kelton Heights and Welleston Village." The two men looked at each other and were shocked at the record once more. "Pretty impressive…That is one smart and amazing girl." John says as Stuart nods.

Then it was Stuart's turn as he read out the Doctors Franklin notes; "Doctor Mark Theo Franklin, PhD and Doctor Paul Angelo Franklin PhD; both successful authors and college lecturers until Mark lost his daughter and wife after Sidney Preston's death. He was blamed and charged with the death until he was cleared by the coroner and the judge ruled the death 'accidental'. The trial destroyed his career and he stayed with his son who was a student teacher at the time and while Paul was away, he took a massive dose of pills and alcohol but survived the attempt when the son came home early and administered CPR. With his son's help, he got back on his feet and took a teaching job with-"

He stopped with a realisation…he just met and was talking to Doctor Franklin's long-lost daughter and John was thinking the same as he looked at the picture taken when she seven years old and now in University. The two men looked at each other in shock and disbelief…both thought the same thing: *'Nah it can't be-can it?'* Stuart was nearly out the door with his jacket as John stopped him, "And where do you think you're going, rookie?" Stuart says as he got his coat on and his phone, "I'm off to Births, Deaths and Marriages in the Town Centre. I'm so sure that this is Franklin's long lost daughter and I will prove it! Besides John, I need to get away from here for a while."

John grabbed his coat as Stuart looked at him, "Where are you going, John. I-I don't need a body guard or a babysitter-"John grabbed his coat and keys to his car, "Oh I know that, I'm coming with you to protect you from 'Dead Eye' Carol at Birth, Deaths and Marriages." The rookie shuddered at the very mere mention of her name as John got his coat, "Yeah maybe you should; I think that woman has it in for me!" John smiled as he went to the door and he claps Stuart on the back and he looked him in the eye with a glint of humour as he puts his phone in his pocket. "I think she likes you…" as he walks to the door as Stuart looked at him and hears him laughing as he shouts back to him while Stuart walked to the front door with his jacket and phone saying: "I would rather face a suicide bomber than her!" John laughed as the duo head towards the Town Centre and 'Dead Eye' Carol in John's car and John told the young rookie that he would treat him to lunch at his favourite hangout as the cops head to the car.

THE KELTON HEIGHTS VISITORS CENTRE HARBOUR AND MUSEUM

At Welling Street, Alyssia is at the Visitor's Centre and Museum looking for the book a student in her class recommended as she showed the young lady the book title on a piece of paper. The young lady shook her head and told her to try the art museum and look for a man named Iain Margarida. She smiled and thanked her politely as she made her way to the museum next door while the girl got back to work. Alyssia walked through a scene of old Kelton Heights there and some other exhibits as there was an Art Fair going on. She thought frustratingly: *'Great…the one day I wanted to talk to the curator and I end up walking into a room full of art critics and hipsters! God, I know how to pick the timing do I?'* She by-passed the art critics and art lovers and went straight to the back of the museum as she looked up at five pictures that peaked her interest in the Museum while an older gentleman watched her with interest.

The Kelton Heights Visitor's Centre and Art Museum was huge and minimalistic as everything was immaculate. Lights were blazing down on the portraits and the small placards had so many small words, even she couldn't see them and she had glasses on! She looked up and saw two men and three ancient maps which drew her attention as she could hear her grandmother tell her stories of how Kelton Heights and Welleston Village in her mind and how the towns were founded while everyone chattered about the new arrival as they sipped champagne and looked at the art pieces as they left her alone and gave their opinion on how this artist represented his work.

Alyssia approached the set of pictures as the Pirate and the Viking looked back at her as if they were having a staring contest while the maps were showing her history itself as if they were telling her; *'This is how it was and you are the only one who can solve the riddles we have before you. Let us see how clever you are. Come on…work it out! We know that you want to.'* She smiled and got out her book of symbols and a magnifying glass but didn't realise that she was being watched by another elderly man who kept his eyes on her as she looked around at all the history of the two towns. The curator named Iain Margarida saw her and excused himself from the melee of the art show as he approached the young girl.

The younger brother is a very strange character; being a curator and an art critic must have their rewards as you are the one that has to keep everything going. Born in Cardiff, the brothers have different views on Kelton Heights and its History while working with the public and arranging events. Being the scholar of the two, Iain is a well-dressed, a bachelor, brash, outspoken, fun, educated, camp, loves his job, and is a "Neat freak" (everything has to be in its place), very understanding man with a soft spot for Alyssia when she enquires about the pictures of the Viking and the Pirate as well as the three maps; turning the art fair into a history lesson. He has dark, tousled hair, brown eyes, round face, skinny frame long hands and fingers and is very tall and lanky. He is a normal bloke and sometimes he wears glasses because he said 'It makes him look smart' sometimes he calls them his "Brainy specs" and he is the most outgoing man you ever have met.

"Hello, my dear young lady?" he replied getting her attention as Alyssia introduced herself to the curator as she shook hands with him. "My name is Alyssia Franklin-Jenkins and hello." She said over the loud chatter of the Art Fair that was happening around them. "Is there anything I can help you with?" he asked her as she told him, "I am trying to learn more about a place called Cassious House and my classmate recommended a book to me."

She heard silence and the couple turned to the crowd who were looking at them and she smiled embarrassingly as she looked back at the crowd as her admirer and the spy smiled. "Um, did I say something wrong?" The spy got on the phone to his employer and told him that "there was a young lady at the museum looking into the history of Cassious House." The Employer was shocked at this news and asked his spy to place the phone on loud speaker and get in as close as he could without being detected. The spy nodded and did what he was told while the admirer watched her and the curator intently.

The spy, meanwhile, got into the act of being an old man and found a chair as a spectator helped him to his chair as he thanked the young person as he placed the phone on loud speaker and sat it in his front coat pocket while he waited for the right moment to get in closer while the curator got his employees to take over the Art Fair as he talked to her as she replied while they went deeper into the museum, "I'm sorry; I didn't mean to shout; I-I came on a very busy day for you." The curator took her to a quiet area and they talked and she pulled out the paper and gave to the curator. "It's okay, sometimes I like distractions and it's just a shock that you live near Cassious House-the most haunted of all houses. Now let's see what book your friend was talking about."

She nodded and pulled out the paper with the title on it as she told him, "A classmate at Kelton University recommended it to me." He looked about and whispered since the crowd was still within listening distance as the spy sat very still as he was a mannequin on display in the museum as the phone was sat on his knee and her admirer listened in as well as the curator whispered to her in an audible tone. "I have the book but it's locked away since George Thackeray visited here with a couple of his goons…two country bumpkins that were dirty and very untidy, if you ask me."

She smiled and listened as the curator continued, "He was very crooked and suspicious and my staff was scared to having to deal with him and his goons; so, I politely asked him to leave after he vilified a member of my staff and famous historian of Kelton Heights, my brother Dòmhnall Margarida who is an employee at the City Centre Tourist Information Centre here in Kelton Heights on the East High Street." Alyssia nodded and listened. "He wanted this book that you are looking for but I had told him that I was sold out and told him to leave and never return; he didn't take it very well, but I stood my ground. I never told him to go to the City Centre…maybe he would find it there but I warned my brother about him and he said that he would be on the lookout for him."

Alyssia asked softly, "Well done for you and your staff for keeping your cool under pressure…" he smiled as they kept their voices low as she asked him, "Do you know when this was?" The curator says softly as well, "It was a month ago and I have reported it to the police and they have it on record as we do. We make this place as calm and soothing for the art lover or visitor while they are here." She nodded and said, "So you keep records of all banned visitors? Impressive, Mr Margarida!" The curator says, "Oh yes, Miss Jenkins. We maintain a pleasant experience here at the Museum; and it's also part of our inspection protocol. We are required to show them to our inspector when he pays a visit…especially the guest book so that we maintain a level of customer service within the museum and tourist information."

Alyssia touched his arm and said, "Well I better sign your guest book before I leave to keep your records up to date and I am truly sorry you have had that experience;" Iain smiled as she said, "But I am not here to put your museum at ill repute," The curator smiled and nodded. "I am just interested in these maps and two men; a Pirate and a Viking." She was pointing to a group of maps and two men as the curator nodded and was surprised, "These unnamed pictures and maps here?"

She nodded and was happy at her interest in them as she said; "Yes sir, I have studied Pagans, Celts and the history of Scotland but these maps and two men are of interest to me, for I have studied the different cultures and history of Kelton Heights and Welleston Village and I was wondering if I could get a closer look?" The old man stood up and went to another chair near the pictures and sat down as he continued to watch her while a small crowd of art critics and art lovers gathered to watch her at work. Iain was quite shocked; "Why of course… we have no idea what are who they are, but if you can help us, it would be of great help. What do you need?"

He gave her all the assistance she needed at her request as Timothy appeared in the shadows and watched her as she told the Iain, "I just need a ladder." The curator nodded asked one of his male employees to get a ladder for this young lady; "Right away sir…" and he got the ladder for her, spread it out and he got it as close as he could to the paintings as he could and he held it for her as she thanked him. She climbed to the top, sat down, went into her purse and got out her book on United Kingdom of Old and was opened to ancient maps of Scotland, England, Wales and Ireland while the old man stood up and went to another chair near the pictures and sat down as he continued to watch her as a small crowd of art critics and art lovers gathered to watch her at work as well as her admirer and the museum staff. Timothy, who stood in the corner, watched carefully as she took out a magnifying glass while the crowd gathered around as everyone's interest was piqued at this strange but knowledgeable young lady.

She looked at the symbols and back to the book to make sure she was right as the curator saw the crowd gathering around him as her admirer says, "We are all intrigued at what she is doing, Mr Margarida;" The curator looked around as he saw the tall gentleman and smiled as he continued, "…she looks to be a person of learning and I also know this young lady; she wrote a paper on the Celtic History of Scotland, England and Wales and its culture as well as influence on the modern world; a genius piece of work, I must say, my dear, very interesting and well worth a read." Alyssia was too busy studying the map but gave a smile and kept studying the map as the gent concluded to the group around him, "If you all would like, I can find that paper and give to you to read?"

The others nodded as Alyssia felt embarrassed and flattered all at the same time as she kept her mind on the subject at hand. "Thank you very much sir, very kind of you to say. I put a lot of work into the paper and thoroughly research everything; your kind words are much appreciated knowing that my hard work has paid off." Timothy smiled at her modesty and humility as she continued to look at the maps and the symbols as the gent says, "You are so welcome; I am looking forward to this…" then he was quiet as she smiled and she started to climb down the ladder with a very big smile as she put her book and magnifying glass away as Timothy watched her with interest. "I knew it—Celts!"

She placed her book, magnifying glass into her purse and slowly came off the ladder as she thanks his employee who was holding it for her. She turned to the young man and said with a smile and a hand on his shoulder, "Thank you for the ladder…you can take it back now." The male employee nodded and smiled as he did just that and she turned to the curator while Timothy and the spy with his employer on the other end listened. Iain was confused as were the art lovers who started to mutter at this revelation as her admirer listened as well. "Celts? What on Earth would they be doing in Kelton Heights?"

Alyssia says to the group as Timothy also listened, "Simple…to survive and thrive like all men. But while other tribal groups of Celts went on to Scotland and Wales, this group stayed here-and it must have something to do with the Pirate and Viking, but Celts in Kelton Heights and Welleston Village? But I don't understand; the Celts were a warrior like race; raiding towns and killing many Romans and other armies…why would this tribe just stay and form a town here in Kelton Heights and Welleston Village and why this land on this map?" Then the curator thought of something and told his employee to get the keys and go to the case in the small town scene and bring out the book. The young lady did and went to get the keys as the curator saw her with them and pointed at the key and she went to get the book.

"Maybe this may help; we were looking at an old diaries or journals of both men, but it's in Celtic, Welsh or Gaelic; maybe you can make heads or tails of it; I really pray that you can…" She nodded and with gloves the female art centre employee went to pick it up carefully as the admirer says thinking back on the paper she wrote. "According to history, the most famous of them you wrote about was a Celt named Boadicea who destroyed Colchester and St Albans as well as capturing London back in sixty A.D. Am I right?"

She smiled and said, "Yes sir, well thought of. She was married with two daughters and according to accounts, Boadicea and her huge army captured those cities that you have mentioned. But later, she was captured by the Romans after a failed takeover of another city. So rather being humiliated by her captors, she poisoned herself. But she has no connection to these two men unfortunately; a Viking and a Pirate and their names may be unpronounceable by any human today." The admirer was astonished and asked his fellow group of artists, "Did I tell you she was amazing?"

Everyone nodded as the young lady came back with the book as she showed Alyssia something as she got the gloves on and went through the pages; seeing the same three maps and men as a newspaper headline caught her eye: "Local Archaeologists discover bones, food and sword in a cave around the Celts Settlement" screamed a headline while diaries and pictures were brought to her. "These are all in Gaelic and Welsh and since my employees don't speak those languages," Iain began as the girl smiled; "…we are unable to translate them, it's a big mystery to me and to the archaeologists that found them. Alyssia looked up at the maps and the two men and thought for a moment, *'What would a Viking and a Pirate want with the Celts? This doesn't make sense…'*

Then it hit her as she read the entries contained within the diaries and journals, "TREASURE!" the curator and the art lovers listened as she said, "There's treasure that was buried from pillages and raids of the castles and kings. These two men were part of this Celtic tribe to help feed their families and the treasure was like a vault cave-a bank- like what we have today, but instead of curses and incantations, we have combinations and locks. But back in those days, the tribe gave the treasure to the leader as they used very powerful curses and chants to keep it safe. The Celts somehow knew of all the evil that would be in the world and buried the treasure deep underground-right under Cassious House!"

Timothy was shocked at this revelation as the art critics and lovers muttered with each other as heard the curator say, "But Cassious House was built long after the Celts, Pirates and Vikings…fifty-two years later. If they did exist, they were destroyed in the great fire of 1720 and that was before Cassious House was built too…" She read the entries again as she pulled out her notebook and wrote down something that caught her eye: *'...sa dorcha eadh laigh a-muigh, gus a solast boillsg cuimeanach...'*

"…In the dark it lies, until a light shines brightly…" Iain was confused as Alyssia puts her notebook away. "What does that mean?" asked Iain as Alyssia's mind was going about a mile a minute as the histories of the two towns were passing through her brain like a runaway freight train as she asked the curious curator who was still confused at the entry from the diary or journal.

"I will hopefully find out the answer when I do an investigation into Cassious House and its past; there is more to the story of Cassious House than meets the eye."*…and I was right, it's much more than the spirit of a prince at work here and I will uncover it quickly,*' she thought to herself as she turned back to the curator and the art lovers and the curious admirer. "That Thackeray Feud lasted for two years which one man and his family and followers were exiled to Italy and the other family stayed to set up a police force right here in Kelton Heights for the Lord Mayor and the Royal Carlton Family." Iain says, "Yes, the history books have recorded it, but what does treasure have to with it?"

Then she smiled as a light bulb went off in her brain. "What if I told you that one group of that criminal family was still here in Kelton Heights and is working at the University?" The curator and the guests smiled as it hit them as the curator said aloud, **"GEORGE THACKERAY!"** The crowd were astonished as Alyssia says, "You told me that he came to see you a month ago, and may I ask if it was about the same two gents and the three maps?" Iain was shocked! "Yes! Yes it was!" The crowd and Timothy loved it; this was better than any old art fair and the huge inflated price of art work as her admirer was enjoying it! "You locked the book away, is it your last copy Iain?" She asked as he smiled, "It is. There are no more after this one and it's completely updated with new details…the book was pulled because of treasure hunters' dis…" Alyssia nodded.

"Now you're getting it! The stories of people looking for the treasure has cost many lives…are true. The treasure is protected by chants, spells and other curses as well as other supernatural forces and if you can't do the work or read the language, it was no good and if you wandered around the House during the night or in the House; the Dark Spirits were out and about, you were taken."

The crowd looked at her and were excited the curator nodded, "So that's why there have been so many warnings about Cassious House during the night. By day it's harmless, but by night, it's dangerous as it can be; Stanley Parks warning of entering or trespassing is still true to this day. Those boys that are missing, they must have disappeared." Everyone was buzzing as she smiled at the onlookers and politely apologised to the curator and the group of art lovers, even the staff who found it fascinating, for her ramblings while Timothy smiled and silently cheered her on as he kept the entry in his mind and would ask Marylebarne about it when he would head back to the Tower as she said anxiously.

"I need to find that cave and get into the House itself, but I can't-I'm not allowed," the curator comes to her and asked her why. "Is it the curse of the House or the Spirit that dwells within its walls?" Alyssia remembered, "Stanley Parks survived the House and lived to tell the tale in 1862 and he became the caretaker of the House and their sole duty: to protect the House and the spirit within. Nope the present caretaker, Kevin Parks, is very protective of the House and the spirits and has been for the last five generations. He said that he remembers a log entry written back in late 1862: *'It's had its share of bad luck already—think I should make sure that there's no more terrible tragedies are added to it. -Mr Stanley Parks 1862-'* Then she turned to the crowd and says, "Oh and for some of you adventure hunters, I wouldn't dare go near the House looking for the treasure; you will never be seen again…trust me!" The crowd nodded and applauded her intellect and understanding as the crowd shook their heads in agreement.

Iain smiled and says to her gently as she takes it, "Well, here's my card and if you think of anything of these maps or who these men are, you will tell us?" Alyssia looked at him and smiled as she replied, "I would be honoured thank you, but I better get back home…I need to return some library books to the University. Right now, I want you and your staff to rename that map on the left, with a huge chunk of land in the middle 'Celtic Life in Kelton Heights,'" she said pointing to it; "…and I will get the date for you as soon as I find it; the rest must be hidden somewhere and I will sign your guest book to keep your records up to date."

The curator nodded and the staff got straight to work as he goes and gets that book for her while the young girl closed the book carefully and took it back to the case and locked it up after Alyssia thanked her as she turned back to the art lovers as the curator went and got the book for her as she says as he comes back. "I do apologise for interrupting your event with history?"

The group around her smiled and thanked her, "This was the best history lesson ever;" said one young person. The crowd patted her back as they went back to the event and the curator gave her the book, she paid for it as she wished the staff a wonderful weekend, signed the guest book as promised, picked up more guides and left the museum until the admirer came to her before she left as he called to her as she turned to him.

"Before you go Miss Jenkins; may I say you my dear are an intelligent young lady?" said her admirer who took up her hand and kissed it gently. "Thank you sir," she said, "my apologies for ruining your art fair…" The gentleman bowed. "It was worth the distraction, my dear," and he left her and went back to the art fair without another word. She left with her book and pamphlets that she got from the Museum and Art Gallery as a very impressed Prince Timothy left the Museum to head back home to the Tower at Cassious House and speak to Marylebarne about what he had learned.

The old man who was watching her watched her go, had a broad smile broke across his face as he took off his disguise as the blue eyes and blonde hair shone in the fluorescent light. He got on the phone after turning the recorder off and phoned to his employer; "Sir, did you hear all that?" and his employer says, "I did…well done. Come back to the manor, I have little job for you." The young man hung up the phone and left the museum as the art fair resumed.

Later on, she got home with her groceries and the information on Cassious House placed the book and the pamphlets, on the table. As she was putting things away in the refrigerator and in the cupboards in the kitchen there stood Timothy behind the door. "Hello there!" he says as she jumps, held in a yelp and her carton of eggs. "I'm sorry; I didn't mean to scare you." She placed the eggs on the table and sat for a moment as she checked that her skin was still on her skeleton and her heart was still beating as she fights to put it back in her chest. "Not at all; it's good to check every once and while to make sure that my heart is still beating and I also love scrambled eggs." He laughed as she asked gently, "So scary Prince Timothy, what can I do for you?"

He chuckled as he got straight to the point while he took her into his arms, "Marylebarne feels that it's time for you to see the House and believes that you would be very interested." He took her hand into his, "Will you come?" he asked as she smiled but had her doubts. "I would be honoured but what about Kevin? He is very overprotective of you and the House?" Timothy says, "Marylebarne will have a talk with Kevin Parks to arrange the visit to the House for Saturday night. Alyssia touched his hand on her cheek as she gently says, "That would be wonderful, I am looking forward to it." She kissed his cheek and he smiled as her gentleness. "Till Saturday night?" he asked her and she nodded as he disappeared into shadow leaving her alone to put away the groceries.

He got back to the Tower when Marylebarne called to him and turned to his advisor as they went into Marylebarne's study. He cast a spell on the room as he told Timothy: "Memory blindness…I found it in the Sultan's advisor journals. According to his writings, Memory blindness is linked with this curse and when a tragedy has occurred. So when Mark and Paul Franklin lost his wife and daughter and the loss of his assistant, he became a victim of memory blindness and it can only be lifted when this curse is lifted."

Timothy was intrigued as Marylebarne found another clue; "The other thing, the journal entry you were quoting to me: *'…sa dorcha eadh laigh a-muigh, gus a solast boillsg cuimeanach…* "In the dark it lies, until a light shines brightly…" It was referring to the curse as well and it's about when or if the key is found but it doesn't go any further than that." Timothy was disappointed but Alyssia may hold the answers to his freedom, but she needs to do research and the prince will have to completely trust her now if this curse is to be lifted and after seeing her in action at the museum, he had no doubts after telling Marylebarne what he witnessed at the Art Museum.

"Then she will have to dig deep and look for clues… 'There is something not right at the University,' she told me and I'm starting to believe that she may be right." Marylebarne says, "Then I better look through the family history; there may be something I overlooked. Right now, I want you to get back to your studies, understood?" Timothy nodded and Marylebarne lifted the spell and the men went about their duties in and around the Tower as he got ready for fencing instruction with his tutor downstairs in the ballroom.

Twenty minutes later, she was loading up a trolley full of University library books to take back to the campus library and puts them neatly in the trolley or in the backpack and leaves the House for the library. She reached her destination and got inside Kelton Hall as she wheeled it in and up to the reception desk as the two Coquitlam sisters see her in the form of two old ladies as they watched her unload the trolley. One of the sisters, Celeana Coquitlam, had dark hair and deep dark eyes and a petite beauty in a beautiful German medieval dress when she became a spirit and she was only a young girl with her sister when the curse took hold. At present, she was filling up an old woman that Alyssia met and gave a list of books to as she helped her unload the trolley. She reached into her bag and pulled out some more books and placed them on the counter while the other sister checked them in.

"Hello, Miss Jenkins," says Catherina in her lilting German accent and haunting blue eyes and blonde hair. She was also petite in stature and very quiet as her sister was the excitedable one as she was checking in all the books. "How are you today?" Alyssia just smiled and says, "Fine thank you. These books were a big help for our first week, it made the course easier to understand; very insightful and interesting." Celeana says gently and happily in her lilting German accent, "I'm so glad that they were a help to you and the students and we always recommend these books to first time students new to University and the course." Alyssia smiled suspiciously as Catherina loaded them on to the cart behind her as Alyssia asked the ladies while she got the rest of the books out of her back pack and carry-all bags… "I want to know more about Cassious House for research; are there any books on it?"

The sisters looked at each other as Catherina says to her as she said gently. "There was one but it got lost in transit; if you still want to learn about the House, the original is in the House's library. I wish I could do more for you?" Alyssia thanks her, "No not all, you've been a big help; goodbye for now ladies," she replied and folds up the trolley, placed it in her back pack along with her carry all bag and heads to the door to go home to get ready for a day out with her friends; but Celeana stopped her. "Stop a moment, Miss Jenkins, Please? We want to talk to you."

Alyssia was a bit scared of these two women took her arm and was taken back inside the library as Catherina starts talking to her when all she wanted to do was go home and get ready to see her friends; "Look ladies I have things to do…" Celeana says, "It will only be a few minutes of your time." Alyssia sighs and says, "Okay what is it?" Catherina began first; "Listen Miss Jenkins; in the spring, there is supposed to be a big conference with all the foreign investors," Alyssia listened but started becoming even more suspicious by the minute; "…and they might invest in a huge state-of-the-art facility to study Natural Disasters. If this investment goes through, it will make Kelton University a leader in Seismology and World Meteorological Study." She continued as she says suspiciously, "Hmmm. I have always been interested in Earth Science, but, um—what does that have to do with me?"

At the same time, Prince Timothy had come out of the shadows and was looking for a new book on Shakespeare Sonnets when he spied the Coquitlam Sisters and asked himself: *'What the hell are they doing? Please don't you dare scare Alyssia to death or you will get a right telling off from Marylebarne!'* Celeana continued as Timothy watched from the book shelves as he was looking through the Shakespeare books. "Ah, they will need students to help with the conference; making and distributing leaflets, programmes, setting up and taking down, hosting--all kinds of duties. But one lucky student will be making a presentation to the committee of the project and if they are chosen they will represent the University; it's a lot of pressure." Alyssia thought about it: *'I hope I don't get chosen; I hate being under pressure!'*

Timothy was so furious that he picked the book of Shakespeare plays instead of sonnets as he decided to take the plays and the sonnets as he watched a "non-interested" Alyssia trying to escape the conversation quickly; "Well good ladies," she begins and smiled as she wanted to leave the library. "I hope the lucky student can handle the pressure well and represent the University and the conference with integrity and distinction. Now if you'll excuse me, I have a date with some friends and I have to get home, excuse me." But the girls stepped in front of her as she was about to leave the library as Catherina says, "Yes, I hope you will do good…" Celeana nodded still looking at her as the other students were watching the event and started to gather around Alyssia. "You would make a wonderful speaker at the conference."

Then it hit Alyssia-these "spirited" librarians were trying to recruit her into doing it as Timothy was furious at this attempt to use her fear of being in big crowds as a scare tactic. He took his books on sonnets and plays and quickly headed back to the Tower to tell Marylebarne what he has just witnessed immediately as he thought: *'Marylebarne is going to be so angry at them and when Marylebarne gets angry; he can be a raging volcano!'* Timothy knew this because he had run in with Marylebarne's anger before when he was a boy; you don't make Marylebarne angry.

Celeana said desperately as Alyssia looked at the others around her; "You must do this; you are our only hope." Alyssia turned to them and came closer to the sisters and asked directly, "Of doing what exactly?" The students held their breaths as the sisters look at each other as Catherina says with a smile and willingness; "Why, breaking the curse on Cassious House. Many have tried Miss Jenkins; but have failed miserably—but we have faith in you Alyssia. Please?" The students around her were looking back at Alyssia as to what she would do in this situation. They didn't say another word until Alyssia saw one thing that answered her suspicions: 'SPIRITS!'

She looked at them as the other students dropped their books or almost cried out and backed away afraid of what was happening before them as a light began emanating around the two elderly librarians as Alyssia needed to do something as she says firmly, just as Paul told his students, as she looked at them directly in the eyes with a firm tone says, **"WHO ARE YOU?"** The other students couldn't believe what they were seeing as the spirits didn't answer, but they fled in a ball of plasma from the librarians as the elderly ladies fainted as Alyssia and another female student ran over to the librarians and caught them as both fell to the floor with them and in front of the desk as the other frightened students were moved into action.

"Call the first aiders now!" One of the shocked students nodded and rushed behind the desk to call for the first aiders while the other students gave Alyssia and the other female student gave them their coats to place under the ladies heads. The two of them knew first aid and get the elderly ladies into the recovery position just as the first aiders ran in to offer their assistance as Alyssia explained what happened.

Meanwhile back at Cassious House, the sisters materialised into human-spirit form and as they got back to the Tower, they talked and laughed; until they heard Marylebarne clearing his throat and they looked up into the eyes of a very angry advisor, a very annoyed Prince Timothy, and an enraged Jesterson as the other spirits gathered around them completely and utterly disappointed with the sisters. "In my study now!" Marylebarne exclaimed as the sisters nodded as Timothy and Jesterson followed the advisor to the study while the other spirits gathered around the door and listened to the angry exchanges through the door in the advisor's study and it proved to be the talking point of the Tower as they gathered around the door.

While back at the University Library, a few moments had passed in an instant as her friends rushed in and saw her at the other end of the library drinking water as they came to her. "Are you okay?" asked Amber as her friends came beside her. "We saw a crowd at the front door and came in; what on earth happened?" She was just about to explain when Milton says, "Isn't it obvious? She likes drawing a following around her." Alyssia smiled sarcastically, "Oh yeah," she said to Milton, "I love being the centre of attention…NOT!!!" Milton backed away as she replied to him, "Sorry Milton, I'm just a wreck; I didn't mean to take it out on you."

He smiled and squeezed her hand. "It's okay…" while the girls smiled as he sits down before her and Alyssia explains while they all listened at what was said. She told them about a conference in the spring and how they were drawing her in to do the speaking as her friends sit beside her and comforts her. "I-I just started," she says trying not to cry. "I'm not good in big, crowded gatherings. Why do you think I'm sitting way over here?" Milton says jokingly, "Aww come on Alyssia, admit it! You were a former pop star in a former life."

He stands up and took the bottle from her and pretends to be singing into microphone as he dances about making the girls laugh by doing the moonwalk, Beyoncé dance and shaking his tush at her as Adrianne smacks it hard. Then he says, "Or even a model…" he pretends to walk on the catwalk and trips a bit as he mocks, "Take that tap water away, I only drink vodka!" The girls laugh harder making Alyssia smile and face palm as he then says, "Or maybe a movie star?" as he picks up the bottle again and holds it up as if it was an Oscar, "I'd like to thank Martin Short for making me who I am today; an idiot!"

The girls laugh harder as he sits back down in front of her as Alyssia wipes tears from her eyes and replied to a smug Milton; "You have just chased the stress away even if it's only for a little while, Milton!" He sits in front of her and whispered in his Groucho Marx voice, "I do birthdays, weddings and if you want I can put a 'Barrel of Laughs' in a coffin at a funeral?!" The jester of Kelton University wiggled his eyebrows at her as she giggled and says, "You're too much, Milton!" He stands up and takes a bow as he sits before her, "At least you're smiling," he says "…that's a good thing!" The girls agreed with him until the first aider with the book came to the friends as Amber, Adrianne and Milton leaves them to talk. "We'll be over at the bookcases looking at books on Quantum Physics…" Amber says as Alyssia looked at her strangely but then shook it out of her mind as she talked to the first aider.

The friends hide behind a nearby bookcase and talk; Milton spoke up first as they get deeper into the library. "What the hell is going on? First Thackeray House falls on her, Franklin and his son know that she is their daughter but can't prove it; she must give a presentation in May, now she is asked to speak at a conference in the spring, and she is seeing spirits now? Gals, there is something going on and this only our first week."

Adrianne says, "You're right. We have to protect her and tell Franklin and Dean Winchell what's going on; this new friend of ours is somehow bait in a trap and we have to spring it before she gets hurt. Alyssia has always been the focus since she started and there's something about that we all have to consider." Amber nodded and says, "I still say it's Cassious House and it's doing something to her; I'm worried about her and we must get her away from here even if it's just for a little while, what do you say?"

The trio agree and they go and plan their fun time with her as they saw the first aider having a talk with her as Adrianne was on the phone to the Doctors Franklin and Dean Pharrell Winchell told them what had happened to her as she sat down beside her and asked, "You okay?" She watched her nod while Alyssia took a swig of water while the first aider took her hand into hers and felt it shaking, "You are still white as a sheet and trembling…" Alyssia took in some more water as she says, "I'll be fine, I just needed some water, a place of peace and quiet and to keep out of the way; I don't like crowds."

The first aider smiled a bit and understood how she felt while she tried to make her talk as brief and to the point as possible. "Well, the librarians are going to be fine; they just need some rest and we called in some back up for them and the emergency staff will be here as soon as possible. Can you sign the first aid book?" Alyssia took the book as the First Aider replied, "I wrote some things down but I need you to fill in the blanks." Alyssia did just that in the book as she nodded, looked over her statement, took in a deep breath, signed the book, and choked back tears; she couldn't believe what she saw.

She didn't understand what was happening to her as she was digging deeper into this mystery, there was more to her past than a murder or an inquiry that went horribly wrong. She felt weary, useless, and exhausted with the whole thing and there were so many questions needing answered; why was she a target of all these events going on in her world? What role does she play in this situation that makes her a target and why was she the only person that was being targeted? Why was she being protected and for what reason? She thought of that very first night running from evil dark spirits and a young man protecting her as she thought: *'And I thought a sword-wielding Prince slashing up dark spirits was bad enough; there is something definitely going on here and it lies in that Carlton Royal Family Album…this is a different kettle of fish and I intend to get to the bottom of it.'*

Then the first aider, after reading her statement asked sympathetically; "I know that you're under stress, but is this a true account of what happened?" Alyssia looked at her as she looked at what was written down in the book; the same one that they recorded the fall of the House of Thackeray as Alyssia told her, "Yes I can honestly say that what I wrote in that book is true to the best of my knowledge and you wouldn't believe me if I told you because you seem like a very normal, sensible smart person." The women laugh as her hand started to shake violently and she was not really sure how to answer her.

Sure, she has never seen a ghost or even taken parapsychology or maybe she believes that ghost are all smoke and mirrors. Now she knows about a top-secret conference which has now been revealed which now she must inform a member of staff right away, but right now she must deal with the first aider as she heard her heart saying: *'One thing at a time… okay? Take it one thing at a time!'* said her brain. "All I know," she began after taking a drink of water and a sigh "…is that the librarians fainted as another female student helped me get them in the recovery position quickly after we caught them and fell to the floor with the ladies by the desk and kept them comfortable as I asked another student to fetch you; the first aiders."

The first aider placed a reassuring hand on her arm and said, "I know that you and your friends are taking a parapsychology class and I believe that the presence of ghosts can take over a person and they do strange and funny things to someone. One student, a year ago, thought she saw the spirit of William Shakespeare walking the halls of the University-she fainted dead away." Alyssia says quietly, "Yeah laugh now because you don't see the Bard coming out of two elderly women quoting Hamlet's soliloquy, do you?" She took in a breath and said apologetically, "Sorry, I didn't mean to snap at you, either; you are only doing your job," The first aider says softly, "…its okay; but what about you?"

Alyssia reassured her as she took in a sigh, "I'll be fine; I'm in shock and shaken. I understand what you mean about ghosts and spirits, but this whole first week has me all shook up, that's all." She nodded, "Would you like me to inform your tutors?" Alyssia shakes her head, "No I'll do it, thank you anyway. Mark Franklin and my lecturer's needs to hear it from me; I'll let them know."

The first aider nodded and smiled as she puts down "Heat exhaustion" as the cause and said, "It's hot in here anyway. I'll have a talk with the head caretaker about the heating in the library. The librarians will be fine, thank you and the other student for your prompt response and time Alyssia. Why don't you head home and get some rest?" Alyssia nodded as her friends watched the first aider leave, and then, they came over and sat beside her.

She took in the last of her water and relaxed her nerves which had her glued to the leather chair the whole time until she felt Amber's and Adrianne's hands on her arms as they sat beside her on either side while Milton took her hands in his as she told her friends what the first aider had said as she tried so desperately to fight back tears. Adrianne spoke up and rubbed her back as she asked, "How about a late lunch with us? A bit of shopping and some laughs-it might take your mind off everything for a while and you'll feel better?" Alyssia was about to decline until Milton says, "Besides, I've always loved the company of three beautiful women…"

They laughed as her water was finished and she said, "Okay why not? But do you mind if I speak to Doctor Franklin and put my trolley away in the flat?" Adrianne says, "No need to talk to Franklin, already done. Get your purse, put the trolley away in your flat and come out with us," Milton says, "…I'll get the car ready and we'll have some fun and we'll run over some pigeons and seagulls along the way and learn about Quantum Physics together." Alyssia chuckled with the other girls and agreed as the trio helped "unglue" her from the leather chair that she was stuck to and they leave the library for her House and some fun after they check on the elderly librarians and thanked her for helping them.

Back at Cassious House, Marylebarne was very angry at the sisters at what they had done to Alyssia, as told by very furious Prince Timothy who was a witness to the events. He went to the window and stood there thinking of Alyssia, who had come back to the flat, and was putting away her trolley away and getting her purse, as she left the House and locked the door. She was putting away her keys in her backpack when she looked up at Timothy who smiled and mouthed down to her as Jesterson joined him. "You okay?" She nodded and signed to him, "I'm going out with my friends; be home soon."

He nodded and signed back, "Okay, stay safe…" and he blew her a kiss as Jesterson and Timothy watched her disappear down the driveway after waving at him and she went with her friends who were waiting at the bottom of the drive for her. "She is a good person, none of this is her fault Timothy, and we just have to keep her safe." Timothy agreed as he patted his shoulder as he looked at the jester. "I know Jesterson; just wish I could help her figure out her role in all this." The jester nodded and patted his back as he smiled while two of them were listening to the angry voice of Marylebarne to the Coquitlam sisters as they turned back to a very angry Marylebarne.

"You two are unbelievable… what was the first thing I said to you all when she arrived here? 'No spooking Alyssia' and you scared her half to death. You two could have been caught or worst, killed. You would have had that young girl frightened off then what chance we had, to break the curse and to help the University would move on would be gone…I-I'm so ashamed of the both of you!"

Marylebarne walked away as the sisters defended their actions, "But it's true, Marylebarne" cried out Celeana as the advisor, the prince and the jester looked on them as she cried. "Foreign investors are coming to the campus in the spring." Then Catherina defended her sister's statement. "Yes, and they may want to look inside Cassious House, sir. We must prepare ourselves for the inevitable invasion." Timothy speaks up loud but firm as he looked out of the window; "NOT WHILE THE DARK VEIL OF EVIL REMAINS ON THE FIRST-FLOOR LANDING AT THE TOP OF THE STAIRS!" The Prince said calmly but angry as he turned from the window and approached the sisters; "You haven't realised that yet, have you? Why do you think that we all live in this Tower?"

He calmed down long enough to take in a breath but his voice was still firm, "That veil of evil is the real reason why the curse is still in existence." Jesterson was remembering that horrible day over three hundred and fifty years ago, "When the Prince told the 'Sultan' advisor the truth on that horrible day, the advisor- a good friend to the Prince- told us good spirits to go and run for the Tower and to stay away from 'the veil' because it will contain the spirits of the evil dead. Many people and spirits were lured there by their mournful song while others were dragged in because they got too close or made sudden movements; never to be seen again. So, he made it quite clear to stay away from 'the veil' and we have obeyed this rule for over three hundred years!"

Timothy patted Jesterson's back and says now that he has calmed down; "This is not the place for foreign investors to visit the House because we don't want them ending up like all the others! We have also a caretaker who has defended us and has kept this place safe for five generations and you think foreign investors are going to take or invade the House? THINK AGAIN! The dark evil spirits would have them all for dinner! Besides, Kevin would not allow them access due to the danger it involves and he would be held responsible for their disappearances for the rest of his life and that would be a burden that is very hard to bear or run away from."

Jesterson started to mourn the loss of his family again as Timothy asked, "What is it Jesterson? Please, talk to me." The jester sniffed as he said, "Forgive me gentlemen, I-I don't mean to interrupt...I was just remembering when I watched my father, mother and sister being taken by these evil spirits; and I was also remembering how I was lured in by their song while trying to free my family from their grasp. I saw many who were dragged in screaming or clawing at the floor or hanging on to furniture, while many others were simply grabbed and cries of death and pain still echo in my nightmares and they could not be helped, while many others were simply gone; never to be seen again like all the guards and James. I know this because I was almost ready to be dragged in to join my family when you Timothy and you Marylebarne, slashed at the dark spirits and got me to safety as we all ran to the Tower. Timothy, and you my good advisor, kept the dark and evil spirits away from all of us as we fled; they saved me and I owe them all for saving my life. I'll never forget that…"

He opened his eyes and the tears poured out as he told the sisters, "I don't know what I would do now if the prince and the advisor hadn't saved me and I will stand beside them when called upon---or have you forgotten your loyalty to the Prince and his father that you go around using other people's fears just for amusement?" Jesterson angrily cried out as Timothy comforts him, "Easy, my friend Easy, let Marylebarne handle this, okay?"

He nodded as Timothy held his friend close and he knew how heartbroken he was having to live with that constant nightmare everyday of losing your family and thinking that you should have done more to protect them…it was agony and Timothy knew that as well when his father and mother never came to see him after the curse to provide comfort. "This is what pain is, Catharina and Celeana; the pain of losing your family the fear of seeing that nightmare relived over and over again and waking up in tears and heartbreak to know that when you close your eyes, the pain and fear return until you are driven to the brink of insanity and you are driven to the veil of evil begging them to take you because you can't take it anymore."

Timothy came closer to the sisters as Marylebarne listened knowing that right now, at this moment, he was acting like a Prince; wise and compassionate-standing up for those who are too scared to do it on their own. He was proud of his charge and wished his father and mother were here to witness this- this was day that he grew up as he continued. "This is what Jesterson has to live with; now it's happening to Alyssia. She lives every day with the pain of not having a family; the nightmare of watching her mother die every day in terror and in fear until she sits up screaming in the middle of the night crying out for a mother who died needlessly and a father and son who are missing and not knowing if they are alive or dead and to know that your only family member, the one who raised you, is gone and the crushing pain and to move on without a clear path or vision. So she moves on blindly every day until clarity is found and knowing that she will never be reunited with her lost father and brother so she buries it and moves on; that is what pain can do."

He looked back at the advisor who was almost in tears as he thinks of what was and how it is now being trapped and locked away in a Tower while trying to keep order with a young prince who has taken to his duties rather well and learning what it's like to be a prince or a king in a ever changing world. Timothy told him as he looked back at the sisters and then back at the advisor, "I will take Jesterson to his room, Marylebarne; he needs to rest and pull himself together." The advisor nodded, "Of course my wise prince, you do that…Jesterson needs a friend now more than ever."

The Prince and the jester were just about to leave when the sisters, who were full of remorse, fell to their knees before the Prince and Marylebarne and begged for forgiveness. "We are sorry, your highness and Marylebarne please don't send us to the veil." Timothy felt sorry for them as he left Marylebarne to handle their punishment as he needed to calm down himself and help Jesterson sort out his fears until he heard a door closing downstairs. He took in a deep breath and replied, "That's Alyssia returning from her day out with her friends. I better go check on her and see if she's all right and Marylebarne, go easy on them; they didn't know how we got here and they were just children at the time when all this happened."

Marylebarne nodded as the Prince Timothy rubbed Jesterson's back as they both left the study, "Come on Jesterson; let's leave Marylebarne to deal with the sisters." The jester nodded as Timothy took Jesterson to his room and told him to go and grieve and rest as he went to tend to business after the other spirits left the door and they patted Jesterson on the back as reassurance that they would all be there for him. A little girl told the jester, "Don't be sad anymore…" and he knelt before her and they hugged as the little girl smiled. "Feel better Jesterson for we miss your jokes." Jesterson patted the little girl's head and gave her a small kiss on her hand and cheek. "Thank you my sweet little girl." She smiled brightly at him as he stood and let Timothy lead him to his room so he can mourn the loss of his family.

As for Timothy, he took a deep breath to hide his tears, disappeared into the shadows and headed for Alyssia's home as night closed in on the House once again. After dealing with the sisters, Marylebarne went to speak to Kevin Parks about Alyssia entering Cassious House as he took a deep breath to calm himself before speaking to Kevin. He disappeared and gathered his thoughts as he arrived in Kevin's hall mirror as the Parks were getting ready for a romantic night out. Kevin was fixing his tie and straightening his jacket until he heard, "I'm glad that I caught you before you left Mr Parks, I need to ask for your permission on Alyssia's behalf to enter Cassious House."

Kevin was going to look around, but Marylebarne stopped him. "I would just look straight in the mirror, Mr Parks." Kevin said in a whisper as he looked to the left corner of the mirror and kept his eyes on the wise advisor and asked, "Why can't Alyssia ask us herself?" Marylebarne says, "I guess that she is sort of busy trying to get through this first week of University after a rough time she had on her first week of term, no doubt you have heard what has been going on, my dear Mr Parks?"

Kevin gathered himself and sorted his tie and jacket as he nodded, "Yes, I have heard and I can't believe what is going on. She is only a student Marylebarne, and yet she gets knocked down by a lecturer, Thackeray House falls down on top of her, she is spooked by spirits in the library and told certain things she has no business hearing and will have to sort out tomorrow and solving a couple of mystery paintings of two men and three unknown maps at the Welling Street Visitor's Centre and Art Museum and it's only been a week."

Kevin thought about it for a moment and spoke up, "Marylebarne, I will let her go into the House indefinitely if you promise to watch over her while she is gone from our sight, that is the only way I will give Alyssia permission to enter the House whenever she wants. My wife even feels that she is the one that will change everything; I guess I'm still a bit overprotective of you just as the four generations of Parks before me, and now she is telling me to relax the rule."

Marylebarne says, "My dear Kevin Parks our loyal protector and friend," Marylebarne says as he got closer and puts his ghostly hands on his shoulders. "We spirits are very grateful and appreciative of what you have done for us and your fathers before you are the reason why we are still here. We just ask that Alyssia be allowed to come and go as she pleases and who knows, she may be the one to break this curse and free you from the duty of being our protectors. All we are asking for is a chance to let her prove it to us; that she is the one, *'the key'* that could break this curse on Cassious House and unlock our past and search for the truth among the lies. She has courage, loyalty and is willing to put her reputation and life on the line to prove it and she has already gained our trust, now all I ask of you is to trust her. Will you do that for us Kevin?"

Kevin thought, *'how can I not refuse that offer as you make such a good case on her behalf?'* He took in a deep breath and replied, "Marylebarne, she has my permission to enter the House as long as you watch over her and she is away before midnight, Deal?" Marylebarne smiled and said, "Deal and thank you Kevin." The caretaker smiled and watched Marylebarne back away and disappeared into the shadows as Kevin turned and found no one there as he thought out loud, *"I must be getting senile in my old age…"* Sharlene came behind him and wrapped her arms around him and asked what was going on as he told her everything while they headed out for their romantic evening.

In her home, the numb and shock of this afternoon gave away to crying and shaking as a stressed out Alyssia let the tears fall from her eyes. She was standing by the window, with pain and sorrow so hot and noticeable, Timothy was heartbroken as he came to her and held her close as she told him, "This is how I deal with stress…a good cry." He took her hand and kissed her forehead as he asked her, "Will you be okay?" She could only nod as more sobs began to overwhelm her as he brushed back her hair. "I'm here now and the sisters will be seriously reprimanded for what they did to you. I am so sorry that you got spooked," he said gently. "Please, I beg of you, don't leave."

She looked up with tears pouring from her eyes as he tried to brush them away, but she managed a smile as she reached up and placed a hand on his cheek as he looked at her with love as she asked softly; "Who says I'm leaving? I want to help." He was very happy as she smiled and said, "I think three hundred years is too long to be trapped in here, don't you agree?" He nodded, held her close to him, kissed her forehead and asked as he let her go, "So what can we do to help? Please I would do anything to get to the truth."

He felt needed again as she told him softly, "I need to learn everything about the House, its history, the curse; right down to the last detail…there is more to this House than you and the curse and what happened on that tragic day. The truth is hidden from you and I intend to find it and I want to help you find out the whole story of that tragic day and maybe get some questions you and I want answered." Timothy nodded and thought that was fair as she wrapped her arms around him and he held her close. "I love your hugs…you give the best hugs;" she said to him gently as he smiled.

He thanked her as he said holding her, "Then Saturday night is confirmed," the Prince says as she smiled and stared into his beautiful brown eyes. "Kevin has given you permission to enter the House; Marylebarne has asked him on your behalf and he told Marylebarne, 'as long as you were out of the House before midnight, it was okay with him.' That's if you are up for it? He's still a bit overprotective of us." She sniffed and played with his hand and fingers as she rested her head on his shoulder, "I'll be okay, some sleep and a clear head and I will be fine; honest and yes, I'm up for it…" The couple laughed as she said gently, "Thanks for your concern, Timothy."

He smiled and stroked her cheek and hair as he felt something stir inside him while he held her close again: *'Could this be love? But I have no heart or soul?'* She placed her hand back on his cheek and a shudder ran down his spiritual spine as she then placed her hand on his chest as he held in his desire for her. *'IT IS LOVE! B-But I can't be in love with her… can I?'* She smiled up at him as they stood holding on to each other one last time as he took her hands into his and held them close, "Till Saturday Night?" She nodded as he kissed her gently on her forehead one last time as they let go of each other; telling her that he would be back later as he disappeared into shadows.

As midnight came, Timothy took his fresh book on plays and sonnets to read while guarding her and Mystery while his two girls slept soundly. The dark spirits were singing out in mourning, "She is *'the key'*… *'The key'* to breaking this curse!" It was repeated over and over like a needle on a broken record. Timothy was confused as the song grew silent and they went back into the veil as dawn broke in the East as Timothy went back to the Tower and slept before the sun broke through the window of her bedroom.

Chapter 5

Friday morning came as her alarm went off and she looked outside at the weather; it was cold and rainy as Alyssia was showered, changed, got the bed made and Mystery was up waiting to be fed as they went to the kitchen to have breakfast together. The cat jumped up on the countertop in the kitchen as Alyssia dished out her food while she was having her own breakfast and they ate together as the rain started to fall. After she finished her breakfast and did her dishes, she went to the phone to call Mary Anne to see if it was okay to come over and to visit as Gwen picked up the phone.

"Hello, Mary Ann Parker residence, Gwen speaking…" Alyssia heard as she smiled and thought: *Always so formal, aren't you Gwen?'* Then with a chuckle, she spoke with love and warmth to the daughter. "Gwen, its Alyssia." "Oh hello Alyssia," said Gwen happily. "Nice weather we're having eh?" Alyssia chuckled, "…yes nice weather for the duckies!"

Both girls laughed as Alyssia got straight to the point. "Listen Gwen, I was wondering if it's still okay to visit with you and your mum; if not I will completely understand." Gwen says happily. "Of course you can; she has been looking forward to your visit for a long while and she's been telling her friends about you and so have I…" Gwen then says to her, "But mum has got a doctor's appointment this morning and then, we're off to the grocery store to get some things for the house and you know that I will be hanging around; if that's okay?"

Alyssia chuckled as she replied happily, "It's perfect and yes it wouldn't be any fun without you, Gwen." The girls were happy with the arrangement as Gwen says quickly, "We'll be home about twelve-thirty if that's fine with you?" Alyssia says, "Of course. I look forward to seeing you and Mary Anne and if I'm late, I will immediately call you." Gwen smiled and cheerfully says, "We look forward to your visit; I'll let mum know… Goodbye." and both ladies hang up the phone.

She went to put on some soothing music and then went over to the homework table to look at all her homework from the first week of University. She looked through her homework notebook, went to bookshelf, looked out all her folders that were in her homework notebook, and got started on her assignments for her other classes; while Mystery came up beside her as Enya played gently in the background as she gave Mystery a cuddle and a rub on her ears as she lay down on the glass and relaxed while Alyssia did her homework.

About ten thirty, she put down her pen and started to get ready to head off to Mary Anne Parker's home in the suburbs after playing with her kitten. She was already dressed and she puts on her shoes and raincoat as she went to her car after the rain stopped until she heard a voice calling out to her. "Miss Jenkins, I say Miss Jenkins…" She looked around to see Dean Pharrell Winchell coming up the drive towards her as she closed the boot of the car.

At first, Pharrell is just an outsider with skinny, but bulky frame, brown eyes and brown greyish hair medium height and build; doing his job and looking forward to retirement as well with Edward Mangard, but when he hears that Alyssia Franklin-Jenkins is coming to study at Kelton University, he makes plans for her future and protection with the help of the caretaker Kevin Parks. He is good friends with Mark and Paul Franklin whom he has good, solid friendship with and after Mark had a nervous breakdown after losing his wife and daughter to a disastrous trial that left his career in ruins, he offered him and his son a job at Kelton University. He is very understanding and listens to his students about any concerns that affect the University and will do whatever he can for her; especially after Thackeray House falls on top of her and rushes to make amends by asking her to teach a study group (the first of its kind) at Kelton University.

F"Alyssia, I say Alyssia," he called to her and she smiled and watched him coming up the drive as she waited for him to catch his breath. "Good morning Dean Winchell. How are you?" He got his breath back and said with a smile, "I am fine, but most importantly, how are you, Alyssia? I heard about the incident in the library and I was worried…" Alyssia placed her arm around him as she looked up the sky; it was threatening to pour down rain once more as she said, "Please Dean Winchell, come inside and have a cup of tea and I will drive you back to the campus." He declined but she insisted, "Dean Winchell, you are going to have a heart attack if you keep after me like this." He laughed until she had a terrible feeling that she and the Dean were being watched and she looked through the binoculars and saw George Thackeray looking at them.

She had to think of something fast as she says to the Dean, "Come in to my house out of the rain" and she whispered, *'George Thackeray is watching...'* he looked at her and nodded as she went back to her normal voice quickly. "Come in, have some tea, and get your breath back?" She whispered to him again, *'Act normal and don't let on.'* The Dean says, "Yes of course, thank you." They get into the flat as she closed the door as she went to the sideboard and put her binoculars away discreetly as she says to him, "Have a seat and I will get the tea ready-besides, it's good you came; I need to talk to you about something very important which involves the safety of the University."

The Dean nodded and looked around her home as he sat on the couch as she called out from the kitchen, "I won't be long;" as she waits for the kettle to boil she decided to ask from the kitchen, "But why me Dean Winchell?" He looked at her, "I beg your pardon, Alyssia?" She came to him and sat beside him on the couch while she waited for the kettle to boil. "Why are you so worried about me; I'm no one special?"

Pharrell happily explained as she sat beside him while he took her hand in his as he remembers her mum and dad. "Your mum and dad were good friends of mine and students of the now defunct Kelton Heights Vocational College. They were the last graduates to pass through its doors and we became very close friends. Your parents made me your godfather and I promised your parents on their graduation day, that if anything happened to them, I would look after their children and may I say, you do look a bit like your mum."

She was glad that someone was looking after her; especially after her grandmother passed away and during the drama of the first week at the University as she says sincerely, "Aw thank you, Dean Winchell. That is very kind of you...I still miss her to this day." He patted her hand and felt some comrade-ship with her. Then she heard the kettle; "Excuse me a moment Dean Winchell," he nodded and she went to the kitchen to make the tea and prepare the biscuits as she put everything on a tray and brought it through with two mugs; one with Hot Chocolate, one with tea, milk and sugar, teaspoons and a small tea pot and she poured the hot water into both mugs as she replied, "Since you asked about the incident in the library; I am fine, still a bit spooked," she sighed and said as she set the tray down, "…it's the two elderly librarians I am worried about and I wonder if they are okay? They are the ones you should worry about."

The Dean smiled and said reassuringly, "They are well and are back at work with reinforcements behind them this time. The younger staff decided to give the ladies a bit of a break and do all the heavy stuff for them and the caretaker has fixed the heating in the library." Pharrell explained to her that he was out of the University on business and he was told by the Health and Safety officials and first aiders about the incident in the library and what happened during the week at their meetings.

"I am deeply sorry about your grandmother's passing, that you had a rough first week at University, and that you were involved in these incidents. I must be slipping in my duty as a godfather but your friends seem to take up the duties rather well when they told me what has been happening to you. I heard what had happened with the librarians and I was told you were involved from the head first aider, I came up to the House to see if you were okay."

She was very glad that there were guardian angels around her as she says, "Well, you are busy Dean Winchell and that is really kind of you that you would come all this way to check on me as well as you saving me a trip to the campus. I was just on my way to see you and Edward Mangard; I was told in the leaflet that he is the Principal of the University?" The dean smiled, "Yes he is, but I'm afraid he is away on business for the rest of the day and will not be returning to the campus until Monday." She was a bit disappointed as the Dean reassured her, "But if you would like, I will pass a message on to him for you. I work very closely with him and after the building collapse; I was in talks with building inspectors, lawyers, police and Health and Safety officials for many hours, so you can rely on me for relaying a message back to him about safety or any other concerns to him."

She hands him a mug of tea and she had hot chocolate as she says, "Thank you, Dean…oh and please help yourself to a biscuit, sugar, and milk." He nodded and they enjoyed their hot drinks and each other's company as he said, "This is such a lovely, cosy home you have made for yourself." Alyssia chuckled, "Thank you Dean Winchell. My grandmother thought it very weird that when she told me to clean my room, I actually did 'clean my room!'" they laughed as she continued.

"She watched as I got cleaning supplies and cloths out of the cupboard and she had a weird look on her face as I told her, 'Okay I will bring these back gran.' I never thought I say this but my gran never had a bother with me after that because I was supposed to be a rowdy teenager, stay out till all the wee hours with friends, come home with weird tattoos, smoking, drinking, partying, taking drugs, shout and argue with her... like a typical teenager."

The Dean and Alyssia share a laugh as she said, "But I wasn't; which was weird! Anyway, after about an hour or two, I brought back the cleaning supplies and her jaw would drop as she would come into my room and see me sitting on my bed, reading Shakespeare with Enya on my radio and the room shining and sparkling. I just like everything in its place, that's all. She even checked under my bed to make sure I didn't pile any dirty clothes there...there wasn't any. It would stun my grandmother when one day while I was out doing some chores for her, a friend who was visiting, asked her if she ever had any trouble with me; she would tell her 'No not a spot of bother'...her friend didn't believe her until and she would show her my room as proof!"

The dean smiled and said, "She didn't really?" Alyssia chuckled, "Oh yes she would; her friend would come to visit and she would look into my room and hear Enya playing softly in the background. I think that her friend was more stunned as my grandmother." They chuckled as the dean pulled out a pen and notepad after he sets down his mug. "Anyway, you wanted to hear my concerns about the University, not talk about how boring I am."

The dean and the student got down to business, "Yes, and you are never boring, always a delight to speak to." She smiled shyly and puts down her mug on the table's coaster as they got down to business; "So now what business can I sort for you?" he asked as Alyssia took in a deep breath and says, "I know about some foreign investors coming to the University in the spring... and before you ask, the librarians would NEVER give anything like this away to any student at the University." The dean nodded in agreement as his sigh was more of relief than anger as she continued. "So, I thought I better tell you about this in case there were any safety or security concerns."

The dean was very understanding as he drank more of his tea; "Yes, Alyssia, I do appreciate your concerns…" he replied after he placed his mug down on one of her coasters displayed proudly on her coffee table and says gently. "And yes there is to be a top-secret conference; it's hard to keep a secret or anything in a small town, let alone on a very small University campus" he confessed as he finished writing down her concern on the security and safety of the University and the top secret meeting.

"I want you and Edward Mangard to know that I am not interested in or what the conference is all about or what it might entail. But most of all, I have no intention of betraying trust or secrets. I would like to stay on good terms with you and his staff…" she said as Dean Pharrell Winchell was impressed as she had shown great resilience into not getting involved in top secret affairs that were none of her business. Dean Winchell put his pen and pad away in his pocket and took up his tea again. "Alyssia," he began, "you are a very good person and I thank you for bringing this to my attention and for detecting wrongdoing and raising security issues about the conference."

Pharrell says with no malice and confusion, "Edward Mangard has made this conference very hush-hush…even his own staff doesn't know about it; do you know any more about the conference?" Alyssia takes in some hot chocolate. "All I know about it was something about a new state-of-the-art Natural Disaster Research Facility-that's about the extent of it, Dean Winchell." The dean sighed with relief; "Well that's okay then; at least the spirits didn't go too far, but how did you know they were spirits?" They chuckle as Timothy came into the flat and hid in the shadows after he saw a man there talking to Alyssia.

"The librarians, I spoke with, talked with an English accent when I asked them to put aside some books for me on Wednesday afternoon for the study group's reports on ghosts. Then when I came back with those books yesterday afternoon, they were talking with a German accent with a bright glow emanating all around them; that's how I knew they were spirits. So I did what Paul Franklin told me and they left their bodies. Some of the students who were with me couldn't believe what was happening as they stood there gawking at what they've just seen. Anyway Dean Winchell, when they started talking about a top secret meeting and a State of the Art Research Facility, it rang alarm bells. So I thought I better let you and the principal know before I headed off to Mary Anne Parker's home for the day."

Pharrell was really impressed with her and decided to confide to Alyssia what is going on and what the facility would mean for the University as the Dean began, "It's good that you brought this to my attention Alyssia and I will tell you what I know about the facility but you must not mention it to anyone else." Alyssia understood and replied, "Dean Winchell, whatever is said here will stay within these walls and go no further; you have my word." Pharrell took in a deep breath and told her in a low voice.

"Thank you Alyssia, I really appreciate your discretion." Pharrell sighed and began as Alyssia listened to what he had to say. "The Natural Disasters Research Facility will be the first of its kind for the University; and its quite amazing, exciting and most of all universal. It will bring experts, students, visitors, and dignitaries from all over the world. Global Warming, Earthquakes, Tornadoes, Tsunamis, Hurricanes, Flash Floods, and the Ice Age-all types of study; you seem interested?" She smiled "I am," she says gently as the Prince smiled and listened. "I've always been fascinated with how the Earth works." She said happily but then she saw the dean's face drop. "But by the look on your face, there's a catch…"

The dean nodded and steadied himself as sadly smiled as Timothy kept hidden and listened carefully to every detail. "Yes there is…Thackeray House must be sacrificed to make room for the facility and his land is just perfect for the facility so George is not happy." Her thought to that statement: *'Huh, when is he ever happy? If he cracked a smile to anyone, he would probably give someone a heart attack!'* Timothy must have read her mind as he chuckled while the couple talked on about her concerns as Pharrell continued. "He has threatened everyone; including the faculty with death if we went through with it; so we have until the end of this year to make our decision to go ahead but George is going to stop it in every way he sees fit and that's why we are holding the meetings somewhere secretive and if George ever found out, he would be right there to stop it."

The dean was downhearted but Alyssia simply says as she placed her hand on top of his as Timothy watched as he heard her say, "My dear Dean

Winchell, may I be firm yet kind to you?" she asked as he nodded, "Yes of course;" as Alyssia says, "You are his boss and Edward Mangard is your main boss, am I right?" he nodded as she continued. "He pays your salary, makes you aware of any University issues that affect you, the students, staff and lecturers and the rest of the community around the University whether it's on campus or off campus?" He nodded and she said gently, "I would never like to attend a University where everyone is afraid of each other. I believe that you are a good person and if Edward Mangard wants his Natural Disasters Facility, build it over George Thackeray's and his goons dead bodies; just don't let him intimidate you!" *'That's my girl,'* the prince smiled and thought as he nodded while he stayed hidden in the shadows of her home. The dean had renewed faith and courage as if his fears and worries were snatched away from the jaws of a lion with in him and he patted her hand. "Thank you Alyssia; sometimes I need to be reminded of who's in charge at this University."

Pharrell smiled as Alyssia did thinking out loud as worry was temporarily etched into her young features. "Foreign investors mean tight security checks, terrorist checks or sympathies to prevent attacks, media attention..." but now it was Dean Winchell turn to calm her he touched her hand and says reassuringly as if he was reading her mind. "Not to worry Alyssia," she looked back at him; "...this campus is way too small to house a conference this big so we have a very secret location of where it will be already booked. The investors will be told on the day they arrive and then escorted to the secret location by secret security force in plain clothes with official badges."

She sighed with relief as he concluded quite happily; "You let us deal with all of that; all you need to worry about is the homework, assessments, reports, assignments and exams, okay?" She nodded as they were just about finished with their business as the dean looked at his watch and was shocked; "Oh my look at the time...I've kept you too long." They both stood as she grabbed her purse and coat and says, "I will make sure that the principal is told of your concerns and if he needs to see you, I will let you know personally."

He stood up and stretched as she thanks Pharrell while Timothy went back into the shadows and into the Tower to tell the others as Alyssia grabbed her keys off the hook as she went outside with the dean and locked the door to her flat. "Come Dean Winchell, I better drive you back; it looks like the heavens are going to open up." He looked up and saw that she was right as her car was in the shelter of the trees but it would not be for long. Alyssia and Pharrell reached her car and as they got in and just in time too as the rain got heavier and the wind was colder as she looked up and smiled to Timothy as she waved to him quickly. He did the same as he watched the car disappear down the drive as he told Marylebarne what he heard and that the sisters were right about a research facility being built.

The advisor called the sisters to his room, "I want to apologise to you two for being angry with you…Prince Timothy has informed me that you were right about a research facility, but the only thing that he and I are not happy with is how you went about it." The sisters smiled as the Prince asked them gently, "Has Marylebarne has assigned you a punishment?" Catherina nodded and said sadly, "We meant no harm to her your highness, and we thought that if she is *'the key'…*'" Timothy stopped them confused, "Wait a minute, what do you mean, *'the key'*?"

Celeana reached into her gown pocket and gave him a parchment out of her studies as he takes it and he read with Marylebarne: *'The only way the curse will be broken is if 'the key' is found. She must be true of heart, loyal, love and have a child-like demeanour about her…'* The Prince and the advisor looked at each other, "Are saying that Alyssia Franklin-Jenkins is *'the key'*?" The sisters nodded but said, "It may be her or someone else, but all I know is that Alyssia is so nice and what we did to her is unforgivable, but we think that she is the one that will break this curse so there was only one way to find out and that was to talk to her."

The Prince smiled as they weighed up all the evidence, "Well, there is another way to find out; listen and wait. I've already saw what she is like when I looked around her home and I think it's time to put my plan into action to look for more clues." The advisor says, "…and she said to you that she wants to help us, she is very intelligent and is the only one that hasn't run away from the House since she met you. You seem quite smitten with her, my dear Prince?" He cleared his throat and changed the subject as Marylebarne smiled and chuckled as the Prince turns and asked the sisters, "Do you know anything about family trees?" The sisters looked at him oddly, "Well yes," said Catherina with puzzlement; "My sister and I have been raised to understand them from our father, why do you ask, your highness?"

He smiled as Timothy asked Marylebarne to close the door. "I need a favour…I need you to find the Carlton and Thackeray family trees and start looking for clues on Alyssia Franklin-Jenkins; see if there is anything we missed or any surprises that may pop up. If you do, see Marylebarne or me right away; I need everything you can find on the families I have mentioned. But first you need clues…" The sisters listened to what he has in mind and why it's important to get it right; "This may be the only chance we get to help reunite her with the missing father and brother, Marylebarne." The advisor nodded and he listened to his idea. "We will go back to her home as soon as she is away and look around for any evidence of her family besides the photos…look for anything that I may have overlooked."

He looked at the sisters and said to them calmly, "I want you to gather as many spirits that are not busy or bored and tell them to follow me and Marylebarne to her home I need as many eyes as I can get." The sisters bowed and hurried off to find his search party until there was a gentle knock on his study door; it was Jesterson who opened the door while the sisters left Marylebarne's study. "Sorry to bother you sirs," He said bowing to them as the jester came in to the study, "…but Alyssia and the man from the University have left." Marylebarne says, "Thank you Jesterson;" the jester was about to leave as the advisor called him back. "Oh Jesterson," the jester poked his head back in the door as the advisor asked, "Are you doing anything right this minute?" The jester said, "No sire…why?"

The Prince and the advisor smiled as the Prince asked with his hands on his arms, "Will you come with us to her home to look for clues? I may have overlooked something and I need as many eyes to help me look." Jesterson says as he smiled, "Of course, sire…" he says as he bowed and came into the study, "Anything for her and you, sir." The Prince smiled and placed a hand on Jesterson's shoulder and says to the sisters as they see the search party gather around him, "Wonderful work, Coquitlam Sisters, come we only have very little time till she comes home. She doesn't like driving in the dark so we have to move fast." They all bow before him and the search party left the Tower for Alyssia's home at the other end of Cassious House.

In the car, the dean asked her as he puts on his seat belt, "How is the study group going?" Alyssia says as she drives down the drive. The Dean rolled to the end of the driveway while the rain lashed down and the wind blew heavily through the trees as if a huge fan from a movie set was used. "The students are enjoying it, but its early days yet…" Pharrell smiled and listened to what she had to say. "The students seemed less stressed when we do the group and one student commented to me is that I talk to them in plain English as most of them fear answering questions in class or are wary about speaking up or just giving their opinions because they would sound foolish or dumb. So, they write them down ask them to me; either in class during break time or at the study group."

"While we are working on the "big" report on 'ghosts', one student came to me and says to me that she was unsure of how to word her report to make it sound 'sensible' not only to her, but to the Doctors Franklin. I told her that we would go over it together and I made up a game to help them gather ideas and that's when Mark, Paul and Cecilia came in and gave me a hand; they were so nice, helpful and understanding; and by the end of the class, everyone had a finished report… I believe that they are more relaxed when they are away from the campus and classroom."

She turned on to the road and drove over to the entrance of the campus then the car drove slowly through the campus until she found the road up to the Administration Building and got the car under a canopy as she stopped the car and put the brake on as she concluded her observations to the Dean. "I find that when we are in the classroom with the Doctors Franklin; they tend to be quite formal, but outside the classroom the students can be themselves." The dean says as he unlatched his belt, "I quite agree…things have to be very formal on campus but I am happy that the students are doing very well and I hope that they keep up to good work and if you need anything; at all, you'll let me know?"

Alyssia nodded, "I will, Dean Winchell; oh, Cecilia Lambert from the Communications Department will probably come and see you about some pamphlets that I have given her for the students to keep them from plagiarism. I use the pamphlets as a reminder of what is and what's not included in reports and others written material. I believe you have something similar and she will be asking about them," she says with kindness as he looked around and saw that he was at the Administration building.

He took off his seatbelt and says, "Thank you for bringing it to my attention, we forgot to put them in the fresher's bags so I will make sure

Cecilia and the rest of the teachers get them for all the students, thank you the ride up here to the campus, I really appreciate it." Alyssia smiled as she watched him unbuckle his belt as he sees the rain coming down in sheets as Pharrell and Alyssia heard the rain on the canopy roof and looked out as Alyssia replied, "That's why I gave you a ride, it would have been impossible for you to get back here in time and you would be soaked and at least you are dry when you come back to work."

The dean says, "Quite right. Thanks again for the lift, tea and your concerns; I'm sure you'll do well in your classes and that you will keep the conference to yourself?" Alyssia says as he opens the car door, "Of course Dean Winchell, I'll do anything for you even it means keeping the conference a secret. It would be a disaster if anyone like George Thackeray knew; good day Dean Winchell and I will see you on Monday." He smiled as he slowly got out of the car, "And to you Alyssia," she smiled as he got out of the car and she locked the door as he disappeared into the Administration Building of Kelton University.

The next stop was Mary Anne Parker as she pulled out slowly from the Administration Building's canopy and made her way, slowly, through the rain soaked campus car park to the road that will lead her to Mary Anne Parker's residence in the suburbs. As she was on her way, she stopped halfway and picked up some things and called Gwen quickly to see if she was home and to also let them know that she was on her way to them when she left ASDA.

Back at the caretaker's hut, John and Stuart were looking over the photocopies that 'Dead eye' Carol gave them on the Franklin Family. Stuart wasn't talking to John after Carol gave him a slap on his behind and John did nothing to stop it, but now was not the time to be angry as John made it up to him with a large coffee of his choice and he paid for it. Stuart thanked him by threatening him on their way back to the campus; "You so much say anything about this to the others, and I will murder you myself and make it look like an accident!" John laughed and promised as the officers got down to business as they were looking over police reports and comparing notes.

They were back at caretaker's hut and looked at all the paperwork, there were copies of everything; but there was something missing as he asked John as he was reading up on a police report and taking notes while Stuart looked through all the papers around his desk and in the files.

"John, I can't find any legal separation papers, divorce papers…nothing, do you have them?"

John looked in his pile of papers and said, "Well spotted Stuart, what's your take on it?" Stuart had to word his sentences carefully. "I believe that Emily and her daughter were going to go back to Mark and Paul after she found out that her lover had murdered Sidney Preston, your brother." John followed along his line of thinking as he nodded, "You may have something. I remember I was at the station and walking past the witness rooms and saw her talking to two police officers. She was in tears as they asked her if she was anywhere near Cassious House at the time of Sidney's murder and I remember her saying: *'No I was at work and I was on my way to the other side of town to pick up my daughter at school…'* She wanted to tell the officers where she was that day until I heard her say this: *'He was bragging to others about how he killed Mark's assistant and that Mark and Paul were next. I was in no way involved in Sidney's murder… He was our best friend and John's brother.'*

Just as she was leaving the station to go and pick up Alyssia, she saw me in the hallway and gave me this letter and photo of his daughter to give to Mark if we ever found him. He showed the picture and letter to Stuart as John said with a sigh as Stuart looked at them. "…but according to the son, they were away out of town at a mental health clinic after Mark attempted to commit suicide; so the police let her go that very night and cleared her of all wrong doing. The very next day she was killed; murdered in her own home in a fiery explosion and I blame myself every day that we should have done more to protect her and I felt like that I failed her." John said sadly to Stuart. "It wasn't your fault, John." Stuart replied sympathetically as John looked at him as the rookie concluded, "You were only following procedures…" John smiled and thanked him. "So I was right John," says Stuart carefully, "…she was going back to her husband and son to support him and return his daughter to him and be a family again?"

John's rage boiled within him as he broke a glass, "But our local lecturer decided to silence her; it seemed that Thackeray didn't want his secrets exposed, so he beat her, filled the home with gas and blew the home up with her in it! Cold blooded murderer!" The young rookie felt for his boss and vowed to get Thackeray after this assignment as he hated the man even more than when he started this undercover assignment.

John's rage knew no bounds as he took in a deep breath and called the sarge after he calmed down as he told Kohl; "I want anything more you have on George Thackeray as well as Ted and Ed Ezra. I'll be by later to pick up the files and I also want Stuart back inside Thackeray House to complete his undercover duties. After that sarge, he will stay with me until this case is wrapped up…I will make sure he is safe sir; I promise."

The sarge knew that the John and Stuart were on to something and told the officer to get those files quickly after he hung up the phone. He calmed down and saw his frightened friend Stuart as he calmed himself down and told him with a hand on his shoulder. "First of all, I'm sorry about my temper, I didn't mean to frighten you; I'm just frustrated at this whole case in general and the lack of action we have to go through." Stuart smiled and accepted his apology as John continued, "Second, I want you back in Thackeray House and then report back to me everything you hear or are told and I will speed up the process of getting those search warrants to get into the classroom and we can see what's in there. I will question Alyssia, Mark and Paul Franklin next week; but as of now, you are under watch."

Stuart nodded as John pulled out a listening device as John said as he fit the device on to him, "You are not to mention this to anyone-not even to George Thackeray; do I make myself clear?" he asked as he placed the Viridian Patch in the lining of his jacket. Stuart says as John brought the wire up and Stuart fit it into his ear, "I wouldn't dare, I don't want the 'Death Stare,' John." That made him smile…even for a little while.

John got him ready as he looked up at the clock, "Noon time, want to go to our favourite hangout for some lunch before we go through more files and you head back to Thackeray House? And not to worry; the device will not be activated until you are inside Thackeray House." Stuart sighed with relief until his stomach rumbled and says as he rubbed his eyes, "I thought you never ask! I also need to stop off at the grocery store… pick up some tea and milk." John nodded and the cops went to the front door and got their coats as the police officers headed into town in John's car.

Back at her home, Timothy and the other spirits arrive and spread out as they looked around at how her home was laid out and they split into teams. Marylebarne watched as Timothy picks up a picture of her and run his fingers across the glass as the advisor asked him, "What are we looking for, my dear prince?" Timothy looked back at Marylebarne and the other spirits as he says, "Sorry was lost in thought," the others smiled as he placed the photo down where it was. "I want to look for her family and the truth; I'm looking for clues-anything that could tell us what her family was like…" His heart broke as he sadly replied to the others. "I want her to be happy, not sad and lonely; I can see through her façade and it isn't pretty."

He looked to the others as he continues, "I can't change her past; but I can change her future and give her back what she really wants; her family." Marylebarne says as he puts an arm of support around him as he looked at his advisor, "Then let's get to it!" The prince smiled as the spirits bowed to him as they all looked around and searched the place for any clues as the Prince soaked up everything around him while they searched high and low for clues and found photo albums and memories, photos of the family in happier times as Timothy asked them to bring the albums with them and he would return them when he was on guard duty. The other spirits nodded and take the photo albums through to Marylebarne's room and then went back to the search at her home.

Then, Marylebarne reached through the sideboard and pulled out a diary as he looked at it oddly as the Prince and the other spirits looked at him, "Did you find something?" Timothy asked as he walked over to his advisor as Marylebarne gave the book to him; "Yes, a strange book with a lock and key;" he started to chuckle and concluded. "…my goodness, these humans are strange."

The others chuckled as Timothy took the book, patted Marylebarne's back and placed the book in the palm of his hands, he held it close, and his other hand was on top as he closed his eyes…he was inside the pages of her past which passed right through his mind. He delved deep into a happy childhood, playing with her dad and brother, baking cakes with her mum, playing games, singing and laughing…deeper he went as the family had a picnic, walking in the park then away to the amusement park where she looked at him and said, "Daddy angel man" and the child waved at him and he smiled and waved back at her.

He turned back into the shadows and there he looked into her present day, her mother crying as she got beaten badly, then her tortured screams of being burned alive in her own home. Suddenly, he saw an evil person watching all this in the circle of fire as the flames were high and the sadness was strong but the evil person didn't look him as he drew his sword. "Who are you?" He turned and it was George Thackeray's face as he drew his sword. "Thackeray you coward, fight me!"

The Prince and George drew swords and they fought in the circle of fire as steel clashed against steel like thunder until George knocked the blade out of his hand and sent him sprawling across the floor. "Cassious House will be mine and there is nothing that will stop me from getting it!" George said wickedly as Timothy found his sword and ran to it but was kicked away again as he kicked Timothy in the kidneys and to the floor once more and hit him on the head with the butt of his sword. Timothy tried to stand but he was weak and tired from the fight until he heard George's laugh and him saying, "DIE NOW PRINCE TIMOTHY ANDREW CARLTON!"

George cackled once more and he ran towards him with his own sword and was about to make the plunge with his sword as he looked up with him with fright and was ready to roll away until Timothy opened his eyes quickly and dropped the diary as he shouted, "Thackeray destroyed her happiness and family! A family that was so happy, a bond that was strong, lively, active, caring, full of happiness and life; pulled apart by Thackeray." The others were horrified as Timothy began to feel sick to his stomach and his head as he rubbed his neck and felt his stomach as his battered spirit rejoined his human form. Then he felt weak and tired as his spirit came back into his body as he felt very faint and started to fall over.

"Your highness…" they cried as Marylebarne and the other spirits stopped him from falling over as the other spirit grabbed a chair for him. "Easy my boy…come and sit down here." One spirit grabbed a chair as the prince sat down as another one gave him some brandy and he got his balance back as he thanked them while Marylebarne asked angrily, "Doesn't that man have any shame?" Jesterson replied, "No Marylebarne, shame isn't in his vocabulary; I think he thrives on break ups and the unhappiness of others. He needs to cause pain and misery just like they did in the bloody Thackeray Feud of 1725-1726 which almost wiped out both families until Mario was ordered banished to Italy."

The search party members all agreed with him as Timothy sniffed and looked at the jester while he dried his tears, "You might have something there; we're dealing with the Italian mob Thackeray, not James Thackeray." The others looked confused; "The mob boss?" Jesterson says as the Prince listened, "Mario Angelo Sabacini Thackeray was a big problem and he was the one, along with the 'Sultan', who ordered the assassination of you and your father. Sorry these memories are painful but it was James and I who alerted you and your father," Timothy patted his arm, "...it's quite all right!"

Timothy then gave the glass to one of his fellow spirits helped him up after placing the tankard into his pocket as the prince took the drink and sat for a moment. A few minutes later, Timothy stood up with his help, bent down, and picked up the diary, dusted it off and placed it in the drawer as he looked out the window with tears in his eyes while everyone talked. Timothy replaced the diary in the sideboard as Marylebarne started to understand.

"Yes I remember now, it was James and your father's idea to have the good Thackeray name changed to keep the families separate so that the wrong family would not be blamed----**FRANKLIN!** That was the name James changed it to." Timothy started to understand, "So when the attempt happened, my father wouldn't blame the wrong family for the assassination. JAMES WAS BRILLIANT!" Jesterson says, "He was also the one who ordered his own brother and his family and followers banished from England to Italy after they were exposed!" The spirits were finally getting somewhere as Timothy asked, "But what does this have to do with Mark and Paul Franklin? Are they the lost descendants of the James Thackeray-Franklin clan?"

Catherina says as she piped up, "My sister and I can find that out for you, your highness," he came to the sisters and they told him with remorse; "...it would be a sign of repentance for what we did to Alyssia. We have enough clues to start searching the family trees and get the required information for you," said Celeana. The Prince says with a smile, "Okay you do that and also look through the photo albums that are in Marylebarne's study. When you are done with them, put the albums in my room on my dresser and I will return them to Alyssia when I do guard duty." The sisters were excited and said, "We'll start right away, your highness..."

They bowed and ran back into the shadows and to the vaults of the House as the Prince said to the others. "The rest of you listen to me carefully and pass this on to the others around the Tower. I want you to search high and low, deep and wide of the House for anything on the Thackeray-Franklin clan. I want diaries; secret papers, records and hidden documents like birth certificates, marriage certificates, death certificates and other legal papers given to the sisters as soon as they are found…leave no stone unturned no matter how insignificant they might be!"

All the spirits bowed and left as they spread the word and they searched high and low in the House's libraries, vaults, living quarters and hideaways for all clues as he watched all the spirits vanish in the shadows and started their search. Timothy felt sad for her but vowed to make her future a happy one as Marylebarne saw him still staring back out the window as the advisor came to him while he nursed a stitch in his side. "What is it my boy? I thought you would be happy?"

Timothy nodded and looked at him as he said as he took up her picture once again and rubbed the back of his neck, "I am," and he drew a deep breath as he was still puzzled about his feelings for her as he asked his advisor, "But why does she affect me so? Why is it that every time I see her; I want to feel her touch, hold her close, kiss her and just be a part of her life? I have no heart and soul but I keep feeling something moving within me."

He looked at his advisor, "What's wrong with me, Marylebarne?" He asked as he looked at his advisor, "Tell me Marylebarne, what is it that makes me smile every time I see her? I want to comfort her when she cries, I hear talking in her sleep; one night she woke up screaming out her mum's name and I calmed and hugged her. She looked up at me and she told me her nightmare then she fell back asleep after I gave her some water and I just held her and reassured her that she was not in any danger. What is wrong with me?" he asked as he drank down the rest of his water that Marylebarne had given him.

"You, my dear Prince Timothy Andrew Carlton are in love!" Marylebarne says as Timothy looked at him with tears in his eyes, "My dear boy, this is no secret as to what this feeling is. You feel like you can walk on a cloud every time you see her, you delight in her smile and you feel like your feet aren't touching the ground. You want to do everything to be with her, you guard her, you make sure that she's safe, you hold her when she needs a friend or when she's afraid, you talk with her and laugh when she laughs; my boy that's love."

Timothy looked at his advisor confused as the advisor continued. "Don't be afraid of it, embrace it. Let it fill you and when you get back your heart and soul, you will feel alive again. Let the feeling come so when you kiss her lips, it's true, pure and unadulterated love. You my boy, feel human when you're around her; Jesterson and I watched how you shared that love with her and she felt secure knowing that you were there when she had that nightmare and she was appreciative of it, so hold on to it and don't let go of it."

Timothy smiled, "Thank you Marylebarne." The advisor smiled as Marylebarne slapped his back after he stood; "Now how about we join the others in looking for clues, hmmm?" Timothy smiled happily as he placed her picture in his pocket, dusted the table quickly, replaced it with another picture and disappeared into shadows as they went back to the Tower and joined in the search while the rain gave way to sunshine and blue skies.

On the other side of town, Alyssia makes a pit stop to pick up some flowers and treats along the way to Mary Anne Parker's home and gets back into the car and starts driving to her destination after filling up with petrol. The rain had finally stopped and she saw the sun come out and as she got out of the car, she took in the fresh air and smiled after Alyssia makes it to Mary Anne Parker's home as Gwen tells her mother that Alyssia is here as the old woman smiled.

Just then, a ball of spiritual energy enters her body while her eyes lit up and a broad smile broke across her face as it settled within her. Mary Anne Parker says to herself in Emily's voice: *"my daughter comes; now it begins-'**the key**' has arrived; she is the one that will break the curse!"* Gwen brought the tray through as she went to answer the door to Alyssia who came in with flowers for them as well as some treats as Gwen thanks her and takes the treats and flowers to the kitchen as she gave her a hug and lets her in to the house after opening the door.

"Hello Gwen, it's so good to see you," Alyssia says giving Gwen a hug and kiss as Mary Anne woke from a dream. "ALYSSIA!" Mary Anne cries for joy as Alyssia comes to her with hugs and kisses in her chair and gives Marigold a rub on her ears. "It's good to see you again Marigold and Mary Anne…" she tells the cat who purred happily then she heard Gwen in the kitchen. "The flowers are very lovely Alyssia, thank you so much," Gwen says to her mum, "I'll put them in water, mum." Mary Anne nods and motioned for Alyssia to have a seat. "Gwen, there are two sets of flowers, one bouquet for you and one bouquet for Mary Anne." Gwen nodded and says, "Why thank you so much; awfully kind of you." Alyssia smiled as Mary Anne asked her excitedly, "How's University? Did you make lots of new friends?" Gwen called to her, "Mum, let Alyssia get in and take off her jacket and get comfortable…" Alyssia chuckled as she placed her jacket on the hook by the door then she came to the old woman as the student answered her questions in order as she took her hand, "University is wonderful and yes I made lots of new and wonderful friends, thank you and my lecturers-Doctors Mark and Paul Franklin-are really nice."

Mary Anne clapped with glee as Emily sighed lovingly within her body as Alyssia smiled as the old woman took her hands. "That is wonderful to hear; I am so glad that you, Mark and Paul are getting along well so well… Is he well?" Alyssia looked at her and says, "Ah yes he is," Mary Anne was smiling from ear to ear and chuckled with glee but Alyssia said with a sad smile, "but is still upset with losing his wife and daughter though. He still thinks of them, but it looks like he is doing well now and doing a job he loves so much."

Mary Anne's face had a sad smile as Emily cried within her knowing that Mark and Paul still miss her as Mary Anne asked, "…does he still talk about them?" Alyssia nodded. "Yes he does," Alyssia says, "I think he feels responsible for not standing up to fight for his wife and daughter." Emily took in a sigh and felt her heart breaking as Alyssia told Mary Anne, "But I am here to make you and Gwen smile…" Mary Anne patted her hand. "Yes, of course! Let's have some fun and laughs Alyssia." The student kissed the old lady's hands as she smiled as Alyssia let them go and sat on the couch next to her.

Timothy had come to Mary Anne's home and watched over the family from the shadows as Alyssia saw a piano as a memory came flooding back and she heard her young self say as her mum came over to her sad daughter who sat at the piano and brushed away tears, "…but mum, I don't want to play the piano; I make too many mistakes!" Her mum echoed in her head, "It's okay to make a mistake, sweetheart; that's how we learn, Alyssia." But her child like self said as she looked at her mum with tears in her eyes, "… but all the kids call me names," then she heard her father's voice gently say to her as he dropped his paper. "Then they are not your friends…" and then her brother came to his little sister, put his hand on her shoulder and says, "If they hurt my little sister, then I'll hurt them!" The family laughed as she started to play with the keys as her mum says gently as she stroked Alyssia's hair, "…go on and I will guide you." The child smiled as she dried her tears and says, "Okay mummy."

The child played as Alyssia came out of the memory fog as she shook her head, stood up and went over to the small upright piano. "I didn't know you had a piano, Mary Anne?" Alyssia asked as she dried some tears and the old woman says, "Oh yes, I was a piano player in a local orchestra, in show business, and then, a piano teacher while studying to be an archaeologist; I tried very hard to teach Gwen but she didn't do well." Then Gwen replied, "Yes," said Gwen chucking as she came out of the kitchen with the vases of flowers and placing them somewhere on the window sill.

"I didn't have a musical ear but mum, and dad were happy when I became a nurse instead." Alyssia smiled as she looked back at the piano as Mary Anne asked, "What about you Alyssia, do you play?" Alyssia smiled as she could feel her mother sitting beside her giving her comfort, "I used to but it's been so long since-" she stopped as she tried not to shed tears as Mary Anne asked her as she was trying to lift her spirits. "Will you play something for us?" Alyssia was hesitant but she agreed and went to the piano as Timothy watched from the shadows as she sat down on the bench near the piano as her mother came out of Mary Anne and sat happily beside her.

The Prince saw her and she motioned for him to keep silent as he nodded while Alyssia says as the keyboard cover was lifted. "I'm a bit rusty because I don't have a piano at my flat so I can't practice as much as I used to." The women smile but Mary Anne says gently as her mother smiled, "Alyssia, just do your best, that's all I am asking of you." Alyssia smiled and nodded as she started to play "A Day without Rain[33]" by Enya as they listened. Timothy thought as he listened to her play and smiled: *First a study group teacher and now a pianist…you're always are full of surprises, aren't you Alyssia?'*

She started to play as tears filled his eyes; - but they were not the only ones to hear it.

---

[33] "A Day without Rain" by Enya ©2000 Warner Brothers Group plc

John and Stuart were working away in the greenhouse as they took a break from police files until they heard the piano and both men took it in knowing without a single doubt this was her; *'the key'*. Now they stepped up their plans along with the whole police force who also heard it and to keep her protected and they from that moment on, they knew that she was the one to end the curse once and for all.

While in the University, the whole faculty jumped for joy at the revelation and knew that freedom was eminent as the music continued to saturate the air and the woods were filled with joyous rapport as the piano filled the trees and leaves as the branches soaked up its melody and danced with joy in the strong winds as the birds signalled throughout the land that *'the key'* was found. At Cassious House and the caves, a guard at the mouth of the cave was just about to have lunch with his buddy when he perked up his ears when the melody drifted through the rain soaked streets and filled the air around Cassious House

The guard told his friend who also heard it too, was also speechless and the young man stood up and told his friend, "I'll better inform the commander, be right back and no munching my sandwich!" The friend agreed and ran to his commander deep inside the cave as he heard the music. "Sir, begging your pardon," The commander looked at him and said breathlessly, "...but you must listen."

Everyone quieted even Cassious House listened as they heard Alyssia playing as the commander stood up speechless, "It can't be...but it is!" Marylebarne heard it too as he paid a visit, "I knew she would come. She is the one!" Marylebarne thought as he cried tears of joy: *The Coquitlam Sisters and Jesterson were right! They were bloody right! I could kiss them!'* Every spirit cheered, but the dark spirits heard it as well, ***"SHE IS THE KEY!"*** the king hissed to his people as they all cheered and chanted a song of joy as the king told his guards, "Let all the innocents go now!" The guard bowed to him and let the innocent people go as the Dark King called to Marylebarne.

The advisor came running down from the Tower and into the main hall and saw all the innocents as he cheered and welcomed them as he led them to the Tower after the Dark King called to him. "Here are all the innocents, Marylebarne; safe and sound as promised. Take them home and see to them." The overjoyed advisor replied happily, "Thank you and yes; I will make sure they are well cared for." The Dark King smiled as all the innocents looked all around them wondering what had happened as they saw Marylebarne and asked him, but he called more strong and able bodied men down to come and help the innocents to settle into life in the Tower. "I will explain everything to you when you are settled and rested with food and drink in your bellies. Come and follow these men and women to the Tower; there's room for everyone!"

Just then, he saw Jesterson's family and came to them as he says, "I know someone who will be overjoyed to see you. He's been grieving all this time that he couldn't save you, now seeing you alive and well," Marylebarne was at a loss for words as he simply said, "...come, let's get you to the Tower to rest, give you food and water and a long overdue reunion with your son who never gave up on you." The family nodded as the father says, "I would like an ale sir," The family and the advisor laughed and said to them and the others, "Welcome Home and you can have all the ale you want as soon as you are settled and rested!" he cried as the confused, frightened innocents smiled and greeted Marylebarne with hugs, handshakes, and relief.

Meanwhile, "The Three Stooges" Nathan Baines, Dylan McAnelly and Ross Queronaille were lying on the ground outside wondering where they were as two neighbourhood watch patrol men helped them stand. "What the hell? Where are we?" Nathan asked as the officers, "Never mind where you are come on...we'll take you boys home; your mothers are worried sick about you." They looked as Cassious House and grew fearful as they told the officers, "Get us away from here!" The Community Patrol Officers called the police and told them that the "Three Stooges" had been found... unharmed! The police were stunned as they were driven to the station and questioned as their parents were called and the doctors examined them. It was a happy ending these mothers wanted to hear! They told the police and the Community patrol that they will never touch alcohol ever again after their brush with the Dark Spirits in Cassious House and they sought for help to stop drinking alcohol and pay back the money on the credit cards.

Inside the Tower of Cassious House, it was a different story as the good spirits helped the new arrivals settle in to their new life in the Tower as Marylebarne cried out to all that were there, "We got company!"

Marylebarne called out to the others as they saw the innocents coming into the big area of the Tower while the other spirits called for help and everyone assisted them and cared for the injured and ill. Jesterson ran towards the main hallway and into the main room of the Tower as he saw all the innocents until heard a familiar voice, "JESTERSON!" and he turned around to see his family who were taken away from him. He ran and greeted them as he hugged, cried and brought them into the Tower to his friends and family.

"But how?" Jesterson said with shock as his mother says, "The Dark Spirits let us go, son…they heard something and they let us go." Jesterson shed tears of joy and held his family close as he took them to his room and gave them food and water while down in the cave; the guard went back to his duties after his commander thanked him. Marylebarne had come from the Tower and he heard from all the guards and the one who first heard it before the music ended saying gently, "After all these years, we've found '*the key*'!" Marylebarne says, "Yes we have and now all we have to do is keep Alyssia safe!" They all agreed and bowed to their advisor as they returned to their posts and took a vow of secrecy of who the key is and swore they would never tell anyone until the curse was broken. Just as it started, the music stopped and faded in the wind as the guards returned to their posts.

While back at Mary Anne Parker's residence in the suburbs, Mary Anne, her mother, Gwen and spirited Prince Timothy applauded her. "That was beautiful! Bravo!" Mary Anne cried out as her mother Emily said goodbye to Timothy as she went back into Mary Anne and they had tea and treats as Timothy left the ladies to talk and he left for the Tower and his studies not knowing the excitement the Tower was feeling as Alyssia put the keyboard cover down gently on the small piano and came over to the couch for tea and some chatter. "Well done, my dear," said Mary Anne as Alyssia smiled and Gwen patted her shoulder as the girls had their teas and a chat.

At Cassious House, excitement was in the air as all the spirits were jumping for joy around the House while they searched for clues to the Thackeray-Franklin clan. Joy and happiness were all around them as a cautious Marylebarne calmed the excited spirits down while The Coquitlam Sisters and Jesterson were praised by Marylebarne as he said very firmly while they looked for more clues; "Now that we know that Alyssia is *'the key'*, we must keep her safe at all costs! No scaring her away, no tricks...she must not be told and must be able to make up her own mind and not be pressured!"

Jesterson nodded and said, "If she is pressured, she would be frightened off and all our hopes of being rid of this curse and for the University to move forward, would be dashed. Am I right Marylebarne?" The advisor and Coquitlam Sisters nodded and went back to their work as the advisor patted the sisters' backs and says, "You are right and welcome to Jesterson's family and others who was freed from the dark veil. Tend to them and get them back to full health; we'll need all the help we can get." The other spirits agreed and started to nurse the sick and injured back to full health as everyone cheered and made Jesterson's family feel welcome as were shown to their new room down the hall from the Tower until Prince Timothy had returned from Mary Anne Parker's home and was told the news as all the new faces greeted him with a bow as he greeted each of the innocents and they talked with him about their experiences and treatment within the veil.

It was a pleasant, yet unexpected surprise to the Prince who was very happy to see the innocents who were glad to be out of the darkness as they told the others what it was like to be in the veil as Timothy listened and soaked up all the information that was given to him. After talking to all the innocents and listening to their experiences, Timothy looked to see Marylebarne coming towards him as he replied, "My God, she amazes me every day; it's almost time to show her the House properly tomorrow night but in the meantime, we mention nothing of this to her; understood?"

Everyone, including Timothy, agreed and they went back to work looking for clues as Marylebarne took his charge aside and asked, "How is she?" Marylebarne asked the Prince who smiled as he whispered to his advisor. "She is well and I saw Emily inside Mary Anne Parker." The advisor looked at him oddly as he sighed and said with a chuckle at Marylebarne's facial expression, "...and no I haven't been drinking bad ale!" The men chuckled as he told his teacher and friend, "Come with me, I'll explain as best as I can." Timothy and Marylebarne walk past the new arrivals and welcomed Jesterson's family as he walked with Marylebarne to his room and told him everything that he had witnessed at Mary Anne Parker's residence as the day wore on into the middle of the afternoon.

Back at Mary Anne Parker's home, the early afternoon wore on as the ladies had some tea and something to eat as they laughed as the day moved into late afternoon. Mary Anne says while drying away happy tears, "Oh my ladies," Mary Anne said happily. "I have never laughed so much in my life…" Alyssia whispered cheekily, "Then you haven't met Milton Russell; the jester of Kelton University." She told Gwen and Mary Anne what Milton said and did at University so far and it made the girls chuckled happily as schoolgirls looking at boys in the mall as she calmed down. "Alyssia, your visit has made my day; thank you for coming over and making me and Gwen smile…"

She smiled and replied, "Why thank you, Mary Anne and Gwen; I'm enjoying my time here with you, too. But I need your help ladies," she said as she pulled out the book she got from the curator. She hated ruining their day with History as Alyssia witnessed that Mary Anne was an archaeologist and she may even have clues. She took a deep breath and said; "I need you to help me solve a puzzle. I hate ruining your day with History, but I really need your help and advice." She opened the book to the page she needed and says, "The curator, Iain Margarida was very kind to take me around his museum at the Kelton Heights Visitor's Centre and Art Museum during an art fair and I came across these three maps and two men, and please ladies, don't worry if you don't know who they are."

Mary Anne and Gwen nodded as she showed them the brochure which was on the table and got to the page of the three maps and the two men; one of the maps was already named; all she needed was a clue to the men in the two pictures and the name of the two remaining maps as she explained to the women what the curator was wanting and what it would entail. "The curator wants to do an exhibition of old Kelton Heights before it was a lively town; the map on the left is a Celtic settlement with a huge mass of land in the middle and according to the ancient writings which he showed me, 'A huge, magnificent House will be built…'"

Gwen was astonished, "You mean Cassious House?" Alyssia nodded. "The House was to be cursed to protect something beneath it; what it is… we don't know; but if the curse was lifted, then we could go in and see. According to the history books at the museum, when the Celtic tribe left Kelton Heights and Welleston Village, there were very little clues as to who they were fifty-two years ago; the only clue was left was a solid gold necklace that is worth a king's ransom. Then when the 'Sultan' advisor cursed the House after the Prince's phoney 'murder rap,' he remained to make sure that the Prince told the truth, the curse would only be on what's below; but that never happened; EVERYONE WAS CURSED IN THE HOUSE!"

Mary Anne began to understand, "The Celts must have known that all the greed and evil would soon inhabit the world and would take over so they cursed the land the House would be built on to protect what is below. "Exactly, Mary Anne…but what they didn't count on was the inhabitants being cursed along with it. According to ancient writings, it was only supposed to be the House itself and when they blessed the land and placed their villages around it, it was deemed sacred and holy and if anyone stepped on to that holy site, it was sacrilege or desecration as the Bard; the leader of the tribe, would deal with the trespassers and marauders harshly. Now in that once beautiful manor on top of that hill near Kelton University, stands a very sad, haunted, cursed House that is sitting on their treasure and I don't think the Celts had this in mind when they blessed the piece of land which was sacred to them."

Mary Anne began to understand as she said, "Alyssia, I may be able to help you and the curator out;" Mrs. Parker pulled a key from around her neck and gave her daughter the key as she told Gwen, "Go to my bedroom and in my closet behind all my clothes, you will find a locked cupboard. There in front of you after opening its doors, there will be a huge lever arch folder full of pictures, articles and other goodies, will you please bring it here?"

Gwen was confused but went to get the folder as she left the room leaving Alyssia with Mary Anne as the spy, who also heard the music along with his employer was lead there and he watches the ladies as a small phone was on the ledge of the window sill while his employer listens to them on the other end as Mary Anne says, "I loved Ancient History and I was a graduate at the University of Kent with my husband before I went into show business and played in the orchestra, that is where I met Mr Parker," she told Alyssia. "…and my husband was one of the archaeologists that were on the dig near the caves as he and I headed up the Archaeology department when the museum was just being built."

Alyssia nodded and the spy had a sneaky suspicion that this wasn't Mary Anne Parker but Emily Anne MacPherson-Franklin; the wife to the missing Mark Franklin who was a teacher at Kelton Heights Vocational College; she had lived and was living an obscured life but he would not give away her secret; not while George Thackeray was around. He watched the student stand and take her hands as she told her, "I will go and get the dishes cleaned up and washed while we wait for Gwen to return…is that okay with you?"

The old woman nodded, "Aww you're a dear, Alyssia. But you are a guest; I don't expect you to clean up the dishes." Alyssia smiled as she replied humbly, "I insist Mary Anne, besides I need to stretch my legs." The old woman smiled as Alyssia chuckled gently, "I'll go and start on the dishes while we're waiting for Gwen and then we'll take it from there." Mary Anne smiled and nodded as she patted Alyssia's hand as Alyssia packed all the dishes on to the tray, took the tray into the kitchen, filled up the basin and started on the dishes. Mary Anne relaxed as Marigold slept soundly in the old woman's lap as she stroked the cat gently; purring away very contented as Alyssia cleaned up the kitchen after all the dishes were put away in the cupboard and the teapot sat shining like a new penny.

A moment later, with all the dishes washed and put away, and while Alyssia sat with Mary Anne and talked, Gwen came through with the binder as she held it up and asked her, "Is this it, mum?" Mary Anne clapped with glee. "Yes, Yes, bring it here my dear." Alyssia came to them again and Gwen set the binder down and gave Mary Anne back the key. Mary Anne opened it and found the same two men and their names as well as the names of the maps that hung in the museum. Alyssia got out her notebook and brochure and started to write away all the information she could for her report on Cassious House, making sure that she wrote down the sources and dates, newspaper and author of the piece, as well as the name of the newspaper. After all the needed information was collected and stored in her notebook, she thanked the elderly Mary Anne Parker. "This is such a big help, thank you" as she wrote the names down until Mary Anne then asked a strange favour of Alyssia.

"Alyssia, I want you to take the binder away to the curator at the museum; I won't need it; besides my daughter won't need it either, she's a nurse!" The girls laugh as Gwen nodded, "She is right, Alyssia, I know more about History than I do about politics…nil." Alyssia and Mary Anne laughed as she closed it up as she said to her, "If you are sure Mary Anne, I will make sure the curator gets it and he puts it away safe until its needed." Mary Anne thanked her in her mum's voice who said, "That will be ideally gracious of you, my sweet Alyssia."

Alyssia looked at her in silent surprise as Emily continued through Mary Anne as she touched her cheek; "You look so beautiful, look at how much you've grown! I knew you would make me proud, Alyssia, my sweet girl." Alyssia was shocked as she whispered, "Mum, is that you?" Mary Anne glowed and smiled as she nodded, "It is and I want you to know that I will always be with you; no more tears, no more nightmares; I will drive them all away, I promise." Alyssia almost choked on her tears as her mum bent down to Alyssia's ear and she heard her mum whisper, *"Tell Mark and Paul I love them."* All Alyssia could do was nod as she sat shocked as her mum smiled. Mary Anne sat back in her chair as she smiled and stroked her face and her hair until the spirit ball left her and Mary Anne almost fell over as Alyssia and Gwen caught her and a frightened Marigold jumped down scared that her tiny body and tail would be crushed.

Alyssia held her close as Gwen said firmly but gently, "Alyssia, she needs to rest; it's been a long day for all of us;" Alyssia stood up as Gwen touched her arm and said with gentleness, "I'll be right back." Alyssia nodded and smiled as Gwen picked up her frail mum, who was light as a feather, and carried her to bed as she puts her under the covers and leaves her to sleep as Marigold leaped up out of Alyssia's lap and on to Mary Anne's chair as she curled up and fell asleep while Alyssia calmed her down by stroking her body and rubbing her ears as she calmed the kitten down and purred happily at the rub on her ears and body.

Gwen came back through and saw Alyssia, who was getting her coat on and saw her out as she got the binder and her purse as Gwen walked with her out to the car after she gave Marigold a small kiss and a rub on the ears. Alyssia was still shocked at hearing her mum's voice as she dried some tears away as Gwen touched her arm gently. "Are you okay?" Alyssia looked at her, "J-Just heard my mum's voice through Mary Anne and now I miss her all the more. These memories and this house…I-I can't fathom what's going on; I wish someone would tell me Gwen, I-I'm so confused." Gwen had nothing but sympathy for her as she replied, "Come on, I'll walk you to the car. Alyssia looked at Gwen as she took Alyssia by the shoulders and they left Mary Anne's house. The girls were outside as they walked to the car as Alyssia got her keys still in shock as Gwen broke her out of it. "I'm so sorry that I was a bit brash with you, Alyssia…she does this every nap time; she is so stubborn for doing that."

Alyssia understood and says as she smiled, "Not to worry Gwen and you weren't brash with me…I can understand how frustrating it must be to have her take her nap." Gwen smiled but was a bit concerned about Alyssia upon hearing her mum's voice. "Thank you Alyssia; I appreciate it, but are you going to be okay? You seem a bit emotional," she softly replied as she opened the car door, placed the binder on the backseat and covered it with her coat.

After that, she puts her mobile phone in the front drink caddy for some weird reason that she may need it and her purse was put into the boot as she came back to Gwen. "I'll be okay; you may be right, it's been a long day for all of us." She smiled as she continued, "Just tell your mother that I will be back at the end of the month and that I said 'thank you' for the time we had together." The nurse nodded but Alyssia felt there was something more, "But Gwen I have a strange feeling that I'm missing something; is there something more I can do for her?" Gwen sighs and shakes her head as Alyssia took her hand, "She's old, Alyssia and for some unknown reason, she wants to stay alive long enough to see the curse lifted."

Alyssia was puzzled as she asked, "You mean on Cassious House?" Gwen nodded as Alyssia and the spy, hiding close by with his phone on full speaker and his mysterious employer listened as well. "It's her mission to 'see the House free from its darkness.' Her great, great, great grandmother died in that House after serving the Carlton Royal Family for generations. She has been at death's door a couple of times but came back to life feistier than ever…and I don't know what else I can do for her?" Alyssia touched Gwen's arm gently as the daughter had tears in her eyes as Gwen says, "If that's what she wants to do, then who am I to deny her?"

Alyssia closed and locked the back door of her car as she tells her, "I'll see what I can do and make sure that her wish is fulfilled. Tell her that Alyssia will be back to see her at the end of the month," She pulled out a piece of paper and wrote her number down, "…here's my phone numbers and if anything changes call or message me;" as she gave the frustrated Gwen her home phone and her mobile number as she took her hands gently as if to say that everything would be okay but down deep, she knew it was asking for too much. "Tell her that I will make sure the binder is given to the curator and that he must keep it safe," Alyssia promised as Gwen and Alyssia exchange hugs as she continued.

"I promise that I will do everything I can for her but you have to trust me and with winter setting in, stay warm and safe." Gwen was happy for her concern as she replied, "I will make sure mum and I are safe with lots of heat and warmth this winter. A lumberjack has promised my mum free logs so he is bound to show up and stock pile wood. We'll be just fine, I promise." The girls hug once more as Alyssia gets into the car while Gwen sees her buckling up. "Take care Gwen and God bless your mother and your family." Gwen gave her the biggest smile and said, "You too Alyssia, take care of yourself and don't work too hard." The ladies smiled and waved good bye as she points her car towards the museum and its curator.

About an hour in a half later, she arrived at the edge of Kelton Heights and art the Visitor's Centre and Museum near the Harbour and parked the car near the door. She was just about to unbuckle her belt when she saw someone staring back at her in the bushes so without taking her eyes off them, she reached for her mobile, made sure that she locked the doors, called the police and kept eye contact with the bush invader as she sat very still and silent after hanging up her phone while she took off her seatbelt and waited for the police, never once taking her eyes off the intruder in the bushes.

Later, the police arrived just in time as an officer came to her car with a K9 unit as she saw the officer and the dog coming towards her in her rear view mirror and she rolled down the window and told him, "There someone in the bushes right behind me, officer; I believe it's that escaped rapist you have been looking for?" The police officer looked in her mirror and saw the eyes as he whispered, "Roll up your window and keep eye contact; he knows you're watching him and he won't attack unless you're not looking." He signalled the other officers to go around and cut off his escape and search the bushes. The officer pretended to keep talking to her as she kept her eyes on the man in the bushes as the cop gave the signal as he said, "Don't move, I'll tell you when." Alyssia nodded slowly as the police was in position as the officer drew his gun as he said into his radio, **"GO!"** The police ambushed the bushes and had the man in custody within moments as he told her unlock her door and come out.

She did as the police puts the man in the van with his hands and feet shackled as he struggled against his restraints, yelling and cursing at them as she was being questioned after he put in the call that the escaped rapist had been apprehended and is now in custody. "We have been after this man for three days after he dug out of prison right under the guard's nose; are you okay?" The police officer asked as Alyssia smiled, "Yes just a bit shaken but I'm fine; thank you and thank you for your service to the community, stay safe officer." He tipped his hat to her and he left her to do her business as she got into the back seat and got the binder still tucked under her coat and goes inside the museum.

She holds the binder close to her as she walks into the museum and saw the young secretary, "I'm Alyssia Franklin-Jenkins, and I came in here a while back when there was an Art Fair on." The young lady nodded and recognised her as she welcomed her back as Alyssia thanked her as she asked, "Is Iain Margarida, the curator in?" The young secretary told her as Alyssia signed the guest book, "One moment and I will check for you." She called him in his office as she mouthed to the young lady after putting the pen down, "I'll just look around." The young secretary nodded as Alyssia waited and looked again at all the artwork in the museum still not making out the small words on the placards as she looked around.

A moment later, the young secretary pointed the curator to Alyssia who was looking at some other historic relics because she couldn't make heads or tails of the artwork on display as Iain came to her and he smiled as Alyssia turns to see him. "I'm glad that you are here and it was very surprising when my receptionist told me. To be honest, I didn't expect to see you back so soon." They shook hands and she said softly, "Well sir, I am just about to make your day but can we go somewhere private to talk?" He nodded as he saw that she was holding something very close to her; something of importance and didn't hesitate to grant her request. "Of course follow me, Amanda hold all my calls." The young lady nodded and he led her to the back of the museum into room which was private and secure.

She looked around as he flicked on the light in a very white room and saw that it was completely closed in with no cameras or listening devices. "Come in and don't be alarmed; we only use this room for very private meetings." Iain made sure that the door was properly closed while Alyssia gave her eyes a chance to adjust to the bright lights in this closed room as she sat down at the table which was also white. Iain came over and did the same as he asked, "So, what can I do for you?"

She uncovered the binder and sat her jacket on the back of the chair as Iain puts on his gloves to view the contents and he was very excited and happy as to what he found in there. Alyssia then pulled out the brochure with the names of the two men and the maps as she gave it to him; he was jumping up and down like a joey in a kangaroo pouch. She told him, "Mary Anne Parker used to work as an archaeologist before the museum and visitor's centre was built and she wanted you to have this binder and everything in it. The man standing there," she began as she uses a pen to point to a certain male in the picture of the newspaper while the curator looked closely with a magnifying glass, "...is Mary Anne Parker's husband; he also worked as an archaeologist. They were both head of an archaeology department at the time before they got married. They were at the excavation of 1927 in Welleston Village standing behind some pillars."

Iain said, "Then you should go and see my brother Dòmhnall at the City Centre Tourist Information Centre in the West High Street. He knows more about "The Standing Plinths of Welleston Village" than I do and he will give you all the information you need including the address. The plinths are located on a piece of farmland about fifteen miles north of Welleston Village; my brother will give you the exact location. He's a bit of a square but quite knowledgeable in this area than I am. I am curious to know what you might find out if you go out there as the place is on some private farmland owned by a farmer and his wife. But this is the best news ever and I thank you, Alyssia and I am happy to take this off your hands, if you want?" He asked her for Iain was interested as she told him as continued to view the contents, "The strange thing she told me was, 'to take it far away from her.' I couldn't understand why but then she told me with a smile; 'that this might make your day,' so I came bearing good news." Iain was elated, "This is wonderful news," he said. "You have truly made this curator so happy and my Friday; we will keep it in here for safe keeping as well as the names of the gents and the two names of the remaining maps that you can correct just now."

Iain was excited and felt like a kid in a candy store as she thought: *Glad that he didn't kiss me; Milton would have a field day if he ever found out.* She shook off the thought and told him," I may need it again if the need arises, is that okay with you?" The curator smiled and looked at her, "I just don't have room for it at my house and it must stay under lock and key." The curator says to her, "That's just fine; return anytime to use it and yes, it will remain under lock and key. It will take some time for exhibition to open to the public, but you will be the first to be invited here when it does."

Alyssia smiled as they stood up while he placed the binder into a plastic box and placed a lid on it, then he opened the security door and switched off the lights as Alyssia needed to close her eyes to adjust her vision to the normal lighting in the hallway as they left the room and then she opened them slowly as Iain waited beside her. "Shall we get back to the front of the museum?" Alyssia chuckled and said to him, "I am, just needed to adjust my eyes…" Iain understood as he took his private key and locked the door while she pulled out a piece of note paper as she wrote down some details and handed it to him while they headed back to the museum.

On the paper, it had her address and Mary Anne's address Iain and Alyssia concluded their business as they reach the front of the museum as she told everyone after signing the guest book, "All of you have a wonderful weekend and now I must head home to do some housework and homework! Talk to you very soon and that address is where I can be reached. I also gave you my phone numbers, mobile and home, to contact me if anything should come up." They all nodded and said their goodbyes as she leaves the museum in peace with a couple more brochures as the afternoon wore into early evening. She was glad the she made his and Mary Anne's day as she thought with positivity: *'Two for two…not bad for a Friday.'*

Back at the University in the caretaker's hut, the officers return to the University after getting groceries and the files from the police station as John tests Stuart's listening device and the men prepare to part ways as he slips something with a letter in Stuart's pocket as he tests the listening device after turning it on and looked at the computer screen. "Look we have done enough for tonight, come on over if you are bored; I'll put you to work on some gardening plots tomorrow." Stuart says, "Thanks Mr Preston…I'll remember that," as the rookie gave him the thumbs up to let him know that the device is working after watching the lines dance across the screen and the officers' part company as the rookie heads back to Thackeray House with a deep breath and groceries.

Stuart gets to the back of Thackeray House and took his keys to the back door out of his pocket. He didn't need to as the door already fell off its hinges this morning and he rolled his eyes, goes inside and upstairs to the kitchen with the groceries. He begins to put them away until George comes in to the kitchen in haste with rolled up plans of the area around Cassious House. Stuart wondered where he got the plans but instead he held his tongue as George replied with happiness, "Ah, Stuart my boy; where have you been?" George asked as he clapped Stuart on the shoulders. "I was at the grocery store; we were, um... running low on milk and tea."

George was lost in his delight to care; "That's wonderful, now listen Stuart, my boy...I've discovered some caves near Cassious House; so you, I, and the students are going to see what's in there." He patted the plans and slapped Stuart on the back again as he put the groceries on the littered counter and walked him over to the table as George spreads out the map and shows him the caves were and they go over the plan. Then he asked, "Any questions?" Stuart says, "Yeah one; ah aren't those caves cursed as the House?" George shot him a look as Stuart says, "I'm just saying..." But a smile broke across George's face as he told him, "Smart lad, always on your toes," he claps him on the back again as Stuart felt them stinging and replied, "Yes I know those caves are cursed but I just want to check them out that's all. Are you with me?" Stuart nodded and says, "That sounds okay, I guess we wear black?" George rolls up the map and takes it with him. "Yes and be ready before eight pm and we'll go exploring...I'll bring the flashlights!" George left the kitchen with the map close at hand as he whistles a happy tune. Stuart waits until it's all clear and quiet as he quickly texts John. *'Did you get all that?' -ST-* He waits for John's reply as John texts back, **'Yeah good work. My God George is so stupid. Stay safe and tell me all about it tomorrow morning.' -JP-** He heard a sound but it was nothing as he texted back to John, *'Will do... till tomorrow goodnight'-ST-."*

He then deleted all the messages and then shuts off his phone and puts it away in his pocket as he hears the Ezra brothers fighting again and he rolls his eyes while he puts the groceries away after he shuts off the listening device and he would turn it on again when he is near the caves. *I'll be glad to be back in the Caretaker's Hut when this all over. This place gives me the heebie jeebies...'* he thought as he leaves the kitchen and goes to his room as he gets ready for the cave exploration until he discovered John's note, which simply reads "Just for you-good luck" and a small hidden camera in his coat pocket that John slyly slipped on him as he gets ready to do some cave exploring as he said to himself quietly, "Always looking after me, aren't you John?" as he shoved it back in his pocket.

As the eight o'clock hour drew closer, he fits the small hidden camera on to his collar of his jacket and leaves his room to head to the kitchen as he flicked on his listening device so John could hear everything. George and his goons join in as John watched them leave Thackeray House and head for Cassious House property while John has his dinner and writes down in his notes 'trespassing on private property' to his long list of charges against George Thackeray and the Ezra Brothers, Stuart flicks on his camera discreetly as they get near the House and the caves as the quartet cut through bramble and thorns to see the caves before them as George turned and asked Stuart to stay back and he nodded as the trio get a closer look.

While at the House, Alyssia has her dinner, cleans up her dishes, and finished her housework and then she relaxed on the couch with her feet up and her book "Young Sherlock Holmes" as some "Lord of the Rings[34]" music is playing in the background. Mystery came to her, hopped into her lap, curled up and went to sleep as Alyssia rubbed her ears gently.

An hour later, Prince Timothy came and she jumped at his sudden presence as he sits beside her while he placed a book mark in her book. "Hey, I was reading that!" she says grinning at him as he took it from her hands, closed it with the bookmark in place as he looked at the cover and said comically, "Sorry Sherlock, I'm working this side of the street" and puts it on the coffee table as she chuckled. "So, my dear Prince, how are you doing? I see you don't like Sherlock Holmes?" She asked as he invites her to cuddle in and she does as he takes her hand in his answering her questions in order. "Oh not bad, studies, studies and more studies but I can't complain but I always found Sherlock a little bit dry but interesting, and I tend to

---

[34] "The Lord of the Rings" ©2001-2003 "The Fellowship of the Ring", "The Two Towers", and "The Return of the King" The books written by JRR Tolkien 1954/5 and "The Hobbit" by JRR Tolkien 1937; the movies "An Unexpected Journey", "The Desolation of Smaug" and "The Battle of the Five Armies" 2012-2014 directed by Peter Jackson for New Line Cinema Film Company and Universal Pictures. Enya appears courtesy of Warner Music Group (WMG) ©2012

get jealous when another guy has your attention." The couple laugh as he wiggled his eyebrows and says, "What about you? How was your day?"

She plays with his hand and says, "Well, let's see..." she began as she gets her head on his chest as he sees Mystery purring away and gently rubbed the kitten's ears. "I made and old lady and her daughters' day; made a curator's day and had some University business which has been sorted." She smiled as Timothy asked, "The incident in the library?" she nodded as she looked at him. "Marylebarne has seriously reprimanded The Coquitlam Sisters for spooking you and now they are doing some detective work for you." She sits up and looked at him confused as he began to explain; "...we may have evidence that links your lost father and brother to a forgotten family called Thackeray-Franklin." She was now curious as he tells her everything from the time of the assassination attempt to the family changing their name to weed out the guilty.

When he finished, she tried to make sense of what he told her asking, "So, what you're saying that James may have changed his name? My brother and father may be part of that forgotten family?" He nodded as she lies back on his chest and says, "Cool! But still so many questions..." He nods as they play with each other's fingers until light dances across the window as they stood up and went to her window.

"What the---?" as Timothy and her look out into the darkness after Alyssia puts Mystery on the warm couch as she sleeps on and she says to him, "We better go and investigate; can you go outside?" Alyssia asked him as he tells her while she gets her jacket on, "I can go out at night but not during the day; I would disintegrate into dust." They go to the front door as she gets a flashlight out of the top drawer of her sideboard as she jokes; "So a trip to the park for a picnic on a sunny day is out of the question?"

He laughs and says, "Yes," as the Prince sees her wiggle her eyebrows and zips up her jacket and laughs and he gets serious as he telepathically sends a message to Marylebarne, "...we better go out and see what's happening." She opens the door and flicks on the flashlight after she closed it without locking it as they head in the direction of the caves as Kevin Parks joins them as he too saw the lights dancing across the window and were about several feet from the House as they hid in the bush near the homes and watch three men approach the caves as they are stopped by a ghostly guard as the others snapped off their flashlights.

Kevin wanted to approach them but Alyssia held him back as the ghostly guard asked them, "Who are you and why have you come?" Then Alyssia recognised them. "Thackeray and his goons, what the hell are they doing here?" she asked in an audible whisper as they stayed out of sight while George replied with flair, "I have come to see what's in your caves and to claim what's mine, let me pass!" The ghostly guard just looked at them as if he was born yesterday as Alyssia held in a giggle, and shook her head and thought: *'Really Thackeray, is that the best you got?'*

Timothy read her mind as he chuckled and sends the ghostly guard a message through his thoughts; *'Don't let him pass. He is evil and will take the treasure for himself…'* The guard got the message and sends the gruesome threesome back home until Stuart comes over to them. "Stuart," asked an angry Kevin Parks; "What the hell are you doing here? Don't you know that these caves are cursed and off limits?" Timothy and Alyssia looked at each other as Stuart and the others watched George argue with the ghostly apparition as he says, "George says that he found some caves around here and wants to see what's in them. I told him that these caves near the House were cursed and off limits but he didn't listen to me…I am truly sorry, Mr Parks; I did try to stop them."

Kevin felt sorry for him as he did try and the others patted his back and shoulder as they nodded, "I stayed back as a look out; so I better get back to my post." The Prince says, "Good idea and we better get in before 'The Death Song' begins which will start in a few minutes. I have put a forgetful spell on Stuart and the others; as soon as they all fall asleep, they will forget everything they have seen here tonight…but for right now let's get back to the House before 'The Song' begins."

Alyssia, Kevin, Timothy and Stuart leave quietly as they get back to their homes and lock themselves in for the night and shuts the door and windows while Stuart waits for an angry George and his two goons leave for Thackeray House as the wind becomes cold and Dark Spirit's 'Song' grew in intensity as the duo get inside, Alyssia turns on all the lights and Timothy pulled the curtains as she quickly goes and gets ready for bed. As he waits, she comes through to see Timothy as the Prince takes her hand and they share their love and talk through the night right up until bedtime. Finally the song ends and he helps her into bed as he guards her until dawn.

Chapter 6

THE END OF THE FIRST WEEK OF TERM

Saturday morning started out cold and rainy but then cleared leaving sunny spells and blue skies. Alyssia had made her bed, got showered and changed, had her breakfast and fed her beautiful, gold-eyed, lucky black cat Mystery who always made her laugh and gave her lots and lots of love. Then she returned to the homework table and did her report after playing with Mystery who was tired of all the fun as she settled down for a cat nap.

Alyssia was looking over all her work from the first week of classes; proof reading, correcting mistakes as she was typing it up on her computer, saving and printing all her work-until finally, she was finished as her fingers were hurting. She saves her work and takes in a deep breath of relief while Alyssia puts everything back in the folders then replaced the notebooks back on the bookshelf until Monday as she checks off all her home work in her other spiral notebook.

She looked at Franklin's report on ghosts and on a case file given to her by Mark and as she looked at it, she felt that she did all she could with her reports as she makes sure both reports were saved on to her memory stick, along with all her notes and ideas were put in separate folders. She stretched as she makes sure that the information for both reports was stored on her memory stick in separate folders that she created, safely ejects it from the drive and shuts down her computer. It was time to concentrate on getting a new outfit for her visit to the House tonight and since the House was built in medieval times; she would have to get a costume to match that time in history.

While the spirits and Mystery slept soundly, she left the flat for the town centre with pictures she found on and printed off the internet while searching for a medieval costume shop which was near the City Centre of Kelton Heights after looking on Google and getting the address and the pictures off the Internet. She parked her car near the shop, paid for the parking ticket and placed it on her windscreen inside the car. After she locked the door of her car, she reached into her handbag and pulled her three pictures as she went into the shop to look around while the shopkeeper finished with a previous customer.

The shop was amazing and it boasted as having the biggest selection of medieval clothing; it was crammed with all types of outfits and accessories from the middle ages; crowns for the gentlemen, tiaras for the young ladies, swords, spears, jester outfits, prince and knight costumes, and beautiful veils and capes to accessorise each dress for the ladies or a manly costume for the men with elegance and style. She saw a fair maiden outfit and smiled as she looked that the picture-it was exactly as she wanted; simple without being overly complicated and she hoped that the shop keeper would have something like that in her size.

Finally, it was her turn to be served as the shop keeper smiled approached her, "May I help you my dear?" asked the kindly lady shopkeeper. The shopkeeper was also a costume player as well as the pictures behind her saw her in many re-enactments from a jousting tournament to the king's royal court. She saw her in many other pictures dotted around the till and shop area such as the signing of declarations to the king's feast to acting in dramas and pantomimes[35] as well as serving the community by supplying the costumes for these events. She was in her late thirties with a round oval face, fiery red-auburn hair and green eyes. Small but bulky, and with gold-rim glasses that she wore to fit her delicate features and very beautiful-she could have easily come out of one of those fairy tale books as Alyssia

---

[35] A Pantomime (if you are wondering) is a type of musical comedy stage production designed for family entertainment. It was developed in England and is still performed throughout the United Kingdom, generally during the Christmas and New Year and to a lesser extent, in other English-speaking countries. The 'panto' (for short) includes songs, gags, slapstick comedy and dancing, employs gender crossing actors and topical humour with a story loosely based on a well known fairytale, fable or folk tale.

smiled and showed her the pictures of what she was looking for as well as the costume. "I was wondering if you have these types of dresses that I could try on…" Alyssia asked as she gave her the pictures of the dresses as well as showed her what she was asking for. The shop keeper loved it; because she was the kind of shopper who knew exactly what she wanted and wasted no time of looking about at something that she would feel uncomfortable in or was over complicated; she chose a simple fair maiden outfit with a necklace to match.

The kindly shop keeper said with a bright smile, "This is a good choice of costume; simple but not over complicated." She came to her and placed her hands on her shoulders as she whispered, "Come dear, let's get you measured up, okay?" Alyssia smiled and followed the shop keeper to the back of the shop as the kind lady pulled out a measuring tape and measured her for the skirt and blouse while the ladies discussed what to wear under it as Alyssia brought her own black flat shoes.

The kind and helpful shopkeeper talked to her about what she liked colour wise as she looked around and found the perfect outfit for her and gave her the costume saying, "Follow me and I'll show you to the dressing rooms where you can try it on." Alyssia thanked her as she followed the lady to the dressing room as she went in and changed from modern to Medieval.

While that was happening, the shop keeper heard the bell to her door and told her that she had a customer waiting as Alyssia told her from behind the curtain of the small dressing room, "You go ahead…I don't want to keep you from your work;" and the shop keeper smiled as she went to help the customers while she tried on the costume and slipped on the flat black shoes. About an hour later, she came out in full costume as the shop keeper was helping another customer; she and the customers were startled at the transformation.

The lady shop keeper gave her the matching necklace and placed it around her neck as she stood back and admired her beauty. "Well, what do you think?" she asked everyone around her with a nervous sigh of anticipation as the shop keeper says with joy; "You look beautiful!" The lady hugged her and got a picture of her in full outfit as everyone applauded and took photos of Alyssia on their phones, including a medieval cosplayer who would take the photo back to her group to show everyone as she gave Alyssia her a cars and told her in a whisper, "Give me a call if you're interested," and said goodbye after renting a costume and leaving the shop. Alyssia was flattered and bemused by the invitation, but until her studies were over and the evil curse was broken; she will have to keep her waiting.

But on the other hand, she loved what she was wearing and told the lady that she would take it; "Wonderful, I'll just get a ticket written up for it; you look so beautiful in it…and keep your hair down, it makes the outfit that much more beautiful." Alyssia was hugged by the lady again as she smiled and went to change back into her modern clothes as she thought: *'Well its back to reality again; I really felt different in these for a while and I hope Timothy likes it.'*

After she got back into her modern clothes and brought the costume out, Alyssia helped the shop keeper fold up the clothes and place them in the bag along with her shoes and the small necklace which was placed in another small bag and put in with the costume. The shop keeper gave her the total and paid the lady by card as she thanked her while she placed the flat black shoes into the bag with her new medieval costume.

But before she left the shop, she had one more favour to ask her; "I was wondering if you do something like these formal Celtic dresses." The lady looked at the two pictures and smiled, "Leave these with me and I'll scc what I can do for you. I know a lady that docs thcsc and shc is surc to help you, so if it's okay with you, I will give her your measurements and she can make replicas of the ones pictured here." Alyssia got her measurements written down in a small notebook for another tailor was asking for them and thanked her as she gave her the address of where she could be reached by phone (home and mobile) or email as she thanked her, got her bank card as well as her medieval outfit and left the shop as she went to the tailor and gave the lady her measurements and thanked her as she got busy on making her a pair of trousers and skirt and thanked her as she left the dressmakers and went to her car.

She got to the car and placed the costume in the boot as she had other chores to do in town before she went home after picking up some other things like cat food, cat litter and a cat litter tray for Mystery which she so desperately needed for the House as she drove to the local ASDA to pick them up. She looked around for a craft shop to pick up some plastic canvas or something close to canvas and three balls of white yarn next door to ASDA and found the shop as she puts them in the car and drives home.

Back at Cassious House, the spirits had woken up and were busy preparing for Alyssia's arrival as Timothy came into the ballroom to see how everything was going after waking up and having breakfast. Marylebarne could see that the Prince was very anxious for everything to go perfectly as the advisor said to an anxious Prince; "Everything is well, your highness..." Timothy was taking a break from his studies as Marylebarne says to him gently while he took some fruit from the fruit bowl; "You must not worry, this is going to be the best celebration yet--now go back to your studies and let us handle everything."

Timothy tried to help as the advisor pushed his hand away and pointed him back to his chambers to continue with his work and as he left the room, he stuck his tongue out at Marylebarne who just smiled and shook his head as the prince disappeared from the doorway. The advisor giggled and the prince went back to his studies as Marylebarne took in a sigh and went back to helping the other spirits set up the ballroom for Alyssia's visit to the House.

Meanwhile, the Prince came back to his room and to his studies; but couldn't concentrate...he couldn't stop thinking about Alyssia Franklin-Jenkins as he looked at her picture on his desk. She was the best thing that ever happened to him in all these long, lonely and hopeless years and everyone, as well as Marylebarne could see that in him; he was totally head over heels in love with Alyssia as he stroked the picture with his fingertips, kissed it, and smiled happily after taking it from her home while he lay on his bed and held the picture close to him.

Just then, Timothy heard the door close downstairs and he smiled, got up out of his bed and made himself presentable as he grabbed his sword, strapped it on and went into the shadows thinking of playing a trick on her as he came from the shadows and into her bedroom. She was humming a song that was dancing around in her head while he hid behind her wardrobe door and saw her place her costume neatly on a hanger and hung it inside the wardrobe as she sighed gently and went through to the living room as he thought, *'she is going to look so beautiful in that.'*

He came from behind the side of the wardrobe and followed her, mirroring everything that she was doing and smiling like a wild man from the jungles of Africa. But when she stopped to do something, he bumped into her from behind and he played a game of "Now you see me, now you don't" sneakily laughing as he followed her around once more. After the game, he bent over her shoulder as he said in her ear, "Hello there beautiful!"

She let out a cry of fright and jumped out of her skin as he laughed; she was totally livid with him as he was still grinning like a Cheshire cat who just met Alice and laughing at her discontent at the trick he played on her! She smacked his arm a couple of times as she angrily said, "I-I really hate it when you do that, Prince Timothy Andrew Carlton!" She exclaimed as he took her into his arms while she slapped his chest playfully as he kissed her forehead and held her hand in his. "You sounded like my mother there for a moment!" He said laughing but she didn't think it was funny as she pushed him away, turned her back on him and walked away to the kitchen as he followed while he came up behind her, wrapped his arms around her as he kissed her neck and stroked her hair. How could she stay mad at him with a cheeky grin and a wiggle of his eyebrows after she turned around to face him as he caressed her hand and touched her cheek?

He watched her laugh as he held her close with a hug that she couldn't resist; he knew just the right thing to do when she was scared or just needed a cuddle. "There you are, Alyssia..." he replied with a small chuckle as he watched her smile and rested his forehead on hers while he stroked her hair and cheek gently. He wrapped his arms around her gently, pulled her close, and he replied with a giggle and a kiss, "Look, I'm very sorry I scared you..." She looked at him and she said sarcastically, "No you're not!"

He chuckled happily as he hugged her tightly while she tried to put her heart back into her chest and took a deep breath. "Well, tonight's the night..." he replied as she looked him still a bit annoyed as he continued to nuzzle her neck gently while she tried to fight her desire for him as she placed her hands on his chest then slid her arms around his neck as he replied, "I can't wait for you to meet everyone." Alyssia felt him letting go as he kissed her hands but she was still annoyed with him for scaring her witless. "I have a mind not to come; but you did say you were sorry so okay, I'll come...as soon as my skeleton comes back from outer space."

He chuckled happily and kissed her cheek as he whispered in her ear, "I really am sorry, I won't do it again, promise. I'll behave myself at the party tonight," she looked back at him angrily and said, "You better, mister!" he gave her one last cuddle and said with a hug. "I will see you later tonight… dress beautifully and I'll come for you at the appointed time." He kissed her cheek, gave it one last stroke as he left her desiring him more and disappeared into the shadows and made it back in time to his room and to his studies in the Tower just as Marylebarne came to see him about a certain letter he wrote and they discussed it happily as he continued with his studies on writing letter to other royal members.

The early morning wore on into the early afternoon as she was reading up on the history of Cassious House, the veil of evil and other material that she got from the Kelton Heights Visitors Centre and Museum in which the curator happily gave her. She also paid a visit to main library in the city centre and got the books from the library in the town centre as she was doing her research as she tried to match all the evidence to Cassious House and writing the notes down from other books in the library she was reading taking notes, writing down books and sourcing them for future use while the spy, who was watching her all that time, sat across from her and read his newspaper as she took notes from more books and referenced them for Franklin's independent report for a case and others for the Cassious House report.

She had just finished the last reference for her notebook, closed it quietly, returned all the books to its proper place, closed her spiral bound notebook and placed it back in her handbag as she left the library without another word. The spy followed her out and went the other way as she felt the wind in her face and went to her car. Back at home and with pamphlets, notes from books and official guides scattered all over the table, she took off her glasses and set them on the table, she was getting tired at looking at all the small print as her eyes were ready to close; so she took off her glasses and rubbed the tiredness from her face.

So she placed her book face down and went to her homework table and read the brochures instead and written up some notes which collaborated with the history books from the library. Another few minutes passed as her brain screamed 'INFORMATION OVERLOAD!' and she agreed and put down her pen as a signal to her tired brain that she had stopped reading the brochures and stretched up to the ceiling. *'I couldn't agree with you more, brain…'* she thought and she went over to the sideboard and took out her mum's diary, for this was all she had of her mother Emily and she treasured it immensely. Her mum's diary had pictures and scribbles from her days when she was a girl and smiled or chuckled at some of the things teenage girls did.

For instance, her first crush and how she met her father as well as her wedding dreams and happiness for the future. Then she talked about the birth of her big brother and her being born as well as all the adventures they had; picnics, cooking and baking cakes, dressing up, performing... all this brought a smile to Alyssia's memories.

But that smile turned to disbelief when she came across an entry that so distressed and confused her as she thought: *'Mum, oh my God, no...this can't be true.'* She could hear her mother's voice in her head dictating this entry and Alyssia pictured in her mind what her mother was like when she was a teenage girl living happily in Kelton Heights with her friend Madeline Gratin; her old school chum. Then, as if she was sitting beside her, she heard her mum's voice reading this entry as she read from a very frightened teenage girl's point of view. Tears came to Alyssia's eyes as she tried not to picture the terror within her mum's words but to no avail as she grasped her diary firmly and read on:

Emily MacPherson Diary   *March 1989*

"A Prank that went wrong"

"I was with my friend Madeline on the street on our way to the shops; we were talking about this cute guy who was in our class in school and laughing happily as I needed to pick up milk for my mum, when a group of bullies intercepted us, said hurtful things and seized us. Scared at what they might do, they marched us into Cassious House, pushed us inside and barricaded the door with heavy rocks and cinder blocks.

We banged on the door, called out to them to let us out, but they were gone and they were laughing as Madeline came to me while we held each other close-it was no use. With the door not budging and weary from crying and being scared, we had no choice but to accept our fates."

"Just as we sat on the bottom step of the stairs and I tried, in vain, to get a signal on my phone, there was a Dark Spirit upon me and Madeline. We tried to run and hide but it was too late; she was taken immediately but the King looked at me as she screamed and begged for me to help her.

I begged his majesty, on my knees, for his forgiveness and for our lives as I cried out and told him quite anxiously; "Some bullies locked us in here...please, your majesty, w-we don't want what you are guarding; P-Please give her back to me...I beg of you."

I pleaded with him with tears in my eye, and he did the unthinkable; he released Madeline unharmed and I held her close to me. But when she saw the Dark Spirits, she fainted dead away as the King looked upon me and said gently as I tended to Madeline.

"Emily Macpherson," I looked up at him still scared of what he might do as I answered him back, "Yes s-sire?" He then replied gently as he came down to our level and knelt before me as he touched my arm and I didn't flinch as his touch was gentle for he knew I was scared and said, "When you are married you must train 'the key'; you must teach the child the piano, Gaelic/Welsh and to sing...will you do this?"

"I was a bit confused but I agreed in exchange for our lives," Y-Yes your majesty, I-I will do as you say... J-Just don't harm us!" He smiled and agreed and with a nod from him, we awoke outside the House unscathed and bewildered as we felt the cool air on our faces outside Cassious House. The police found us dazed, confused and unharmed as they told us that the bullies were apprehended and charged with aggravated kidnapping after a neighbour witnessed our kidnapping while Madeline woke up in an ambulance being looked over to see if she was hurt.

I praise the dark spirits for my freedom and all I can do is raise the child the way they wanted; but I will go a step further and teach her compassion, love, sincerity; all the attributes that will make her human...I hope the Dark Spirits will see this and consider their wish fulfilled." -EM-

Alyssia found this alarming as she said out loud as she dried some stray tears, "My mum was in Cassious House? She was almost snatched? But what changed their minds while others were being snatched left, right and centre? The agreement that she made with them, was it about me?" She started to cry as she read the entry again. "Who is *'the key'* and why was it important for that child to be 'trained'?" she asked herself as all these emotions and questions ran through her like a raging river heading down the Amazon and straight to the sea.

Alyssia had to find out and she had to do this alone; there was no other way as she puts her mum's diary face down on the coffee table and went to the door of the cursed House, unlocked it with the key given to her from Sharlene Parks, the first day she moved into the small home next to them, took in a deep breath, and she opened the door carefully and quietly, not to make any sudden movements and went into the dark main hall as she placed the key around her neck.

She saw the dark veil which was moving around like as if the wind was gently blowing on it and approached the dark veil at the top of the first-floor landing and wondered what the veil was made of; but she dared not touch it or get too close. She was scared but she slowly approached it slowly and carefully keeping her eyes on the veil at all times, she found a small rug near the landing as she went to it, knelt upon it, and waited for something to happen and meditated as to what she wanted to ask the Dark Spirits.

As she came out of it, she thought of her mother while she looked around the dark main hall as she looked up at the dome above her. The white clouds raced by and she heard the trees tapping on the windows next to her while her mother screamed in her brain, *'Save yourself and leave now...forget me, please sweetheart.'* But she refused and stood her ground as she thought of how she should address the Dark Spirits directly. She also knew that the Prince was going to be angry with her, because he risked his spirit life to save her. But down deep, she had no choice...she had to ask the Dark Spirits about her mum and get her answers or this mystery would never get solved.

But who she didn't notice was Jesterson who was in the library and was headed back to the Tower with a book he liked to read as he was humming a tune. He was just going away to the Tower until he saw Alyssia waiting in front of the Dark Veil as she was still a bit scared and nervous as she sat on the mat waiting for the Dark Spirits. The jester thought as he watched her: *'What the hell are you doing? Get out of here while you still can...please just leave.'*

But it was too late to turn back now as she gathered her courage, swallowed her pride, and said with unwavering bravery as the veil flapped around like the British flag flying over Buckingham Palace as she told the veil; "I-I wish to speak to your leader or king..." Just as she said it, a Dark Guard came out and floated above her as she took in a deep breath and released it as she showed courage before him as she stood up slowly and showed her respect by humbly bowing before him while the guard did the same.

"Please guard of the darkness; ask your leader if he would come forth and speak to a human named Alyssia Franklin-Jenkins and she requests his presence as a matter of urgency." Alyssia said to the Dark Guard as his skeletal-human features and body glowed as if he was a glow in dark figure. His skeletal hand was wrapped around a rusty spear as a rusted sword sat at his side in his broken leather sheath with the sewing becoming unravelled and the handle was brown as charred metal protruded from each side and soaked with his blood probably from long forgotten war that he fought before joining the veil. He never touched the ground as if wires were holding the guard up in the air yet she saw none and his voice was in a snake-like hiss and his tongue was forked and he was tall; towering over Alyssia as she looked at him with awe and fear. Jesterson watched as the Dark Guard was getting closer and he was prepared himself to defend her after putting his book down gently on a table near the library as he watched the Dark Guard come closer and looked her up and down and all around as he sniffed her but she didn't move from her spot but a bit shaken up at how fast they moved and she uttered not a word as he returned to the front of the veil.

The Dark Guard looked directly in her eyes as his cloak blew in the wind like the veil on the landing while his skeletal fingers were tightly wrapped around his spear and his human-like face stared at her angrily as he asked while Jesterson watched in horror. "Why do you make such a request, human?" she told him firmly but gently, "Because I feel I can help set you free just like your king did for my mother who bore me, for which I am eternally grateful. All I ask of your king is what it is that you want so I can release you from your prison...what say you?"

The Dark Guard came in her face but she held her ground as Jesterson wanted to cry out but couldn't-he was too paralysed with fear to move. All he could do was watch and listen as the Dark Guard angrily hissed to her, "I can easily take you right now, human for making such a demand of my king;" she retorted back to him still scared but with some courage; "Then no one is set free; you will remain trapped in this prison forever. Is that what you want? You have been here for over three hundred plus years, what's another three hundred plus years?"

The Dark Guard growled and was taken aback by her response but he knew that she was right; It's been too long and he longed for freedom from this darkness; from this House and if this was the only way to get his freedom then so be it as he calmed down and he hissed in a calm tone. "You seem very eager to help us; human. I will let my king know that you request an audience with him; wait here!"

She bowed to him as he left her to fetch his king while Jesterson watched from the shadows; fearing that what she was doing would get her snatched away and the Prince would lose the love of his life. So he sent a telepathic message to her: *'He has waited so long for you, Alyssia...please be careful. I just hope you know what you're doing.'* She felt his message as she sent back telepathically as she looked in his direction but didn't see him: *'I have to get some answers as to why my mum was trapped here and why she was spared all those years ago. She was talking about something called 'the key'. I will be careful...I promise, Jesterson.'*

The jester thought out loud, "Your mum? Training *'the key'*? I don't understand..." as he stayed hidden, he watched what will happen next, but he didn't have long to wait as the Dark King and his two Dark Guards came before her out of the dark velvet veil. He stayed hidden as he saw them and was amazed at how majestic and regal they were. They were just like the Dark Guard she spoke to before, but these guards were like him and the Dark King was taller and had a rusted crown upon his head. His torn royal cloak danced in the wind, as he too, spoke with a snake-like whisper as she bowed before him with respect and authority as he returned the gesture. Jesterson returned to his hiding place and closed his eyes to what he had seen and then he heard the Dark King speak as he had to think of something.

"You wish to speak to me, human Alyssia Franklin-Jenkins? I do not like to be awakened at this hour of the day!" She nodded and understood his grumpiness and was not going to insult his intelligence as she had answers to get about her mother and got straight to the point as she replied gently not to rile his annoyance any more than it was. "Please, your majesty, forgive me for waking you but this is a matter of urgency. I am the daughter of Emily Jenna Franklin, better known to you as Emily Jenna MacPherson; the one you spared all those years ago?" The Dark King thought and says as he remembered and his features grew soft and kind; more father like than evil as he knew something that she didn't but he listened to what she had to say. "Yes I do remember. What is it that you want Alyssia Franklin-Jenkins?"

She knelt back on the rug before him as she replied gently but firmly; to show him that she wasn't backing down until she gets the answers she so desperately needed. "The truth; I wish to know why you are snatching people who get too close or are taken away when you sing 'your song'." The Dark King nodded as she said with a plea in her voice, "Please, your majesty, I beg of you to speak the truth…" The Dark King prepared to speak out to her gently and truthfully; she was entitled to know the truth while a frightened Jesterson had heard enough as he grabbed the book he picked out to read from the library and ran into shadows to fetch Marylebarne and Prince Timothy.

The Dark King then replied to her, "The Sultan's advisor put us here to guard this house and what's below it. We have done that, but a greater evil imprisons us here and his name is George Thackeray!" She repeated back in her mind, *"George Thackeray? What of him, your majesty?"* He grinned as she stood up slowly and came down to her level and placed a hand on her cheek as he was about to tell her the truth of her mother and of George Thackeray, for if anyone could thwart the plans of George Thackeray, it was Emily's daughter Alyssia. All she needed to do was trust him as his guards watched him lower himself to her level to talk to her and give what she needed; the truth about her mother, her friend and what happened that day.

At that moment, Jesterson had come back to the Tower and found Marylebarne and the Prince talking in his room as he said white with fear as he knocked frantically and called to them, "Your majesty and

Marylebarne come quick! It's Alyssia; she is talking to the Dark King of the veil!" Timothy and his advisor both got their swords, dropped everything as they were horrified…he had to rescue her in his mind, "Let's go Jesterson…" The jester nodded as he made sure that he had his sword and ran to her rescue.

While downstairs, Alyssia speaks to him, "It always comes back to George Thackeray, but why?" she thought aloud as The Dark King looked back at her as she asked him, "Sire, what would you like me to do for you? Name it and it shall be done." The Dark King was just about to speak when another voice said, "I would like you to stay away from her!" The King and his guards shrieked angrily as they saw Timothy with his sword already drawn as Alyssia cried out, "Timothy please…*Don't*!" But it was too late as the prince raised his sword and ran to her aid as Jesterson and Marylebarne tried to stop him. "No my prince, let him speak to her." But he was ready and he ran towards her ready to defend her as Marylebarne cried out "Timothy, come back!"

He charged to her rescue as the Dark King nodded indiscreetly and two more Dark Guards came from the veil and stopped him in his tracks as she cried out, "Timothy No!!!" She, Marylebarne and Jesterson covered their eyes for a moment but then opened them to a surprise. She watched as the two Dark Guards were holding him fast with his wrists grabbed and the other two Dark Guards holding him by the waist. She begged the King with tears of mercy and fell to her knees, "Please my Dark Lord, don't hurt him…he thought I was in danger; he's only trying to protect me."

He looked at the Prince and his two friends hiding in the shadows as Marylebarne, Alyssia and Jesterson watched as the Prince struggled but the Dark Guards grips got tighter as the Dark King nodded to her and reached down to dry her tears. "Leave her alone! Let her go! I'm warning you…don't you dare touch her!"

But the Dark King touched her cheek and dried her eyes as he hissed back to Timothy, "She called on us Prince Timothy and she wants to help us!" The Prince looked at him and then back at Alyssia who was almost in tears as he struggled and she told them why she summoned the Dark King as they saw that she was close to tears and she stood up with the help of the Dark King. "Go ahead and tell them, my dear girl," he said kindly to her. She took in a sigh and replied, "My mum, Emily Jenna MacPherson and her friend Madeline Gratin were seized as teenagers and they were barricaded in here by bullies as recorded in her diary so I wanted to ask the Dark Spirits and its King why Emily and Madeline were spared while many others went missing or were lured in here by the 'Death Song'! Please Timothy, if I'm going to get to the bottom of this mystery and break this curse once and for all, I have to know the truth. Please I beg of you, let me do this."

Then Jesterson said out loud, "...in her diary;" Jesterson recalled as Marylebarne and Timothy listened, "it said something about 'training '*the key*'?" Alyssia then said as the three friends looked back at her and nodded. "I called upon him to ask if this was true...please Timothy, Jesterson and Marylebarne; I need to know." The Dark King says in a kind but firm tone as he placed his skeletal hands on her shoulders, "I promised her the truth as well as you." The prince, the advisor and the jester were shocked as they came from the shadows and stood before the king of the dark veil as he repeated to them gently after he gained his composure.

"As I was saying to the human Alyssia, The advisor of the 'Sultan' put us here to guard whatever is below the house but George Thackeray had another agenda...he ordered us to snatch anyone who tried to find or take what's below!" Then Alyssia replied, "My mother Emily Jenna MacPherson was spared saying that she was locked in here by some bullies with her friend but she and her friend were spared, why?" Alyssia asked as the Dark King says as he nodded, "Yes, your mum and her friend was locked in here by mistake so we saw pity and compassion within your mother for her friend and we told her that she must train '*the key*' to read and speak Gaelic and Welsh, play the piano and sing and she agreed in exchange for her and her friend's life." He came from around her and touched her cheek gently as the Prince struggled again to get to her.

"We felt your presence near Kelton Heights and heard you playing the piano; you my dear girl are '*the key*'!" Alyssia was shocked at this revelation as she thought; '*Me? But I'm a human...no wonder mum was so adamant about me keeping up with the piano, learning Gaelic and Welsh in school as well as taking singing lessons...me 'the key'?*' She looked up at the Dark King who smiled gently and stroked her cheek, "Don't you touch her!" The Prince cried with tears of fear and love as well as for her safety as he struggled to break free of his captors to get to her.

The Dark King snarled at him as she saw the sword still clutched in his hand and she had an idea as she told distraught Timothy after seeing the sword in his hand in Welsh, ***Timothy, os gwelwch yn dda! Erfyniaf arnoch, gadw eich cleddyf...maent yn ei weld fel bygythiad!*** "Timothy Please I beg of you! Put your sword away...they see it as a threat!" Marylebarne and Jesterson looked at each other and were surprised at her perfectly spoken Welsh language. The Dark King was impressed, too... not only that she spoke Welsh, but more importantly; he saw compassion within her as Timothy looked at Marylebarne and Jesterson nodding for they understood what she was saying to him and he did as she asked.

The Dark Guards saw and felt him backing down as they let him go and he sheathed his sword while the Dark King nodded to his Dark Guards to back away and they did. Alyssia sighed with relief as she looked at him and saw the disappointment in his eyes as the Dark King saw more than that as he came to the Prince and said gently as he looked at the Dark King with a steady gaze as he sheathed his sword.

"We would never hurt *'the key'* Prince Timothy..." The Prince and the Dark King nodded as she looked away from him but he looked on her with love rather than disappointment and anger. The Dark King floated over to Timothy then said, "You must know that her brother gave up but his sister stuck with it and she is here, is she? You must be proud of her; my guards were wrong to leave the veil and attack *'the key'* the first night she came into the house, and you saved her and I thank you."

Timothy was confused as he gave him a courtesy nod as the Dark King floated back to Alyssia and she stood in front of him as he placed both hands on her shoulders. "She had the courage to stand before us; no other would do this except *'the key.'* Never be angry, Prince Timothy for Alyssia is the one we have looked for all these years and we have kept her and her family safe," as he placed both hands back on her shoulders as Timothy had a news flash for the Dark Spirits and their King.

"Her father and brother are missing and her mother is dead in a gas explosion and her grandmother has passed away; yeah...some protection!" The Dark King was saddened by this news as he looked Alyssia with a fatherly gaze as she was still confused as to what the Dark King had told her: *I'm 'the key' but to what? God mum, I wish you weren't so cryptic!'* Just then she broke out of it as she heard Marylebarne say to very angry

Timothy, "He is right, dear Prince..." Timothy looked at him as the advisor continued as she looked up at the Dark King and he smiled gently at her. "She is only looking for answers just as we are looking for a way to break this curse; we have to work together and if the dark spirits are looking for freedom, at least we must try."

Timothy looked to them and the King bowed before him as he looked to Alyssia who looked away with shame at what she was doing as Marylebarne continued to quell his Prince's temper while the Dark King comforts her. "At least my dear Prince, she has the courage to do what she needs to do; look at her!" The Dark King had her hand upon her shoulders like a father looking after his daughter after she brings home a boy she wants to date.

"I am sorry for all the trouble that I am causing him; I bet he hates me right now?" She told the Dark King as he looked to the Prince and then back at her as he says gently, "no he doesn't hate you; he is worried about you, that's all, Alyssia. Please do not be depressed or hurt; like you said 'he was only trying to protect you.'" She looked at him and asked, "Then why do I feel like I betrayed his trust?" The Dark King could only smile and stroke her cheek gently as she bowed her head with guilt.

The Prince looked at Alyssia who was talking to the Dark King and he loved her even more as Marylebarne asked the Dark King as the Dark Spirits look back at him, "What does George Thackeray have to with all this? It seems that we keep coming back to him?" The Prince thought for a moment and says as he turns to the Dark King, "Correct me if I'm wrong my Dark Lord," The Dark King and Alyssia looked at him, "But may it have something to do with what's hidden below the House?"

He looked back at Alyssia as her head hung low in shame but the Prince was looking at her with eyes full of love. "Yes, my dear Prince..." the Dark King says as they all looked at him. "If he can get what is hidden below, he can take this house, the two towns and worst of all, he can restart his criminal empire-then nothing or anyone can stop him!" Alyssia couldn't bear the hurt and disappointment that she had put on the Prince as the Dark King came and consoled her as Alyssia lays sobbing on the floor as the Dark King lays her on the mat until he heard Timothy call to him. "Please I beg of you, Dark Lord let me go to her."

Timothy cried out with tears in his eyes as the Dark King nodded as the Dark Guards stand aside and let Timothy, Marylebarne, and Jesterson pass while the Dark Guards returned to the veil. The trio came and surrounded her with hugs and love as the Prince and held her close to him. "Ssshh, now I'm here and so are Marylebarne and Jesterson." She said through her tears, "I'm sorry, I just wanted answers and I ended putting you all in danger." They consoled her as the Prince held her close and kissed her forehead gently, "I see why you did."

She looked at him as he took her hand and held it close to his chest as they consoled her as Timothy said; "Come on, stand up." She nodded and they all stand as she looked at the Dark King and replied to him, "I will do anything that you want to set you free, just name it and it shall be done." The Dark King says in a soft voice while he touched her cheek, "Bring us George Thackeray and his goons so we can drag them into hell-that's all we ask!" She sniffed and bowed to him and his guards "Consider it done, my Lord…" He smiled and bowed to her as his focus was on the Prince who was holding her close to him. Timothy looked back at the Dark King as he replied, "Now that it is settled, my dear Prince, there is a way to set you free; but you must follow these instructions carefully and to the letter…"

The Prince nodded as Marylebarne got out a pen and pad and wrote down everything the Dark King was going to tell him. "By the light of the first full moon of spring, you must wear the necklace of pure gold and confess your love. Your lips will be loosened and she must kiss you in the moonlight when the moon is high in the sky…only then can your heart, soul, and this House can be set free from the curse." Timothy bowed to him and said, "Understood, my Dark Lord!"

Alyssia looked at Timothy and he kissed her forehead gently as Timothy nodded and thanked the Dark King as he tended to a saddened and shamed Alyssia. She told him, "I'm sorry for betraying you…" Timothy says to her as he stroked her cheek, "You never betrayed me, I will always love you for your courage and compassion, never forget that." He held her closer to him while Marylebarne put his pen and pad away as he said a low voice. "Now all we have to do is find that necklace and we'll be all set," Timothy and Jesterson nodded as he replied, "But Marylebarne, we looked all over this House, there is no sign of it…"

Marylebarne was just about to say something until another Dark Guard came, bowed and whispered to his King his watch report to his King. "Impossible. Thank you for bring this to my attention!" The watch guard bowed as the quartet looked at the Dark King, while the watch guard stood aside and waited for orders as Alyssia asked, "What is it my Dark Lord? You seem distressed and agitated?"

The Dark King looked at the quartet with anger as he told them: "My guard is telling me that someone has been digging in the basement-but how they are getting in to the lower part he doesn't know." Alyssia dried her eyes and says to the Dark King and his Watch Guard waiting beside his king, "Point or show the way and maybe I can help you." The Dark King bowed to her and the Watch Guard nodded and led the way while the Prince, Alyssia, Marylebarne and Jesterson follow the Dark Guard and the King into the basement.

The group found and lit two gas lamps as they get in to the dark, narrow stone stairwell of the House. She looked down and sees a burlap sack with tools, a flashlight, a pen and pad, a drill (battery powered) and heavy wooden screws inside the sack. "This will do the trick!" she said aloud as the group looked at her and she followed once again as the group got closer as she slung it across her body and looked back at Timothy who was still in love with her as they get near the basement with the Dark Guard leading the way.

Marylebarne carried one of the gas lamps while Jesterson carried the other down to the dark basement and she opened the door with a creaking sound as the lock was rusted away with the chains and they fell before her feet as they looked at each other as she opens the door. Marylebarne and the others got inside the basement and found another oil lamp as the advisor helped her light it and the group looked around the dark, dingy, dark cold basement as the gas lamps were hung from the ceiling.

Inside the small basement were some digging tools, huge plastic blue tarps and mounds of dirt as they crowded inside the basement which opened out in the massive underground area as water was dripping from somewhere. The cold winds blew onto the spiders' webs that covered every beam at every corner of the basement as the eight-legged arachnids scurried for the dark shadows quickly, angry at this intrusion while the group came closer. A small mouse scurried away from the light and hid in its hole as

Alyssia had some cheese in her jacket and placed it in the hole for the small, hungry creature that saw it and ate it happily with its family.

As they look around at the tools, she saw another blue tarp and slabs of stones nearby as they all looked at each other. "This is new…" Jesterson says as he bends down and she lifts the tarp, and found some newly dug up dirt as she passed the soil through her fingers. "This is recent, your majesty," she said as she clapped her hands of the soil while the Dark King growled at this invasion of privacy. She looked around and saw even more slabs and another mound of dirt as she stepped on another tarp and felt something wooden under her feet as the group looked at each other.

She tapped on it again as she got the tarp off to find the trap door hidden underneath; "Well, well, well…what do we have here? Now we know how they are getting in; Good work, Watch Guard!" The Watch Guard bowed before her as the Dark King nodded to his guard in appreciation for a job well done. The Dark Spirits watched as she grabbed the heavy handle of the trap door, "Can you help me lift this?" She asked Timothy as they nodded and gave her a hand with the trap door and opened it to see a ladder and a tunnel as she got the light and looked at it. "A tunnel; what sorcery is this?" The Dark King said with gritted teeth.

She started down the ladder with the burlap sack hugging her body and looked at the Prince who looked at her with love and as he stroked her cheek lovingly, "Please be careful down there," and he lets her go as she gave him a small smile. She reached into the sack for the flashlight as the Dark King watched the couple with interest while Timothy went over to a crate and sat down.

"Jesterson, Marylebarne, and Timothy please stay here; I'm going to see where this tunnel leads and I'll be as quick as I can," she said as they smiled while she snapped on the flashlight. "Okay be careful," Jesterson says as she smiled and he went to sit beside the Prince who was almost in tears as she prepared herself for the walk and then she told the advisor as he came closer, "And Marylebarne please tell the Prince, I am sorry for disappointing him and I will give him back his love if he wants…" Marylebarne nodded sadly as she sighs, dries her eyes, and plucks up her courage as she heads down the dirt tunnel with the flashlight shining the way.

The Dark King and the advisor looked at Timothy who was crying quietly in the corner as her footprints echoed down the dark tunnel as she ran down the narrow passageway. "I think he heard her..." Marylebarne told the Dark King while Jesterson tried to comfort his Prince but he couldn't be consoled. The Dark King came to the lovelorn Prince and says with a hand on his shoulder as the Prince looked at him. "You love her; I admire you and I am a bit jealous of you too..." The Dark King and the Timothy smiled. "But she is a wise and a beautiful young lady; she's only trying find answers." He nods and says to the Dark King, "She mentioned to me a binder that she took away from an elderly lady she was visiting..."

The Dark King replied, "Yes, her name was inside the binder and if George Thackeray had taken it and saw her name, he would have killed the young girl and nothing would change. Events are now set in motion that we cannot stop; we must follow them to its logical conclusion. This is one for the history books, Marylebarne, and no one should forget this for as long as they live; about a brave girl who risked everything to set us all free." Everyone nodded as they waited for her return as Timothy couldn't let him forget her family who suffered for what she has gone through as Marylebarne wrote it down in his small notepad along with the date. "So let me get this straight; her mother died to protect her son, husband and daughter all because of that binder, did you know that this was going to happen?"

Timothy asked the Dark King who knew his bitterness and anger as the dark king says with defeat and sadness as he went back to the trap door; "No I did not, your highness. But her mother will not die in vain; I can assure you of that; for her husband and her son are very close at hand." Timothy was bewildered and confused as they waited for her return until it hit him: "Oh my God Marylebarne, Paul and Mark Franklin-the University lecturers! That's her family and they don't know it!" The Dark King nodded and replied, "This curse has blinded them to the truth, my dear Prince!" They all looked at each other with shock as they waited for her to return. "Then it's more important to get those documents of a forgotten family now; she needs to be told the truth and break this curse once and for all." Marylebarne said as everyone nodded as the advisor explained to the Dark King what is happening as he told him what had discovered as they talked while waiting for her to return. "If this is true then that forgotten family shall also be remembered and honoured within the Royal Carlton family history…I will never forget them and neither will my men."

The Dark King understood what was at stake and he agreed to help as much as he could as the advisor thanked him and said, "We need all the help we can get, my Lord." He signalled to his guards to go and keep an eye on the veil and the guards bowed and did their duty for their king as they left the group in the dark, dank basement as they waited for Alyssia's return.

While down in the dark, dirty, unstable, narrow passageway, Alyssia got near the end until the flashlight hits another ladder at the far end of the passage as she lifts the flashlight to find another trap door. She climbs up the ladder, opens the lock and quietly lifts the trap door slowly into… "Thackeray House!" she exclaimed in a low voice. "So, this is how you're breaking in to the basement, you dirty rotten scoundrels! What part of 'Off Limits' don't you understand??"

She was just about to leave a little surprise for them until the dirty rotten scoundrels came down the corridor as she kept low and out of sight until she overhears the trio planning a murder. She was scared as she thought: *John has to know about this, it's imperative that I get their exact words or Thackeray and his dust buddies will get away with murder!'* She grabbed the pen and pad that was in the burlap sack and listens carefully and writes down what was being said for Detective John Preston who will need to be told after this is all over.

These two crazy bullies are now invading the campus for their promise of being George's bodyguards and now live in Thackeray House as George's thugs after they were evicted from their farm for growing poisonous plants that killed a little boy. Their unkempt sandy blonde hair, cold blue eyes, dusty, dirty, smelly, sweat soaked clothes, overbearing tall frames and muscular build are used for intimidation and their fights are to build bad character. Already wanted for numerous murders and violent beatings, Ted and Ed Ezra are not to be messed with. They are merciless, unforgiving, bullies, uneducated, illiterate, bad teeth; smelly, stupid ignoramuses that are supposed to feared by all but end up being big chickens when confronted women that stand up to them like her friends Amber and Adrianne.

"Aww come on boss," said one of the Ezra brothers in his 'country bumpkin' twang; "…just one small killing, please?" Who she didn't see was Stuart lurking around the corner listening as well as George shot the Ezra brother a look of anger and snapped back at the brother, "No!" He regained his evil composure as he snapped back. "You either follow me and we do the killings together or I leave you to rot in jail! Once we kill everyone in the University, John Preston and that 'so-called' son of mine Stuart, those blasted friends of hers, Alyssia, the Franklins and the caretakers of Cassious House; we will rule this town!" They all laughed as Stuart was livid at him as he listened as the other brother asked, "But what about Cassious House? How do we get past all them ghost and spirits, boss?"

George brought them together as he slapped their backs and coughed at the dust coming off them, "I have poison bombs that will kill all the ghosts and spirits; you throw them into the House wait 20 seconds and the gas is released throughout the House and it kills them all…then after an hour or two, we move in and claim what is ours."

They all laugh and leave for the 'classroom' as an angry Stuart slips away quietly and goes to the hut to see John, who has heard everything as well as he texted him that he was returning to the gardening hut and John thought it was a better idea and he could protect him until this assignment was over. Alyssia closes the trap door quietly as George says in a very evil tone, "Come on boys…let's go and make some bombs!" They all laugh and head down the hall to the 'classroom' while Alyssia had put her pen and pad away in the pocket of her hoodie after writing the last sentence and got the battery powered drill along with some heavy wooden screws and screws the trap door shut to the wooden beams and securely fastened the locks. Then she climbs down the ladder after putting the drill away; and with the flashlight pointing the way back, she heads back down the narrow, unsafe passageway.

While back in the basement of Cassious House, everyone waits for her return as the Dark King paced back and forth as he waits around the tunnel entrance. Marylebarne and Jesterson was comforting a distraught Prince Timothy who was still reeling from her words as he prayed that she didn't mean what she said because he was so in love with her despite what was happening in this point in time. The ghostly Dark King was in the dark passageway and he had seen her and she snapped her flashlight off and put it into the burlap sack after seeing the Dark King and he came up to tell the others, "She is coming!"

The trio rushed over to help her up as they helped her up the ladder and she clapped the dirt off her hands. She thanked them as she knelt down, closed the trap door, took the drill and some heavy screws and screwed the door tightly into place and secured the locks as the drill finally lost power as she replaced it in the burlap sack as she stood up and said to the Dark King, "Your Lordship, that should keep them from breaking in to the lower part of the House and see if you can get your men to work together to replace all those slabs quickly; it will keep pressure on the trap door and to keep them from ever opening the trap door again until I get the police and the Council of Kelton Heights down here to refill the tunnel when this curse is broken."

He nodded as she stood up with his help and then she hid the burlap sack so well that no one will ever find it as Alyssia then says to the Dark King as she claps the dirt from her hands, "Let me know if there is anything else I can do for you in the meantime..." He said while placing a hand on her shoulder. "All we ask of you deliver George Thackeray and his goons to us dark spirits first; then to break the curse on this house and set us all free." She smiled and says, "Then consider it done, my Lord. Everyone at the University wants rid of him, so you should have the honour of making sure he is never seen again."

The Dark King smiled and barred his skeletal teeth as Jesterson asked as he turns to her, "Have you found out anything of interest in the tunnel?" Alyssia said with a sigh after she gets her breath back. "I have Jesterson... the passageway before you; it goes directly to Thackeray House at the University. They are using the tunnel below to break in to the House and steal whatever is hidden below Cassious House...whatever is down there; they are risking a cave in to get it."

The Dark King calls his guards and gave them instructions as the advisor became firm as he says to Alyssia and the others, "I will warn the guards at the caves to be extra vigilant and Jesterson, you must warn the other spirits; they need to be ready to fight for what is theirs...this House is our home and the Prince's rightful residence and I will defend it to the death!" He nods and was about to leave as she says with a sigh, "But that's not all;" They all look back at her as she continued; "I've also overheard a murder plot on how he plans to get rid of my friends and how he plans to get rid of you. He plans to gas you all out by letting off poison bombs within Cassious House. The gas would kill every spirit who dwells here in the House and the he plans to "take back what is his" after the gas has dispersed-Cassious House."

The trio were shocked and bewildered as the Dark King bristled with anger like a porcupine ready to attack a predator; "While the curse is still intact?" The Dark King asked angrily while the Prince and the others sat on the crate in shock and horror as she answered his question. "Yes, he believes that no one would oppose him if he had a cursed House and everyone would have to bow to him." Alyssia says with an angry but worried tone in her voice. She needed to get this message to John Preston quickly to back up Stuart's story as the Dark King angrily hissed, "The selfish, murderous fool! I will warn my people and they will be on their guard always!" She nodded as the Dark King came to her as his voice softened to a gentle father-like tone again, "Thank you again, my dear girl..." He placed a skeletal hand on her cheek and said lovingly. "May your love always be a beacon of hope to those who need it!" She looked to him and replied back as she smiled, "Thank you my Dark Lord. I will deliver... I give you my word."

He nodded and gave her a kiss on her forehead for luck. "I know you will do me and my people proud!" She smiled and bowed to him as the Dark King and his guards left the quartet in the basement. Marylebarne says to Jesterson, "Come on my boy; we have got to warn the others and then I will see the guards at the caves. They need to be on their toes if Thackeray is going to strike." Jesterson was going to ask Marylebarne about Timothy and Alyssia but there were more pressing issues to worry about as Jesterson nodded and they left for the Tower disappearing in to the shadows leaving Timothy and Alyssia alone in the dark, dank basement as she looked at him.

She was waiting for a telling off from the Prince, but Timothy just stood up to come to her but she stopped him. "Go to the others and warn them of what you know; don't waste your time with me and then after I set you and the House free," Timothy smiled as she started to cry. He wanted to hold her but she kept him back as she continued; "I will leave you and never bother you again." Timothy's smile faded as she cried harder and concluded, "I'm not worthy of your love, your highness." He was shocked and shaken at her last six words as he wanted to tell her that he wasn't angry at her but she couldn't look at him as she ran from him before he could hold her as Timothy called to her as she kept on running never looking back.

He sat on a crate and cried too; his body was slumped and his tears were running down his face as he heard the last of her sobs and foot falls fade away from the basement while she ran back home on the other side of the House. After a few minutes of tears and contemplation, he felt a hand on his shoulder and a whisper in his ear, "Go to her and let her love be your light she has come so far for you to give up on her now; she's been hurt too much; enough is enough."

He looked up into the eyes of her mother, Emily Jenna MacPherson-Franklin, who smiled at him happily and she stroked his tears away on his cheeks and then stroked his hair for she had heard what her daughter had said to him and she came to reassure the Prince that all was not lost. "But Emily…" he began as she stopped him by placing a hand on his lips. "I've seen how you care for her, guard her; making sure that she is safe. Dear Prince; you love my daughter I can see it when you look at her, and now you have my blessing to love and take care of her. Go to her-she has shed enough tears…" she then placed a hand on his cheek, "and so have you, my Prince."

He smiled and reached to touch her cheek as he looked to Emily as a source of comfort. "I'm scared," he told her. "…she says 'she was not worthy of my love;'" as he tried not to shed tears but Emily says gently. "Because she thought you would be angry, disappointed, hurt, and ashamed of what she has done here just now."

The Prince said to her gently, "I would never be angry at her!" Emily smiled as she reassured him by taking his hand into hers as she sits with him, "…then prove it to her. I taught my daughter how to respect and honour those who have fallen in wars and I watched as she placed poppies on the graves of servicemen and women with tears in her eyes as she whispered a 'thank you' to them. I taught her to love humanity, to sing, to play the piano, speak and read Welsh and Gaelic and to understand history. Dry your tears, dear Prince…welcome her into the family; she needs us more than ever if we are to defeat George Thackeray once and for all."

The Prince smiled as he replied to her, "I see now where she gets her kindness and compassion… thank you, Emily; but one thing I need to ask before I go to her, is Mark and Paul Franklin her father and brother? It seems the curse has blinded them to the truth…" Emily nods and says, "Yes they are, but until this curse is lifted, you must keep this to yourself; I want the truth to be revealed to her when her father and brother are reunited with her." He nodded as she kissed his forehead and stroked his cheek once more as she lets him go as Emily started to disappear into shadow saying, "Goodbye, my Prince… go to her and may you be courageous in all you do." He watched her disappear into nothingness as he went back to the Tower to think things out before he went to see Alyssia because he knew that just going to someone who is very vulnerable and trying to sort things out in their head, is not wise just now; but they needed to be apart so both of them could think.

Alyssia finally got back to her home, locked the door, hung up the key as she sobbed long and hard and leaned against the door and slid to the floor while she sat with her arms on her knees and her head on her arms crying as Mystery came to her and climbed into her lap and offered her a rub on her cheek and a paw of comfort as if to say, *"You still have me… no more tears mummy; I hate to see you cry."* She smiled at Mystery and she held her close and stroked her coat gently as her purring calmed her while Mystery put her paw into her wet hands. "Oh sweet kitty, you always know how I feel, don't you? I don't deserve you," and she held her close as she cried.

After a little while, Mystery was sound asleep on the couch as Alyssia tried to do something to take her mind off of what had happened and what she had done. But whatever she tried to do, all she could see was Timothy's smiling face looking back at her because she loved him so much and it tore her heart into pieces which made it harder to concentrate on her studies as well as other things. She thought: *'This is why I never wanted to fall in love…it hurts too much. Now what am I to do?'*

Back in the Tower, Timothy was a broken man as he thought of the seven words that stabbed at his heart like a jagged piece of broken glass in his heart. He sat on his bed thinking of her with a tankard of water beside him as he tried so hard to not shed anymore tears and looked at her picture which sat on his desk and ran his fingers across the glass and held her picture close to his chest.

He cried bitter tears as the cup of water was thrown across the room in anger as he stood still holding her picture in his wet palms because her love was all he craved every day and night and right now he couldn't concentrate on his studies as teardrops fell on her face like soft rain on to the glass as he stood up from his desk and looked out the window of his study thinking of her all alone crying in her home still holding her picture close to his chest as Marylebarne came to him as he watched him replace her picture on the desk and cleared his throat as Timothy dried his eyes and found the battered cup he threw across the room and replaced it by the pitcher on his night table until he heard a gentle knock on his door and his advisor slowly came in.

Timothy didn't have to turn around to know it was his advisor who wanted to check on his broken-hearted charge. "Yes, Marylebarne…what can I do for you, my friend?" he sniffed and dried his eyes with his sleeve of his tear drenched shirt. "The Spirits have been told and they will be extra vigilant; I've also told the guards in the caves and they will also be on their guard; the commander has told me that he'll put extra guards on if necessary." Marylebarne knew he was down as he filled up his cup with water and said without looking at him, "Thank you Marylebarne."

Timothy took a huge gulp of his water and told Marylebarne what she said as the advisor was willing to listen and offer his wisdom as he sat on his bed after closing the door; it was the last six words that rang in his ears and tortured his brain and thoughts, "She told me that she-she…" He couldn't say them as he took in more water while he fought back more tears as Marylebarne came to him and placed his reassuring hand on his shoulder.

"She did this for herself and for us, and now she needs us more than ever…she needs you to be strong; this the ultimate test of love." Timothy looked at his wise advisor as he says, "Go to her and make amends. I know down deep you love her; just don't make the mistake of letting her go unless you are willing to wait another three hundred years?" The Prince closed his eyes at that prospect and Marylebarne patted him on the shoulder gently and left him alone to think saying, "I'm going to go back to the search of the missing Franklin Family. If you need any more advice, just search me out." Timothy looked up at him and Marylebarne smiled as he went back to the search for the forgotten family with the other group of spirits while the other spirits got the ballroom ready for her arrival.

After thinking long and hard for an hour, he came to the conclusion that his advisor and Emily were right as he drank down the last of his water, washed and dried his face of the tears, grabbed his sword, strapped it on, left his room, walked down the corridor, with renewed faith as the spirits bowed and cheered him on. "Go and get her Timothy!" he heard… "Bring her back, your majesty!" said another voice as he passed them and they cheered him on, many of the spirits patted his back and touched his arm with encouragement and love while a little girl gave him a flower to give to her and gave her a hug as he picked her up.

"Thank you my sweet girl. I want to give this flower to Alyssia, may I do that?" The child says, "Yes you may, sire. She is the best thing to happen to us and the House so go and get her." He gave her a small kiss on her small cheek as he put the child down and walked away as she watched him leave the Tower for her House on other side as others wished him luck as he felt very determined to win back her love as Marylebarne watched him come in to the Tower and walked right past him. "And where are you going young man, as if I didn't know…" Timothy said determined, "I'm going to go and win Alyssia's love. I'm not waiting another three hundred years for someone else!"

Everyone cheered as the advisor smiled and said to him with a smile and a laugh, "That's my boy, go and get your girl and show her that you love her!" The Prince heard his message, took a deep breath and disappeared into shadows while everyone cheered him as he left for her home on the other side of Cassious House. Marylebarne and the spirits went back to their duties as he looked at all the busy spirits hard at work looking for clues to the forgotten Thackeray-Franklin family or setting up for the party. He heard a noise behind him and felt a touch on his shoulder as he turned to see Catherina come to him with happy news as she bowed before the advisor and gave him the paper and she went back to work.

"Thank you Catherina, why don't you and your sister go and help the others with the party and continue the search tomorrow? You have worked very hard today…" Catherina thanked him, bowed, and left to rejoin her sister to tell her what Marylebarne said. He read the paper and laughed happily and says to them all, "Make haste, we have a guest tonight to welcome into our family…" as he jumped up and clicked his heels with joy at the news as the spirits nodded and made the ballroom look presentable as he laughed gently and folded up the paper and placed it in his pocket as he waited for Timothy to return with news of Alyssia.

Back in her flat, Alyssia was sitting on the couch heartbroken, alone and without love while she thought of Timothy's disappointment and hurt look which made her cry even more as she held on to a cushion, because it was the only thing that had no reflection or mirror. She wanted to clean, read a book, sleep—do anything to take her mind off that look on Timothy's face; but no matter how hard she tried, she saw Prince Timothy staring back at her whether it was in water, or in glass, or a mirror… nothing helped and it broke her heart into pieces. She cried out, "What's the use?" as depression set in, "no one cares or loves me!"

She puts the cushion onto the armrest, lies down on the cushion and sobbed hard as her heart broke as tears fell like rain. Timothy came out of shadows and saw her sobbing; tears filled his eyes as he lifted her up, cuddled her into his chest and he held her while Timothy gently took her hand into his and whispered, "I do and I forgive you." She sat up and looked deep into the eyes of Prince Timothy who also had tears of love while he dried her bitter tears as Mystery jumped up and sat beside her and wanted all the attention as she purred loudly, *'please stop my mummy from crying'* the kitten seemed to say as she lays between Alyssia and Timothy as the Prince gave the kitten a rub on the ears as she gave the kitten stroke on her long body and looked at her Prince.

"But I did wrong…" she told him with a quiver in her voice but he stroked her hair; "No, you did the exact opposite." He said as he dried her tears and replied, "You saved us and gave us a reason to fight for our right to exist and for our precious Cassious House-how can I not love someone like you?" He held her tight as he took her hand into his, kissed it and told her with a smile, "You complete me, Alyssia, and you alone deserve all my love."

He smiled as he stroked her cheek and hair while he dried her tears. "I do? I complete you? I make you happy?" Alyssia asked as the Prince nodded and she touched his cheek gently. "I-I-I didn't know that-honestly…" He held her so close as though his touch was mending her broken heart and spirit as he quieted her fears and sobs with his finger on her lips as he stroked them gently. She placed her hand on his cheek and his lips while he kissed her forehead softly and said, "No more tears now; go and get ready I will send Marylebarne to fetch you and to bring you to the ballroom before 'the song.' I await you-and so does everyone else for tonight we make merry before midnight. Go make haste…" They stood up as he gives her one last hug, then without another word, he placed both hands on her cheeks and looked into her eyes. "I await your arrival for tonight you become family."

He kissed her forehead once more and lets her go as he disappeared into shadows leaving her standing there wondering what just happened as she goes to the bedroom, showers and changes into her costume; all the while she was thinking about what he meant about her being family. The early evening turned to night as she was in full costume, she was trying to remember her manners in front of royalty while she waited for Marylebarne to come, and she fed a very hungry Mystery who scoffed down her tuna as soon as Alyssia put it in her bowl. She had something light to eat while she tidies the House and the hour had come as the clock chimed the eight o'clock hour as Marylebarne came from the shadows.

He stopped in his tracks to look at her and he laughed with joy as she spins around and shyly said, "I wasn't sure how to dress so I thought I better dress in the appropriate costume. Hope you don't mind?" Marylebarne says, "Mind? My dear girl, you look beautiful!" The advisor said as he looked at her, took her hand and kissed it as he patted her cheek; "You definitely belong with us, my sweet niece. Now come along…" She stopped him, "Niece? What?" Marylebarne chuckled, "You my dear girl are my great, great, great grandniece and so was your mother; but come now, enough talk… The Prince is waiting for us, come on."

She was still a bit confused and unsure as Marylebarne took her by the hand and they went into the shadows until they came upon a set of doors which Marylebarne opened into a very large room at the far end of the House and he ushered her inside as her uncle shut the doors and offered his arm to her as she took it and looked around at the most beautiful decorated ballroom ever as there was one; a cosy fire, all the food you can eat, music, dancing, water, ale, wine, laughter and good company as Marylebarne and Alyssia are welcomed by the other spirits.

"Welcome to the Family my dear," he said with a warm smile, "Come in and make yourself at home." Marylebarne introduced her to all the spirits who greeted her and some toasted her while others complimented her dress and her manners. Many of the ladies gave her a hug or a smile, while others bowed to her as she did the same. Marylebarne saw that she was completely overcome with the immensity of the ballroom which had a huge spiral staircase with animal sculptures on top of its plinths and there were family portraits and a small piano off to the side while the floor was tile and polished. There were French doors which opened out onto the terrace where a small stone bench awaited for anyone to come and sit. The fireplace was huge as it stretched from wall to wall and it required three people to light it as the chimneys were glad to be used again, burning out the straw dropped by birds while building their nests while moss and dead leaves were burned up and turned to ash. At the top of the stairs was a huge vase filled with flowers and a huge round table while pictures which hung behind it, seemed to take in its fragrances once again where the cold, stale air used to be as it looked at all the ghostly guests were celebrating as the pictures seem to smile for the portraits had not seen this much cheer in over three hundred years.

The advisor comes to her and takes her hand and leads her into the crowd as she looked around letting the sights and smells entangle her senses as she goes deeper into the ballroom and sees all children running about while drunks and musicians were being merry as they tune up their instruments and their voices for the festivities. She saw the Coquitlam Sisters approached her and they apologised to her for what they did to her that Thursday afternoon in the library. "I hope we didn't hurt those poor elderly ladies, Alyssia?" Celeana replied in her lilting German accent as Catharina says to her, "Honestly, we meant no harm to anyone…" Alyssia smiled gently, "Apology accepted," she said to them as the sisters looked at each other rather puzzled. "The ladies will be okay; the first aiders put it down as heat exhaustion."

She touched their cheeks gently and left them happy but shocked as Marylebarne smiled as she smiled; "We'll talk later, promise!" The sisters thanked her and they let her go with the advisor after they bowed to them. Marylebarne came and he takes Alyssia's hand and leads her over to the bench while everyone from young men and merry makers made her laugh; "Come in my dear, make yourself at home…" She asked him, "I see that you have a piano too. May I play it every now and again to practice my playing one day?" Marylebarne said as he patted her hand, "You are always welcome to come in and play it when you want, except when the Prince is doing his fencing instruction on Thursday afternoon."

She smiled and thanked him as more of the spirits began to arrive and others made her laugh as Jesterson told her some jokes and she laughed as they awaited for Prince Timothy to join in on the fun, even Marylebarne was having a laugh and a good time as he drank his mild ale until a little girl comes running down the stairs and shouts, "The Prince is coming! The Prince is coming!" then the child runs to her daddy who was sitting near the table of booze as he scooped her up into his arms and enjoyed his drink as she sat her in his lap and they enjoyed music until he stood with her in his arms as Marylebarne puts his tanker down on the table and takes Alyssia beside him as the Prince comes to the landing in his dress uniform and everyone bows before him as he stands at the top of the stairs.

He smiled and greets all his guests with a small speech after they all bow before him, "Tonight we welcome into our family Alyssia Anne Franklin-Jenkins. I hope you have or will make her feel at home for she has given us a reason to fight for this House and for our survival and for that; we owe her a debt of gratitude." She smiled as everyone cheers as the Prince says, "Come on my friends, let's have some fun and forget our worries, strike up the band!" The music begins to play and the ballroom is filled with cheer and laughter as the Prince comes down the steps to Alyssia and Marylebarne who waited for him at the bottom of the stairs and she bows before him.

Timothy reached out his hand to her and helps her stand as Marylebarne replied formally to him, "Prince Timothy Andrew Carlton, may I present my niece, Miss Alyssia Anne Thackeray Franklin-Jenkins, James Thackeray's great, great, great grand-daughter." Timothy was shocked as well as Alyssia while Marylebarne smiled and the couple looked at him in shock. "Y-You found evidence?" the Prince asked as the advisor nods and says, "...thanks to the Coquitlam sisters and the entire search party. It turns that Paul and Mark are my great, great grandnephews and Emily and Alyssia are my grandnieces; they are all from the same family. But enough pomp and circumstance my boy, let's have some fun and celebrate our newest family member."

Marylebarne gave her hand a small kiss and then he passed her hand to Timothy as the prince held her close to him and leaves them. She waited until the advisor was out of earshot and whispered rather embarrassingly while they watched the advisor greet everyone and get his tankard of ale; "If I knew that you were going formal…" He laughed as he looked at her fair maiden outfit; "I'm full of surprises, fair maiden." The couple laughed as he kissed her hand and said, "But come, the night is young so let's make merry;" she nodded as the couple had a wonderful time dancing, laughing and making merry through the night. The Prince was glad to have her back in his arms as he danced her around the room while the night was young and slowly turning to late night as the clock chimed the hour.

The food was almost gone and the liquor and the spirits flowed as he came to her, "Having a wonderful time?" He asked her and she looked at him and said, "The best time ever!" He took her plate, puts it down and with his hand around her waist, he lifted her up and twirled her around the room as they joined in the lively dance around them. "You are terrible…" she chuckled as he let out a hearty laugh danced until the music stop playing. The midnight hour was fast approaching and the party was ending as the Prince and her go out on to the balcony and into the moonlight and stare up at the stars as they sat down on a bench on the terrace as the couple talked, shared their love, and held each other tightly.

"We are safe here…the Dark Spirits never come over to this side of the House-they don't like the moonlight." The couple chuckled as she rubbed her arms of the cold she felt and he gave her his jacket and walked her back inside as the prince closed the French doors as he held her close by the fireside while they warmed their hands and talked until the clock rung out the half past chimed. Timothy took her home as she looked all around them; some were drunk, others fell asleep; especially the children as the parents picked up their sleepy heads and headed back to the Tower after everyone said their goodnights to the happy couple as the Prince and Alyssia were more in love than ever.

But for Marylebarne and Jesterson, it was so good to see a smile on the Prince's face again. "Ah love," says Jesterson as Marylebarne added as they watched Timothy and Alyssia leave the ballroom and head to the other side of the House. "Yes, love repairs the damage heartbreak can cause." The jester nodded as they head back upstairs to the Tower as Marylebarne told him, "...come on, better get ready for tomorrow." Jesterson nodded as he watched Timothy escort Alyssia to the other side of the House.

They came into her modern flat as he took her close, "I never told you this, but you looked so lovely tonight and yes, sorry I should have told you to dress formally, but I love you in this. In fact, you looked beautiful in anything or with nothing on at all." She slapped his chest playfully as he laughed and hugged her, as he picked her up and twirled her around. As he puts her down, he kissed her neck passionately as she closed her eyes... "I'll have to change my whole report you know?" she says as his breath was on her skin and he kissed her cheek. "Forget the report for now...let's make this moment ours."

He whispered as he went behind her, held her waist and stroked her hair as he reached around her front and pulled the string to her costume and helped her undress. He slipped off her blouse and kissed the nape of her neck as she fought her desire for the lovelorn Prince while he worked his way down her shoulders as he holds her hand in his and placed it on his cheek as ran his hands down her arms and her body. Her heart beats like drum for him as she felt his touch on her making each moment theirs as time slowed down for just them and were lost in each other's love until the midnight chimes rang out and beckoned her to bed and Timothy to guard duty.

He cursed the chimes as he says still drunk on her love; "I could do this all night, but I have guard duty in an hour." He said whispering in her ear as she told him gently as she turned to face him, "You looked very handsome tonight, your majesty." He smiled as they sat on the bed after she went to change into her night wear. He looked deep into her eyes and saw his love for her inside his hungry touch and in her eyes while he took her tiny hand and kissed it as his passion for her grew hotter, but right now, she had to go to bed and he had to return to his people as he left her wanting more of him.

"Here..." he stood up after he watched her yawn, "into bed now;" but she told him as she lies down as he got her under the covers, "...but I'm not sleepy" and she fell asleep quickly as he pulled up the covers and said with a chuckle. "Yes you are" and he kissed her forehead while he left her to dream as he went to change for guard duty as Mystery came into the bedroom, leaped up onto the bed and curled up beside Alyssia. He came back to her room and had his book on Shakespeare sonnets as he guarded her till dawn...keeping watch while the House fell silent.

Chapter 7

Sunday Morning was upon Kelton Heights and it was a cloudy, cool morning as she got up, made the bed, took a shower, fed Mystery, and changed into her clothes. She could feel Timothy's hands all over her from last night and she felt rather warm and happy inside. After she got ready and came through to the living room and dining room, she looked at her messages on her phone and found one from Adrianne which made her giggle; *'Hey you…what's up? Amber, Milton and I are going to ASDA to get groceries after church. Want to come out with us for a while? Forget the report and have some fun and you are paying for the teas this time.'*

Alyssia chuckled and thought for a moment as to why her friends are at church while she looked up on the Google Search Engine for "The Gaelic Connection"; it was a place she, Catriona, and her grandmother Jessica went to for some lunch, dinner or high teas after a day of shopping in Kelton Heights. She looked back at her screen and found out that the Gaelic Connection was open today and she would take them there. Going on their page, she looked up the number and times of opening, wrote it down, and waited to call them to make a reservation for four.

She texted Adrianne back to say, *'I would love to join you and yes afterwards I will take you all to "The Gaelic Connection." 'It boasts of some of best food and music and it opens at noon. But I have to go to the Kelton Heights Visitor's Centre and talk to a Visitor Centre's employee named Dòmhnall Margarida so why don't you all meet me there. What do you say, do we have a date?'* She waits for a reply and then gets one back from Adrianne, *'Of course'* Adrianne replied back, *'We'll text you when church is over.'*

She was going to text back "You go to church?" but thought better about it and puts her phone away then went back to her homework table as she worked away on her Sociology and English Literature reports. Mystery came up on to her lap and purred happily while Alyssia rubbed her ears gently to Enya's music as the early morning slipped into early afternoon.

Just then she felt two hands rubbing her arms and a whisper in her ear, "Good morning Alyssia," She turned and looked into the eyes of Prince Timothy who rubbed Mystery's ears as well. She felt his head on her shoulder and she placed her hand on his cheek as she said, "Good morning Prince Timothy." She lifted up Mystery into her arms as the couple continued to pet her as she says with his arms still wrapped around her as she turned to face him, "I had a wonderful time last night Timothy; I won't forget it."

Alyssia said as her hand ran down his cheek and touched his lips, "I'm so glad that you have had a great time and all the spirits are happy to have met you as well, they can't stop talking about you; especially the Coquitilam sisters; they were surprised that you forgave them for what they did to you;" she smiled as he asked her, "But why would you forgive them? They are just curious, that's all." She said with a loving tone, "I forgave them because life is too short to hold grudges and that the elderly librarians were suffering from heat exhaustion, not fright. It seemed that the spirits of those sisters cooled them while the caretaker, who had heard about the incident, had seen to heating in the library. The librarians fainted; not because of the spirits, but because it was too warm." Alyssia told him.

Timothy started to understand as he nodded and she continued. "So when another student and I got them in the recovery position; they were alert and both ladies thanked me for helping them. The staffing has changed and so has the situation, they have bottles of water beside them at all times; plus, there are young people behind them doing all the heavy work while they deal with the students. So Timothy, Prince of the Spirit Frontier," he chuckled at her sense of humour as she set Mystery on the couch, as she took her dishes to the kitchen and washed them up while he followed her to the kitchen; "the sisters are forgiven, the heating is fixed and everything is back to normal...well so to speak. I'm living near a haunted house and talking, dancing and laughing with spirits." He laughed happily as she asked, "Is that normal?" He giggled as she came out of the kitchen after leaving her dishes on the drying rack as he took her into his arms, "Nope, but I'm not going to risk a pillow to the face to say otherwise."

The couple laughed as he smiled; "So what's on the agenda today, besides me?" He had a silly grin on his face as she giggled like a school girl with her first crush as she looked into his eyes. "Well I have to meet Milton, Amber and Adrianne in town after I see this man a historian named Dòmhnall Margarida and then we'll head off for groceries and High Tea. Speaking of which…" She let go and picked up the phone as she called the Gaelic Connection and made a reservation for four at three o'clock. "That's that," she said putting the phone down. "…the reservations are made and now I need to get ready and do some shopping and get that meeting with Dòmhnall over with; I hope its open." She turned back to him and held her close as she asked him as he gawked at her, "Don't you have studies to work on, young man?"

Just then, the advisor as he shook his head while he came out of the shadows as Timothy kissed her neck. "Yes he does," another voice replied as a quite annoyed Marylebarne was standing behind them and they turn to him, "Good morning Marylebarne," she said as he came closer. "Good morning and before you ask, everyone has recovered from last night." Alyssia smiled and replied to her uncle, "That's wonderful, Marylebarne. I hope we can do it again sometime, would you let the other spirits know?"

Marylebarne says, "I will my sweet niece," then he came to his charge as his tone, "I have been looking for you all over the place, young man. You have two letters to write and your fencing lesson is scheduled for this afternoon." Timothy's demeanour turned to a moody teenager in his puberty years. "Aw, do I really have to, Marylebarne. I thought we had the day off today?" Marylebarne was just about to say something as she hid a chuckle in her throat as she took his hand into hers, "Look Timothy, go and do what Marylebarne wants you to do and I will see you later tonight; I promise. Being royalty is a twenty four hour job and I would not want Marylebarne angry at me if I kept you from your studies, just like you don't want Doctor Mark Franklin mad at you for keeping me from my studies." That cheered him up and she gave him a kiss on his cheek and he smiled after she whispered in his ear, "I'll see you later tonight."

He smiled and left them as he disappeared in the shadows back to the Tower as Marylebarne turned to her with a sigh, "I don't know what I am going to do with him…thank you my dear," he said to her as he took her hand and kissed it as he began towards the shadows but she stopped the wise advisor. "Uncle Marylebarne, I'm very curious-why can't I kiss Timothy's lips?" Marylebarne sighed with sadness. "When we were cursed with spirit-like powers, his lips were poisoned and he was not able to say those three words that he wants to say. If he had kissed you on the lips just now, he would have killed you right where you stand."

She was horrified as he touched her cheek and smiled, "That's why I urge you to kiss him on the cheek just like you did there; he is so smitten with you and he would do anything for you, Alyssia. Until this curse is lifted, just kiss him on the cheek, okay?" She nodded and he patted her cheek, "Better go and make sure he doesn't do another runner," she chuckled with him, "...so until later my sweet niece." She touched his cheek and he parted ways as he disappeared into shadows while Alyssia sighed and got to work on some homework.

In the Caretaker's hut, John Preston and Stuart Thackeray are getting ready for next week as John takes the listening device and the hidden camera off his clothes as Stuart said anxiously and horrified after hearing a murder plot. "I'm not going back in there! He plans to murder you, me, Alyssia and her friends, the Doctors Franklin, Mangard and Winchell, the Parks and all the spirits of Cassious House. We can't let him get away with it, John!" John stopped him and said calmly, "I know, but we can't do anything until we get those search warrants and see what he's hiding and you are to remain here under my orders so I can keep an eye on you." Stuart wanted to argue but he almost fainted in John's arms with his anxiety levels being too high as John tells him to breathe, gives him a seat and gets a bottle of water for him and thanks him as he rests. He pats him on the chest and calmly says to him, "Now buddy, I'll get a pad and pencil, and you tell me what you know right from the beginning..." Stuart nodded anxiously as he nervously opens and closes his hands by his side, he was sweating and he was shaking with fright. John gets his legal pad and pen and Stuart tells him everything; but without any written evidence or someone to back him up, John would take it as speculation so he made sure that he tells him every detail.

In town, Alyssia makes into the City Centre and sees the Kelton Heights Tourist Information and Visitor's Centre on the West High Street is open and goes inside to look and ask for Dòmhnall Margarida as she told the young lady gently; "...I was told by his brother Iain that I would find him here. The young lady says, "He's with someone, he should be…" just then the couple whom he was dealing with walked away as Alyssia acknowledged them and she called him over. "Dòmhnall Margarida, this is Miss Alyssia Franklin-Jenkins" they smile and shake hands. "She is here at the request of your brother Iain over on Welling Street?" Connie explained as Dòmhnall began to understand, "Yes, my brother was just talking about you, come in Miss Jenkins" they start to walk away as he turned back and quickly said, "…thank you Connie."

She smiled and left the couple to attend to more customers as he takes her to back to the office. "He told me that you are investigating Cassious House, so come in please." He gets her into the office and tells her to have a seat and she does and gets comfortable. The older brother is so unlike Iain but he has same frame as him, tall, lanky, long hands and fingers; in fact you could say they were twins. His hair sits very neatly and likes to wear every day clothes, kind, considerate, loves his customers, quiet, reserved, loves to laugh, married with two children, loves Subway Restaurant down the road, and exercises regularly. He works with the public in the small City Centre Visitor's Centre and Tourist Information Centre in Kelton Heights and he deals with mostly with walks, tourist sites, walking expeditions, arranging tickets, the best way to see the city and information on attractions. He has a soft spot for Alyssia and loves to act in his Drama troop around Kelton Heights, Welleston Village and other cities around the area.

"I'm so sorry for all the privacy, Miss Jenkins, but George Thackeray has been coming in here for sometime claiming that he was banned from my brother's museum and he has been in touch to warn me so are you from him, Thackeray House I mean?" Alyssia said with a puzzled look on her face, "No, I don't think so; I would be thrown out of here if I was. May I ask if he has been in here asking about Cassious House?" Dòmhnall sighed, "Yes he has," says Dòmhnall adjusting himself in his seat at his discomfort. "His goons scare off our customers with intimidation and their dress sense and body odour, it's very unpleasant I can assure you…" she chuckled gently as she says, "I know how you feel, on campus, you can smell them from a mile away."

He chuckled in spite of himself as she continued, "But getting back to Cassious House, your brother whispered to me that you have the complete story of Cassious House? I was wondering if you have that book; I am doing some research on the House and I need as much information as you can give me." Dòmhnall nodded and he got up and went to the safe and opened it up and got it off the safe's shelf as he gave it to her and says, "This is my last copy and I kept aside for you alone as I don't trust George Thackeray as far as I can throw him."

Alyssia chuckled and says, "Believe me, you are not alone!" The couple laughed as he gave her the bag and she placed it in her back pack but she had an idea. "What other books do you have on a House beside Cassious House?" He nodded and says, "I have one on Kelton House near Welleston Village which sits to the south of the village…so you want to trick him by swapping books, is that it?" She nodded; "You're catching on," she said winking at him. "I placed the book on Cassious House in backpack so I would have Kelton House in my hand." He looked at her and says, "…you are one shrewd young lady, Miss Jenkins." Dòmhnall says with a wink and a smile as she smiled, wiggled her eyebrows, and paid for both books and placed Kelton House in a plastic bag for her to hold in her hand so George would steal that instead since he is so desperate to find out where the treasure is hidden as the couple left his office.

As they headed back to the main Visitor's Centre; he then told her, "There may be something else that might peak your interest; there is a trio of stone plinths that have writings on them and they are from very long time ago they are to the north of Welleston Village and east of Kelton Heights; I'll give you the exact location and a piece of local history; it was also where a group of archaeologists and a museum curator from Ireland found weapons like swords, preserved food, and other items in 1927." This piqued her interest as he continued, "According to legends, the Celts were just "passing through" on their way to Scotland to settle in their new home in Ireland, but this particular tribe discovered sacred land near the sea. It was said that the sacred land was given to them by the Gods and a magnificent House would be built over its caves. Inside would be all the riches and treasures the tribe had stored; gold, jewels, important sacred items like goblets, platters of pure silver and gold, weapons made from the finest steel and other precious items…"

Alyssia then asked him, "Was this House to be built on sacred land called Cassious House?" Dòmhnall was surprised, "Yes, yes it was Cassious

House; but how did you know?" She told him gently, "A local, retired and dying archaeologist named Mary Anne Parker was on that dig with her soon-to-be husband; both were students at the time of the discovery."

Dòmhnall was surprised at this revelation as they made their way out of the office to the Tourist Information Centre as they came back through to where the small children were playing and colouring in the pictures while lovers, mums and dads, young people, college students and amateur historians were picking up everything on Kelton Heights for their classes or just to take them home to look over as she asked; "What more can you tell me about the pillars?"

She asked as he continued while the couple navigated through the crowd as Dòmhnall continued his story. "As far as I can make out, they never pillaged or plundered from royalty or castles; they only took the wealth of Mayors or Lords who were rich and would not share their wealth with the townsfolk, or became too proud or too flashy with their wealth. So a villager came to the Celts leader, the Bard, and told them the name of the official, gave them a map of where they lived and that they should not harm him or the family, they would deal with them in their own way."

She opens the brochure and shows the two men; the Pirate and Viking and these men seem to be important to this mystery as he told her; "The Bard seems to look to these two men because they seemed to know what the villagers wanted and knew the layout of each of the towns with maps that were drawn and given to them." The historian looked at Alyssia who was deep in thought as she said, "This is very odd, and I was never told this by your brother, Dòmhnall."

He said quite fairly, "I think I know why; my brother didn't want any trouble with Thackeray because he was kicking up quite a fuss when Iain refused to tell him anything. He asked him to leave as his staff grew quite frightened of him and he threatened to call the police if he didn't leave. He was probably afraid that you would take it back to Thackeray…that is why I asked if you were from him; I meant no disrespect." Alyssia understood as she said, "That's quite all right, Dòmhnall; I was just a bit puzzled, that was all. I also heard that you were vilified by Thackeray in his goons and I am so sorry that you had that experience."

He sighed with relief and he replied, "Thank you and yes I was quite annoyed and my brother was great to stand up for me like that." She whispered to him, "I would have him kicked him in the canastas!" The couple laughed as they got back to the subject at hand as she asked quite curiously. "Now all I ask is; could you provide me the location so I can look at the plinths up close?" Dòmhnall nodded and got out a small piece of paper as he looked up the information until Milton, Amber and Adrianne came in as Milton sneaked up on her and jumped on her back almost scaring her as she hears monkey like noises while Milton started picking at her scalp as he was looking for bugs and acting like a chimp as the girls kept telling others, "He's not with us!" as everyone chuckled, including the children as Alyssia felt Milton climbing higher on her back and he looked at her upside down as he made chimp noises. "Oh great, I got a monkey on my back..."

Everyone around the quartet chuckled until he clears his throat and lets out a 'Tarzan' yell as the whole shop lets out a laugh, including her girlfriends. Alyssia clears her throat and sarcastically says, "Hey Brian Blessed, mind getting off my back?" He does and she turns to her friends who gave her a hug and a laugh as they greet each other; "I'll be right with you...I promise. I'm taking you to a place called "The Gaelic Connection"; my granny and her nurse, Catriona and yours truly would end up there after shopping or a day out."

The friends nodded, "Sounds like a plan, Alyssia," Adrianne says as Dòmhnall gives her the location to where the plinths were located and shoved them in her front pocket along with a symbols book--then he is introduced to Milton, Adrianne, and Amber from Kelton University as she thanks him in Gaelic and he does the same, and she picks up the bag and they leave. ***Tapadh leat, a Dhòmhnall. Uileag mo mùimgu do ciad-bhean agus muirichinn agus teaghlach.*** "Thank you Dòmhnall, all my love to your wife and children." He smiled and replied back, ***Sibh gu...agus mi dis.*** "You too... and I will" as they head to ASDA and "The Gaelic Connection" for high tea.

Milton and the girls wondered, "Are you speaking in tongues?" Alyssia looked at them oddly, "What do you mean?" she asked her friends as they gathered around her as the friends looked her over, turned her around which made her dizzy. "Well, she doesn't have a long pointed tail with horns and a pitchfork..." Milton said with a weird look on his face as the girls laughed as he motioned for her to open her mouth and stick out her tongue which she did, "Nope no forked tongue, either! And she is definitely not half human/ half horse..." Alyssia said with a shake of her head. "Milton, I was speaking Gaelic to Dòmhnall. He is from Ireland and he lived in Wales for some time; he is Gaelic like his brother, Iain. So, I was telling him, 'thank you and all my love to his wife and children'...and no, I don't breathe fires either so stop checking Milton!"

They all laugh as they were leaving the shop as she turned back and waved to Dòmhnall as he and the others laugh as the quartet were about to leave. Just then like bats out of hell, George Thackeray and his goons came in scaring the locals as Adrianne said, "Oh look what crawled out of the woodwork-the demolition trio!" Adrianne whispered to her as they look at George pushing through the crowd as she told Milton, "Want to bet that he's the Devil Incarnate?" Alyssia takes off her backpack and tells Dòmhnall to hide it and to keep everyone calm and not to antagonise him.

He did as he was told as George came close while the staff of the small Visitor's Centre kept the crowd calm and backed off as he comes into her face with an angry snarl while his goons looked at her friends. Milton stood before the girls protecting them as George smiled with a sneer and a look of disgust before them. "Well, well, well what do we have here boys; Franklin's pets..." he said sarcastically as his goons laugh. "So are you becoming a smarty pants like this wimp behind you? He is reserving me a copy of Cassious House book and I am here to make sure he would have it."

Dòmhnall was frightened but kept his cool as Alyssia says, "You leave him out of this; I have the book right here so you will leave this shop without any more of you and your goons nonsense so take it and leave the shop or I will call the police on you for disturbing the peace." She hands him the bag as he swiped it from her as she is pushed to the floor by Thackeray as her friends were held back in fear of the goons. He starts to leaves but turns back and gives her one warning as he comes into her face once more. "Stay out of my way and out of my business, Miss Jenkins...Cassious House belongs to me and I will take back what is rightfully mine and not you or the fright bunch can stop me." Her friends look at each other in confusion as he stood up as the goons spat upon her as the trio left the Centre's office without another word while patrons looked on in horror.

Milton and her friends as well Dòmhnall gave her hand up and gave her the backpack as he wrote down the incident in his log for his boss and he calls the police to make sure it was reported. Milton helped her up and with her backpack as her friends dust her off and the Centre gets back to normal after the rude awakening and she took in a breath as Adrianne vowed that she would find Thackeray and kill him but Alyssia told her, "Don't antagonise him, Adrianne. He's the kind of person who holds grudges and never gives up until that person is dealt with."

The group dust her off as Adrianne says, "It's not that Alyssia, he needs to be taught a lesson on respect and politeness...look at the way he treated you. You haven't done anything to him and he seems to be picking on you for no apparent reason, Alyssia I wouldn't take that kind of abuse from him. No Alyssia, he needs to be taught a lesson about how to treat people and those goons need an attitude adjustment; they simply can't go around bullying people like that and think that it's okay."

Alyssia smiled, came to her, gave her friend a hug as she whispered, *"I just want you to be safe. I love you too much to see you hurt."* She lets Adrianne go and said to Dòmhnall, "The book swap worked but if he ever threatens you or intimidates you, call the police; you all stay safe and thank you for the help and information." Dòmhnall smiled and told her quietly as she adjusts her backpack on her shoulders while Amber helps her as Dòmhnall says in a whisper. "I have left the information on the standing plinths for you in the front pouch of your backpack along with a symbols book of ancient Celtic. I hope it will help you in your search to find the truth of Cassious House and if you find out anything more or what the plinths writings are, just call me here at the Centre or ask for me."

She smiled and thanked him as he patted her arms as he left Alyssia in the care of her friends. "Come on you three, off to ASDA and I have a reservation for us at the Gaelic Connection and I'm buying like you said Adrianne." She said with a smile and a calm voice as the quartet left the Visitor's Centre for ASDA as the old man who was watching her and her friends from the back of the Visitor's Centre, watched the quartet head for their groceries and High Tea.

He smiled and then disappeared down the street as he got back on the phone to his employer saying, "Sir, Dòmhnall has just given her information on something called "The Standing Plinths" outside Kelton Heights or Welleston Village, I forget which; if she goes, shall I follow her?" he asked as the voice says, "Yes but keep out of sight and don't give yourself away. If she is the one to set my son free, I want everything you can get and stay on top of her whereabouts; she holds the key to set both towns and the House free." The young spy says, "She is from Kelton University sir and is in Franklin House; according to her, she is doing research on Cassious House and Franklin's court case." His employer says, "Good, keep tabs on her and stay out of sight. If she thinks she is being followed, she will be scared off and keep me informed and call me when she goes to the plinths." He hung up the phone as well as his employer as the spy disappeared into the crowd on the High Street in Kelton Heights.

Back at Cassious House, Prince Timothy was finished with his letter writing exercise and he took a break while he changed for his Fencing class down in the large ballroom until he heard a knock on the door and saw a head peeking around the corner of the open door as Jesterson came to him, "Marylebarne wants to know if you are finished with your letter writing exercises? I have to deliver the lessons to him while you go to your fencing lessons." Timothy smiled and went to his cluttered desk with Alyssia picture on top of a shelf and gave Jesterson his two letter exercises as he makes sure that's all of it. "There you are, my friend…" he gives it to Jesterson. "Thanks" says the jester as he reads it and says with a nudge on Timothy's tummy. "So did Alyssia have a great time at the little welcome party we threw for her?" Timothy says as he nodded, "Yes she did; the best time ever then I stayed with her and helped her undress as she changed into her nightwear. Oh Jesterson I have never been this much in love before; she makes me float on air and I hope one day you will feel the same way I do when you meet that special someone after we are all human once again." Jesterson says, "I really hope so too; but I'm looking for a shy and respectable girl, Timothy; nobody too wild. She has to be the one who make heart beat uncontrollably and make my heart leap when she walks into the room and her smile must be bright and beautiful."

He looked at Timothy who is smiling and then cleared his throat as he broke out of daydream as he cleared his throat. "Well, I will make sure Marylebarne gets these, thanks your highness…" and he left the room in his haste, slamming into the door as Timothy tried not to chuckle while an embarrassed Jesterson opened the door and left Prince Timothy's room. Timothy shook his head and smiled as he got ready for his fencing practice as he grabbed his sword, strapped it to his side and left his room after kissing Alyssia's picture and met with his instructor in the ballroom.

At ASDA, Alyssia is in a private place with her groceries and she gets out a card that Stuart gave her as she was resting when she first came to Kelton Heights. She gave him a call as she was still affected by Thackeray's threats as Stuart answered the phone and she said to him, "Stuart, it's Alyssia, I'm sorry to call you on a Sunday but I need to talk to you; I'm so scared." Stuart says to her as he puts her on the loudspeaker on his mobile phone. "It's okay Alyssia, I am with John and we're working on a case, what can we do for you and don't be scared, we are only here to help and protect you."

She was a bit confused but thanked him as she told Stuart everything; from meeting with the historian and his threats. The two officers listened and John wrote everything down as she was near tears as he asked where she is and where she was going. She told them as she asked, "Shall I come back to see you or not? I really don't know what to do." John came on and said, "Alyssia its John, listen to me, just go about your business and don't be scared. We will always make sure that you are safe and that you are free of George Thackeray and when you come back, we'll come and see you at your flat and I'll have a few men go and chat with Dòmhnall and the staff at the Visitor's Centre and at Welling Street. We have asked all the business and attractions to keep a log of all the troublemakers due to the history of the town so they are bound to have records of the disruptive George Thackeray. Just go to the Gaelic Connection and have a wonderful time with your friends and we'll talk later."

Alyssia told him, "Okay, I just wanted to let you know, and I feel better now; goodbye John and Stuart and thank you for the advice." They hang up the phone as Stuart turned off his loud speaker as they make plans to go and see her later on at night as the trio found her and they left ASDA with their groceries. A little while later, the quartet arrived at the Gaelic Connection.

It was a small restaurant/tearoom filled with the charm and warmth to all that come through its doors. The small but cosy place boasted of hospitality and a comfortable atmosphere with a pub/restaurant/tearoom where decent people can have a drink and a few laughs; while the walls were jammed packed with decorations of Celtic symbols and history, there were many pictures of Enya that that were dotted around the place as the customers took their teas and cakes in absolute peace and quiet. Enya was one of their favourite customers and she was also a prominent figure in the restaurant as most of her music was proudly on display and on the radio playing softly in the background. Her music soothed even the fiery of Gaelic souls and tempers as Alyssia came in with Amber, Adrianne and Milton as the host came to her and spoke in Gaelic to her.

Latha bréagha is fáilta gu luis Gáidhlig Ceangal, a Alyssia is caomhnach; do bòrd is eárlaidh ionnas gu lean mi mas e do thoil e. "Welcome to the Gaelic Connection, Alyssia and friends; your table is ready so follow me please." The quartet followed Mòrag to their table as Milton whispered to her, "Do they always speak this way?" Alyssia smiled as she said to the trio while walking to their table, "I should have told you that they speak mainly Gaelic here so it's best to let me do the talking. Do me a favour and throw your comments my way; I will translate them into Gaelic to Mòrag, and one day I will teach you Gaelic; how does that sound?" Milton says, "Okay sounds like a deal, but we want to help pay for our high teas, we will not allow you to pay for us all. If I knew that High Tea was only two pounds ninety-five, we would have not bothered asking you to pay." She smiled, reached up and patted his cheek gently as they reached the table and they all took off their coats and set them aside.

Tapadh leibh, a Mhòrag. Ciamar a tha thu eadar dá sgeul? Is do fear-taigh uill? "Thank you Morag. How are you by the way? Is your husband well?" Mòrag watched the group settle as she says to Alyssia, *Mi áis is fer-taigh a bhiel uill, tapadh leat. Mi cluinnte a'Chatriona feum rachte muin gu Uibhist?* "My husband and I are well, thank you. I heard Catriona went back to the North of Uist…" *Seadh, I clì déidh luis tiomnadh nigh seatlaigte. Mi áis ás leat a h-tuig asibh bi a'gabhail a h.* "Yes, she left after the will was settled. I will let her know that you were asking for her.*" Mi áis fair a-mach árd teatha do sib; Mi áis bi coir muin.* "I will bring out the high teas for you, I will be right back."

Mòrag leaves the quartet as she says, "I do apologise on leaving you out; Jessica my grandmother, me and Catriona were good friends and regular customers to Mòrag and her husband Alastair McLeod who run this place so I was just filling in Mòrag what has been happening. I know you all were looking at me rather odd while I was speaking to her, so pardon my rudeness." Milton pats her hand as the girls smile as he replied, "She has promised to teach us Gaelic so we can talk to Mòrag and not look like dummies."

Adrianne was about to say something until Milton shot her a look which made Amber and Alyssia laugh as if to say: *'Don't you dare!'* Adrianne says, "That sounds like a deal and you can tell us what to say, curse or reply back in Gaelic." The others laugh as Mòrag and Alastair bring out the High teas while Alyssia had hot chocolate. *An seo a bheil mi áis; ceithir árd teas...* "Here we are; four high teas..." Alyssia smiled and looked to the couple as she replied, *Tapadh leat, a Mhòrag and Alastair.* "Thank you Mòrag and Alastair." Then Alastair then said to her, *Alyssia, mi ionnas gu luis cluinntear da do seanmhair* "Alyssia I'm so sorry to hear about your grandmother." She said sadly, *Tapadh leibh, mis luachaich eadh. Faod mis páigh luis cuir gob ri gob?* "Thank you, I appreciate it. May I pay the bill?" Alastair nodded as the trio got out their money and gave Alyssia their share of the bill. She took the money as she asked, "Are you sure? This was supposed to be my turn to pay, you know."

Milton says, "Nope, after the rough time with Thackeray at the Visitor's Centre, we thought that we should put up our fair share." The girls nodded as he concluded, "Besides, I really like it here and the people are very kind and welcoming. The High Teas are amazing as well...I mean look at what you get. It wouldn't be fair on you and these lovely people if you pay for all of us and I would come in here again with my family." Alyssia told the MacLeod's what Milton said in Gaelic and they were eternally grateful as she got the money and Alastair told her, *lean mi gu luis clár-malairt...* "Follow me to the counter," She nodded and told them as she took the money to the front of the tearoom, "...be right back." They nodded as they watch her go and then they start talking about George Thackeray quietly as they have their tea.

"What the hell was wrong Thackeray today? He acted like he owned the place," Amber asked the others as she had her cake. Adrianne replied as they watch her and Alastair talk, "I know and his goons need to bathe more often;" she waved her hand in front of her nose as they laughed. "But he did say something about Cassious House about 'taking back what is rightfully his...'" Alyssia overheard them as she listened and got their attention. "You heard right," says Alyssia who came back as Milton lets her in to the booth as they talked quietly and gave Amber and Milton their change. "According to the story I have in my backpack, the family were under Mario Angelo Sabacini Thackeray, who was head of the criminal Thackeray. The feud between the Thackerays lasted for only a year but it almost wiped out both families. But what really ended them was the attempted assassination of King Stephen Carlton and his son Timothy that exiled them to Italy and it was George's family who carried on the legacy and he wants the House and he will use murder and intimidation to get what he wants."

The trio shook their heads; "But why, I don't understand? Why would he think you would get in his way, Alyssia? You're not a threat to him," Amber asked as Alyssia takes a sip her hot chocolate and said, "My mother and George were lovers." The trio spit out their teas when they heard those six words as Adrianne, who was still in disbelief was cleaning her mouth with a napkin; "You're joking; please tell me that you are joking. You just made that up…" but Alyssia took a bite of her cake, wiped her mouth with her napkin and replied, "It's no joke I'm afraid, Adrianne. Remember I told you that I was taken away from my father and brother at age seven and forced to live with her and her lover until the trial was over?"

They all nodded as Alyssia said, "George Thackeray was Emily MacPherson-Franklin lover... but she was murdered because she went to the police and told them that it was George who killed Sidney Preston," her friends were still in disbelief as she continued. "Those nightmares are real you all; I watched my mother burn to death in an explosion and I still have nightmares of that day. I wake up through the night screaming her name wishing the nightmare would go away, but it never does and I would be in a cold sweat, feel a scream choked in my throat. I would be shaking and I'm constantly looking over my shoulder and I know that is no way to live, I know, and without my family to comfort me, I even jump at the slightest touch when I am not expecting it; so I get really down." The trio were surprised at the revelation, "Wow, that's insane!" Amber said very stunned; Milton could only come out with "…that's really weird!" while Adrianne was quite amazed as she asked Alyssia, "George has a heart?" The trio looked at her as they all laughed and they toasted to their new friendship.

Later in the afternoon, she got back with her groceries and started putting things away in their place until her mobile rings and she answers it after getting her cold groceries in the refrigerator put away where they belong. It was a text from Amber to come over to see Mark and Paul at Franklin House and she texted back saying that she would be right over after she gets the dry goods away. A few minutes later, she made her way over to Franklin House and rang the front doorbell. Paul answered the door with a smile as she tells him, "Hello Paul, I was told to come here… what's up?" Paul said, "Yes come in Alyssia, we are expecting you."

He escorted her to the living room and there she sees John with two other police officers who stood up to greet her as well as Amber, Milton and Adrianne who were also there talking to Police and Mark Franklin. The elder Franklin saw her as he went to her after giving her a hug knowing that she was not hurt. "I heard from your friends that you were threatened by George Thackeray today; I have invited the police to sit in as well."

She looked at her friends but surprisingly she wasn't angry…in fact, she was grateful as John came in and a couple of cops were standing with him as her friends sat beside her on the couch as she got reassurance from everyone around her as Amber says, "We had no choice but to call the police, Alyssia; it was Paul's idea." She says, "It's okay really…I wanted the police here anyway. I had called John earlier…shall we get started gentlemen? I know your time is valuable and so I will not waste your time."

She looks up at the police officers and the caretaker was also there to also offer support as he pulled out his small notebook while Alyssia sat down beside Adrianne and began his questioning. "I'm ready when you are, sir." John and the officers asked the questions while the other officers around the group wrote down what she was saying as she told them everything down to the last detail. After the interview, they told John that they had enough to write up a report and it collaborated with Dòmnhall's story as John nodded and he asked them to send a copy of the report to him. The officers agree as he turned to Alyssia and replied, "Thank you for everything, Miss Jenkins, I need you to sign this statement so we know that this statement has come from you," one of the officers said as she nodded, read her statement, and she then signed it and gave the notepad back to the officers. They thanked her for her time as they were shown out by Paul as Mark says after the police were out of earshot as he knelt before her, "Why is he after you, Alyssia? Tell me…"

She told him as she shook her head, "I don't know Mark, but I believe that since I am researching your case and the House itself, George is probably frightened that I would uncover something. I have done nothing to him Mark, honestly." Mark stroked her cheek gently as he told her with love, "Well whatever it is, you carry on what you are doing and we'll give you all the help you require, okay?" She nodded until Paul was pushed to the ground by George Thackeray who told Paul, "Get out of my way!" as Mark and Alyssia stood.

John helped Paul up as saw that he was okay as Mark said in a calm but angry tone, "What is the meaning of this intrusion George? I'm asking you quite nicely to leave!" But he said angrily, "Not until I speak to this little urchin…" Thackeray pointed to Alyssia as he came at her fuming. George backed the frightened Alyssia against the wall as he replied angrily, "You little brat! You really think I would fall the old switcheroo?" He took the tour guide of Kelton House and ripped it apart in front of her as he said with venom in his words as he backed her into a corner as she slid down the wall. "I want that book on Cassious House and I won't take 'no' for an answer. I know for some unknown reason that you purchased the book and I want it…NOW!"

She was too scared to move or speak as John says to Thackeray calmly, "George move away from Alyssia and leave her alone; she has not done anything to you but to be a student at this University." He looked at him, "Stay out of this, gardener; this is none of your business!" George then saw John reaching for his gun that sat in the back of his trousers as placed his hand behind his back on the hilt of his gun as he said calmly and firmly. "Leave now Thackeray; don't make me do something that I'll regret! I'll tell once you again, step away from Alyssia and leave Franklin House… now!" George did as he was told as he wanted no trouble from John, the Franklins or her friends or even the police. If he wanted the House he would have to keep his nose clean.

Paul, her friends and Mark looked at their frightened student as she was on the floor in tears as George turned and started to leave while Milton went to her and held her close to comfort her as he says to them angrily walking away with a snarl and anger; "Don't any of you get in my way, or I will make it the last thing you will ever do!" He shoved Paul aside again as left Franklin House with a slam of the door as they all breathed a sigh of relief while John lets his gun go and helped Paul stand up once more. "Thank you John, I'm fine…" Paul said with a smile and her friends, Mark, Milton, Paul and John came to her.

Alyssia turned into a frightened little girl as they all heard her crying, "I want my daddy and big brother!" The girls tried to hold back tears as did Mark and Paul as Milton held her very close and said to her as he held back tears, "It's okay, you're among friends…you are safe." They stood her up and walked her to the couch, "Come on over to the couch and sit down." The couple walked over to the girls who came to her and gave her a hug as she cried like a little girl again, "Where's my daddy and big brother?"

Mark left the room in tears as Paul followed him to the kitchen and closed the door as he told Paul and John who joined them as he tried not to break down in tears. "I wish I could hold her, tell her, dry her tears; but the truth is blocked and I…" he starts to cry as Paul held his dad. It was driving his dad insane not being able to tell her that she was her father and that he was alive and standing right in front of her, but that memory block was in full force and showed no signs of letting up. "Its okay dad," he said with gentleness that his father loved, "The wall will fall and the truth will be revealed at last…just hang in there." He cried hard and long at the memories of his long-lost daughter he wanted to be reconciled with so desperately was branded on to his brain and his heart as Paul sat his father down and put on the kettle. "How about some tea to calm your nerves dad; I know that you could use some right about now?" Paul asked as he looked at his son and said with an aching heart and sad smile, "I would like that, thank you son."

John came over and calmed a distraught, pain ridden lecturer while Mark rubbed his face with weariness, "Doctor Franklin, I know that I'm only a caretaker but I am curious, how long have you had this memory block, sir?" Mark looked up at John and thought for a moment as he replied "…for about a year, I think." John nods as Mark quickly asked him, "Since when do caretakers carry guns?" He gave Mark a quick smile as he replied, "Since I joined the police force and the army…this is just a part time job."

The men laugh "Touché!" Mark said and felt that he could trust him as he began, "The memory block started when my wife took my sweet, precious daughter away from me so she could go and live with that leech George Thackeray. After the trial when all the charges of murder against me were dropped and the ruling of 'accidental death' at the Coroner Office, I had a terrible nervous breakdown over the breakdown of my family and the death of my friend and assistant Sidney Preston and my son had to take care of me; on a teacher's salary."

John nodded as Paul gave the caretaker and his father their teas as Mark leaned forward as he grieved. "I guess that was when the memory block took hold; I couldn't take the pain anymore… so I tried to take my own life and I failed at that too. My son rushed me to hospital where I got my stomach pumped and after all that, after all I have put him through John; he was never angry, never raised his voice, never told me off; he stayed with me all night and studied for his exams and finals. Then, I was put into a mental ward for evaluation and they helped me get my life back together along with Paul. That was when Pharrell came to the hospital to see about tests and he saw my son who briefed him as to what had happened to me. Pharrell came in to see me and told us that he was willing to give us jobs at Kelton University. I told him that I would love to have something to help pay my son back for all I had went through and due to my credentials, I was given a place after the interview and with Paul finished all his exams and passed, he was able to help me get my life together but the University would not be ready for a year so he gave us his home and there we stayed until Franklin House was built. I went for the interview and got the job as well as Paul who was by my side. He went to hell and back with me John…I owe him everything."

Paul puts down his tea and patted his father's back as Mark rubbed his face of the tears and ran his wet tear-stained hands through his hair as he looked back at John and asked him as he sniffed. "Why do you want to know, John?" Paul looked at him as John said with a sad smile as he stood up and replied solemnly, "Sidney was my brother, Mark. I was just curious of what had happened to you and Paul, that's all."

The lecturers were shocked as John sighed and gathered his emotions and told them after he finished his tea, "I will leave you now and get Alyssia and her friends safely home…excuse me gentlemen." They nodded and he left them for the living room to check on Alyssia and left him with his sorrow as Paul told his dad after getting his attention, "Dad, if you want, I will take your class tomorrow so you can rest, sounds fair?" Mark was grateful that his son was there with him as she said, "I haven't told you enough how grateful I am to have you by my side? You are the best son ever Paul, and how I wouldn't be able to manage without you?"

Paul pats his dad's back and gets the tea for his dad as he hears a gentle knock on the kitchen door and sees John with a very frightened Alyssia close by his side as he says, "I'm taking Alyssia home, she needs to rest and to get ready for tomorrow morning. Would you like to say your goodbyes to her before she heads out? Paul nods and says to his father, "I will be right back dad, just going to say good night to Alyssia." Mark nodded and went with him, "I want to as well." Paul thought: *'Good for you dad.'* Mark and Paul came out of the kitchen and saw her friends; Alyssia and John were at the door ready to leave as they came to her.

Mark came to her first as he said with his hand on her cheek and with words of encouragement, "I want you to know that out there is a man missing his daughter and he longs to be reunited with her. I hope that one day, he will be and when he is reunited with her at long last, he will be so happy to have you back in his arms to have and hold. He longs to walk her down the aisle, share a father-daughter dance with after she married, and watch her become a mother for the first time and to get the chance to hold his grandchild. But until that day he finds you, I need you hold your head high, stand tall and not let George Thackeray get to you; he is not worth it and he will one day reap what he sows. Will you do that for me?" She nods as Mark takes her close and Paul smiled, "Be brave for me, please? Don't let George get the best of you; you my sweet girl, are stronger than him."

They held each other tight and he dries some loose tears falling from her eyes and lets her go as she tells them. "I hope to see you tomorrow, Doctor Franklin?" He smiled and says, "Please, call me Mark." They share chuckle as Paul gets in a hug and they let go as John and her friends take her home. "Good night you two have a good rest," They all leave after they say good night as John gets her and her friends safely home.

A few minutes later, Sharlene and Kevin Parks heard the doorbell go and opened it as John asked if they had a spare set of keys after they were told of what happened at Franklin House. Sharlene ran to the kitchen and got the spare keys and they get her into the flat as the friends help her lie down with a cushion at her head and a blanket on her feet as she closed her eyes and slept soundly.

The Parks were shocked and appalled at Thackeray's behaviour and they whisper to them, "We'll make sure the doors and windows are locked and get her settled down for the night... thank you all for bringing her home and keeping her safe." John smiled as did her friends as Amber says pointing to the old-fashioned door, "Is that the door..." Sharlene says, "No it isn't. It's just a door that leads nowhere Sharlene closed the curtain and helped them out as Timothy stayed in the shadows and breathed a sigh of relief that everyone was gone as Amber tried to ask again as John then says to the trio, "Come on you three, let's get you back home."

They all nod as Kevin shows them the way down the back steps as Sharlene made sure that the House is secure and Mystery is fed. She quietly leaves the house and locks the door with the spare keys after turning off the lights and making sure everything is locked tight as Sharlene leaves Alyssia to her peace. Timothy heard the door locking and he came out of the shadows as he sat beside her, stroked her hair and she awoke to see Timothy sitting there stroking her hair and said with a sob as Marylebarne and Jesterson hid in the shadows. "I want my daddy and big brother Timothy; I need them more than ever." He comes beside her and lays her head in his lap as she talks about her day. They talk until she was in bed and with Marylebarne and Jesterson beside her, she felt safe as Timothy gets the throw blanket and placed it over her feet and shoulders as she fell asleep in his lap up until the dawn.

End of Book One---Book Two coming soon.

Printed in Great Britain
by Amazon